THE QUANTUM SOLUTION

BY ERIC VAN LUSTBADER

THE EVAN RYDER SERIES

The Nemesis Manifesto
The Kobalt Dossier
Omega Rules
The Quantum Solution

THE SHADOW WARRIOR SERIES

The Ninja
The Miko
White Ninja
The Kaisho
Floating City
Second Skin
The Death and Life of
Nicholas Linnear (ebook)
The Oligarch's Daughter (ebook)

THE TESTAMENT SERIES

The Testament
The Fallen
Four Dominions
The Sum of All Shadows

THE SUNSET WARRIOR CYCLE

The Sunset Warrior
Shallows of Night
Dai-San
Beneath an Opal Moon
Dragons on the Sea of Night

THE JASON BOURNE NOVELS

The Bourne Legacy
The Bourne Betrayal
The Bourne Sanction
The Bourne Deception
The Bourne Objective
The Bourne Dominion
The Bourne Imperative
The Bourne Retribution
The Bourne Ascendancy
The Bourne Enigma
The Bourne Initiative

THE JACK MCCLURE NOVELS

First Daughter
Last Snow
Blood Trust
Father Night
Beloved Enemy

THE PEARL SAGA

The Ring of Five Dragons
The Veil of a Thousand Tears
Mistress of the Pearl

THE CHINA MAROC SERIES

Jian
Shan

OTHERS

Sirens
Black Heart
Zero
French Kiss
Angel Eyes
Batman: The Last Angel
Black Blade
Dark Homecoming
Pale Saint
Art Kills
Any Minute Now

ERIC VAN LUSTBADER

THE QUANTUM SOLUTION

HEAD
ZEUS

An Aries Book

MIX
Paper | Supporting
responsible forestry
FSC® C013604

Head of Zeus
First Floor East
5–8 Hardwick Street
London ECIR 4RG
WWW.HEADOFZEUS.COM

For Linda and Tom,
my North Stars

And everybody knows that it's now or never
But nobody knows that it's me or you

—After "Everybody Knows" by
LEONARD COHEN

PROLOGUE

On one of those increasingly frequent climate-crisis-warm days in December, Brady Thompson, Unites States secretary of defense, was about to tee off on the third hole of his favorite golf course. It was a 460-yard par five, dogleg left, the fairway guarded by a pair of bunkers left and right at that juncture, as if daring the intrepid golfer to defy them.

Waiting patiently for their boss's shot were his regular "partners in golf crime," as they liked to call themselves, Wes Connerly, head of the National Geospatial-Intelligence Agency, a math-analytics savant who looked like a former tight end running to middle-aged fat, and George Wilson, chief of the Defense Threat Reaction Agency, small, intense—a man who took his golf game as seriously as he did his job. Thompson just hoped George wouldn't have a heart attack on one of the greens one day.

All three men were colleagues and, latterly, friends, mainly due to Thompson's indefatigable bonhomie. Neither man had worked for someone like Thompson before, which made them appreciate him all the more. He was one of those people born to be a career pol. He knew the right people, knew how to make the right deals, networked without seeming to. This essential asset served him well as the defense secretary. It served him even better in his other life, hidden away from even the most well-trained prying eyes.

The trio of golfers was surrounded at a discreet distance by their usual young caddies, fully vetted of course, and, just behind, quartering the immediate vicinity with gimlet eyes, their Secret Service contingent.

Fluffy clouds rode across the sky but hardly interfered with the sun. It really was unnaturally warm. Not that the trio cared. Summer in December. Okay!

The secretary of defense was about to start his backswing when Wilson said, "Exact moment when Bill would have made one of his groaners."

"Ah, yes, Bill. Our missing fourth," Connerly acknowledged sadly. "Was it only last week we buried him? He was too young to die."

"So are we," Thompson said, resting on his driver. "But a coronary could hit any of us . . ."

Connerly nodded at Wilson. "Go on, George. Do you remember one?"

"Must? Well." Wilson cleared his throat. "Three vampires walk into a bar. First one says, 'I'll have a pint of blood.' Second says, 'Sounds good. I'll have the same.' Third says, 'And I'll have a pint of plasma.' Bartender says, 'So, that'll be two Bloods and a Blood Lite?'"

The three men groaned and laughed at the same time.

"Well, someone's got to assume the reins," Thompson said as he prepared again to tee off. "George, you got this."

"Tapped out." Wilson turned to Connerly. "Wes?"

"Wait a sec." Connerly thought a moment. "Okay, I've got one." His forehead wrinkled as he made sure he'd got the joke right. "A three-legged dog walks into a saloon, his spurs clinking as he walks, his six-shooter slapping at his furry hip. He tips back his ten-gallon hat as he bellies up to the bar, eyes the bartender, and proclaims, 'I'm looking for the low-down varmint who shot my paw.'"

Everyone laughed. They laughed until tears came to their eyes. All except Wilson, who uttered, "Heh!" Connerly's cheeks had gone pink.

"That's so good!" Connerly managed to gasp out.

"Yeah. Bill loved telling that one." Thompson rubbed his forehead vigorously.

As if by silent mutual consent, the three men then fell silent, bowed their heads in memory of Bill Fineman, who up until a week ago had been the administration's director of human resources. As one they came out of their reveries, and, going into his stance, Thompson swung into his dimpled ball. He wasn't a bad golfer but he wasn't particularly good, either. His handicap was higher than he would have liked.

As he shaded his eyes against the low-lying sun, Connerly said, "Has distance."

"Yeah." Wilson smirked. "But left into the sand trap."

"Lawrence," Connerly sang, terribly off-key. "Lawrence of Arabia."

In due course, both Wilson and Connerly hit their balls, neither of which found the traps, but that was because they weren't as long as Thompson's. Because of this it was Thompson who was smirking as he asked for his sand wedge from his caddy.

Taking his first step into the sand trap, Thompson almost stumbled. He held out his arm, stopping his agent from coming to his rescue and thus shaming him in front of his pals, who would doubtless rib him mercilessly for the next week. Without further incident he traversed the shallow slope to where his ball nestled in the sand, thinking how good a lie he had. That was when the ringing in his ears ramped up. It was this, at a very low level, which had caused his almost stumble. Now it was so loud he couldn't put two thoughts together. Pain shot through him, such pain as he'd never felt before. He shook his head, trying to dislodge the ringing, as if it were a physical thing. To him it was physical, or in any event felt that way.

Bent over the ball, he could scarcely breathe. His heart was racing so fast he was sure he was about to have a heart attack. Then his vision went red. He felt flayed from the inside out. Pressure inside his head was building, as if there was a foreign body in his brain expanding exponentially. He couldn't escape the pain. Was there no way to cut it out of his head? The agony ratcheted up further. He thought he screamed, though maybe not. He couldn't hear anything over the ringing filling him up with an insupportable pain, but he kept jabbing his forefinger against his temple, as if to say, *Here! It's in here!* People rushed toward him, staggering in the sand, but it was too late. What could they do? He was beyond help. If only . . .

A path opened up. His mind, ragged and disjointed, seemed to squeeze a trigger. He thrust the handle end of his club through the roof of his mouth, jamming it harder and harder. There was a maelstrom of desperate activity all around him, but he was deaf and blind to it. The ringing was gone, light was gone.

Echoes fading.

Blessed silence.

Nothing remained.

■　■　■

Snow began to fall in the crepuscular hour before dawn when the world is without color, white light, black shadow. In any case what sunlight there might have been had it been a clear morning would be watery and distant.

It was cold in the pine forest half a day's drive north of Moscow. The flakes, swirling like desert dervishes, were small, hard, perfectly crystalline; had they been granules of sand they would have stuck in every crease, crevice, and nook. So ferocious, so unrelenting was the snow it had completely covered the forest floor by the time the gray wolf emerged from its den. Its nostrils flared; it scented the red stag and trotted off in pursuit of the spoor. Russian gray wolves were large, but this one's size outstripped that of the other males in its territory by a wide margin. It had been trailing the stag for days now, following it down from the highlands, losing its scent now and again, never quite being able to catch up, but this morning was different. It could feel the stag as well as scent it. Loping ahead, it began to close in.

■   ■   ■

Ivan Levrov passed the first outlying trees. He carried a Sako A1 .220 hunting rifle balanced in the crook of his left arm. It was loaded and ready to fire at a moment's notice. A pair of military-grade binoculars through which he had first spied the red stag bumped against his chest. The stag was a twelve-pointer, would make quite a prize. He imagined its head over the brick fireplace in his dacha as he sat at a table slicing through the stag's butchered and roasted flesh. He could already taste the richness of the meat. His mouth filled with saliva and he swallowed compulsively.

Levrov was a lieutenant colonel in the GRU, the Russian military intelligence service. At forty-seven, he might have been at a higher rank, but a decade ago he had chosen the path less taken. He had been trained as a mathematician—the new math that kept evolving the more became known about quantum computing. As a consequence, he was commanded to a generally unknown branch of the GRU, Directorate KV. Even to those inside the GRU, the letters meant nothing, but like Levrov those inside Directorate KV knew it stood for *kvant*, the discrete particle of energy that was changing the face of the world. Quantum.

A flash of antler through the snow-laden pines caused Levrov to swing the Sako into position. His forefinger lay alongside the trigger, alert and ready to perform its duty. Levrov was as fine a hunter as he was a mathematician. Even so, this particular buck would be a career high for him.

He moved forward, leading with his left side. He breathed through his nose to minimize the smoke from his breathing in the chill morning. His hands gripped the cold steel, but he didn't feel it, just as he didn't feel the polished wooden stock against his shoulder. The backs of his hands and fingers were carpeted with black hair, wiry as a boar's. In this forest, so familiar to him, he felt freed and alive—almost an animal. All his senses were unleashed. He saw the stag, he inhaled the scents of the pine, the snow itself—a combination of ice and raw cotton; he heard the rustle of a crow somewhere above his head, then heard its cry as it took off. At this sharp sound the stag froze, its great head lifted, slowly turning this way and that for the smallest sign of a predator. Had the crow spotted Levrov's stealthy, silent advance? Had its caw been a warning? Or was it calling to other members of its family?

Levrov had frozen at the same time as the stag. This close up the animal was more impressive, more magnificent than it had seemed at a distance. It stood in a small clearing, its left front leg raised, body poised, ready for flight at the least little sound it recognized as out of place. The snow speckled its back, as if it were slowly vanishing into the forest itself.

The crow was long gone, but Levrov felt uneasy. Something was wrong, but he couldn't put his finger on what it might be. There was only him and the stag; the empty forest loomed all around them. But still . . .

Wiping away his vague apprehension, he raised the long gun to shooting position, sighted slowly, without making any sharp movement. Now was not the time to spook his prey. His finger found the trigger, curled around it. Just as he was about to squeeze the bullet home, he caught a flash of gray out of the corner of his eye. His brain registered the close proximity of the danger. His forefinger jerked reflexively, the shot went off, the bullet wide of its mark. He cursed silently, looked, but the flash of gray was gone. He'd missed his chance; surely the buck had bolted.

But no. There it was in the same position it had been in when he'd sighted down the barrel. How peculiar, he thought. Why hadn't the animal bolted at the sharp report of the firing? It was unprecedented in his time as a hunter. It was unnatural. Then he saw the blood on its flank, the trembling of its hind legs. He'd missed the kill shot but not the target.

It was at that moment he saw the wolf—gray, large, and powerful. In its yellow eyes he saw a challenge, unmistakable in its enmity. He was deep within its territory. As he swung the Sako in its direction a ringing arose inside his head. Like the buzzing of ten thousand wasps, strident, angry, inimical, rising like a tsunami, undercutting the ground beneath him. Groaning, he staggered.

At the sound, the stag's great head swung in his direction. It saw him, lowered its head, and thundered toward him. Levrov was on his knees, one hand pressed violently against the side of his head, which throbbed as if his heart had migrated to his brain. Here came the stag, crashing through the pine branches, out of the clearing into the space he occupied. And there was something behind, quartering in, an enfilade. The gray wolf.

Levrov tried to react, but the massive pain inside his brain made it impossible to think, let alone move. Ironically, he knew the cause of his pain, though he was baffled as to how he could be subject to it, or why. He understood the method of attack but even his own project was incapable of such an attack. Who . . . ?

This unanswerable question was his last thought. His brain exploded and his heart shut down. Consequently he was unaware when the stag's four tines drove into him simultaneously. His body danced in galvanic action, but this too was far beyond his ken.

■   ■   ■

The stag had backed away at the wolf's approach. It stood for a moment, flanks quivering, bleeding, bleeding. It stared at the wolf as if hypnotized as the beast wheeled, leapt onto the stag, sinking its jaws into the meat of the stag's neck. Blood flowed freely, pulsing down the stag's shoulders and chest. It lifted its head, tossed the wolf high into the air with its great thorny antlers. The wolf hit the snow hard, its back broken, and yet it lifted its head, looking after the stag. It tried to rise, could not. Its tongue lolled, stomach empty, hunger clawing at it even in its last moments. Such was the life of an animal. Not long after, panting briefly, it died.

PART ONE

QUESTION

Three things to keep in mind when it comes to quantum computing. One: It is an entirely unexplored universe. Two: The race to build the fastest, largest, most powerful quantum computer has already been won. By me. Three: In this new universe, we humans are nothing more than mole rats, all blind and unknowing. [Pause] If number three seems to contradict number two then you have grasped the essential nature of the quantum universe.

—from a TED Talk by Marsden Tribe

1

Far off, the Sea of Marmara was a sheet of beaten brass, but closer to the Bosphorus, the Golden Horn was churning with packed ferries, net-laden fishing boats, pleasure craft of all sizes and shapes carrying wide-eyed tourists, looking wide-eyed, always looking. But upon closer examination, in among the sleek yachts one could make out smaller craft that were battered, torn by high seas and storms, crowded not with tourists at all, but Syrian refugees fleeing destruction, fire, and famine, yearning, clinging to whatever life awaited them, hoping to scratch out an existence in Istanbul's alleys, byways, and criminal dens. Southwest of the Horn, in Muğra and Bodrum, the summer's seemingly endless conflagrations had finally burned themselves out, leaving the kind of destruction all too familiar to those exhausted refugees.

Istanbul. One leg in Asia, the other in Europe. And yet Istanbul was neither Asian nor European in character, but something all its own. Overrun by the ancient Greeks, then the Roman legions, fierce, invincible, the leaders renaming it Byzantium until it was taken by force by the Ottomans, fiercer still, unafraid to die. In one way or another the city possessed attributes of all its conquerors. Even becoming part of the newly formed Turkish Republic in 1923 did nothing to rub the rough edges off the palimpsest of Istanbul's disordered history.

All of this had rushed at Evan Ryder the moment she returned to the city she loved and hated in equal measure. Over the time she had been in harness to the world of espionage death had ridden her shoulders almost every day and night she spent in this splendid metropolis. Now, back again, she wended her way down a narrow side street near the Kılıç Ali Paşa Mosque in Tophane. After passing a tinsmith's shop and a storefront showcasing rugs for wholesale export, she pushed through a discreet door and entered a hammam. Fragrant wood, mineral stone, old, from the time of the Ottomans. Historic, but hidden away from the tourists, unknown to the guidebooks. For Turks only. Almost.

After being divested of her clothes, she was given a *peshtemal*—a thin cotton towel—by her *natir*—her female attendant—a short, powerful Turk of indeterminate age with dark skin and an unexpected softness. Evan was, after all, a *ferengi*. A foreigner. She was then taken to the temperate chamber, domed, skylit stars sprinkled around its crown, where she was dutifully washed, scrubbed, massaged. The chamber was lined with mosaics laid during the reign of Abdul Hamid II, the last Ottoman sultan, the tiles telling a kind of story in Arabic, if you knew the language and took the time to pick your way across the letters. After an hour she was shown the way to the heated baths.

There she found Lyudmila Shokova waiting for her, soaking in a far corner, away from three other women enjoying the heat with washcloths folded over their eyes and foreheads. Beautiful, striking Lyudmila, her long legs extended, crossed at her trim ankles. Blond, ice-blue-eyed, she would not have been out of place on the runways of Paris or Milan. Lyudmila, who had once risen through the ranks of the FSB until she was elevated to become the first female member of the Politburo. Lyudmila, who had cultivated her power within the elite governing body to the point where she became a perceived danger to the Sovereign himself. Fleeing Russia just ahead of the purge, seeding clues of her death behind her. Now she ran the largest and most sophisticated anti-Russian network in the world.

The two women kissed in the European fashion, briefly stared into each other's eyes, touched foreheads in private celebration of their reunion.

"How is your first year with Marsden Tribe?" Lyudmila asked as Evan settled beside her.

"You know how it went."

"Ah, yes. But underneath. Where even angels like me are blind."

Evan waited a moment, the steam from the water a thin, twining mist between them. "He likes me."

"Ah."

"Nothing has happened."

"Yet." She swung her head, her damp hair slapping her shoulders, left, right. "Watch out for him."

To this Evan said nothing. So. Time to move on.

"I've made a dangerous move," Lyudmila said so softly Evan had to take a moment to process the sound into words. "Someone in a very secret section of the service—" She meant the Russian intelligence services, FSB or GRU, maybe. "—he did a very stupid thing. He called out his superior for a mistake—a serious mistake—that would set the program back at least a year. His opinion. Marius Ionescu."

"A Romanian."

"Extraction. Russian born and bred. But I believed him when he reached out to one of my contacts. I believe him even more now."

"So now this Marius Ionescu is my problem?"

"No. Not at all. Oh, well, peripherally maybe. But, no, I'm taking care of Ionescu. But . . ."

"But what?"

Her hand covered Evan's, squeezing it with some urgency. And Evan thought, *She's vulnerable. For the first time since she disappeared from Moscow she's vulnerable.* A quicksilver shiver of fear lanced through her.

"We're friends," Lyudmila whispered, leaning close. "More than friends." Wreathed in mist and sweat. "Sisters. Under the skin."

"Of course we are." Evan would not refute her. Anyway, she was too busy wondering what this was all about.

Lyudmila relaxed visibly but her eyes turned inward. Always full of surprises. "In the days of Abdul Hamid he had of course a harem. The last sultan so the last harem in Istanbul, in all of the Empire. Before Turkey was Turkey. Not all the women in the harem saw Abdul Hamid let alone were led to his bedchamber at night. No. But these women longed to be *gözde*—in the eye—noticed by the sultan. Once to be desired. Now to be feared."

Lyudmila turned a little, the heated water stirring, eddying languorously out from her.

"After being 'dead' for so long," she continued, "I am now *gözde*. In the eye of the Sovereign."

Evan was shaken. This was bad. Very bad. "But why would you take such a chance?"

"As I said, I took him," Lyudmila said. "I have Ionescu. And I will keep him."

Evan spread her hands, droplets of water running down her wrists. "That is the foolish thing. Offering him sanctuary."

"In a way I had no choice."

"Becoming *gözde*. For him. Is he that important?"

Lyudmila's eyes clouded for a moment, once again turning inward. Then her direct gaze returned, spotlit on Evan. "Marius Ionescu is a particle physicist of the first rank. He was second-in-command of Directorate KV. Embedded in the GRU."

"So military."

Lyudmila nodded. "Yes. But."

Evan shook her head. "I've never heard of Directorate KV."

"You see?" Lyudmila took a breath. "Directorate KV. Shorthand for *kvant.*" Her eyes slid away for a moment. Uncharacteristic. At last she came to the point. "*Kvant,* a very singular particle of energy. Quantum."

Evan stared at her. "Full circle. We're now back to Marsden Tribe."

"Perhaps," Lyudmila said, her voice softened like butter in sunlight. "Peripherally. I don't know. Yet." She moved closer so their foreheads touched. Lowered her voice even further. "I was forced to take a calculated risk. Ionescu is that important. But in spiriting him away I exposed myself. Now the Sovereign knows I'm alive and well." Her eyes searched Evan's. "They've put a black flag out on me."

Black flag. A death warrant. What did she want? Help? Sympathy? Something else altogether, hidden from Evan. That was Lyudmila's way, despite their deep and abiding friendship.

"They?" Evan said.

"The GRU. But of course with the Sovereign's blessing."

"You slipped through his fingers. He hates you."

"Because I am still alive, he hates me. Because I gathered to myself so much power in so little time, he fears me."

"It seems to me," Evan said, "that hate and fear are the same thing. Especially in this circumstance." She frowned. "But why the GRU? What he's ordering is an SVR remit."

Lyudmila's pale eyes glittered. "The Sovereign assigned a certain GRU officer, once captain, now major, to track me down and kill me. As to why, it's a story old as time."

"She's the Sovereign's mistress?"

"One of," Lyudmila said. "Her name is Juliet Danilovna Korokova. But in any case it won't be easy. She's a very nasty piece of work."

"You know her?"

"By proxy only. But I know a great deal about her. Enough anyway to beg you not to underestimate her. Whatever it seems she can do—be assured it's ten times worse. And now of course she has the Sovereign's imprimatur. Everything is open to her. Virtually all resources."

Evan considered for a moment. "So. Another thing I must know. How tightly is Korokova bound to the Sovereign?"

"She is *kadife*," Lyudmila replied. "Velvet, directly translated. But not its meaning. In the parlance of the Ottomans she is his favorite." This unsettled Lyudmila more than Evan could ever know. Some things were too vital—secrets cut too close to Lyudmila's bones.

The steam rose more thickly now, making it difficult to see the other side of the pool, let alone the series of blue translucent windows rimming the inverted bowl of the space.

"Have you any more intel on this Major Korokova?"

"I'll send what little Alyosha Ivanovna has been able to scrape together to the sandbox on your mobile."

A line of sweat ran down the side of Evan's face. "Does she have any leads as to your whereabouts?"

Lyudmila's head swiveled. "You're asking if there's a leak in my cadre."

Evan nodded. "That would be my initial concern." Droplets plopped into the water, one by one. "Especially since you've incorporated von Kleist into your scheme."

"He's the leak, you mean."

"Or one of his people."

"He has no people within my cadre. Apart from his daughter, and during your time in Nuremberg last year you got to know Ghislane better than I do."

"She's not the leak," Evan said firmly.

"Neither is von Kleist." Lyudmila spread her hands. "He's currently in Zurich, working his own patch. I've never let him near the heart of my organization. He's peripheral."

Evan waited, but when it became evident there would be nothing more forthcoming, she sighed. *So there's another explanation,* she thought. She closed her eyes. Bones jellied, the heat relaxing all her muscles, the steam warming her insides as her breathing slowed. Drowsiness descended.

Lyudmila drifted, and into her loosened mind came an image of Bobbi Ryder. Bobbi Ryder, now known as Kata Hemakova, had defected five years ago. The FSB had worked their magic so that everyone—even most within the FSB—believed Bobbi to be dead. That included her sister, Evan. Kata was a stone-cold psychopath. Someone who loved the kill—lived for it if Lyudmila was any judge. But Kata had been invaluable; she was Lyudmila's mole inside the FSB. And what a successful mole she had turned out to be, working her way up the hierarchy—no small thing for a female, especially one who did not use sex to advance her career. She had cleverly and systematically exterminated everyone in her path until now she reported directly to Minister Darko Kusnetsov, head of FSB.

One of the women on the other side of the pool slowly morphed into Kata. Lyudmila imagined the catastrophic encounter—Kata staring at them, gimlet-eyed, hatred stirring her until the moment Evan locked eyes on her, recognized her as Bobbi, the sister she thought dead and buried. Kata, reacting to the recognition in Evan's eyes, launched herself through the water, clawed hands at the ready. The idea of Evan becoming aware of Bobbi's continued existence working for the Russians, the possibility of Kata meeting Evan were unthinkable; the two sisters would destroy each other, there could be no other outcome. Lyudmila would move heaven and earth to prevent that from occurring.

Across the pool, two of the women, sisters possibly, removed their washcloths, climbed out of the water. Wrapped in oversized towels, they disappeared through the arched stone doorway.

A ripple lapped against Evan's chest, and she opened her eyes to slits. The cloth over the eyes of the remaining woman had fallen into the water. Evan could make out smaller ripples arcing away from the spot when it had hit the surface. How such little things could affect you when you were in still water. The slightest movement . . .

That was when the woman across the pool canted over, slipped face-first into the water. It took a moment for Evan to react, as if the heat had made her sluggish. She pushed off, using more effort than usual, not that that occurred to her in the moment, though it should have. Halfway across, she faltered. An acrid odor scraped the back of her throat. Her nostrils dilated. In the back of her mind a warning alarm sounded, but it was dampened by the mist coming off the water. She awoke sputtering and coughing water out of her mouth, pulled her head up from the water. How had that happened? She could have drowned.

Struggling forward was like dragging herself through quicksand, but at last she reached the woman, hauled her back out of the water. But two fingers to her carotid confirmed she was already dead. Overcome by vertigo, Evan sank down again under the water. Her limbs seemed to be all but useless. With a jerk of terrified consciousness she whipped her head and upper torso out of the water. Sucked in the thick air in convulsive breaths. But that only increased the burning in her throat. And then her brain registered the noxious smell, and, with a soft cry, she turned, made her way back the way she had come.

Lyudmila's eyes were closed when Evan reached her, her breathing dangerously slow. She was about to slip under the water. Evan caught her in her armpits, drew her back up so that the back of her head rested against the lip of the pool.

"Lyudmila." Used one hand to slap her hard across the face. "Lyudmila! For Christ's sake, wake up!" And again, even harder this time, leaving a white imprint that soon turned pink as blood rushed in under her skin.

But the physical actions somehow caused Evan to lose whatever focus she'd had. She hung onto Lyudmila, her forehead resting against the hollow of her friend's shoulder. Her thoughts were clouded. She tried to string one to another but she seemed to be lost inside her own mind. A darkness, sticky as tar, curled around the periphery of her vision. She tried to lick her lips but her tongue refused to move. The inside of her mouth had dried up.

In desperation she pinched the inside of her arm, rolled the skin around, then dug a nail in. Drawing her own blood had a startling effect on her. Her eyes opened wide and she resisted the urge to suck in more air. Instead she held her breath. Then, bending into the water, fingers interlaced, she took a grip on Lyudmila's bottom, shoved her as far out of the water as she could manage. A soft pulsing had started up behind her eyes, and she realized she was feeling the pumping of her blood.

She rested her head against Lyudmila's belly until she could catch her breath. But she started, knowing she couldn't take a breath—not one more. She had to pretend that she was under water. No oxygen until she could surface.

Pushing and shoving, she finally got Lyudmila all the way out of the pool. But then her strength failed her. Even her iron determination seemed paralyzed. Her head nodded; the water was rising. Or she was falling toward it.

Just as her nose pierced the skin of the pool she felt a lurch upward, a fierce tugging as Lyudmila hauled her out. Together, staggering, lurching, once going down on their knees, the two women made their way to the circumference of the room. Evan's fingers, feeling like sausages about to burst their skin, fumbled with the old-fashioned lock, swung the metal clasp free. Together, they lifted the window, shot their heads and shoulders into the cold clean air, took gasping breaths deep inside them, working the oxygen in and the gas that had filled the pool room out.

"What . . . what?" Lyudmila finally gasped. Her voice had deepened an octave.

"Ether." Evan's voice, too, was deeper, ragged, almost a rasp. Her throat felt scoured, as if she had been forced to swallow a mouthful of iron filings. She coughed. "Crude but effective."

"Very Russian," Lyudmila said a bit breathlessly.

Evan leaned further over the thick stone sill and heaved while Lyudmila held her hair back from her face. "Just like high school," Evan said thickly. Her face was pale, washed out.

"Yours maybe," Lyudmila said. "Not mine."

Evan took several minutes to breathe in prana, oxygenating her lungs and bloodstream, expelling the last of the ghastly ether. At length, she turned her head and looked at Lyudmila. "This the major's doing?"

"Korokova." Lyudmila nodded grimly. "Juliet Danilovna Korokova."

2

Major Juliet Danilovna Korokova stood ankle-deep in snow, amid towering pines. Blood spattered the otherwise immaculate white clearing, glaring in the spotlights ranged around the body of Ivan Levrov, sprawled facedown. On Major Korokova's orders, no one had touched the corpse. Even the forensic technicians were held back. They watched her with a combination of lust and fear. She was big, blond, and busty: wide of hip, narrow of waist, with the muscled legs of a runner. The GRU pathologist, Morokovsky, had been directed to come out here, a two-hour flight from Moscow, with a GRU cadre under her command, with no imminent hope of getting back there anytime soon. It was on Korokova's orders that they had set about erecting a tented village. Supplies and all his medical equipment were on their way. Now, standing beside her, he revealed his impatience by rather showily shifting his weight from one foot to the other.

"*Prekrati!*" Korokova snapped. *Stop it!* And he did. Immediately. No one on the team would risk getting on the major's shit list. It was easy to get on; almost impossible to get off. This was known, and feared, even before she became one of the Sovereign's favorites. Her temper was as legendary as her prowess at winkling out rotten apples no matter how deeply they were buried inside the GRU. Had she been another person with a different temperament she would have been admired. No matter. She'd rather be feared than admired. Fear was the best motivator. This she had learned from her father, towering over her like some god out of the writings of Nietzsche. She aspired to be like her father in all ways, at all times.

As for Morokovsky, the GRU's chief pathologist, no one knew his first name or his patronymic; no one bothered to look them up. He was simply Morokovsky, had always been Morokovsky. To say that he and Korokova did not get along was an understatement. They despised one another.

Why, no one seemed to know, only that the animosity was deep-rooted. Morokovsky was at the top of her shit list, never to be dethroned— although within GRU there was a thriving business in wagering on that eventuality.

Korokova, surveying the scene as if with a stethoscope, searching for a pulse hidden from every other observer, still had not moved. Forbidden to rock back and forth, Morokovsky began to grind his molars with such force the resultant squeal was like the braking of steel wheels against railroad tracks.

Korokova circled the clearing and then at a certain spot crouched down. "All right," she said, "turn him over."

"About fucking time."

"What did you say?" Her eyes staring at a fixed spot in the thin layer of freshly fallen snow.

Morokovsky flinched as if he had been slapped. "Just because you run your own directorate inside—"

Her head swiveled on her swan's neck. Her Medusa stare stopped him cold.

With an effort that terrified him, Morokovsky jerked his eyes away. He barked an expletive-laden order to two of the forensic team, who stepped forward and with a minimum of effort turned the corpse onto its back, revealing a large pool of blood, black as oil in the spotlights. Then, "Well, that's interesting."

Korokova, still in her crouch, said nothing.

"I think you'll want to see this, Major." The pathologist could not keep the smugness out of his voice.

Korokova kept her focus on the crust of newly fallen snow.

Miffed, Morokovsky went on. "Ivan Levrov was gored to death by a very large stag."

"Perhaps." Korokova appeared unperturbed.

"No 'perhaps' about it." He pointed to the ragged wounds. "It's fact."

She rose and, snapping on rubber gloves, passed around to the far side of the corpse. Bending down, she picked up Levrov's hunting rifle, all but fully hidden beneath the snow. She checked all aspects of the rifle before she said, "Look here. His Sako A1 .220 is a first-rate hunter's weapon. It's been fired recently." At last, she looked at the corpse, picking her way carefully over to it. "Levrov was a first-rate hunter of red deer. He shot it but didn't kill it. Two of your men ran it down and finished it off. They brought it to Cook. It's so large it must have excited Levrov to no end; it did Cook." She shook her head. "The gray wolf with the broken back was the largest my men had ever seen. Very possibly that's why Levrov's shot was wide of the mark, how, distracted, he allowed the stag to run into him."

Morokovsky chuffed. "Circumstances don't concern me, Major. Just the modus of death. Which in this case is four stag tines to the midsection, puncturing upper and lower colon, causing Levrov to bleed out."

"But then there's the gray wolf. A wolf, a red stag, here at the same time as Levrov. Odd. Why didn't he shoot them both? Even odder."

Morokovsky shrugged, but there was a bitter edge to his voice. "There's no answer for you here. Obviously."

Major Korokova's laugh was like a razor blade slitting flesh. Morokovsky shuddered despite himself. Though this was the first time he'd been in the field with her, he'd had plenty of experience with her inside the cold room—the mortuary—where bodies found a kind of peace following the violence of their deaths. She never shied away from either sight or smell. He hated her for that strength, which diminished his superiority over the outsiders—even those who outranked him—that entered his domain.

"No," Juliet Korokova was saying now, "something's definitely off here—an element that doesn't track."

"And you don't know what?"

At that moment she turned away from him, put her satnav phone to her ear. She listened for a full minute before speaking.

"Even so," she said in unaccented Turkish so none of the Russians could understand her, "circle back. You need to make sure. I need proof. That's right. Something tangible." She thought back to the severed finger of Thoth Abramovich Novikov that Kata had given her. Novikov, whom Korokova had seduced in order to obtain intel. "A finger will do quite nicely," she continued. "Her fingerprint will provide all the proof I require." *And,* she thought, *it will tickle the Sovereign's fancy. Oh, what a reward I'll receive from him.*

Quitting the call, she turned back to the pathologist. "Isn't it possible," returning to Russian, "that something happened to Levrov *before* he was gored. Something that froze him."

These were not questions, and the pathologist knew it. Nevertheless, he felt compelled to say, "He could have had a massive myocardial infarction."

"A heart attack."

"Yes. But I won't know for sure until I perform an autopsy back at—"

"A *complete* autopsy."

Now Morokovsky was truly offended. "Major Korokova, in twenty-three years of service to the GRU I have only ever performed *complete* autopsies. I pride myself in never once cutting even a single corner."

Korokova gave him a steady gaze, as close to an apology as he was going to get. "If the wolf came out of nowhere . . ." She stalked around the clearing. "Yes, the wolf." All eyes were on her, even Morokovsky's. "Why was the wolf here?" she said to herself. "Assume it was tracking the stag. And . . ." She tapped her forefinger against her lower lip. ". . . the stag saw it, saw the hunter with his rifle. Two threats, one more immediate than the other. So it went straight for the hunter."

"You're ascribing a human level of intelligence to an animal."

"Not at all," Korokova replied. "I speak of instinct. And memory. This stag was very large. This encounter with the hunter was unlikely to have been its first. It had learned, as all animals do. Often faster than humans. Why? Because their lives depend on surviving in a hostile world."

She whirled, looking at the pathologist. "A wholly unexpected move. Another explanation for Levrov's inaction."

"A wild one, surely."

"I don't think so." She stalked toward him like a wolf. "You'll send your autopsy findings directly to me. And only to me. No copies."

He shook his head. "You know that's not how it's done."

But she was right up in his face. "It is now."

3

Steam, but of a different kind now. Fragrant with fresh mint and melted sugar.

"The two women who left the pool together." Evan's voice was low. Nevertheless, it penetrated the animated conversations coming from the tables around them. They were the only women in the café, par for the course in Istanbul; as much as modernism had come to the city, tradition still held—the streets belonged to men, especially as darkness fell.

Lyudmila nodded. "That would be my guess."

From the rear of the café they could hear the click-clack of tiles, as two old men played dominoes. Four others, heads leaning in, spoke in hushed tones of politics and religion, which for Turks were inextricably combined. Beyond the shadows and light of the café the world buzzed and jumped as sellers hawked their wares, street vendors shouted through the fragrant smoke of their charcoal fires, boys, their pockets stuffed with stolen fruit, ran down the winding street. Beneath the café's striped awning Evan sipped her sweet mint tea, feeling her knotted muscles start to relax. But it would take more, much more to relieve her twanging nerves.

"Agents sent by the major?" That was how the two of them spoke of Juliet Korokova, a demeaning device that pleased them both.

"That would be my guess." Lyudmila's gaze darted here and there like a dragonfly, searching, always searching.

The server, a long, lean, dark-skinned Turk, arrived to refill their cups, which meant he'd been keeping an eye on them. Was he simply doing his job or did his job encompass more than waiting on tables?

When they were again alone, Evan said, "The question then becomes how did the major know where to find you?" When Lyudmila made no reply, Evan went on. "You have successfully evaded them for three years. What has changed?"

Lyudmila made a guttural sound in the back of her throat, an animal that has encountered a foreign scent. "You have a one-track mind."

"I only met von Kleist once a year ago, as you know. I hardly know him." Evan tilted her head. "But I have to wonder how well you know him."

"Why do you say that?"

"Because you need him. His money. His connections." Evan sipped her tea without taking her eyes off her friend. "*Need* makes dangerous bedfellows. *Need* makes people careless."

Lyudmila's eyes sparked. "You know I'm not careless."

"And that's what worries me," Evan set her cup down. "There's a mole in your organization. A very smart, very clever mole."

Lyudmila's gaze darted away again. When it returned to Evan, she said, "So we'll tackle this from both ends. Clearly I must leave Istanbul as soon as possible. But you're already here. Can you stay?"

Evan nodded.

"I'd like you to find those two women." She cocked her head. "The steam. Did you get a good look at them?"

"Good enough. Sisters. Twins, maybe."

Lyudmila nodded. "Good for us; bad for them." She ruminated for a moment or two while in the rear of the café the two men, old and sun-blackened like bricks of charcoal, began another game of dominoes, their arthritic fingers moving with surprising dexterity. "This city's lousy with Russians, has been since the forties."

"You think the twins are Russian?"

"Not born, maybe, but perhaps Russian Turks." She waved a hand. "They had to buy ether. Not so easy to obtain these days. And if they aren't Turkish born then they're marked coming through immigration, here or Ankara."

Drawing out a small notepad, she scribbled down an address. Ripping off the top sheet, she handed it to Evan, who memorized the address, then put a match to it, turning it to ash.

"This man, Hamit—he's a goldsmith. His work is excellent. Because of the wide range of his powerful clientele so is his intel." She put a hand over Evan's. "He knows me as Rakel. You will be Fiona, sister to Rakel."

Evan laughed. "He won't believe me."

"Why, could we not be sisters?" Lyudmila squeezed Evan's hand, left in the center of her palm a small token. "He will believe this," she said.

As one, they rose, kissed in the European manner. All at once, Lyud-mila drew her close, whispered fiercely in her ear, "The endgame has begun. Don't forget."

Evan began to ask her what she meant, but, suddenly in a rush, Lyud-mila pushed away and strode out into the narrow street.

Evan watched Lyudmila quickly vanish into the seething crowd. The endgame. The stakes for Lyudmila—and by proxy Evan herself—were ratcheted up. *Don't forget.* Don't forget what? She didn't know, and now she wondered if she would ever find out. Whether she would ever see her friend again.

■ ■ ■

In Karaköy, Lyudmila went down to the water. A sleek, polished wood speedboat waited for her, rocking gently in the swell. She climbed in with-out assistance, took a seat aft. The engines engaged fully, the nose of the speedboat rose, and they made a shallow arc, rushing beneath the gate-way under the two-decker Galata Bridge, past the ferry terminal, the shops and restaurants, the neon signs, already gaudy as the sun hung low and swollen, sinking behind the minarets. The speedboat slowed only when they came in sight of a seaplane, resting on its pontoons. The pilot cut the engines and they drifted alongside the starboard pontoon. The door was open and a woman emerged, handed Lyudmila up into the plane. She set-tled into a seat, staring out across the Golden Horn to the European side of the city that had caused her so much joy and pain in equal measure. Well, she thought, that was life in a nutshell, wasn't it?

As the seaplane took off she was alerted to a one-word text on a sepa-rate cell phone. She pressed a speed-dial number. Kata answered at once.

"Our issue still has yet to be resolved successfully."

That was Kata, always "issue," never "problem." For Kata problems did not exist, only solutions, often at the business end of a weapon. "Tell me."

"After a year of trying every which way I know to grow close to him I still haven't been able to make any headway with Minister Kusnetsov."

Lyudmila closed her eyes against the brassy flash and dazzle of sun-light off the waters of the Golden Horn. She wasn't surprised, given the latest intel she had been given about the Sovereign. "That's extremely unfortunate." She was not about to tell Kata that Major Korokova's people had just tried to kill her. Kata's ultimate remit was to use Kusnetsov to get to the Sovereign, but now that wasn't going to happen. In the years since

Lyudmila's self-imposed exile, the Sovereign had cleverly and systematically consolidated his power so resolutely, so unequivocally there was no
one who dared stand against him, even Kusnetsov. In the years since her
exile something had happened to the Sovereign. Possibly the latent insanity that now guided the increasingly intemperate moves he had made
during the last three years was always there. Such a diagnosis would
scarcely surprise Lyudmila, having come to the same conclusion months
ago. The only person who might know for sure and whom they could
actually ask was Evan and Kata's birth father, Dr. Konstantin Reveshvili,
but events had gone far beyond any assistance Konstantin could provide
her. No one inside the Kremlin, no one inside all of the Russian Federation was capable of stopping the Sovereign, no matter what they might
believe of his mental state. He had quelled all the pockets of resistance,
jailed all the ringleaders, would-be ringleaders, supposed ringleaders. He
had taken down more than a dozen oligarchs, who now resided behind
bars in disgrace. These measures were enough to ensure that the rest of
the oligarchs who had amassed their fortunes through his brutal klep-
tocracy fell in line behind him, not one of them daring to wield their
immense fortunes against him. Russian sports figures, opera stars were
also closemouthed when asked about him. His reach had always been
long, but now it was virtually complete.

A month ago the moment had overtaken her. She knew it was now or
never, the goal toward which she had been working for five years. How
dangerous not only for her, but there was now no help for it. She thought
of Evan then. How many times had the opportunity arisen for her to tell
Evan the truth. Earlier today had been the last of an uncounted number
during the last five years. But however much part of her wanted to, another part—the stronger part—forced her to bite back the words, adher-
ing to the strict protocol she herself had created.

"Are you still there?"

Lyudmila snapped out of her rumination. "Of course."

"Because there's more." And Kata told Lyudmila about the call she
had received from Major Korokova, the mysterious death of Ivan Levrov.
"He's—"

"I know who Levrov is." Lyudmila's attention had sharpened a couple
of notches. She had a keen interest in the progress of Directorate KV. Kata
knew only that she needed to keep a sharp eye out for intel going in and
out of the directorate.

"I'm about to helo out to join Korokova at the death scene."

Lyudmila's brain snapped into overdrive. "No," she said.

"What?"

"Not you. Given what I know about her and the frosty aftermath of your first and only meeting with her I very much doubt that the good major would appreciate you stomping all over her territory."

"We can't just let it go."

"Of course not. You'll send someone from your cadre."

"Do you have anyone in mind?"

"Naturally." It was a curious thing, Lyudmila thought. She had been expecting the familiar razor edge to Kata's voice but there was no hint of it. She put it down to Kata's yearlong intimate entanglement with Alyosha Ivanovna. Even as she worked in Kata's Directorate O, a small cadre created by Minister Kusnetsov, head of the FSB, Alyosha spent a majority of her working hours at her old job at FSB SIGINT, where she gathered intel for Kata and, by proxy, Lyudmila. Alyosha served as a grounding agent for Kata without, thankfully, blunting the killer instinct that made Kata so valuable to Lyudmila. "Send Rodion Stepanov Molchalin."

"Captain Molchalin?" Kata was incredulous. "He's the newest member of my group."

"Yes, but I think he's most likely to make a favorable impression on Major Korokova."

"The Ice Queen?" Kata laughed. "I don't think so. I'm not even sure she has a functioning sex organ."

Now it was Lyudmila's turn to laugh. "Send him in, Kata. At the very least he won't rub her the wrong way."

"Like I would." Kata knew it and acquiesced. "Of course, who among us can know human mysteries?"

■ ■ ■

Putting away her phone, Lyudmila stared out the Perspex window, her thoughts turning to Bernhard-Otto von Kleist. He was handsome in the strict Prussian aristocratic sense—gray eyes, patrician nose, wide mouth, the close-cropped hair in the brush style of his long-deceased illustrious grandfather, General Robert von Kleist. He revered the general above all others, save perhaps his daughter Ghislane and, of course, Lyudmila herself.

He was an expert fixer. Every prominent pol in the EU came to him when they needed help of the sort only he could provide. As such he shunned the spotlight, not unlike Marsden Tribe, though their motivations were vastly different. Getting close to von Kleist was the relatively easy part; convincing him of their closeness and mutual trust far more difficult. She knew she had needed to be patient, to inculcate him over time. She had liked him and at times she convinced herself they were close. But then everything changed. Using him had been a calculated risk—one she had little choice but to take.

When she had gone rogue she had promised herself that she would never take on a partner. Partners were nothing but trouble. Not in the beginning, of course, when the romance was in full bloom—but as soon as they'd got their claws into the mechanism you yourself had created they were hell-bent on changing it under the rubric of "making it better," when what they were really doing was refashioning the mechanism in their own image. Because of course they knew best; why else would you have hired them.

This line of reasoning was unfortunately what motivated von Kleist. She had met him in Malta eighteen months ago, when she used him to suborn Konrad Mischler, a Swiss German, director of a prominent Zurich bank with clandestine ties to the FSB, subsequently using him to feed disinformation to the Russians, particularly those who had turned against her. Von Kleist had had such a good time at it he'd refused her payment of his Everest-high fees. Over drinks they got to know each other, over dinner they became fast friends, in bed they forged a partnership over and over again.

Stupid, stupid, stupid, Lyudmila berated herself now. But she was in dire need of what he could provide; no one else could do what he did, not with his level of expertise, contacts, and favors extracted from grateful former clients. Now she had successfully maneuvered him to the sidelines. It hadn't been difficult: he was in love with his own image as a top-of-the-line fixer, and in this regard he had more than enough business to keep him happily occupied.

She had lied to von Kleist, just as she had lied to Evan and Kata; lying was endemic with her, a way of life that might have been initially forced on her but for which she discovered she had an extraordinary talent. Plus, lying was addictive as cocaine or heroin.

Two years ago, she had convinced Kata that her birth parents were dead—even going so far as to take her to the graves of a couple she had passed off as Kata's parents. She had done this even while Evan was meeting their birth parents, Konstantin and Rebecca Reveshvili, who ran a psychiatric clinic in the countryside northeast of Köln, Germany.

Lyudmila didn't want Kata anywhere near her birth parents. Kata's two children were there, safe and sound, along with Ben Butler's daughter. They must be protected at all costs. *I don't like Kata. In fact, I despise her, but then that's not so surprising: I created her. I did the initial intake when she arrived in Moscow. I saw something in her, something despicable, something horrendous. After only an hour with her I realized I was sitting across the table from a psychopath. A homicidal maniac. But perhaps I misjudged just how much she loves to kill. During the act of murdering someone is when she feels truly alive.*

She was the polar opposite of her sister. It was Evan who had saved her niece and nephew. It was Evan whom Lyudmila loved above all others. *I want to save her. I want her to live, I do,* she told herself. *And yet I keep sending her off to do my bidding where she will be anything but safe.* As quickly as tears rolled down her cheeks she flicked them away with a contemptuous gesture. *The trouble with me,* she thought, *is I like too much to play God.*

Outside the seaplane the engines roared, water became land, then water again, a deeper shade, the surface more restless as the sun extinguished itself in the west.

4

"So it's reversed now," An Binh said.

Ben Butler, close beside her, said, "Is that so terrible?"

"Benjamin." Her beautiful lips quirked into a smile. "Everything in life that is terrible has already happened to me. That cup is full. There can be nothing terrible for me now."

They were down in the basement gymnasium where she had helped Ben recover from the wound that, but for her, would have caused him to live the rest of his life in a wheelchair. He was watching as An Binh did sets of leg lifts. She used a weighted barbell rather than one of the state-of-the-art machines Isobel Lowe had installed. An Binh was definitely old-school when it came to physical workouts.

The two of them had become fixtures in Isobel's magnificent newly renovated mansion, surrounded by its garden of hollies, pear trees, and Japanese maples; by beds of roses that in the past would have been in the throes of winter's anorexia but that were now half-leafed, sporting tiny flowers like a child's fingernails. Tulip bulbs slept peacefully under the earth, and azalea bushes poked their labyrinths of spiky arms toward the unaccustomed warmth of the sun. The whole was screened in from the street by twelve-foot-high evergreen hedges embedded with electric wires guaranteed to bring down a rageful lion, let alone a human intruder. AI cameras, small as gnats, surveyed every square inch of the garden with the relentless persecution granted only to machines.

Isobel Lowe was the head of Parachute's two-year-old industrial-espionage arm. Who she didn't know inside the Beltway wasn't worth knowing. Her home, situated near the corner of California Street NW and Massachusetts Avenue, in which they had become something akin to family, was a cream and butterscotch Italianate mansion, where Ben worked and lived, and An Binh recuperated.

Ben had for some years, many years ago, been Isobel's partner when she was a field agent for Mossad. Later, Evan had been his partner in the field when they both worked for the US DOD, and then when he ran his own shop as part of the DOD. Until it was summarily shut down last year. Both he and Evan had come to work for Isobel then and, by proxy, Marsden Tribe, the genius founder/owner of Parachute, whose major business was constructing and utilizing quantum computers. They were of Tribe's groundbreaking design; they were far and away the best on the planet—faster, more stable, more utile in the service of any number of tech spheres, including one supervised by Isobel.

"Join me for a cup of tea," An Binh said, after the last set. Just because the woman didn't sweat didn't mean she wasn't working hard. The amount of weight she had instructed Ben to load onto either end of the barbell was more than most men could tolerate. She had completed a third set of fifteen leg lifts.

"Of course," Ben said, looking her straight in the face. He was like that. He looked you in the eye when he spoke. She appreciated that in him.

Ben, who was used to her silences, knew they were as significant as her words, went on because he knew she needed an explanation. She was feeling strong, but feeling strong and being fully healed were two separate issues; he knew that from personal experience.

"Time and practice," he said as she stood up. "There's no need to rush it."

"But there is," she said. "I know I overstepped boundaries last year."

"You had a debt to settle. It was understandable."

It was difficult to believe that just a year ago she had been shot, on the very precipice of death. But from deep inside herself she had worked on her ravaged body with the same curious combination of Eastern modalities she had used on him to get him back on his feet when medical experts swore he'd never walk again. When she was strong enough it was Ben who took her through the increasingly rigorous physical regime she had designed for him. That began three months ago; her recovery had been fully as astonishing as his had been. They were locked now—the two of them—because of shared near-death experiences, caring for one another in body, mind, and spirit. In short, they had been through a war together and the experience had changed them both forever.

"For you perhaps, but for Isobel, I don't know." She shook her head. "I'm not altogether comfortable taking advantage of her hospitality."

Isobel, refusing to give up even in the face of the surgeons' dire prognosis for Ben, had hired An Binh, who had been urgently recommended by Evan's father, Dr. Reveshvili, to be his physical therapist. It turned out she had skills far beyond anyone's imaginings. Discovering the problem in Ben's hip after he had been shot, she guided him back to health.

"I want to earn my keep, Benjamin."

"Absolutely not." He knew what she meant; she wanted to work with him and Evan, be part of his team.

Her voice softened, lowered. "You know I have resources you don't. I can do what you can't."

He found himself actually considering this. Since last year he and Evan were no longer a team; Tribe was now the one she reported to. He didn't know how Isobel felt about the change; they'd never discussed it. As for himself, initially he'd been dismayed, but change had become a part of their lives the moment they signed on to Parachute. If that's what Tribe wanted, that's what he'd get. It was either that or resign from Parachute, a path he was unwilling to take. Besides, Evan seemed fine with her new role; their trust in each other remained a constant.

Just then Isobel burst into the gym and hurried toward them. With her was a tall, beefy man, a little overweight but still retaining most of his athlete's form, whom Ben recognized as Wes Connerly, head of the National Geospatial-Intelligence Agency.

Out of the side of his mouth Ben told An Binh who Connerly was. "Never a good sign when he's around," he said softly. "Especially when he's accompanying Isobel. Most especially when he's here inside the DC Parachute grounds."

"I can stay," she said. "Start now." She was entirely serious and he knew it.

He sighed. "Now you'll have to drink your tea by yourself."

"Don't worry." Her voice was carefully neutral. "I'm used to it." Then she stepped away, crossed to the far side of the gym, exited through the door to the sauna.

Isobel and her guest approached Ben. He glanced at Isobel, saw she did not seem well pleased, before his gaze fell fully on Connerly.

"Butler." Connerly did not offer a hand; both were plunged deep into the pockets of his too-heavy tweed overcoat.

"Wes," Ben said with a hint of irony. He had worked for people like Connerly and he didn't like them. More tellingly for him, he didn't trust them.

Connerly's eyes narrowed. His cheeks pillowed out before he pushed out an audible breath.

In order to keep matters from turning into a pissing match, Isobel injected herself into the conversation. "Mr. Connerly has come here specifically to—"

"Who was that?" Connerly overrode her.

"Who?" Ben said. He was determined to make Connerly work for every little detail.

"That woman. The Asian."

Ben stiffened, looked Connerly in the eye. "What does her ancestry have to do with anything?"

"Asian-born," Connerly said. "Is she Chinese by chance?"

Even before Isobel put a hand on Ben's forearm she could sense the tensing of his muscles. He was far from a hothead but she knew he and An Binh had a special relationship. Even if Wes Connerly was a racist, she knew it was not politic to call him on it. Not here, not now. Maybe never.

There now fell a silence heavy as a blanket of snow.

Interestingly, it was Connerly who broke it. Perhaps he sensed that he had crossed a line. "Listen, you two, I have hundreds of Chinese and North Korean cybercriminals trying to break into every government database. They're like a swarm of fucking locusts, so excuse me if I'm a bit overprotective on this point." He shrugged, then appeared to think it was time to get to the point. "Brady Thompson was a friend of yours."

"Hell, no."

Connerly pursed his lips. He didn't like to be contradicted. "Still . . . You knew him, yes? Knew him well."

Ben nodded.

"Okay, then." Connerly gestured curtly as he turned on his heel.

With a last glance at Isobel, Ben followed him.

■　■　■

Later, when he was sitting beside Connerly in a government-issue black Navigator, the head of NGSA said, "We haven't exactly gotten off on the right foot. I know that the president pulled the rug out from under you, but I assure you I'm one of the ones who saw that as hasty."

"Sure," Ben said, a sharp edge to his voice. "Let's go with that."

Connerly stared out the window at the passing buildings. "Wouldn't by any chance be interested in coming back."

"I'm completely happy where I am," Ben said.

"I could make it worth your while."

"I very much doubt that."

"My agency has many perks on offer. Unlimited funds, as well."

"I had no idea you had a sense of humor, Wes."

At that, Connerly turned back, fixing him with his mild, entitled gaze. "We're not on a first-name basis, Butler." Then he shrugged. "Took a shot."

"Seriously? It didn't seem like your heart was in it."

Connerly made a wry face. "That attitude, I assure you, is as carefully cultivated as an African violet." He shifted from one buttock cheek to the other. "Allows me to stay within spitting distance of the snake pit without getting bitten."

But it was Ben who, like a dog with a bone, kept the subject alive, possibly because it wasn't only the DOD that had done him dirt but a member of the FBI as well, and that betrayal still burned like a match struck in a bale-filled barn.

"It wouldn't matter anyway, Wes," he said now. "Even if I agreed I wouldn't give you what you want."

Connerly, with a dead-eye stare, said, "And what might that be?"

"Access to Tribe. Or more accurately his secrets."

"Come on, Butler. You don't have them," Connerly said flatly and as if the answer wasn't of the gravest import to him.

"You can't know that," Ben replied blandly. He was enjoying immensely Connerly's growing discomfort.

Connerly made a sound of derision. "I knew this fishing expedition was a waste of time."

Ben ignored him. "The point is if I did I wouldn't give it to you people."

"Yes, Marsden Tribe's exalted quantum computers."

"They're a damn sight better than what you have. Or IBM, or Amazon, or Cambridge. Or everyone else scrambling to unlock the secrets of quantum space, for that matter."

Connerly closed his eyes. "How much easier my job would be if I could have the use of Marsden's marvels."

"You do have the use of them," Ben reminded him needlessly. But a knife turn nonetheless.

"Limited use. For a fat fee," Connerly groused.

"We run a business, not a charity."

Connerly kept doggedly on point. Maybe he'd been given a script. "Fraction of the whole. Glimpse of the promised land. What he SaaS's to other companies." He meant Software as a Service. "But we are the US government. On another level entirely. Entire platform is required. Whole nine yards." The SUV had slowed in piling traffic. He pushed himself forward, presumably to give the driver alternate instructions. When he again sat back in his seat, he rumbled on. "Trouble with all these billionaires. Not a drop of patriotism in their blood. They owe us—all of them. Big time. Giving them the freedom to make their billions."

"How neofascist of you." Ben had ceased playing around with this putz. He meant what he said and in the change in Connerly's posture and expression it was clear the other man knew it. A government putz Wes Connerly might be, but unlike so many senators who approved his department's annual budget he wasn't stupid.

But just like him he ignored Ben's thrust. He licked his lips. "And paying not a penny of taxes."

"Send Congress a memo."

Again, Connerly contrived to ignore Ben's slings and arrows. "Let me tell you, Butler. Hell of a thing when the United States government can't get what it wants."

"Democracy in action," Ben opined dryly.

"Piece of work," Connerly said, clearly disgusted, "you are."

They had finally left the snarl of traffic behind and arrived at their destination: a sprawling white building a stone's throw from CIA HQ in Langley, Virginia. The façade was as anonymous as the side of an Egyptian pyramid, its interior just as mysterious.

"Change your mind soon enough," Connerly said as they exited the Navigator. "They think." With no indication of who "they" were. Ben figured he'd soon find out.

"Hold that thought," Ben said.

Connerly eyed him with a glimmer of a smirk. "Stranger things have happened, my friend."

Ben remembered what happened when the FBI turncoat, Jon Tennyson, started calling him "my friend." Bad things happened, nearly costing Ben his life.

5

ISTANBUL, TURKEY

The goldsmith Hamit's shop was on a wide boulevard in Sultanahmet. Evan came upon it quickly as she rounded a corner of a side street and entered the vast and heaving flow of the boulevard. The marble and glass shopfront looked quite posh. Lyudmila had mentioned that Hamit's clientele was firmly upper-class.

Instead of heading directly in, Evan moved off to the opposite side of the boulevard. She sipped on pickled cucumber and cabbage juice in a plastic cup bought from a street vendor. She waited twenty minutes, marking the people who went in and out of the shop, as well as anyone hanging about, other than shopkeepers, street vendors, and the like. Having witnessed nothing untoward, she picked her way through the throng to the opposite side and entered the shop of Hamit, the goldsmith.

It was large for a shop in Istanbul, with high ceilings and plenty of light via lamps. On either wall hung black-and-white blowups of Hamit's handiwork: jeweled necklaces, rings for both fingers and toes, thick chokers, drop earrings made from clusters of jewels. It seemed odd to have these fine works of art in black-and-white until Evan approached the three-tiered glass case three-quarters of the way back. Then the eye was dazzled by the colors of the stones, deep and rich. It was, Evan thought, like stepping out the front door of Dorothy's home in Kansas into the Technicolor of Oz. A neat trick, meant to entice the eye, speed up the pulse, and open the wallet of prospective buyers.

Two young men in traditional Turkish outfits stood behind the cases, removing items from their velvet beds as well-heeled women in French and Italian designer clothes pointed to them. The odor of too much money and privilege surrounded them like a haze of overpriced perfume.

Evan looked beyond the young men, to the back wall. To the right she saw an opening obscured by a curtain of golden beads that now clattered as a man who must be Hamit held aside the beaded curtain for a woman of estimable means with whom he had been conferring. Hamit pressed a buzzer, and without breaking stride the woman passed through a panel in the long case that ran from one side wall to the other. She looked neither to the left nor right as she traversed the thick carpet in her high-heeled pumps. It seemed as if the two young men relaxed their shoulders the moment she was gone.

Hamit, standing with a clutch of design drawings in his left hand, watched Evan as she slowly approached the counter. She could feel him sizing her up as to whether she would be worth his time.

He was a tall, slim man in his midsixties, handsome, dark of mien. He sported the slicked-back hair and pencil mustache of an old-world impresario. He moved like one. Though he was wearing an imported tan summer-weight wool suit, his footwear was strictly Turkish—thin blue calfskin loafers imprinted with gold Arabic letters.

Seeing that his two assistants were still busy helping customers, he put the drawings aside and approached Evan. "How may I help you, madam?"

"Rakel sent me," Evan said softly. "I am her sister."

"Rakel's sister." Hamit raised one eyebrow, deliberately theatrical. "Mm."

She showed him the token Lyudmila had given her.

He took the token, inspected it as if it were a diamond, then dropped it back into her palm. His expression lightened enough for the semblance of a smile to form on his lips. "Yes, of course." He moved to the gate in the case, gestured. "This way, madam."

He led her through the beaded curtain into a cozy, overheated space. Again he gestured and she sat on a wooden stool facing him across a lacquered table. He turned his head subtley toward a wooden screen at the rear of the space and in a moment a girl of no more than thirteen emerged with a tray on which stood a tea service. She poured the steaming liquid the proper way, from high up, into a glass encased with a chased gold server with a handle. She set a small plate with a variety of sweet cookies on the table, then withdrew.

It was only after they drank, after Hamit asked after Rakel and Evan replied, that she got down to business. "I'm looking for a pair of sisters. Turkish. Late twenties, early thirties. Probably twins."

"Madam," Hamit spread his hands, "I am no magician. These sisters could be anyone and everyone of that age of the female persuasion."

She described them as best she could. "It's possible they're of Russian descent."

"Ah."

"You know them, then."

"I do not." He raised a long, elegant forefinger. "However, two young women similar to the ones you described were in this very shop yesterday. They spoke Turkish to me, but Russian to each other." He shook his head. *"Aptalca şeyler,* they were." *Foolish things.* "They were looking at my most expensive pieces. When I asked them if they could afford these pieces they laughed. Laughed, can you imagine!" He shook his head. "They claimed they were about to come into an inheritance, but to tell you the truth I didn't believe them. I shooed them out of the shop and that's the last I saw of them."

"As it happens," Evan said, "they were telling the truth." But only, she thought, if you substituted "payment for a murder" for "inheritance."

"I think those are the young women I seek. Do you know their names?"

"They never introduced themselves. Part of the rudeness of the younger generation. All the old standards have been washed away." The goldsmith shrugged. "Now. I don't see how I can be of further—"

"They would have been looking to buy a good quantity of ether."

Hamit's eyes opened wide. "Ether, you say."

Evan nodded.

He did not have to gesture again for the girl to pour them more tea. The sweets remained arrayed on their plate, untouched. Evan was full up with tea. What she longed for was a lamb tagine and the flatbread to scoop up the fragrant stew. Failing that, an iced vodka would do. *I've been hanging out with Russians for too long,* she thought wryly.

"Well," he said, after taking a sip of tea and putting down his glass, "that puts an entirely different spin on the matter."

Evan cocked her head. "How so?"

"Ether must be imported, you see. Also, it is hardly a common item." He tapped an exquisitely manicured nail against the tabletop. It sounded like a maestro's metronome.

"But you know about it. Ether."

"I? Apart from working gold and precious stones I know nothing." He gave a sly smile. "It's my customers who know just about everything."

"Not by pillow talk, yes?"

He gave a silent laugh, something she'd never seen before. "This room we're in, it's like a confessional. Only better. The judgment of God or Allah is far from here. There is only me. And they trust me, my customers. Here as I design the exquisite jewelry they will display on their fingers, wrists, around their necks they tell me their deepest frustrations, fears, desires, wishes."

"And you provide the solutions."

"Ah, no, sister of Rakel. I am but a goldsmith."

"Hardly humble."

He spread his hands. "What would be the point." It wasn't a question. "No, I merely suggest someone who may provide a solution."

Evan found herself liking this man. He was both smart and clever. Better, he was confident in his own abilities. He also knew his limits, which precluded arrogance, a weakness she could not stomach but upon which she could prey.

Evan took one of the sweet treats, popped it into her mouth, enjoyed the taste of ground almonds and honey. "And so." She licked powdered sugar from her fingertips. "To ether."

A certain darkness seemed to come over Hamit, clouds across the sun. "Only one man—one man in all of Istanbul. The Syrian."

"An importer-exporter."

"After a fashion." Hamit made a face. "Abd-El-Kader is that." He took a gulp of his tea as to wash a bitter taste from his mouth. "Here he is known as Örümcek."

"The Spider."

Hamit nodded. "The spinner of webs." When he set his glass down, his hand was not altogether steady. "Abd-El-Kader smuggles Syrian refugees into Turkey."

Evan felt an uncomfortable prickling at the nape of her neck. "For a price."

"No, you don't understand. These Syrians—these refugees—have no money. They are barely hanging onto their lives."

"So then . . ."

"He makes of them indentured slaves. Ten years of their lives they give up to him in exchange for the promise of leaving the war behind. They think of Turkey as the promised land. This is what the emissaries of Örümcek tell them. They believe, of course they do. Desperation makes them perfect marks. They sign a document and then here they are in Istanbul. Put to work. What pitiful wages they receive go to him."

"Then how do they live?"

"Abd-El-Kader provides for them, after a fashion. Stores them in old, abandoned warehouses his company has bought up for next to nothing. He crowds them in. Like the cattle cars of the Nazis on their way to the camps. They die like flies in there. What matter to him? There are always more coming, like a tide, endlessly lapping at the Golden Horn."

Hamit's eyes had grown markedly darker. They alit upon Evan's face like the gaze of a crow. Intelligent. Inscrutable. "This is the man you must confront if you are to find the young women you seek." He cocked his head. "Finding them is this important?"

The insidious sickly sweet stench of ether. "It is."

"Is your life, then, so unimportant to you? Rakel, your sister, will wail and tear her hair at your funeral."

The hairs on her arms stirred. "I will manage," Evan said.

He continued to stare at her, as if taking the final measure of her, as if she were a new piece of jewelry he was designing. Then he gave a quick nod, gave her an address in Karaköy. "An extremely run-down area of the city." He pushed away his empty glass. "Altogether fitting, as you will discover to your grief."

6

The interior of the Defense Threat Reaction Agency looked like a mausoleum, if said mausoleum was clad in ferroconcrete blocks instead of Carrara marble. In any case, the white color was almost the same. Interesting, Ben thought, that Connerly wasn't taking him to his own lair.

Ben lost count of the number of checkpoints he was required to negotiate—his cell phone, keys, wristwatch, metal credit cards, and pocketknife were all confiscated at the first one—until he and Connerly arrived at the elevator bank at the rear of a lobby that appeared to be as big as a football field. As it turned out, the elevator bank wasn't Connerly's objective at all, for they turned left just before it, went past two unsightly columns where a warehouse-size elevator gaped open, waiting for them. Connerly swiped his key card, the doors slid soundlessly shut. They went down instead of up, three floors, Ben judged, though the elevator's descent was elephantine in its pace.

When the doors opened, they stepped out into a corridor that seemed to stretch endlessly in either direction. There were few branches and no corners that Ben could discern. The constant hum of very large engines and exhaust fans filled the air.

"It's as if we're inside an enormous beehive," Ben said.

"Wasps," Connerly replied without turning his head. "They're all wasps here."

It didn't sound like a joke. It seemed clear that Connerly didn't have a sense of humor, Ben thought. But then humor for most of these government types was as vestigial as an appendix. He also noted Connerly's use of "they" when he might have been expected to say "we." Ben filed that bit of data away.

Connerly turned smartly to his right, marching down the corridor at an unexpectedly fast clip. He was like a horse that scents the finish line.

Ben wondered who or what was lashing his withers. He did not ask Connerly where they were going, and for once Connerly was silent as the tomb.

The corridor was odd on many levels. It was rounded at its top, as in a tunnel. The source of the lighting was mysterious, and oddest of all, there did not appear to be many doors, just blank walls, as if the spaces beyond were as vast as the lobby above their heads.

At length, Connerly stopped before a door on their left. It was as over-sized as the entrance for an emperor. It was steel-clad. It reminded Ben of a door to a bank vault. Connerly used his key card, but that wasn't enough. He stood still as stone as the reader recognized the unique design of his retina.

At once, the door swung open of its own accord on well-oiled hinges the size of Ben's forearm. Inside the doorway stood a man Ben recognized but had never met. George Wilson, the head of the Defense Threat Reaction Agency, into whose bailiwick Connerly had taken him. He was small, dark, intense, bookish. His eyes were a pale blue, set wide apart. He sported a prow of a nose. If his chin were any more pointed it could be used as a weapon.

During the introductions, brief as they were, he grasped Ben's hand, enfolded it with long, white fingers, knuckles the size of dice. And he held onto Ben's hand, trapping it, Ben would say later to Isobel, while with laser eyes he appeared to be looking through skin, fascia, and muscle searching for Ben's bones.

At first, Ben thought to pull his hand away as if from a faulty light switch, but then he reconsidered. Let him acquiesce to this silent interrogation, or rather let Wilson believe that. And Ben's smile was so warm, so genuine that at length Wilson had no choice but to let him go, stand aside so that he and Connerly could enter the inner sanctum. It seemed odd to Ben that Connerly was being used as nothing more than a messenger boy, tasked with bringing Ben to what appeared to be Wilson's fortress of solitude.

The lighting was soft here, the insistent whirr in the corridor muted if not banished altogether. The room was generously proportioned and, to Ben's surprise, furnished neither as an office nor a lab. With its over-sized leather furniture, burlwood side tables, shaded lamps, it looked like a men's club somewhere in London. All that was missing was a fire-place and just above it a mounted stag head on the wall. There was also a highly polished mahogany table with a baize top where, Ben imagined, a group might play Texas Hold'em beneath the green-glass lamps, swathed in aromatic cigar smoke.

In fact, there was a figure seated at the head of the table, farthest from where Ben was standing, smoking a Churchill Imperial. Blue smoke drifted languidly from his half-open mouth.

"Benjamin Butler," the figure said. "Come on over."

Now that he shifted in his chair Ben could see that he was in uniform. Closer to, Ben could see the shoulder boards: four stars. He entered the fragrant haze, saw a square-jawed man with small, keen eyes, a Roman nose, a generous mouth with the plush lips of a woman. Face was lined, wind- and sunburned. A man not one to sit behind his desk in the Pentagon. Out with his men, despite his exalted rank.

"Benjamin Butler," Wilson said, "meet General Philip Johnstone Reade."

"General," Ben said, "I don't know whether to shake your hand or salute." The eyes, staring up at Ben, crinkled at the outer corners. Reade held out his hand. Stepping up, Ben shook the four-star's hand, which was heavy, callused, and dry.

"How about a cigar." A command, not a question. Reade pushed over a wooden humidor laminated with lacquered tobacco leaves, watched as Ben opened it, extracted a cigar, and lit it with a heavy brass Zippo.

When it was going, the general, eyes on his cigar, rolled it in his fingers, inhaling the scent it was giving off. Several moments later, a young woman, long of leg with dark gleaming hair, entered from a door Ben had not noticed. She was carrying a tray. She was not in a uniform of any sort, he noted.

She glided to a halt beside the general's left elbow, set down a plate and a cup and saucer. She wore a little black skirt that looked like nothing but must have cost four figures, a sleeveless oyster-colored silk shirt. In other words, not an outfit that the usual E-5 or E-6 could afford. She had long, slightly upturned eyes, wide lips, and high cheekbones. Her arms were toned, her shoulders broad as any swimmer's.

"Dry toast and tea, Mr. Butler," Reade said. "Special diet. Nothing you would be interested in, of course. So do tell Daisy what you'd like to eat?"

Daisy? Ben thought. Why not Daisy Mae while we're at it? He felt like he'd tumbled down the rabbit hole. Briefly, he turned, saw Wilson grin at him like a totem before fixing his eyes on Daisy. Connerly looked as if he was trying his damnedest not to say what he very much wanted to say. No matter. His eyes said it all.

With a chill down his spine, Ben turned back to the general, who had already taken an enormous bite out of the top slice of toast and was chewing it contemplatively.

"Snap to it, man. We don't have all day."

Ben, smiling, took his time addressing the young woman. "I'll have an egg cream, Daisy."

The general's jaws halted in midchew. His eyes narrowed. "What the hell's an egg cream?"

"Special diet," Ben said without a hint of irony. After toiling under the weight of the federal government for years, he suddenly felt free as a bird in flight. He didn't have to answer to these people, did not even have to be civil to them. He would because that was the sort of person he was. But that didn't mean he couldn't have a bit of fun along the way.

The general's eyes seemed to narrow even more, like slits in a castle wall behind which stood soldiers armed to the teeth.

"Vanilla or chocolate?" Daisy asked, unfazed by her master's consternation. Clearly, she knew what an egg cream was.

"Chocolate, Daisy." Ben's smile was relaxed, amused even. "Thank you."

The smile was returned before Daisy made her silent exit. Wilson's avid gaze followed her all the way. Connerly seemed not to have noticed her at all. He came and sat at the table, across from where Ben sat. His choice of chairs appeared deliberate. Wilson followed him to the table only once Daisy had passed through the doorway from which she had come.

The general began to chew again, frowning so deeply the horizontal lines across his forehead turned into fissures.

"Well," the general said, struggling to recover, "now that we're all seated and geared up . . ."

"Except for my egg cream."

At once, Reade's gaze snapped to Wilson, then to Connerly and back again. "You clowns failed to tell me Mr. Butler was a smart-ass." He grunted. "I don't like smart-asses." Pushing his chair away with the backs of his thighs, he arose the way a volcano pushes through the crust of the earth, with vigor, heat, and menace.

It was at that moment Daisy chose as if by magic to emerge through the door with Ben's egg cream. All eyes were fixed on her this time as she moved to Ben's left elbow, set down the tall old-time fountain service glass filled to the brim. Needless to say, she hadn't spilled a drop.

"Here you go, sir." She had set the glass in front of Ben. "I trust it's to your satisfaction."

"No doubt," Ben said. "No doubt."

When she had taken her leave, General Reade cleared his throat. "On the other hand, I've studied your record, which is exemplary."

"Thank you, General."

"You've accomplished a great deal in service . . . a great deal." He cleared his throat again, then spread his hands wide. "Mr. Butler, this all may seem like some kind of wonky circus to you, but I assure you the men around this table are deadly serious."

Ben savored his egg cream, wiping his upper lip of foam after each sip. "Much as I enjoy this treat, General, I'd be obliged if you'd tell me what I'm doing here."

"I'll fucking tell you." Connerly, cheeks spotted red, raised his voice as he made to stand up. But Reade's bladelike hand stilled both his voice and his motion. He subsided back into his chair, but his cheeks were still aflame.

"To your point, Mr. Butler." The general pressed a button hidden by the baize covering. A large print hanging on the wall behind him rose noiselessly, revealing a flat-screen. At which point the general pressed a second button and the screen lit up. It showed MRI images of three human brains, or possibly, on Ben's closer inspection, three different views of one brain.

"This," General Reade said, "is why you have been brought here." He nodded toward Wilson. "George, since this falls under your bailiwick, why don't you start us off." Again, a command rather than a query.

Wilson rose, a small laser pointer in his hand, which he aimed at the images. A red dot appeared on the left-hand image. It moved to the center image, and on to the right-hand image as he spoke. "What we're looking at here are three images of the human brain." The pointer clicked and clicked again. "But not just any human brain, Butler. This is the brain of Brady Thompson, Unites States secretary of defense. At least he was, until forty or so hours ago."

"You sure got these results quickly." Ben could not keep the skepticism out of his voice.

"Need engenders speed," Wilson said. "Believe me, this is the *emmis*. You are indeed looking at Brady Thompson's brain."

"Oh, for the love of God," Connerly said, clearly disgusted.

The general blew smoke rings, the hint of a smile finding the corners of his mouth as he watched Ben with a circumspect gaze. To Ben's way of thinking, he sported the expression a father has for a son who had proven his brilliance among his peers.

Connerly had gone rigid. "Tell him already." He was near to shouting. His entire neck was lobster red.

The general's head swung slowly as a monastic lantern, his gaze baleful. "Hey, Mr. Connerly, you are entirely out of order. Do you understand? No, I doubt you do. Asking that we start with the dog's ass instead of with its head is neither logical nor wise."

"I'm a mathematician at heart," Connerly said, but in an altogether more muted tone. He couldn't get his gaze to meet the general's, instead examining the green baize in front of him. "I look for equations which I then solve. I must take a straight line to the solution. Anything else is anathema to me."

"We are dealing with a human being here, Mr. Connerly," the general said, "not a string of numbers." He pointed. "You'd do well to remember that."

That final admonishment seemed to shut Connerly up, at least for the moment. He crossed his arms over his chest, his gaze looking inward, perhaps at the face of the punishment just meted out to him.

Reade gestured. "Continue, George."

Wilson nodded. "Okay, so listen, Butler, our initial assessment was that Thompson died of a massive heart attack. The initial autopsy appeared to confirm that. His heart just about exploded." Here he stopped, seemed to go off on a tangent. "For the record, Ben, we know you and Evan Ryder were acquainted with Brady Thompson and—"

"The trouble is," the general interrupted, "we don't know quite what your relationship was."

"It was like any other—"

"Come on, man." Connerly's voice overran Ben's, and this time Reade did not wave him to silence. He had risen up, bending his torso toward Ben, knuckles pressed hard against the baize. "Don't bullshit us. It's too late for prevarication."

"What he means," the general said, "is that we have an exceedingly serious situation on our hands."

"Some would say a full-blown crisis." Connerly was staring hard at Ben.

A small silence ensued, which meant neither Reade nor Wilson disagreed.

Ben considered for a moment. His and Evan's relationship with Thompson could scarcely be called an acquaintanceship. But with Thompson's death the secret was null and void. "What Evan and I discovered three years ago is that Brady Thompson was a FSB asset."

The silence was so absolute the general's crunch on the last piece of toast sounded like a gunshot, the grinding of his teeth like pestle on mortar.

"The secretary of defense was a *Russian mole.*" Connerly seemed about to go apoplectic. He sat down suddenly and hard. His gaze skittered around the room like a cat on a hot tin roof, afraid to alight on anything for very long.

"That's right," Ben said. "But Evan and I found out. Instead of rumbling him we decided to turn him. He became our asset, a double agent, feeding the Russians factoids embedded with disinformation."

The general's eyes had narrowed again. "And you two took this action on your own?"

"At that time, General Aristides had oversight of my shop. He knew. We briefed him extensively. In the end, he became Thompson's de facto handler. He was the only one we could trust."

Reade ran a hand across his brow. "So to summarize, the secretary of defense, once a Russian asset, turned by you and the Ryder woman, was murdered forty hours ago."

Wilson nodded. "That's correct, General."

"Wait, what?" Ben looked from one to the other. "Murdered? Who said anything about murder? You just told me he died of a massive heart attack."

Wilson stood unnaturally still. "I said those were the preliminary findings."

The general leaned forward. "Mr. Butler, this dog and pony show was necessary. In order to prepare you."

"Prepare me?" Ben's head was buzzing like a swarm of enraged wasps. "For what?"

The red dot on Wilson's laser pointer began to move, and with a sense of deep foreboding there came into Ben's mind a quote from Omar Khayyám he had learned as a child, "The moving finger writes; and, having writ, moves on: nor all thy piety nor wit shall lure it back to cancel half a line, nor all thy tears wash out a word of it." He felt as if what he was about to see he would never be able to unsee.

"You see here, here, and here," Wilson was saying. "These dark areas. They look like tiny explosions, don't they? And here and here are more— over a dozen to be precise."

Ben's heart was hammering in his chest. "What are you saying? What does this mean?"

"It means," the general said, "that something of unknown origin attacked Brady Thompson's mind, detonating in these areas George has just showed you."

"The general has sugar-coated the cause of Thompson's death," Connerly said, his voice quite reasonable now. They had reached the point in the meeting where his expertise was not only welcome but required for guidance. He rose and came around the table, held out his hand until Wilson dropped the laser pointer into it, ceding the floor. "The fact of the matter is I am confident I know the origin of this attack," he said. "The fact of the matter is I have been studying the so-called Havana syndrome that has been affecting our field agents and diplomats first in Cuba, hence its name, then in Moscow, Stockholm . . ."

"And most recently here in Washington," the general said with the pursed lips of a man at last showing his distress.

"For some time, the prevailing wisdom has been some form of weaponized microwave emitter, principally because all the incidents occurred inside buildings. But the most recent incidents here in DC have been out in the open, which makes microwaves less likely."

"So no one knows what's caused these attacks on our people." Wilson drew out a dossier from a briefcase on the floor beside him, opened it onto the tabletop. "In fact, the CIA doesn't believe these are attacks at all. In their latest press briefing they claim—" Here he paused to read from the dossier. "—'that it is unlikely to be the result of a worldwide campaign of attacks by a foreign power against US diplomats and spies.' Blah, blah, blah." His finger moved down the page. "Here's another quote, this from a senior admin official: 'findings of a CIA investigation have found that the majority of cases could probably be attributed to a preexisting medical condition, or environmental factors, or stress.'

"This is what the CIA has been saying from the get-go. They don't want anyone thinking that these are enemy attacks. Too fucking scary." Wilson turned over a page in the dossier. "Now here's the kicker. It's from a group of Cuban scientists. Don't laugh, please." He tapped a finger on the document in front of him like a professor calling a class to order.

"In this one instance, we—meaning us chickens in the airtight coop—believe the Cubans were correct when they wrote, and I quote, 'Havana syndrome theories violate the laws of physics.'"

"No one is interested in getting to the bottom of the naïvely named 'Havana syndrome' except us." Connerly sniffed, his upper lip curled. "We know they are indeed attacks. And we now know the *origin* of the attacks—at least the newer ones, and possibly all of them." The red dot moved from one tiny explosion in Thompson's brain to another. When it landed on the last of them, he turned to Ben. "We recognized these as signature probabilities of our own experiments in weaponizing quantum states."

"What?" Ben jumped up, his body gone rigid. "That's crazy."

"Why would you say that?" Wilson pushed out his lips. "The only thing we know of that doesn't obey the laws of physics is quantum states."

"Granted," Connerly continued, "we still know next to nothing about quantum states. But that handhold is enough for us to ID these." The red dot flickered over the spots in Brady Thompson's brain.

There was that grin on Wilson's face again, sardonic, knowing. "There is only one person whose expertise in quantum computers is advanced enough to make this happen, Butler, and that's your boss, Marsden Tribe."

Ben felt a lurch, as if it were his heart that was registering the ground opening up beneath his feet. Wilson's grin expanded as he kept his gaze locked on Ben. "Now there's the face I was looking for," he crowed.

7

Abd-El-Kader's headquarters was in Karaköy, south of Galata, a large warehouse on the waterfront. To its right was a cheap-eats restaurant called Donkey Kong. Istanbul was a big city; though Evan possessed at least a passing acquaintance with most neighborhoods, this one between the Atatürk and Galata bridges was an area unknown to her.

The Syrian's company was called Alila International, its name emblazoned in red across the front of the dilapidated façade of the warehouse. But below it, the brickwork was covered with a rainbow scrum of graffiti.

It was around nine in the morning. Someone at Donkey Kong was sweeping the pavement, kicking around the plastic chairs as if angry with them. She paused, touched her new passport and documentation. Lyudmila wasn't the only agent who had contacts in this city. Late yesterday afternoon Evan had visited Dr. Enamiy, a dentist whose instruction academy used the indigent as guinea pigs for young would-be dentists. It was never pleasant to be in the large workroom where his cadre of students practiced on people who had nowhere else to go to alleviate their pain. Lots of pulled teeth, lots of blood, the reek of decayed dentin and infected gums.

Like most businesspeople in Istanbul, Enamiy was as venal as he was clever. Never have one profession when you can have two, the modern Turkish saying went. Enamiy's side hustle was forging documents for those in need and with sufficient cash—half down, half upon completion. Evan had used him several times before and had never had cause to complain. His workmanship was impeccable. He forged any and all documents desired, even the new ones that used holography and were supposed to be forge-proof. "For me nothing is impossible," Enamiy liked to say. And always backed up that boast with the goods. He handed her a sheet of paper on which were typed out names in two columns. The one on the left contained given names, the one on the right family names.

"Take your pick," he said as soon as he had taken a series of portrait photos of her. He was already getting to work.

"When opting for an alias in the field pick a name without ethnicity," one of her instructors at Langley had told her. *"One that's easily forgotten. And don't get cute—no Jane Smith or anything of the sort."*

Amanda Schneider, regional director of Ruhr Trading Partners, complete with passport and documentation, stood in the shadows across the road from Abd-El-Kader's warehouse. It seemed a wholly unprepossessing building, clearly having seen better days, but of course that was the point. Like her, Abd-El-Kader had no desire to call attention to himself.

Apart from the restaurant's street sweeper and the new-model dark blue Mercedes sedan parked up the street around which loitered a man in a shiny black suit, smoking furiously, the street appeared deserted. Amanda Schneider was quite certain it was not. She felt observed the moment she stepped out of the shadows and into the slanted sunlight reflected off the water.

Ignoring whatever was moving in her immediate surroundings, she strode purposefully toward the warehouse without looking to the right or left. The entrance was on the building's right side. She opened the human-size door, stepped crisply into the interior. She was immediately hit with the assertive aromas of Assam tea, cinnamon, and stone. Judged by the shabby exterior, the inside was shocking: oiled teak floors, black granite counters, the intricately patterned walls of a Mandarin's palace. There was no resemblance to a warehouse whatsoever. Curbing her surprise, she crossed to the closest counter. Around her men, and several women, went about their mysterious tasks laden with briefcases, armloads of files, trays holding pyramids of square lacquered boxes. It was from these boxes the scent of the freshly dried tea escaped like a prisoner on parole.

It did not take long for her to realize that the laborers, of which there were many, were all Syrians, whereas the people behind the counters were invariably Turks. She approached a heavyset man with a long curved mustache and a dour countenance. His dark eyes flicked over her incuriously before he went back to whatever he was doing before she showed up.

"I'm here to see Abd-El-Kader," she said in Turkish.

"Is that so," the man answered in a voice lacking in affect.

"I have an appointment."

He did not move.

She spread her credentials on the countertop for him to see. Though the man glanced at them cursorily, his glowering expression did not change.

"Please do me the courtesy of letting Abd-El-Kader know that I have arrived." She smiled. "And right on time, I might say. As I was instructed."

She placed her business card on the countertop, pushing it toward him.

The man plucked it up, glanced at it, then looked at her as if he were taking a long, lingering pull at a glass of raki. He grunted, then, shrugging, picked up the receiver on an internal line, spoke softly for several minutes as his eyes roved over her credentials. He nodded, spoke one word in reply, put down the receiver.

"Please be good enough to wait." His tone had softened like taffy in the sun.

She upped the wattage of her smile. "*Teşekkür ederim.*" *Thank you.*

■   ■   ■

Ten minutes later she was stepping off an elegant elevator the size of a freight car run by a wizened woman in traditional Turkish clothes. Immediately, two men in black suits identical to the man guarding the Mercedes up the block stopped her, ran a portable metal detector over her, had her open her purse. While one of them rummaged through it the other stood back, sneering at her.

Unlike on the ground floor there were no Turks here, only Syrians, perhaps even members of Örümcek's, the Spider's, extended family. Following this security search she was escorted down a short hallway paneled in Syrian chestnut. It had a peculiarly low ceiling. Anyone six feet or over would have had to stoop.

At the end of the hallway were a set of double doors, also made of chestnut, with three horizontal brass bands affixed to the wood with iron studs. One of her escorts knocked on the right-hand door and, without waiting for a reply, opened it. He stood aside for the regional director of Ruhr to walk through.

She entered alone. The door closed softly behind her. She stood on the edge of what might have been a soccer pitch—long and wide with a ceiling so high she could not clearly make out its design. Light flooded in through windows through which the water could be seen, filling now with boats, ferries, barges, and pleasure craft of all sizes. Below, glass-fronted cabinets lined the walls, most filled with books, others with what seemed to be artifacts unearthed from ancient Middle Eastern ruins. Without looking more closely she couldn't be sure, but she suspected they were all part of past Syrian cultures.

At first she thought she was alone, but gradually she made out a mammoth desk at the far end of the room and a man sitting behind it. She began the trek across the expanse, clearing her mind of expectation: mind/no mind. Learned from her martial arts master.

Örümcek, the Spider, was a bulldog of a man, perhaps forty or so. He sat behind the desk the way a judge sits behind his bank, but unlike a judge he jumped up as she approached, came around his desk, and beckoned, "Come, come, Ms. Schneider. Please."

When they had exchanged traditional Muslim greetings, he held up her card. Perhaps this was the reason for the delay in her appointment time.

"I apologize for keeping you waiting."

"You needed time to vet me." Of course he had. Deep backup for her legend was part of the complete package Enamiy provided. On Google search and phone calls, she was Amanda Schneider, just as her credentials claimed.

He smiled. "Nothing personal, Ms. Schneider." He lifted a hand. "Standard operating procedure. I have never done business with Ruhr Trading Partners."

"That's quite all right," she assured him.

He swept a hand out, indicating a chair. "Please."

She sat, one leg crossed over the other knee. Her hands folded in her lap. He called for tea.

"Now, tell me why you have arrived at my doorstep?" He had small eyes, perfectly black. His oiled hair was thick and lush, combed back from his wide forehead. He had small, almost round ears, a nose with the large nostrils of an animal, and rather feminine lips, like rose petals. He wore a dark suit, like his minions, but this one was clearly made-to-measure, of very fine cashmere.

"My company is an old and well-respected one," she began. "Electrical machinery and equipment is our specialty."

He stepped to the window nearest him, looked out at the harbor, hands clasped behind his back. The sky was bright, the sun already too hot for this time of the year.

"Arming the Nazis in the forties, I have no doubt."

She was expecting this. Syrians, and Syrian Turks, had no love for Nazis, or for Russians for that matter, whose spy networks all but took over Istanbul in those same midforties. "We survived," she said in a neutral tone.

"And thrived, I am given to understand." He turned back to her. "Is this what you want me to buy, electrical machinery and equipment."

"Ah, no." The corner of her mouth quirked up in a smile. "You already have your resources for those things."

"Indeed we do," he said. And then, taking an entirely different tack, "You speak Levantine Syrian like a native."

"I spent time in Damascus. I had a very good teacher."

"And an even better ear." He tapped his right ear with his forefinger. "The best linguistic teacher in the world will fail if the student does not have the ear for languages."

"Ruhr has branched out since the forties," she said, in an attempt to get them back on track. "Electronic—"

He spoke over her, as if to cut short the time he was wasting on her. "For electronics we also have our resources."

"Branching out, I said. Abd-El-Kader, I'm here to sell you chemicals."

The door opened behind her, light footsteps across the floor.

"Ah, our tea has arrived. Just in time, eh?" He smiled. "What kind of chemicals are you speaking of?"

"Potassium, bromides, resins high in urushiol for lacquers."

"I know what urushiol is."

"Of course you do. My apologies." She could hear the glasses on the tray rattling, the sense of someone approaching just to her left, the unusual scent of myrrh.

The Syrian waved a hand. "Continue with your list, if you would be so kind."

"Surely." She nodded. "Ethylene, propylene, sulfuric acid, nitrogen, sodium hydroxide."

"The big five," he said.

"And, of course, ether."

His eyebrows raised. "Ether?"

"Yes, I have it on good authority that you can use regular shipments of ether."

"That's her." A female voice from over her left shoulder.

Her head whipped around. She had just enough time to recognize one of the young women from the hammam before something entered her upper arm. An unnatural warmth swarmed into her and she saw the young woman as she had in the baths, through a shimmering scrim of steam, before it all lost focus. Her head fell forward, someone grabbed her under the arms, but that must have been somewhere miles away.

8

Captain Rodion Stepanov Molchalin, tenderfoot in Kata's Moscow cadre, stepped off the helo, jumping two feet into the snow. His first impression of the semipermanent camp Major Korokova had erected was of the absolute order in which the personnel went about their various duties. He counted twenty or so GRU soldiers and an older man he surmised was the GRU medical examiner. As the only member of FSB in the area he felt exposed, a fish out of water. The helo pilot waited until he was well clear of the rotors before he ramped them up and took off, swinging the gunship back toward Moscow.

Before he had left, Kata had briefed him on Juliet Korokova—everything she knew, which, so far as he was concerned, wasn't a whole helluva lot. In fact, he climbed into the helo without any real sense of her at all. Perhaps, he thought now, it was better this way; he was free to make his own assessment without bias.

Then he saw her from the back and a shiver went through him. All at once he felt as if Kata had thrown him to the wolves. He'd never been much of a ladies' man, never met a female officer he could relate to—until Kata. For whatever reason, he had taken to her immediately, had no problem taking orders from her. In fact, he barely thought of her as female at all. She was simply Kata Romanovna Hemakova, a colonel in a newly formed directorate of the FSB he had not even known existed until he was summoned to the colonel's office to be interviewed for recruitment. He had as little idea who had recommended him as he did Directorate O's raison d'être. Apparently, no one else outside Directorate O knew it even existed. That's the way it was, Kata impressed on him, and that's the way it would remain. If he was honest with himself, he liked the secrecy; it was like hiding in plain sight, a game he used to play with his father when he was five, maybe six. It was his father's game. He always lost, of course, but each time they played he learned something more about hiding in plain sight. He won his first game on his eleventh birthday, and from that time on he never lost again. So Directorate O suited him down to the ground. He was where he wanted to be, and if that meant Kata was throwing him into the deep end of the pool it also meant she was trusting him with an important mission. He knew Directorate KV, of which the dead man was a member, was important, even if he had no idea why.

That was all right with him; in due time he would find out its importance, perhaps even while he was here. Looking around as he approached the tent village, he could sense that the dense forest around him held many secrets, not the least of which was why Major Korokova had taken over the case.

"Whatever you do," Kata had told him at their last rendezvous, *"do not step on this woman's toes. She's liable to bite your head off."*

"You mean figuratively, of course."

He was about to smile, but Kata crossed her arms over her chest, said, *"Do us both a favor, Rodion Stepanov, and make sure you don't find out the answer to that question."*

His boots crunched into the skin of snow that had hardened over the ground. No more snow had fallen since Levrov's demise. An omen? But he had to remind himself that he didn't believe in omens, only his mother did. That belief was what drove a stake through the heart of his parents' marriage.

He was close enough now that Korokova should have heard him. But she was in a contentious conversation—or perhaps "argument" was a better term—with the GRU pathologist, a man who looked like he was more intimately acquainted with death than life. Life was bitter, his expression said, while death had no flavor at all.

"This is insanity," he was saying, "to make me set up shop here in the godforsaken wilderness instead of taking the corpse back to my lab in Moscow where it's nice and warm and I don't have to keep looking over my shoulder to see if I'm being shadowed by a fucking wolf pack. Plus—surprise—I can do a real autopsy."

"Morokovsky, you shock me. I didn't know you had water running through your veins instead of blood." The major's words dripped contempt.

"Please." The pathologist waved away her response. "There's simply no precedent for this. I demand an explanation. What the hell is so special about Ivan Levrov anyway?"

"He's a close relative of the Sovereign," Korokova said, as if that were a joke only she was in on. "That's all the explanation required."

As Morokovsky's eyes flicked from the major to Rodion, Korokova turned around. Rodion's heart seemed to stop, then to hammer furiously like a kettledrum being beaten. The reckless throbbing reverberated deep within him.

"So you're Colonel Hemakova's creature," she said without affect. Then in a hiss, "My FSB ball and chain."

He had the presence of mind to give her his name, standing tall and straight. He tried not to blink from the golden light coming off her like an aurora borealis.

"Frankly, I don't give a rat's testicle what your name is."

She stood arms akimbo, which made his heart drop into his stomach, from whence it fell farther—much farther.

"Let's get one thing straight, Mulchan."

"That's Molchalin," he corrected. The words were no sooner out of his mouth than he realized his mistake.

"What did I just tell you, Mulchy," she snapped.

This time he bit his tongue.

"That's your name from now on, hear me, Mulchy?" She threw him a smile he could only categorize as evil. He found it thrilling.

Behind her, the pathologist chuckled. "Why don't you have him kiss your boots while you're at it?"

She whipped around. "Why don't you get the fuck out of here and do your job."

He smirked, and without any warning whatsoever she slapped him so hard across his face that he lost his balance. Staring down at him as he squirmed in the snow, she said from her height, "You've yet to learn your place here, Morokovsky."

He ground his teeth, gathering himself onto his knees. "I'll report you. I swear I will."

"That too has been tried." She leaned over him. "But where are those naïve people now, Morokovsky? Butyrka? Matrosskaya Tishina?" She was naming prisons. "Or perhaps Black Dolphin?"

At this last name, the pathologist shuddered, and well he might. Black Dolphin in Siberia housed the country's most heinous criminals—child molesters, murderers, terrorists, cannibals, and serial killers, all serving life sentences.

The major turned her back on the pathologist. She didn't utter another word until he had risen, sloping away into his medical tent.

"Now, Mulchy, I must ask you to keep your yap shut and stay out of my way."

Still starstruck, Rodion nodded mutely, but still felt compelled to tell her, "I'm to report to Kata twice a day."

The major's eyebrows rose. "'Kata,' is it? Not 'Colonel Hemakova'?" She squinted at him, as if she were training her X-ray vision on him. "What kind of a shop is the colonel running there?"

"Unconventional." When he said it he couldn't help feeling a bit of pride.

"I'll say."

"But then judging by your actions with Morokovsky I'd say you're just as unconventional as she is."

Korokova stared at him. "Are you fucking coming on to me, Mulchy?"

He was taken aback. "What?" It was as if she had pierced him, peered into his soul, picked up on his most secret desire. "No. Of course not."

Her gaze ramped up in intensity. How did she do that? he asked himself breathlessly.

"Because that would be a bad idea. A very bad idea."

Her voice washed over him. His mind blurred the words; they did not apply to him.

She gestured. "Walk with me. I could use a stiff drink."

"It's breakfast time."

"As you've already discovered, I'm as unconventional as they come." That evil smile again, making something deep inside him turn to taffy. "If you can't drink vodka at nine o'clock in the morning you might as well go back to the short-pants boys at FSB right now."

9

ISTANBUL, TURKEY

"Ayman Safra." From the master's chair behind his vast desk, Abd-El-Kader, the Syrian, regarded his visitor. "Of Joseph and Moise, the Lebanese Safras?"

Ayman Safra, sitting across from him, simply smiled. He was a large man in every way a person could be large: tall, corpulent enough that his thighs and massive buttocks overflowed the chair into which he had lowered himself in the careful manner of heavy men. He was bearded, light-eyed, with a small bow of a mouth. For such a massive man he had small feet, rather like a ballet dancer. His prodigious jowls folded over the collar of his shirt, obscured the top of his immaculately knotted tie. He was also Lebanese, which automatically put him on the Syrian's bad side. The Lebanese were the most tenacious businesspeople Abd-El-Kader had ever encountered. They were take-no-prisoners types.

What irritated Abd-El-Kader all the more was that Ayman Safra was wearing a made-to-measure suit that, if Abd-El-Kader was any judge, cost upward of six thousand American dollars, cut and fitted in either Milan or Tokyo, where, lately, the Japanese were outdoing their Italian counterparts. On his tiny feet were John Lobb shoes that probably set him back half what his suit cost.

Abd-El-Kader glanced down at the card Safra had handed him when he strode in. There was nothing on it but his name, an internet address, and a satnav phone number.

"Who was it you said you worked for, Mr. Safra?"

That smile that never reached his cheeks, let alone his eyes. Those canny eyes. "Your benefactor wishes to remain anonymous."

My benefactor, Abd-El-Kader thought grievously. "What do you take me for?" he bit off. "Who in his right mind would consider doing business with someone he hasn't met face-to-face, let alone whose identity is unknown to him." He shook his head. "This isn't amateur night at the follies."

"Your benefactor has made you a generous offer," Safra said with serene dignity. "In fact, in my opinion the sum is more than your business is worth."

This Lebanese really knew how to get under the Syrian's skin. He pushed himself forward as if he were about to leap across the desk and physically assault Safra. "You and your master don't know a damn thing about my business."

The Lebanese remained unperturbed. "The fact is we know everything about your business, sir. Everything. Including your illegal trafficking in your own people, smuggling them into Turkey, using them as slave labor until they sicken and die."

What have I done to deserve this? Abd-El-Kader asked himself. But like the last dying ember in an exhausted fire, the last of his self-pity died. He was on the attack now, no holds barred. He reached into a side drawer, took out a 9mm Makarov pistol, laid it on the desktop with the barrel pointing at the fat Lebanese.

"A Russian pistol."

The Syrian's eyes narrowed. "What of it?" he snapped.

Safra spread his pudgy hands. "A simple observation."

Abd-El-Kader did not touch the Makarov, merely placed his hand beside it. "You have thirty seconds to get out of my chair, cross my office, and shut the door behind you."

Ayman Safra ignored the weapon, stared straight into the Syrian's eyes. "A direct threat. I had hoped our negotiations would be reconciled amicably."

The Syrian sneered. "Now you know for a fact that they won't."

Safra inclined his head as if he'd asked for a refill on his drink he was never served. "I feel duty bound to inform you that your benefactor's next offer will be substantially less."

Abd-El-Kader laughed. His forefinger tapped the grip of the Makarov. "Tell your master to go to hell." He lifted the pistol. "With my compliments."

Safra inclined his head again as he levered himself off the chair. "As you wish."

He pointed the Makarov at the Lebanese. "As I demand."

"Pity," Ayman Safra said, and reached for the slim briefcase he had set by his right leg. "I so abhor demands."

Abd-El-Kader's laughter boomed through the room as Safra made to take his leave. He paused, turned back. "I almost forgot." He snapped open the briefcase, the sound bringing the Syrian to his feet, the Makarov aimed at Safra's heart.

"It's only this." Safra extracted an eight-by-ten photo. He slid it across the desk. "I'm so absent-minded these days." He sighed. "Perhaps a sign I'm getting old."

Abd-El-Kader frowned. "What the hell are you talking about? You sound like a foolish old man."

That smile again—a smile that was not quite there, that flickered in and out of existence. "I beg you to take a look at the photograph and tell me—is that your father?"

Almost against his will, Abd-El-Kader glanced down, saw that the photo was indeed of his father, in the wheelchair to which he had been confined since his stroke. There was the familiar tribal wrap he favored across his knees and lap.

The Syrian's eyes snapped up. "What is this?"

"Please be so kind as to answer my question," Ayman Safra said. "Is that or is it not your father?"

A pulsing vein commenced to beat a tattoo in his left temple. "You know damn well it is."

"Good." Safra inclined his head. "Halfway home."

Abd-El-Kader's face held fast to a bewildered look. "What is—?"

But Safra had already withdrawn from his briefcase another eight-by-ten photo. This he placed alongside the first one. It also showed the Syrian's father, but this time at somewhat of a remove, in order to include the two men holding onto the wheelchair from behind. A pair of beefy men smiling into the camera. They must have been outside and a wind had gotten up, because the coat the man on the left was wearing had been caught flapped open, revealing the butt of a handgun in a shoulder holster strapped over his shirt.

"Abd-El-Kader," Ayman Safra said in the same neutral tone he'd used from the beginning. "Do you know the two men with your father?"

"N—" But the Syrian's throat was clogged. He couldn't get a word out. *This is a nightmare,* he thought. It must be. *Any moment I shall wake up, pick my head off my desk, and be alone in my office.* But, of course, he knew that was a pipe dream, for here he was, a man holding a Makarov, vulnerable as a woman, helpless as a child.

"Your father belongs to your benefactor now." Safra scooped up the photos, stored them back in the briefcase. "He will be treated as an honored guest, as befits his status."

"I'll kill you and your master," Abd-El-Kader said through gritted teeth. "There's nowhere you and that sonofabitch can hide, my people will find you and—"

"In that event, all your people will find is your father with his throat slashed, his body and face terribly abused." Ayman Safra withdrew a sheaf of clipped-together papers. "I'm absolutely certain that is not what you want, sir."

He placed the contract on Abd-El-Kader's desk, and atop it a blue Parker Duofold pen he unclipped from his shirt pocket.

"You have thirty seconds to sign the contract, selling the entirety of your business to your benefactor." An active satnav phone was in his hand. "Your father has thirty seconds to live."

Abd-El-Kader realized oh so belatedly that he had misjudged this corpulent Lebanese. Worse, he had underestimated the power behind Safra. Ayman Safra with his moderate voice, his gentleman's manner, had lulled him into a false sense of security. Now the trap carefully laid for him had sprung and it was too late to chew his leg off. As a man in a dream, he flipped through the contract, reading with dream eyes. "This is substantially less than the offer," he said with a voice leaden with dread.

"As I warned you," Safra said entirely without smugness or irony. He was a businessperson through and through.

Abd-El-Kader ran a shaking hand through hair made damp with sweat. Without another word, he signed the contract, even though he saw that the countersigner's line wasn't filled in either in typeface or in signature.

He was about to spin it back to the Lebanese when Safra, saving him the trouble, took it from his hand, along with the Parker, and returned them to their respective proper places.

"Good day to you, sir," he said. "I assure you that the pleasure of doing business was all mine."

10

She moved with a feline's unselfconscious sexual fluidity, which, to Rodion, at least, increased her allure a hundredfold. She led him into the mess tent, one of the larger tents in the semicircle. Two lines of aluminum tables had been set up with folding chairs on either side. In the rear were a portable stovetop and oven, powered by generators. Cook was somewhere around, a hazy figure amid the steam, which was so thick it obscured the ceiling like a marine layer. Rich scents came from his pots and grills, redolent with a perfume of roasted meat that caused Rodion to salivate.

The major seated herself without even a glance at Rodion. He chose the chair across from her. As soon as he sat down, a bottle of iced vodka appeared, along with two water glasses. He looked over his right shoulder at the kitchen, wondered how the major had pulled off the miracle of requisitioning a full kitchen rather than have her cadre eating standard-issue field packets that were nutritious but more or less inedible. Kata had failed to tell him how powerful the major was, perhaps figuring it best he find out for himself. At this moment, he felt himself launched on a journey into the unknown, and the curious thing was that he felt no fear, only anticipation. Possibly that was down to the major herself.

As she handed him his glass, the tips of their fingers touched. Yet for as fleeting as the moment was he felt a needle of heat skitter across the back of his hand, firing the nerves in his arm. He looked at her to see if she had felt the same thing as he had—or maybe he'd dreamed it, because her face was as impassive as it had been since he met her.

"Drink, Mulchy."

Another command, which he obeyed. It was only when the glass reached his lips that he realized it was half full of vodka.

"Down in one," she said, and, tipping her head back, drained her glass.

Rodion had no choice but to do the same. His eyes watered as the liquor turned from ice in his throat to fire in his stomach. At least he stopped himself from coughing. But, to his shame, a single tear overflowed his right eye, crawling down his cheek like the mark of Cain.

For her part, the major was busying herself with refilling their glasses and gave no sign that she had seen the mark of his shame. Even so, he held himself back from swiping it off his skin, convinced the gesture would compound his weakness. So there it sat at the end of its arc, trembling until it subsided.

His second glass of vodka went down much more easily. Possibly because his esophagus by now had been anesthetized. The tear had dried on his cheek and he forgot about it.

"Good breakfast," the major said, capping the bottle. Folding her arms, she put her elbows on the table. "Now tell me why you're really here. What is Colonel Hemakova's interest in Ivan Levrov?"

When he made no attempt to answer, her eyes narrowed. "It can't be personal, surely."

"I would like for you to call me by my name," Rodion said, knees shaking under the table.

The major cocked her head. "I gave you a name, Mulchy."

In for a ruble, in for a pound, Rodion thought. "I reject it."

Now she sat back, palms down on the table, fingers spread. They were long, narrow, and tapered near their ends. "Who are you to tell me what I can and can't call you."

He waited a beat before replying. "You understand what we're discussing."

With a withering look, she rose and without a word strode into the rear. The marine layer had for some reason lifted. He could hear her ordering Cook around, and several moments later she returned carrying two plates and silverware.

All the comforts of home, he thought, *right at her fingertips. She must be some kind of magician, and I'm in her presence.*

She sat down, pushed one plate across to him, began to eat off the other. "Venison," she said, around mouthfuls. "Rendered from the buck that killed Levrov." Her forked stabbed out again, spearing a cube of roasted meat. "Ironic, isn't it?"

That's one word for it, he thought. The vodka had turned him ravenous, which was, he saw now, her aim. All to bring him to this. A second test, worse for him than the first. Under her scrutiny he picked up his utensils, cut himself a piece of meat off the venison strip. It did smell good, damn it, he thought. Tasted even better. He began to eat.

"Finally," the major said, setting down her fork, "getting into the swing of things."

"About your questions—"

"What's your quid pro quo, Mulchy? What do I have to give up to get the answers I want?"

"Call me by my name," he said.

She appeared to consider this for a moment, but he wondered where her mind really was. "Rodion Stepanov," she said at length.

So she was listening, he thought. "Rodion is also fine."

"How very un-Russian of you, Rodion Stepanov." But there was little of the earlier sharpness that had turned each word into a tiny knife thrust. She nodded. "Done." She pushed her plate to one side and interlaced her fingers, making of them a steeple, or a temple, he thought. "Your turn."

He sighed. "Kata knows Levrov works—worked—at Directorate KV. Furthermore, she knows why the directorate was formed and what it does."

The major cocked her head. "Which is?"

"*Kvant,*" he said without hesitation. "Quantum computing."

Silence then, punctuated once by a string of invective uttered by Cook directed at the pot that had burned his hand. He began to thrash it with a wooden spoon.

"Major?"

Her attention snapped to. "I was wondering how it is that your 'Kata' knows all about Directorate KV?"

He watched her with care, wondering whether she was telling the truth or this was yet another of her enigmatic tests. "I'm new to her directorate," he began.

"No one knows anything about her directorate. Like KV it doesn't exist so far as the rank and file inside GRU is concerned."

"The same is true for the FSB." He paused. "As I was about to say, even though I'm the new kid in Directorate O's bailiwick I would bet six months' pay that 'my Kata,' as you call her, knows everything about everything."

Something passed behind the major's eyes, the briefest flicker of amusement if Rodion was any judge.

"Except me," she said. "Well, now I know why you're really here."

"That isn't true," he protested.

"Ah, well, another bit of intel. She didn't tell you, then." She nodded. "Clever of her, I must say. Need-to-know. And you, Rodion Stepanov, did not need to know." Her head tilted again. "You understand."

"Sure. Low man on the pole and all that. But that's all surmise on your part. Paranoia, maybe."

"I cherish my paranoia, Rodion Stepanov." She offered what in anyone else might be a smile. "Learn to embrace yours."

He'd had enough of her trying to make a fool of him. "Listen, Major, I'm here for one reason and one reason only: to find out what happened to a valued member of Directorate KV."

"But why? I want to know why."

"Pass."

"Really?" She pursed her lips. "You disappoint me."

"No, I don't." He had been on hyperalert ever since they had sat down. With each parry and thrust he was filling in the blanks in the façade she presented to him. "If I did you wouldn't be sitting here talking to me."

She took out a cigarette, fired the end with a gunmetal lighter, took a long slow inhale, held the smoke deep in her lungs before releasing it. A small cloud like a word bubble hung in front of her face before dissipating. Not once during these little actions did she take her eyes from him, but he knew her mind was on some other plane, formulating the best response. He was getting the measure of her now, at least the level right below her armor.

"I wonder," she said now, breaking the silence, "how you feel about loyalty."

He shook his head. She'd wrong-footed him again.

"I mean you've just divulged some of your Kata's secrets."

"When we met you called me Kata's creature. You're right. I'm loyal and true. Dogged, as well."

"I see."

"I wonder if you do."

A flash across her eyes, like a tiger sighted in long grass. "What the hell does that mean?"

"I've told you what she authorized me to tell you." A line had been crossed, another useful piece of the puzzle. He'd remember that. He altered his tone, dropping it, slowing his speech. "What I mean is we've just met, Major. We don't know shit about each other, do we?"

"That's by design, isn't it?"

"Mm. But here we are in the wilderness, hours from Moscow, in the grip of extraordinary circumstances, so I'm wondering—"

But what he was wondering would have to wait. At that moment Morokovsky, the pugnacious pathologist, rushed in, his fierce gaze riveted on the major as if she were the only person in the tent.

"I can't do this anymore," he shouted.

"Good morning, Morokovsky," the major said equably. "How's your morning progressing."

"I just told you." He was fairly shaking with rage.

"What exactly can't you do?"

"A proper autopsy, damn it. These conditions are intolerable. You summon me out here, blind me in one eye, tie one hand behind my back, and expect me to give you a full report on the cause of Ivan Levrov's death."

In Rodion's mind there were only two likely reasons why she had insisted on having the autopsy done in situ, not at Moscow Central. One, she already knew or had a good idea what had caused Levrov's death; or, two, she didn't trust the people back in Moscow. Even her own people. Either possibility intrigued Rodion, and he realized this was why Kata had sent him here. There was a mystery attached to Levrov's death and now he was sure it led back to Directorate KV.

"I assumed we knew the cause of his death," the major was saying now.

"Come with me." Morokovsky turned on his heel and stalked out of the tent, the major and Rodion a step behind him. They crossed the clearing, entered a much smaller tent. Even though the cold had slowed the process somewhat, they were immediately struck by the stench of the decaying corpse. Morokovsky had begun the autopsy; Levrov's front was slit open from chest to pubis. He lay on a table atop a thick sheet of plastic. Behind him was an impressive array of machinery, some of it familiar, some not. In any event, Rodion's attention was firmly fixed on the opened-up corpse.

He stood on one side, the major on the other, with Morokovsky at the head.

"You can clearly see the damage done by the tines of the stag's antlers," the pathologist said. "But that's not how Levrov died."

The major's eyebrows lifted lightly. Her eyes seemed to change color, but that might just have been a trick of the light. "Evidence." Once again a command rather than a question. This was one means, Rodion was discovering, by which she continually got her way.

"The volume of exsanguination is inconsistent—"

The major lifted her head. "What are you saying, Morokovsky. There was plenty of blood."

"Correct. But almost all of it was postmortem."

The major's nostrils flared as if she were just now taking in the stink. "Meaning."

"Meaning, Levrov was dead either just before or simultaneous with being gored. The blood did not gush out of him when the stag pulled back. It would have if Levrov's heart was still beating. It wasn't. His blood dribbled out slowly."

"How." She shook her head. "Explain, please."

He sighed. "That's the problem, Major. I can't." He spread his hands. "At least not in this makeshift mortuary. I haven't the instruments."

"Draw up a list. I'll have whatever you need flown in."

But he was already shaking his head. "What is required cannot be moved. The machines are too delicate, too interconnected." He threw her a look of disdain. "Even you, Major, magician that you are, cannot get an MRI out here."

"Why not?"

"For one thing, we will never have enough power. For another, as I said, our MRI instrument cannot be moved. It's huge." He shrugged. "The only recourse is to bring the body back to Moscow for deeper analysis."

"Why," she said. "Why do you need to perform an MRI on Levrov."

"I've told you." Morokovsky scrubbed his tired face with his hand. "This man did not die from being gored, as it was first surmised. He also did not die of a heart attack."

"The fear of death could have brought on a heart attack or a stroke."

"Just before he was gored? Ask yourself, Major. What are the odds? No." He pushed his lower lip out. "To determine the real cause of death we need the MRI."

The major took a step back, turned and crossed to the tent flap, looked out onto the compound. When she turned back, she addressed Morokovsky. She was at her most imperious when she said, "You will pack up your equipment immediately." Her tone was crisp and all business. "I'll make the arrangements. You'll leave for Moscow within three hours."

"Sure." He nodded. "That's more like it. Now you're listening—"

"The autopsy is concluded," she added.

The pathologist froze, goggled at her. "What?"

"Your services are no longer required, Morokovsky. You will go. Levrov will remain here."

"But . . . but you can't," he sputtered. "The autopsy isn't complete."

"It is because I say it is."

"But his family." There was spittle on his lips. "What will I say to his family?"

"You will say nothing." She came toward him, her aura shining like a second sun, almost blinding Rodion, but he must be the only one affected. No one else seemed aware of it. And yet, Morokovsky must have felt something, for he shrank back solely on instinct. "Nothing to the family. You are forbidden to take their calls, forbidden to talk to anyone else concerning your visit here."

"Visit?" Morokovsky said. "You make this sound like a family reunion."

"If that story makes it easier for you, by all means use it."

"Please, Major, this is—"

"Go, Morokovsky, before this becomes difficult for you—and it will, I promise you."

11

Darkness and the sharp cries of seabirds. The hooting of a ferry, infinitely sad; so far off.

She was breathing through a hood, which meant she was inhaling more carbon dioxide than normal, than was good for her. Lack of sufficient oxygen made her weak, as if the lingering weakness from the drug she'd been administered weren't enough.

An entire orchestra of tympani was having it off inside her head. Her temples throbbed, her eyes felt distended. Somewhere close by was terror, but she refused to acknowledge it, knowing giving in would only make things worse. And her situation was bad enough as it was.

The little things. Noting the little things would keep her sane because she couldn't move her limbs. Her feet were numb, her arms stretched above her head, wrists tied tightly together with what felt like a zip tie. She was hanging from either a hook screwed into the ceiling or a rafter. Her legs were doubled up so that her heels dug into the backs of her thighs, tied with hemp as zip ties weren't long enough to do the job. Her knees just brushed the floor.

The strain on her shoulders and neck was excruciating, and she was in danger of losing all feeling in her legs. She had no idea how long she had been unconscious, but judging solely by the state of her limbs it must be hours.

The best—the only—thing she could do. Eyes closed, she sought to empty her mind. She concentrated on the ferry hooting until she no longer heard it. She redirected her mind to the seabirds, hearing them as an agglomeration, then as separate species, picking them off one by one until they, too, were gone. The creaking of the building, gone, the tiny skitter and snuffling of rats, gone.

Nothing remained now. Her mind was empty. She felt no anxiety, no fear. She did not consider what would happen to her or ruminate over the recent past—how she got here. There was only the present, where nothing existed but her pain. Then that, too, was gone.

Nothing, not even silence, disturbed her inward direction. Her essence slipped its leash. Detached from her body, it floated above her corporeal form. Free, seeing everywhere and nowhere at once.

The squeal of a bolt being withdrawn, the scrape of the door being opened, shut, relocked.

Voices.

Two females, both voices in the same register, so similar they must be sisters.

Twins.

She knew who they were.

One stationed herself behind Evan's body, the other stood in front.

"Well . . ."

"What do we have here?"

"Still asleep?"

"Not for long, she isn't."

A bucket of water crashed down onto the hood. Another, then another. The hood became soaked, then sodden. The cloth clung to her face like a mask. More water. Breathing became impossible; she didn't try. She was deep within prana; her body's processes slowed.

"Nothing?" Voice from behind.

"Fuck this." Voice from in front.

A fist buried itself in her solar plexus. Her autonomic nervous system could not help responding. Her body spasmed.

"That's more like it." Voice from in front.

"Now we find out what she was doing with Shokova. Now we find out how the two of them survived. Now we find out where Shokova is." Both voices mingling. Two mouths in one body. One mind. Monstrous.

"So." Voice from in front. "What is Lyudmila Shokova to you?"

She had been taught that keeping silent only engendered escalating pain. She had been taught that to be branded a liar engendered escalating pain. She had been taught to turn an interrogation into a negotiation without your inquisitor's knowledge.

"Take off the hood." Her voice was muffled, but she made it more so.

She was rewarded by a slap across the face so hard it drew blood out of the corner of her mouth. She tasted copper and iron. That side of her face bloomed heat.

"Shokova. Boss? Informant? Cutout?" the voice in front of her said. "Tell us."

"Take off the hood."

Something hard slammed into the back of her head, white pulses blooming and dying like novae. Her head fell forward briefly before she lifted it.

"Yobanaya suka!" Fucking bitch! The voice from behind her. It was harsher, fuller of vindictive rage than the one in front. "Tell us about Shokova."

"I will when you—"

A bucket of ice water sluiced over the hood, choking her. "We tell you. You don't tell us, *blad.*" *Whore.*

Evan, sputtering more than she needed to, said, "I can't talk clearly with this hood on. I can scarcely catch my breath."

"Fuck you," said the voice behind her. "That's the idea."

Amateurs, Evan thought. Or poorly trained professionals. One and the same. And as if to prove her point the hood was whipped off her head. Evan sucked in air, slowly, regularly, taking it deep into her lungs, holding it there, oxygenating her body before she exhaled. She saw one of the twins from the hammam. She looked more Russian than Turkish and seemed inordinately proud of it. Another amateurish misstep.

She came up in Evan's face. A hawkish countenance, prominent nose, Cossack's eyes, a mouth like the slash of a stiletto. Beautiful and intimidating. She wore black designer jeans, a T-shirt of the same color splashed with PUSSY RIOT in slanted white graffiti across the front. *"Ti moy suka,"* she said through gritted teeth. *You're my bitch.* "Don't forget it or you'll be hooded again."

"So, come on." Her twin put a knee in the small of Evan's back. "Spill it."

In interrogations it was of paramount importance to separate what your inquisitor *wanted* and what she *needed.* Give her what she needed and you gave yourself time. Time to find a way out.

"Lyudmila and I know each other for a long time. We're friends. We've gone to Southeast Asia together, spent weeks in the jungles, calming our frayed nerves."

"Fucking each other, you mean," the woman from behind spat. "A pair of asshole lesbos," she sneered.

The woman staring at Evan seemed not to have heard what her sister said, or at least discounted it. The brains of the operation, Evan concluded. Did that make her twin the muscle?

That would be the way a male team would work. But women? Would that make sense? For sure, the one behind her was the hothead, so the answer was possibly yes.

"And what were you doing in the hammam?" the woman facing her said. She had a scar over her left eye. Half-concealed by her thick eyebrows. Interestingly, this heightened her beauty rather than marring it.

"What d'you think?" Evan said. "Relaxing."

"The two of you didn't look relaxed to me." This from behind her. Evan wondered how she could induce the twin to abandon her post so she could see both of them together.

The truth is . . . "The truth is Lyudmila was aware there was a contract out on her. She was too wound up. I was trying to calm her down. It wasn't working."

So far she had not lied; the truth had had its desired effect on the Scar. She had pulled her shoulders down, a sure sign she had relaxed her posture inside as well as out. A beginning, no matter how minuscule.

"How did you escape—?"

"Never mind that, Taissa," Scar said. Definitely the pragmatic one—stronger but easier to negotiate with. Her twin would be vulnerable to constant needling, even if it caused Evan more pain. Sooner or later her anger would open a path, no matter how narrow, to bringing her down, but of course none of these insights were worth a damn if she wasn't able to free herself from her bonds.

Scar leaned in so close their noses almost touched. "Tell me where Shokova is now."

Noting the "me" instead of "us," Evan said, "Certainly not in Istanbul. The attempt on her life spooked her. She left me outside the hammam."

"And where did she go?" Taissa's harsh voice in her ear.

"She didn't tell me."

"I don't believe you." Taissa closed in on her ear, the menace of a cross-cut saw. "You two being friends and lovers, how could you expect us to believe you?"

Evan kept her eyes firmly on Scar. "Those are precisely the reasons she wouldn't tell me. She's already put me in too much danger. She wasn't about to compound her mistake."

"She's full of shit, Inessa," Taissa growled. "I know it."

"No you don't," Inessa said sharply. "It's only logical. She's accurately describing standard security procedure."

"Then we have nothing," Taissa said. "What use is this bitch? We might as well kill her."

"Maybe you're right." Inessa bit her lip. "We can't very well leave her here."

"Right, she'll begin to stink and the Syrian will blame us." Taissa at last came around to where Evan could see her. If they were twins they certainly weren't identical. Taissa was dark of complexion, hair, and eye. Her flattish face had more of the Tatar in it, which made a certain amount of sense. The Baikal Tatars spoke Turkish rather than Russian. She wore the same black designer jeans as her sister but a sleeveless singlet that showed off her cut shoulder and arm muscles. A narcissist, Evan thought.

A reddish spark grew in Taissa's eyes as she studied Evan. "She dies, but I decide the method and the length."

"Well, don't take too long," Inessa told her. "If Shokova has indeed fled the scene we've got to pick up her trail and we won't get that done here in the Syrian's headquarters. He's had enough of us if I'm not mistaken."

Having been given the green light, Taissa grinned hugely. "I'll go find just the right implements."

"And I'll go talk to the Syrian," Inessa said. "The sooner he knows we'll be out of his hair the better."

■　■　■

In her time before Taissa and Inessa had waterboarded her Evan had formulated a plan. Whether or not it would work had yet to be determined. But that was in the future; her concentration was fully in the now; she knew she didn't have much time before Taissa would be back to kill her. The moment she was alone, she released her bladder. Easily done, since it was full and had been paining her for some time. The relief in peeing was massive. So many interior muscles that were involved in keeping her urine in now relaxed, pain and tension draining out of that part of her body.

The urine soaked her trousers, slid down to the lowest point so that she was drenched from knees all the way up to her crotch. But it was the hemp bonds around her thighs that soaked up the most of the liquid. She began to smell it as it dripped onto the floor, made a small puddle where her knees touched the floor.

The rats she had heard snuffling and scratching before were already on the alert. There was nothing they liked better than human urine except perhaps human blood. She had plenty of both to give them but if she was right they'd be going for the hemp bonds first.

She felt them as they sniffed at her, gathered around her. They licked up the puddle, but that hardly satisfied them. It was the sodden hemp they headed for, scrambling up her legs. The gnawing began instantly, their front teeth pulling at the hemp, unwinding the fibers as they continued to suck out her urine with frantic zeal.

The fibers were being rapidly disentangled. She could see the loosening of her bonds, silently urged the rats to gnaw faster, but now another problem raised its head, literally. In their frantic scrabbling at the hemp, one of the rats had nipped through her skin. Blood oozed out. Now there was a mad scramble for both her urine and her blood. But the bonds were being literally ripped apart to get to her flesh. She felt almost nothing, and when the bonds did free her and her lower legs slipped down to the floor the numbness that gripped them made it difficult to stand up. But as her legs changed position many of the rats were dislodged. They squealed their protest, their red eyes savage with bloodlust.

Grasping the rope the sisters had used to suspend her from the roof rafter, she pulled herself to a standing position. Her legs trembled terribly; waves of pins-and-needles made it feel as if they were on fire. The most tenacious rats clung to her, biting into her while their lazier brethren fed voraciously on the urine-soaked hemp.

When her legs were strong enough, she stood fully, and now there was enough slack in the rope for her to move her arms. The zip tie around her wrists was not industrial-strength, thank God—another rookie mistake. Had it been, no amount of strength she could muster would free her.

Putting her fists together, she raised her arms high over her head and then swung them down as fast as she could, slamming her fists—and the zip-tie locking mechanism—as hard as she could into her chest just below her breasts. The locking mechanism was the weakest part of the zip tie and it burst apart under the percussion.

Now she was free, but not yet fully and completely. First things first. She went to work on the rats. She ripped the nearest one off her. Steeling herself, holding down her gorge, she bit off the head, spat it out as far as she could, flung the body as close to it as possible. A great chorus of squealing resulted, with the rats following their dead comrade, falling on it, a semicircle of ravening beasts intent on gorging themselves.

She tried to walk, but immediately her legs gave out and she fell.

Trying not to vomit, she spat out as much of the taste as she could as she rolled toward the far wall, where several plywood sheets were leaning, creating a kind of tent. Once inside it, she pushed her hands into her armpits, massaging the flesh to help mitigate the deep ache. The pounding in her head fell like hammer blows. There was pressure behind her eyes, and even palpating her solar plexus drew a half-stifled gasp from her, made spots dance in her vision. Still, she bent over, her body screaming, trying to massage feeling back into her legs. Blood rushed in but her nerves woke up as well, and the pain from the rat bites hit her hard. It was all too much. All her systems were either on overload or temporarily shut down. Her hands, arms, shoulders were on fire. Her eyes drooped closed. She leaned back against the wall, promising herself a minute or two of rest.

And promptly fell into a sleep so deep she might still have been drugged.

12

When Rodion and the major were alone with the corpse, he gave her a solid round of slow-motion applause. "That was quite a performance. Brava!"

She rounded on him. "I don't know what you're talking about."

"I think you do." He stepped toward her, toward her light. He was no longer blinded by her. He should have been afraid—not of what she would do to him, but what she might think of him—but he wasn't. Something inside him had overridden his reticence—or was it timidity? He had been a timid child, seemed never to have outgrown it. Until now. "You were never going to allow Ivan Levrov to leave here. You were never going to allow an outsider to probe into his death—apart from Morokovsky, of course. You had no choice with him. But when he crossed the line you had drawn you shut him down, sent him packing with a permanent muzzle on."

The sound she made was clearly derisive. "You think you know me so well."

"On the contrary." He shook his head. "As I said neither of us knows the other at all."

"Then . . ."

He spread his hands. "It's what I would have done were I in your place."

"And what, exactly, is my place, Rodion?"

Noting her use of only his given name, he said, "How can I know? But if I had to guess I would say, given the evidence, you were directed to keep the cause of Ivan Levrov's death secret while going through the normal motions of a postmortem with the GRU pathologist. Who, I would assume, has no knowledge of Directorate KV or what it was set up to do." He made a gesture. "Which leads me to believe you know exactly what caused Levrov's death, knew it even before you left Moscow."

"Those are some spectacular deductions you've made."

"Am I wrong?"

Instead of answering, she strode out of the tent with such alacrity it took him a moment to react, and he was thus several steps behind her as she recrossed the compound. A scrim of clouds turned the sun a filthy white, and a wind had sprung up, chanting through the myriad pines like an unholy choir. Dampness was fast invading the atmosphere.

"While you're here with me, in this compound, there's nowhere for you to go. You understand this." She spoke not to him, per se, but to the incoming weather. Or else to someone who was not there; it was difficult for Rodion to tell.

Soldiers were busy in the center of the compound constructing a rectangle made of logs, dead things foraged from under the snow, not newly sawn branches. But Rodion was focused on her.

"Are you saying I'm a prisoner?"

She laughed as she went into her tent. "You sound as if you'd like that." But she had already turned on him so that he had to backtrack in order not to collide with her. "I don't like anyone knowing my business, why I'm here, what Levrov's death means."

"I have no idea what it means," he confessed.

Her eyes shone eerily. "But . . ."

"But I know he didn't die from being impaled by a stag. He didn't die from a heart attack or a stroke."

"Maybe an embolism," she said, but he knew she didn't believe it. Neither did he.

"Or maybe something happened to his brain, something only an MRI would confirm."

The major turned away, crossed to her desk. "We'll be burning his body, pagan style, in an hour. Lunchtime," she added, "if you'd rather take your meal."

■   ■   ■

"She going to burn Levrov on a pyre," Rodion said in Kata's ear. "Who knows? Maybe she'll perform a pagan rite over the flames." His tone had turned facetious.

"Interesting solution," Kata said. She was on her way to meet Alyosha, whom she hadn't seen in what seemed forever but in reality was only ten or so hours. Kata had been in her office all that time.

"What does that mean?"

She heard the concern in his voice, imagined him frowning.

"It means," Kata said, "she's doing the right thing."

"You can't mean that." Rodion was aghast. "How will we ever find out what really killed Levrov?"

"Tell me exactly what's happening," she said, to calm him down as much as to get the maximum amount of intel out of him.

"I'm standing at the edge of the forest, outside the semicircle of tents. The soldiers are finishing building the pyre. All that's left to do is place Levrov's wrapped corpse onto it, squirt some petrol, and toss a lighted match on the unholy thing."

"You aren't a religious man, Rodion." She knew this from his dossier.

"True enough, but I find myself sick to my stomach about Levrov's end."

Silence. Only the nearly inaudible clicks and pops of the security solutions that kept their communications private.

Then the ruble dropped. His voice hissed like a steam engine. "You didn't send me here to find out about a murder. You sent me here to spy on Major Korokova."

"Someone had to do it, Rodion. I chose you."

She heard his indrawn breath. "She's got a—I don't know."

"I warned you," Kata said. "She's dangerous."

"I'm talking about something else entirely."

"Explain."

"I can't. I don't understand it myself."

"Well, then, buckle up, Rodion, and do your job," she said. "You're not getting out of there until you find out everything about her, who she's dealing with, and what it is she really wants."

■   ■   ■

Alyosha Ivanovna, eyes like pale blue topaz gems, walked past the bar of White Rabbit with its vaguely disturbing paintings of rabbits with human bodies, and was escorted by the maître d' to the table by the windows where Kata was already seated, a bottle of high-end vodka stuck in an ice bucket on a stand at her right elbow. Alyosha's legs were long, her torso lithe as that of a big cat, and like a big cat she was strong—stronger than a lot of men. As she was shown to her chair, the maître d' slid the bottle out of its ice sheath and poured them both triple shots. He left them with the menus. Overhead the barrel glass ceiling let in the Moscow twilight. The restaurant was situated on Smolenskaya Square in the Arbat District, its expanse crossed by the Garden Ring Road.

Kata and Alyosha lifted their glasses, downed the vodka. Alyosha, face thin with prominent cheekbones, a wide forehead, rosebud lips, and small ears that Kata inexplicably found endearing, smiled her secret smile that was only for Kata. Her eyes never left Kata's.

They had met a year ago under trying circumstances at a dacha in the forest outside Moscow where Kusnetsov had taken Kata to a party of high-level officers and oligarchs. There, too, they had shared iced vodka. Alyosha had said, *"I saw the anger behind your eyes. It smolders like a poorly banked fire."*

Kata had shaken her head. *"You're mistaken."*

"It's like looking in a mirror. It doesn't matter why we are angry, only that the anger lies deep inside us, sometimes in a place even we cannot reach."

Something had loosened inside Kata. *"And then we feel out of control."*

"Yes."

"We know there is nothing to be done."

"Yes."

Kata's eyes had clouded over. She felt enclosed in a darkness that welled up from inside her. *"I think that's why I kill, Alyosha, why I'm so good at it. Why I love it so much."*

Alyosha had appeared unsurprised. *"It makes sense, doesn't it? For that moment you are in control. No matter how brief, that moment brings release."*

Kata had reached out, taken Alyosha's hand in hers.

Now they were together. Alyosha was the first person Kata had ever lived with as an adult. Oddly, it never felt strange when Alyosha became her lover, and when she moved in with Kata their bond, which had been forged in blood and death, when Kata had saved Alyosha from the abusive predations of a general, became even stronger. Kata had never been one for deep introspection—there were connections missing in her brain that made strangers of emotion—but her love for Alyosha, flowering instantly, had found rich soil in the wasteland of her mind.

A waiter appeared from out of nowhere, poured more vodka for Kata and Alyosha. Though Alyosha was physically strong, Kata nevertheless felt a deep desire to protect her. In fact, she had promised her precisely that when bargaining with Kusnetsov, saving Alyosha a second time. She hadn't minded doing it; in fact, it made her feel stronger herself, braver.

Someone with more inclination to introspection might have deduced that her deep connection with Alyosha was the very thing making Kata stronger, braver.

Her eyes were filled with the striped shadows playing over Alyosha's face and body, firing her like the good vodka they were drinking. She had never loved before, never understood what love was, or if she did in an objective sense she was unreceptive to its blandishments. For Kata, to love was to be weak, and weakness was something she would not tolerate. For her, "weakness" was another word for destruction, death. Obliteration.

Shockingly, Alyosha, *obozhayemyy*, the adored, had engendered an alchemical response within her, a sea change as unexpected as a tiger leaping from tall grass. At first, she had struggled not to be overcome by emotions. Because she did not understand them they frightened her as nothing in the real world could. But then, gradually, because of Alyosha's inherent tenderness, Kata allowed herself to be overcome in brief bursts that caused her a breathlessness. When she confessed as much, Alyosha laughed gently in delight. *"That's elation, Kata,"* she had said. *"Elation."* And held her so tightly their heartbeats merged and Kata felt alive in a way she had never felt before. Was it possible, she wondered, that love was as powerful as hatred, as death? She had based her entire life on hatred—hatred of Evan, of her foster parents, of America, her foster country, and her birth parents, who cared so little about her they dumped her on someone else's doorstep. Too bad they were dead and buried. Wreaking vengeance on them would feel so sweet.

But not, she thought in wonderment, as sweet as being with Alyosha. The rest of the world with its eternal enmities, fears, sorrows, regrets ceased to exist.

Now with dinner ordered, more vodka drunk, the prospect of a string of clubs afterward, she settled in to a niche shiny as a Christmas toy, a respite from the fraught spiderweb of her life.

13

She heard them coming then, their clawed feet skittering over the floor, drawing nearer. Was she dreaming or . . . ? Her eyes popped open, blessed sleep having lasted mere seconds, and all the pain rushed back at her like a tsunami. A powerful shudder went through her. Her limbs felt stiff, but her hands and feet had ceased their tingling. She made fists a couple of times, wiggled her toes. She struck her shins to reassure herself her legs were more or less back to normal. Her trousers were still wet and had begun to stink. They clung to her thighs with an icy clamminess. Briefly, she thought about shimmying out of them, but a concerto of squealing was rising to a crescendo, so not a dream after all. Clearly, the rats had finished with their comrade, had scented her within her hiding place. By this time, her legs were burning from the rat bites, the pain spreading like wildfire.

Looking around her hiding place between the wall and the plywood boards, she found a stash of old tools: bent screwdrivers of several sizes; a nonworking slip wrench; two pairs of pliers, one rusted beyond usefulness; and a battered claw hammer, speckled in old paint.

She curled her fingers around the hammer's wooden handle, waited as long as she could to allow her limbs to get used to blood flowing through them again. Then she crawled painfully out and methodically, relentlessly went to work on the rats.

It was in the middle of this grisly work that the sound of the door lock opening came to her. The door began to swing open. Taissa made to enter, but instead stood in the open doorway, dead still; she'd seen the blood, the unraveled hemp, she smelled the reek of urine, the mess of deaths on the floor. But she didn't see Evan.

Slowly, she backed out, disappearing for a few seconds, only to return with a pistol in one hand, a hunting knife with a wicked eight-inch serrated blade in the other. No time for thought or consequences. Evan drew her arm back, threw the claw hammer straight and true, knocking the pistol out of Taissa's hand and breaking two of Taissa's fingers as well as fracturing her wrist.

But that was it, that one last use of the hammer all her weakened body was capable of. An agonized cry was forced out of her, and she sat back down, half-dazed, blackness rimming her vision. Taissa dropped her knife to grab her shattered wrist, but still she ran at Evan. She came very fast, lips drawn back in silent shock, teeth bared like a wolf. Black lips, yellow-white teeth, elongated canines, courtesy of her barbarian fore-bears.

She hit Evan like a force of nature, slamming Evan onto her back. Her weight, directly on the spot where Evan had struck herself in order to break the zip tie, was a sunburst of pain. Taissa, making the most of Evan's weakness, lodged her knees on top of Evan's shoulders—another rip of pain in Evan's right shoulder. With Evan's right hand incapacitated, Taissa was a lethal adversary. She elbowed Evan in the throat, bent low over her.

"I don't know how you managed to free yourself," she said in Turkish-inflected Russian, "but it makes no difference now. I have you, Amer-ican. I have you where I want you." Her eyes glittered like a wolf's in the forest. "My sister gave me permission to kill you any way I want, and now I will. Know why? I don't give a shit about you, American." She shook her head, beads of sweat flying off the ends of her hair. "Why should I care whether you live? Tell me, you bitch. No, don't bother; noth-ing you say can save you." She appeared to be carrying on a conversation with herself while Evan, mute and helpless, looked on. "Like all your kind you're beneath contempt. You're not human, an animal at best, at worst a cockroach crawling through the world excreting entitlement and excess wherever you go. You think you're destined to inherit the earth, as if you're descended from the pharaohs." She spat into Evan's face. "It's so lovely that you have developed the ability to indulge this delusion." Snarling now. "The reality is the world is better for your death. One less hustler shilling the monetization, the commodification of everything no one needs and all you Americans want."

Respite. This diatribe, seeming ripped straight from Russian anti-West agitprop, had given Evan a chance to regroup. It wasn't enough, not nearly, but she knew it was all she would get. Arching her back, she jackknifed her legs up and over, scissored them, trapping Taissa's head in a vise. Before the woman could fully respond she jerked her legs to the left. Taissa toppled over onto her side.

Evan rolled with her, racked with pain in every part of her body. She needed to expend a great deal of energy to keep herself from panting, keep her muscles from tightening up, going into spasms that would immobilize her. She forced herself to take slow deep breaths no matter how much pain they caused her.

Taissa was up, reaching for her, when Evan delivered a sharp kite with the edge of her left hand to the other woman's shattered wrist. Taissa howled, made to grab her damaged wrist—a clever feint—instead struck a blow to Evan's right shoulder.

The pain was blinding. Evan sucked in her breath; her entire shoulder was aflame, nerves shooting hot needles down her arm and into her hand. Leaning in, Taissa dug her fingers into the shoulder like the talons of an eagle. Evan's head was thrown back, the tendons of her neck standing out, veins pulsing.

"That's it," Taissa crowed, "die slowly. Die thinking of all the expensive treasures you've amassed. What good will they do you now?"

Evan felt as if her pain were crushing the life out of her one cell at a time. Half-paralyzed, her sight black at the edges, her lungs laboring, the shadow of death appeared to her. It was Taissa, of course; the rational part of her mind was sure of it, because Taissa wouldn't shut up. She kept on a tattoo of anti-West cliches, a woodpecker attached to the side of Evan's head.

In fact, it was this incessant chatter that brought Evan back from the abyss toward which the shadow of death was relentlessly shoving her. Twisting her torso in another wave of agony, she slammed her left elbow into Taissa's ear. Taissa screamed like a banshee, grabbing her ear, trying to stanch the blood drooling out of it.

Evan had opened up her defense. Rising, she stamped down hard on Taissa's fractured hand. She went for the knife lying not eight feet from where she stood. She was kneeling, reaching down for the weapon, when Taissa landed on her back, slammed the back of her head so hard Evan must have blacked out for a moment, for an instant later Taissa had the knife, was turning it in her hand in order to hold it properly. The blade slashed through the air. Steeling herself, Evan ignored the knife, concentrated on the length of hemp that had been used to bind her legs. She felt the sear as the knife blade buried itself in her arm. Ignored that too. Grabbing up the hemp, she twisted until she was behind Taissa, then wrapped the hemp around her throat and hauled backward with all her remaining strength. Taissa fought her, dropped the knife after a couple of ineffectual slashes missed Evan completely. She tried to dig the fingertips of her good hand between the hemp and her flesh, but Evan had already drawn it mercilessly tight. She hauled backward again, keeping the hemp right up against Taissa's throat. She heard a soft crackle like a fallen branch beneath a stag's hooves. The cricoid bone had shattered. No air was getting into Taissa's lungs. Her resistance became frenzied as she neared death. Her legs spasmed, her heels beating a spastic rhythm against the floor, sending up tiny dust devils.

Taissa's breathing became labored, stentorian, like a ninety-year-old woman's. Then all at once it ceased completely. All that was left was Evan's deep painful breathing and the settling of dust over them like a shroud.

■   ■   ■

To defend and protect: that was one of the human mind's prime directives. It was hardwired from millennia-old ancestors who hunted creatures three times their size, took them down, either alone or with others, skinned, butchered, and ate them over an open-pit fire. Sharing their largesse with the women and children. Sometimes it was the women who did the hunting, more skilled at finding their prey than the men. Sometimes they were eaten by their prey and never came home. Sometimes they got lost and were presumed dead by those who loved them the most.

Sometimes—but very rarely—they were found.

Evan's dreaming mind took her to such a time, when she was certain that she and her sister Bobbi would never meet their birth parents. The only mother and father they knew were the Ryders, who lived and worked their land and mines in South Dakota. Childless until a nameless couple appeared on their doorstep with the two-year-old girl and her just-born sister.

Evan on her knees, staring from the photo taken in the Black Hills of South Dakota to Frau Doktor Rebecca Reveshvili's tearstained face. As she took in the photo, of herself at five years old, Bobbi at three, she thought of the dream shadows, moving across the walls, the floor of the farmhouse in which she and Bobbi had grown up. Not a dream then? Were they memories?

Two years ago, through Lyudmila's intervention, she had found her parents, Kostya and Rebecca Reveshvili, at their psychiatric clinic in Germany.

Rebecca had placed her hand on the crown of Evan's head. A benediction or a welcome home? Both. The prodigal daughter at last returned to the mother and father who had created her. Home, and yet a very alien place, with two people who had left her and Bobbi with an American couple as the first part of a long-range FSB plan to grow sleeper agents inside the enemy's culture.

That was the moment when she realized that she wasn't American; she was Russian. Bobbi wasn't American; she was Russian. This was the truth that Bobbi had known about their parents, their real parents, the secret she wouldn't share that night in the caves of South Dakota when they had been teens. This was why Bobbi became a spy for Russia.

Rebecca holding Evan's hands in hers. "From the moment I first held you—beautiful pink baby, close to my chest, feeling your heartbeat against mine, your tiny fingers curled around my forefinger—all the defenses I had built against loving you crumbled to dust. That dust tried to choke me, bring me back to where I had begun, but that place was gone, dead and buried. I was no longer the woman I had been passing through immigration in New York, to begin this mission in America, on our way to South Dakota.

"You . . . you changed everything for me. Giving you up ripped out a part of my heart. Now it beats more softly, more erratically. There have been times I thought it would stop altogether. Ask your father; he will tell you. Or perhaps he won't. Kostya is more secretive than I ever was. He holds his secrets close, hoards them like a Tolkien dragon its gold. But, make no mistake, he loves you fully as much as I do."

Evan could not stop the tears rolling down her cheeks. Reaching up, she took her mother's hand in hers, rose to face her. She placed a hand on her mother's cheek, wet also with tears.

"Tell me this isn't a dream."

Her father's eyes were shining as Rebecca gathered her into her arms. "This isn't a dream, Evan."

■   ■   ■

Dream. Memory. Sometimes they were one and the same. So it was for Evan as she opened her eyes, staring blindly at the ceiling, wanting nothing more than to be back with the Reveshvilis—watching Kostya's kind face, wrapped in her mother's arms. But, inevitably, the dream-memory faded. She found herself staring up at the rafter and thick brass hook that still held the threaded remnants of the rope that had bound her, then downward tracking to take in the carnage of blood, rat bodies, stains of dried urine, and Taissa's swollen tongue pushed out between bare teeth. Above, eyes protruding as if trying to peer into a future that would never now occur.

Evan tried to move, groaned. She felt drowned, cast up on an alien shore where all life had fled decades ago. She was alone in this void, somewhere she had never been before and to which she wished fervidly never to return.

She might have stayed like that, immobile, hardly putting two thoughts together, had it not been for the sound of footsteps at the door, which impelled her gaze to turn in that direction.

A figure stood in the doorway, someone familiar, and a sense of warmth, of being found flooded through her. Until the figure stepped into the room and what light there was fell upon the face, eyes burning like beacons in the night. Had she the strength she would have screamed then, recognizing Taissa's twin sister, Inessa, and with her the shadow of Evan's own death.

14

"Yes, it's true," General Philip Johnstone Reade said. "Tonight we have become recruiters." He gestured to the men around the green baize table. "Wilson, Connerly, myself."

Ben was also there, of course, sitting across from Connerly. Reade was on his left, Wilson on his right. Midnight. As he was being driven here it had been all too clear that Langley and the city just across the Potomac were major contributors to the light pollution leaking everywhere, disturbing the natural biorhythms of birds and insects.

"We can tell you—now that you've had your six hours to think—that only we three are in this. All correspondence is handwritten, delivered by a single courier."

"Let me guess," Ben said. "Daisy."

"Daisy is her operational name," Connerly said in his annoyingly officious way.

"Her real name is Margo," the general continued.

"I see that her duties also extend to chauffeuring."

"Yes," Wilson said. "She drove you here tonight."

"If I may," Reade said with a generous degree of sarcasm, to return the conversation to the topic at hand, "any and all correspondence between us is folded into envelopes which are then sealed with wax."

"No chance of your private affair being hacked," Ben said. "Niccolò Machiavelli would be proud. Not to mention Armand Jean du Plessis."

Connerly's face screwed up. "Armand de what?—Who the fuck is that?"

"Cardinal Richelieu," Ben told him. "Best known for, among other coups de main, ordering the destruction of the Huguenots; reforming the French navy and army; crushing any rebellions and advancing royal absolutism. Also, delightfully, he raised money by any and all means. I'm sure you gentlemen understand that sort of thing."

"Looks like we continue to host a hostile witness." Connerly trying too hard to recover.

"He's just showing off," the general said, shifting in his chair. "Making a fool of you, Wes, by presenting his superior knowledge." He turned to Ben with the ghost of a smile playing across his lips. "Very Richelieu, wouldn't you say, Butler."

"I pluck only the best kernels from the best, General." Then, turning to Connerly, "The rest I leave for the chickens."

Connerly lurched out of his seat, jaw clenched, the muscles on either side of his mouth pumping like men frantically bailing a sinking ship.

"Down, boy," the general ordered. "He's just messing with you."

"Why me?" Connerly protested. "Why always me?"

"I don't like you," Ben said without inflection. "You're a fucking bigot."

"Right." Reade nodded. "Take the rest of the week off, Wes."

Connerly looked at the general, neck flushed, skin raised in bumps. "Why are you—?"

"You don't need to understand why I give you an order."

"Yes, sir." Connerly pushed back his chair, overturning it, punishing it because he couldn't retaliate against the man who was now his nemesis. He gave Ben the death stare before stalking out of the room. The door did not fully close at his departure. Daisy was standing in the doorway.

"Trouble in paradise?" she asked.

By way of answer, the general beckoned her in. She came across the room. She was dressed all in black, apart from a wide white belt with twin buckles that accentuated her hips on one end, and what rose above it on the other. A short jacket with three-quarter sleeves over all. She sat down at the table, though not in Connerly's chair, which caused Ben to wonder whether she somehow had been monitoring the meeting from the beginning. *In here, I am surrounded by electronics,* he thought, *all cleverly hidden, all waiting to entrap me or anyone else who sits in my place.*

Daisy—or Margo, if he preferred—smiled at him with all the innocence of a deb at a tea party. "The men treating you well? Have any compliments, complaints?"

She was expert at wrong-footing him, which, he supposed, was the point. "My only complaint has been dismissed."

"Excellent." She enlaced her fingers. "So . . ."

She let the single word hang in the air so that he could absorb every layer of its meaning. He got it now. They'd started with the hard man, switching midstream to the soft man—in this case, woman. He'd bested the hard man. Perhaps they hadn't expected that, but in any event they pivoted to plan B without the slightest glitch. Smoothly run human machinery always impressed him. Possibly they knew that, too. It was difficult to know how much they really knew about him.

Margo leaned forward. In a female of her genetic makeup the change in posture could be interpreted as a provocative gesture. "So, Ben, which will it be? A chocolate egg cream? Or a cup of slow-acting hemlock?"

She had a way with words, that was for sure, Ben thought, smiling to himself. But he didn't allow the smile to spill over onto his lips, let alone his face. He'd made up his mind before he'd stepped into the car they had sent for him at precisely 11:30 P.M. as promised.

"Before jumping into the deep end of the pool I'd like a little more information."

"You have a list?"

Not the general, not Wilson. Margo asking. The two men looked on silently. It dawned on Ben that Reade hadn't gone for his beloved cigars the entire time he had been in the room. A disorienting sensation was rising up from the pit of his stomach.

"Like why was Wes Connerly here? This isn't his pitch at all."

A slow smile spread over her face. Her pink lips parted to show a row of small white teeth that appeared very sharp indeed.

"Wes was read in—"

"And just what the hell is the National Geospatial Intelligence Agency anyway?" Ben demanded, talking over her. "It sounds like administration-speak—a bunch of words thrown together signifying nothing." He said all this to Margo because it was Margo who had queried him. But it was also because he was getting the distinct impression that Margo or Daisy or whatever her real name was was more than an aide to General Reade, more than a courier for this ad hoc group, more than a chauffeur. She was all of them and none of them. She was dead center of the general's cabal, the instigator and the motivator while the general went smugly on, certain that he was in charge when, in fact, he hadn't a clue.

"Wes Connerly is not of import to you—or to us, really," she said, calm as a reptile basking in sunlight.

Then what was he doing here? he was going to ask. But in the next moment there was no need. He knew. Connerly was set up as a sacrifice, someone on whom Ben could take out his anger and disappointment at what they had told him about his current boss, leaving them animus-free. He had been wrong—cleverly misdirected. Connerly wasn't the hard man. He was facing the hard man now.

"I suppose you've worked it out by now," she said.

"Most of it," Ben acknowledged. "Everything but who you really are."

She smiled her toothsome smile, and in that moment, when her personas—Daisy, Margo—slipped, she was terrifying.

15

At precisely 4:45 in the afternoon, Kata presented herself at the Russian State Library on Vozdvizhenka Street. She was precisely fifteen minutes early for her prescribed rendezvous with Comrade Director Stanislav Budimirovich Baev, head of SVR. He was her old boss and she knew him well, knew he was in a perilous cold war with her current boss, Minister Darko Vladimirovich Kusnetsov, head of FSB. She was walking a delicate tightrope high above FSB headquarters, keeping her promise to Baev to inform him of any overtly antagonistic moves against him from above.

She crossed to the literature section, removed a volume of *War and Peace*, stepped to a table, turned on the gooosenecked lamp, sat down and opened the novel. She started reading. *"Well, Prince, so Genoa and Lucca are now just family estates of the Buonapartes. But I warn you, if you don't tell me that this means war, if you still try to defend the infamies and horrors perpetrated by that Antichrist—I really believe he is Antichrist—I will have nothing more to do with you and you are no longer my friend, no longer my 'faithful slave,' as you call yourself!"*

She was well versed in all the Russian writers but enjoyed Tolstoy the most. The original Russian was so much more emotive than the dry English translation.

At precisely 4:50 P.M. she looked up, her gaze quartering the room, her security-minded training urging her to look for any anomalies, no matter how small, in the daily workings of the library. Finding none, she returned to Tolstoy, but this time the words scarcely registered.

Her memory raced backward. Had it only been five years ago that she had been ushered into Baev's care? Baev, who always had her do personal, off-the-grid wet work for him. Her easy expertise had delighted him at first, but as she rose through the ranks of SVR and was poached by Minister Kusnetsov she had a suspicion that Baev had gradually come to fear her. He was desperate to hold onto her, thus this latest in a long line of clandestine meetings. Plus, she had always suspected that he was in love with her, was angered when she did not respond to either intimidation or blandishments. She steadfastly remained an enigma to him, which was just how she liked it.

As for Baev himself, it was one minute past five with no sign of him. He was as prompt as any Russian, especially those within the clandestine services, who'd had punctuality hammered into them from the very first day they were recruited into service.

"Heavens! what a virulent attack!" replied the prince, not in the least disconcerted by this reception. He had just entered, wearing an embroidered court uniform, knee breeches, and shoes, and had stars on his breast and a serene expression on his flat face.

Having read these lines three times without them registering, Kata closed the novel, returned it to its place on the proper shelf, and, striding across the floor, exited the library. It was precisely 5:16 and Baev wasn't coming.

■   ■   ■

Slushy snow was falling as she made her way back to her office. Once inside the building, it was immediately apparent to her that something had changed while she'd been gone. There was always the stink of male sweat, of anxiety, an underlying hint of fear, but this evening it seemed to her these odors were amped up. Instead of heading for her office she made a hard left, went up a floor to Baev's quarters. She was surprised to see the cubicles of Baev's assistants manned by people she did not know, in uniforms, no less—black with gold trim and sigils on the upper sleeves and the shoulder boards, a design unknown to her. They were busy, speaking softly but urgently into wireless headsets. When she asked them if the comrade director was in they made no reply.

Passing them by, she stepped into Baev's corner office and stopped dead. Not only was Baev not present, but all of his possessions had been removed as if they'd never existed. Never one for neatness, his office had always been somewhat of a mess. Not now. What items had replaced Baev's things were neatly placed on the swept-clean desk. A brand-new open laptop and a perfectly ordered pile of dossiers to its left had pride of place. Apart from the old desk lamp that had come with the office, nothing was as it once was.

That included the man standing with his back to her, staring out one of the windows behind the desk. His hands were clasped behind his back. He had a military bearing, though his hair was not cut short but shot up from his skull as if terrified of what lay within. He wore the same black uniform with gold trim as the officers outside. His, though, sported different sigils. A rank designator? That was Kata's best guess, anyway.

Before she could ask after Baev, the man said, "How may we help you?"

The two of them were the only occupants of Baev's office. Was he speaking in the imperial "we"? Really?

As she was pondering this he turned around, astonishing her. Was it her imagination or was he actually sporting Vladimir Lenin's mustache and goatee, Leon Trotsky's round small-lensed spectacles and hairstyle? Kata opened her mouth to say something, almost immediately closed it.

"Kata Romanovna Hemakova." His voice was a deep basso that re-sounded off the walls, which had been repainted the vibrant color of a fresh egg yolk. The color more or less matched the gold trim of his jacket.

She finally found her voice. "And you are?"

"We imagine you are looking for Comrade Director Baev." His eyes, beady, oil-slick dark, were close together, like Trotsky's.

She said nothing. Why confirm the obvious.

"He was your former superior, was he not?" No answer required, she knew. "So have you come here to reminisce, perhaps talk over old times, have a bit of a knees-up as the British say." His smile was as thin as the hair on a nonagenarian's head. "Or was it on business that you have arrived here. Business between you and the comrade director."

He was going to force her to say it, she knew that much. "Where is Comrade Director Baev?"

"Away," the man said.

"When will he return?" But the complete occupation of Baev's office was answer enough. She felt as if she were in an elevator whose cables had been cut. Free-falling.

"No one knows where he is, least of all us. So when—if—he will return is an unanswerable question."

"I'm sure if you did know you wouldn't tell me."

He shrugged, as if to say, *Why would we? Who are you to know anything of import?*

"Who are you taking orders from?"

An eerie smile split his face. "The same person who reassigned Comrade Director Baev to . . . parts unknown."

Kata took a step toward him. She didn't know whether that was a smart move, but she was done playing this jackass's game. "You mean Minister Kusnetsov."

He spread his hands. The gesture gave him the look of a mockingly pious bishop.

"What about Baev's family?"

"Do you mean his wife and children, or his mistress du jour?"

"Is it your contention—" She took another step toward him. "—that you disapprove of mistresses?"

She was almost in his face, where she wanted to be. She needed to establish control of this conversation, to allow her mind time to assess the radical change that had been made. She needed to quell the anxiety growing inside her.

Again he shrugged. "Not our department."

She made a show of looking him up and down. "No, I suppose not." She tried for a smile, nearly made it. "Exactly what *is* your department?"

"Currently we are the director of SVR. Our rank is colonel." A military man.

"Currently," she repeated. "Does that mean you will be moving on soon?"

"Everything changes, Ms. Hemakova," he said. "Except, of course, the Sovereign."

"Of course." Did he even register the mocking tone in her voice?

"Now you will step back to the correct eight-foot distance." The darkening of his voice was noticeable.

"You can't order me around," she retorted. "I work for Minister Kusnetsov."

"You don't. As of this moment Directorate O no longer exists." His eyes seemed to spark through the lenses of his spectacles. "You work for us now. Ludovico Ferranov."

"What, no patronymic?"

"Not for the likes of you, Ms. Hemakova."

Despite her best efforts her cheeks were burning. "Seriously? As soon as I speak with Minister Kusnetsov—"

"We wouldn't waste our time. The minister is in talks with the Sovereign. At the Kremlin. You cannot see him, he will not take your call." He nodded to the cell phone she had pulled out. "Try it. You'll see. He is currently incommunicado." He made a brusque gesture. "Now step back," he ordered, "or suffer the consequences."

Kata had no choice but to obey. She stepped back to mark precisely eight feet from the colonel.

Ferranov went behind his desk, sat, opened the top file. "Dismissed," he said without looking at her.

As she was at the door, his voice froze her. "Ms. Hemakova."

She turned back.

"You will keep your nose out of Directorate KV's affairs. Is that clear."

"It is, sir." Fury mixed with the anxiety of having the rug metaphorically pulled out from under her. She no longer had her friendship with Baev, no longer had the aegis of Kusnetsov to protect her. She was alone, exposed, at the mercy of this strange robotic cipher.

As she was about to turn away, he raised his arm. "Oh, one other thing, Ms. Hemakova."

He paused, forcing her to say, "Yes?"

At last his oil-dark eyes lifted to hers. "A word to the unwise. If we were you"—here he shuddered—actually shuddered—"we would disassociate ourselves from our lesbian lover."

Fury took her fully. A red mist rising.

16

"There is a fly in the ointment."

"A fly," Ben said.

Daisy—in his head she was still Daisy—nodded. "Yes."

"In the ointment."

"A spanner in the works, if you prefer."

They were alone in the sublevel conference room, both the general and Wilson having bid them adieu.

"However," Daisy continued, "in this instance 'a fly in the ointment' is more apropos."

In the ensuing silence, Ben felt compelled to say, "I need to stretch my legs. If you'd care to join me."

"All right," she said, almost reluctantly. But her eyes gave him another answer entirely.

They rose, crossed to the door, went down the hallway. He followed her as she made an abrupt turn to the left, down a dimly lit branch. She brought out a different card, and the door swung inward. He stepped in after her, found himself in the women's bathroom.

She stopped in the middle of the room, turned on her heel to face him. "There's only one security camera in here and I've fixed it."

"They haven't noticed?"

"I've interfered with the signal. There's a constantly running tape of an empty bathroom."

"That isn't suspicious?"

Her smile was knife-edged. "I'm the only woman allowed down here and I notoriously have the bladder of a camel."

The thing was, Ben thought, he needed to keep sizing her up, and every time he did so she became a different person, like a human chameleon. This included her personality.

He crossed his arms over his chest. "Now that we're alone kindly tell me why 'fly in the ointment' is more apropos of your problem."

"Because, Ben, you are the fly *and* the ointment."

"Please be clearer."

"The general likes you. That's highly unusual, unique, one might say. He doesn't like anyone."

"Even you?" he said, trying for playful.

"*Especially* me."

He huffed. "I find that difficult to believe. I mean why would that be?"

"Reade's afraid of me."

Ben tried to take that in, failed, shook his head.

"Reade may like you, but I don't trust you."

"Hm, speaking of trust, Daisy or Margo or . . ." He let the rest of the sentence hang, because she'd already got the idea.

She dug a passport out of her jacket, handed it over. He opened it, saw her photo. Then he checked the bindings, the center crease, did not find it wanting. It was authentic.

He looked up at her. "So your name—your real name is Zahra. Zahra Planck."

She nodded, took the passport back. "My mother is Iranian, my father was German. And, yes, Max Planck was my great-uncle." She sighed. "Somehow my father had delusions of me becoming a writer, but instead I became a scientist. A physicist. A particle physicist, like my great-uncle, and for the past four years I've been specializing in quantum computing." Her smile had now softened slightly. "That's why the general is afraid of me. I'm heading up the government team, and even though Marsden Tribe is still a light-year ahead of us we're making progress."

"So now I see why I'm the fly," Ben said. "You don't trust me. But I'm also the ointment?"

"We need you," Zahra said. "Urgently."

"What you really mean is you need a conduit into Tribe's quantum solutions." He shrugged. "You're barking up the wrong tree, since we're using hoary phrases. I'm nowhere near his team of physicists."

"That's just it." She stepped closer to him. "What Reade is asking you to do is absurd, impossible. But does he know that?" She gave a small laugh. "He and his so-called cabal are Ivory Tower dwellers. They sit in the center of an echo chamber. People tell them what they expect to hear.

What I'm asking of you is eminently doable. What I need is proof of his culpability in Brady Thompson's murder. You're part of his security. You have a long and successful history of being in the field. You know how to get what I want."

He turned away, stepped to the far wall. "This prison cell doesn't even have a window."

"Naturally. Too far underground." But the penny had already dropped. "I know a place," she said.

He turned back, grinning. "Lead on."

■   ■   ■

"Like you," Ben said, "I'm mixed race. American WASP father. Lebanese Jewish mother. They met in Beirut, where I was born."

"A Levantine Jew," Zahra said. "My goodness."

He cocked his head. "Am I your first?"

She laughed. "Shall we order?"

They were sitting in a tiny hole-in-the-wall restaurant. Iranian. The owner-chef embraced her when they arrived. She introduced him to Ben as Babak. They were the only customers. Apparently they opened for just her; she'd called ahead while he was gathering the personal effects he'd surrendered to security. The place was just off Wilson Boulevard, in northeast Arlington. She must have been hungry. She ordered soups, salads, koobideh and soltani kabobs for both of them. A meat eater then, Ben thought, absorbing everything about her.

Babak told them he'd bring Iranian tea later; now something stronger to drink.

"So we're both part Middle Eastern," Zahra said.

"But you must have known that about me already."

She sat back as drinks came, a bottle of Persian Empire Saggi Arak and two glasses. Babak poured them both half a glass, then retreated into the tiny kitchen accessed through a Heriz rug hung as a curtain. On the walls were paintings of Iranian origin, depicting the Persian cities of antiquity. Nothing of modern Iran, Ben noted.

"The general knows. Wilson as well."

He already knew that as far as this situation was concerned Connerly had served his purpose; he had been dismissed from the loop. Maybe he knew nothing at all—at least the bare minimum, which did not include Ben's ethnic background.

The food came all at once, which was no surprise to either of them. Babak, bless him, did not stay around for accolades but returned to his overheated cave. Zahra ate slowly and carefully, shearing off precise cubes of kabob with her knife, taking small bites between her teeth.

"My problem, Ben, is this," she said after a time. She was so neat she had no need to wipe her chin, but she very delicately licked the grease from her lips. "I've done my homework on you. In the field you have repeatedly proved yourself intrepid, inventive, and above all loyal."

He ate even more slowly than she did; he never took his eyes off her. He was studying her features, the microexpressions that flitted across her face in less than a blink of an eye. The concentration was exhausting but, he was certain, worth it. There was no effective way to gain the advantage over an enigma, and Zahra Planck was the greatest enigma he had ever encountered. Next to her, Isobel was more or less an open book.

"These three qualities are what make you so good at your job," Zahra continued. "However, for me, at this particular moment in time, the third quality—namely loyalty—is an issue."

Ben knew there was no need for him to query her; she was going to keep going and it would be counterproductive to interrupt the flow.

"You are loyal to Evan Ryder, to Isobel Lowe, to Marsden Tribe."

Now was the time to step in. "I have histories with Evan and Isobel," he said evenly. "I have personal relationships with them. I trust them implicitly."

She snatched at the opening he had given her. "And Marsden Tribe?"

"What about him?"

"As of a year ago you had no history with him. You have met him, what? Three times?"

"Two actually."

"So we may assume you have no personal relationship with him."

"He pays my salary, my expenses. He's extremely generous."

"With money."

"You're stating the obvious."

She ignored that gibe. "What about with his time?"

"I report to Isobel, not to Tribe. In any event, he's an inordinately busy individual."

"Not too busy to spend time with Ms. Ryder."

"I wouldn't know about that."

"Is that so." She cocked her head. "Is she, like Marsden Tribe, too busy to tell you? Or has she stopped confiding in you?"

Something was rising inside Ben. He could not quite put a name to it but knew he didn't like it. "We're not joined at the hip," he said tartly. "We have our separate lives."

"Within the confines of Parachute security?"

"I don't care what she and Tribe are up to."

Her dark eyes gleamed like obsidian. "So they *are* up to something."

She had neatly led him into this trap. This supposed diversion wasn't a diversion at all. It was a pickaxe to undermine his relationship with Evan. In hindsight it was so obvious that he now wondered why he felt anything at all. But Evan and Tribe? Really? The thought sickened him, but again he couldn't figure out why. Why should he care, and yet he did. Worse, Zahra could see it on his face. A blow well struck.

Babak came and cleared away the plates and silverware. He said nothing, did not look at either of them, scurried away as fast as was seemly.

"We've wandered far afield." It was all he could think of to say.

She pulled herself up. "Quite right." Her voice was clipped, businesslike. "The real question is whether or not you trust Marsden Tribe." She spread her hands. "You must admit the evidence we presented is compelling."

"Is it? You've shown me what you wanted to show me. You've told me what I was looking at. Perception, that's all that is."

She gave him a look he couldn't read, which annoyed him when it should have concerned him. He watched her slip out a file folder from her bag, open it on the table. She turned it around so that the contents were facing him.

"These are photos of the MRI scans I was shown before."

She pointed to the top photo. "This one is, yes." She set that aside, revealing a second photo of Thompson's brain from a slightly different angle. "This one as well." She set that aside to reveal a third and fourth photo he knew he hadn't seen before. "But not these two."

He glanced up at her. "Why not?"

"Because General Reade and his little cabal wouldn't know what to make of them."

"And you do?"

"Yes."

Ben was following the thread she was laying out for him. "But you haven't told them."

"No."

"Again, why not?"

"Because I want to show this to *you*."

"What I'm looking at makes no sense to me."

"That's because I put this scan under a microscope. This photo is the result."

Her hand swept over the scan. "What you're looking at is one of the three detonations inside the late secretary of defense's brain."

He nodded. "If that's what you say it is."

For the first time an edge of annoyance flickered across her face. "You don't need me to tell you anything. Look for yourself at how damaged the brain cells are around the detonation."

He could see that. "All right," he acknowledged.

"Now I want you to concentrate on the precise center of the detonation." Her forefinger stabbed out, the nail touching a spot before moving away.

Ben took up the photo, tilted it so that more light shone on it.

"What do you see, Ben?" she asked.

"Nothing." His brow furrowed. "Nothing at all."

"And yet there must be something there." Her eyes were shining like those of a zealot. "Something caused the detonations. They didn't appear out of thin air."

He shook his head.

"But you're right. Even under microscopic scrutiny nothing is visible."

"Well." Ben's brow furrowed. "It can't very well be *in*visible."

"And yet it is," Zahra said. "To the naked eye, to a microscope. Which means we've got to go smaller still to find it."

"What if nothing is there?"

She sat back. "Fine. Give me your explanation as to how three detonations inside Thompson's brain got there." Her eyes flashed. "We've already precluded all known medical causes."

He looked again at the photo but tellingly said nothing.

"Of course," Zahra said. "There is no other explanation. Qubits—quantum particles—are too small to be seen with either the naked eye or a microscope. Similarly, the holes they made in Thompson's skull wouldn't be picked up by the best forensic scientists." She spread her hands on the table. "My conclusion—the only logical conclusion—is that somehow Marsden Tribe, your boss, has figured out a way to weaponize qubits."

Ben wanted to snort in derision but he couldn't make himself do it. What if she was right? What other way could those detonations inside Thompson's brain exist?

"I've told you, I have no idea what's going on inside Parachute itself," he told her. "Our security team is completely sealed off from the rest of the company."

"Not completely sealed off," she said quietly. "Perhaps Evan Ryder knows."

Now it all came together. Ben sat back, head spinning, the wheels within wheels of the enigma he saw sitting across from him.

"Of course," he said, his voice perfectly flat. "Of course that's what you want."

"No, no, Ben." She leaned forward, placed her hand atop his. Her palm was warm like embers burning, her fingers cool as water. "You mustn't think you're a means to an end." Her gaze grasped his, would not let go until her fingers had curled his around a thumb drive. "There is more— something else inexplicable. It's all here"—her fingers squeezed his lightly—"in what I've just given you. I'm trusting you to get this to the right person, Ben. I trust you. *You* are my end."

17

Ever since he'd returned to Moscow and his cold lab, Morokovsky remained in a mood most foul. Days later, in fact, his rage had grown exponentially. He tasted it in his food, he lay with it sleepless in the night, and since he couldn't take it out on the major, he did the most human thing and took it out on those around him—those closest to him. There was not a person on his team who did not cringe from the full fury of his wrath. That they had no idea why they were being reprimanded made little difference either to them or to him.

He stomped into his office in the square six-story Brutalist raw cement structure that passed for postmodern design these days. Three stories above ground, three below, it was referred to ironically by those who toiled away there day and night as the medical arts theater.

Of course, nothing could be further from the truth. The procedures carried out within its walls were as brutal as the architectural design of the building itself. There were no windows in his office, just as there were none in the mortuary, where the dead and mutilated lay sleeping on their stainless-steel trays. All except Ivan Levrov. What the major had planned for the corpse was anyone's guess. Worse, it was out of Morokovsky's control.

Control was Morokovsky's thing, his guiding light, his god. Within his autopsy room he controlled everything and everyone. So what if they called him a martinet behind his back. He cared more for the corpses than he did his living crew. They were all nitwits anyway. They were clever enough not to ask him about his trip to the Rostov forest, and if they were curious about why he had not brought the corpse back they said nothing. Anyway, they were too busy being browbeaten for standing too close to him, standing too far away, not answering his questions quickly enough, answering too quickly. He picked on their personality failings no matter how minute. They all stood and took it, of course, like good little soldiers. His hands curled into fists at his side; he wanted to punch every one of them in the face.

This harsh methodology had been drummed into him by his father and grandfather, both of whom had been illustrious pathologists with a number of international patents in pathology instruments to their names. Now here was their son and grandson enjoined from completing perhaps the most fascinating autopsy of his career, stymied by a woman no less—a woman with direct connection to the Sovereign. But that was the problem, wasn't it? He wasn't connected to anyone of note, let alone the Sovereign.

He went to work on a pair of corpses—they were backlogged, as usual—dictating his findings into a hanging mic, carving out vital organs and weighing them on a scale as he imagined one of the ancient Egyptian gods of the dead did—never mind his name. After two hours of him playing god of the dead, his stomach began its noisy protest. He washed up, left one of his assistants to write up his dictated notes, and went upstairs to the commissary.

The commissary was on the top floor, flooded with light, and large enough to accommodate the entire staff, though it was rarely even a third full. It was an in-between hour—after lunch and before the dinner service had begun—so there was only a sprinkling of people. Good. It was here he could get away and relax, if only for the twenty minutes he allotted himself for a meal.

If there was one person in the medical arts theater he could call a friend it was Maria Mariskiovna, his assistant pathologist. She was young, blond, with pretty eyes beneath long lashes. She reminded Morokovsky of Tatiana, the daughter he had lost last year to a bacterial infection no one knew how to treat; the terrifying scourge was resistant to every known antibiotic. Frantic, he'd done everything he could think of to save Tatiana, but to no avail. He was consigned to watch her waste away, day by day, each one more painful. As for his wife, she had a complete psychological break and was now shut away somewhere in the German countryside.

As usual at that hour, Maria was just coming off shift. They greeted each other with weary smiles. Slicing open dead bodies, scooping out major organs to weigh them, inevitably took its toll, even on someone like

Maria, who was just starting out. This made Morokovsky sad. Over their time together they had become more than comrades-in-arms; they were confidants.

"You always look like crap," she said in her bantering tone, "but today, I fear, is something special."

That made him laugh. "You're right, I do feel like crap left out in the rain."

He bought them both coffees and some pastries and they sat at a table near one of the windows. He liked the way the sunlight struck her face, pulled all her good features into prominence.

"So why the particularly long face?" she asked.

"Ah, well, I feel like a horse who'd been beaten for pulling a hearse with too much ease."

She looked at him quizzically. "Meaning?"

"So, okay, a horse walks into a bar," he said as she sipped her coffee, "and the bartender says, 'Hey, buddy, why the long face?'"

She laughed so hard the coffee almost came out of her nose.

"Tatiana always like that one," he said with a chuckle. "I began telling it to her when she was seven. She laughed no matter how many times I told it to her."

"I will too," Maria said.

He turned away then, abruptly overcome with a visceral memory of Tatiana's unique scent, the loving way she looked at him. The uninhibited way she laughed at his stupid jokes. Really laughed; she was doing him no favors. *Where are you?* he wondered now. *What I wouldn't give to talk to you one more time.*

Maria put a hand over his. "But really."

He sighed deeply. "Truth?"

"Always."

"I don't much care for being sent home as if I'm ready for the glue factory."

It was at that moment that the pain exploded inside his head. One after another, detonations took him farther and farther away from Maria, the commissary, the medical arts theater, his memories. He could no longer see, could no longer hear. He was unaware when his arm swung out, swiping his coffee cup and saucer onto the floor. Securely locked within the multiplying punctures of agony assaulting his brain he had no idea that

Maria had jumped up, that she was screaming his name, had taken him by his shoulders and then, as his eyes rolled up in his head, began shouting at the top of her lungs for medical assistance.

Moments later he got his wish; he was with Tatiana again.

18

Inessa entered the room where Evan lay, and her eyes opened wide at the sight of her dead sister. Her shout echoed off the walls of the room, rebounding over and over as she gave voice to her grief and rage. She snarled like an animal whose cage door had been left open.

She took a step into the room, nose wrinkling at the thick, gamey stink. Her gaze bounced from her sister to Evan, over and over. The venom in her eyes turned them black as moonless midnight.

"I will kill you." Her voice was thick and hot as the astrosphere, guttural in nature. "But not quickly, oh no. Slowly as I watch the blood drain out of you drop by drop. I'll laugh as your face becomes deathly pale and I'll stop to allow you to recover just enough before I start again. Edging you toward death. But not before pain, agony, and screaming that will rip the lining of your throat."

Evan watched her standing there, not moving. She had heard these words before, or ones like them. She was inured to words; there was nothing to be done about them. Words were the altar of the bully and the coward. Words were meaningless, a weak attempt to intimidate and induce terror. It was action Evan was concentrated on, and there was none from Inessa. Oddly, she simply stood one step inside the open doorway. Seething. Planning her initial attack. What would it be? Evan was suddenly filled with anxiety. What had she been thinking? In her debilitated state Inessa could do just about anything to her, even if she wasn't built like an MMA fighter. Evan had little strength left and all her stamina was lying in a puddle around her. There was no other exit from the room that she could see, and even if there was one it was sure to be locked, and even if by some miracle it wasn't how far could she get without passing out?

These were her concerns, mounting steadily into a silent scream when Inessa, advancing on her, stumbled badly. It was only when she fell to her knees that Evan became aware that she had been shoved hard from behind.

Another figure strode into the room, undoubtedly the man who had pushed Inessa. To Evan's astonishment it was the Syrian, Abd-El-Kader, "servant of the powerful." He stood behind Inessa, though she seemed unaware of him. Her head lifted, her eyes staring into those of her twin. Her mouth constricted into what might have become a feral snarl had Abd-El-Kader not grabbed her forcibly by the collar of her jacket and jerked her backward so hard her teeth clacked together. She went wild trying to squirm out of his grip, whether to get to her sister for solace or to Evan for revenge was impossible to say because she was brought up short by a terrible blow to the side of her head from the Syrian.

"Know your place," he growled. He seemed totally unaffected by the charnel house the room had become. Maybe it wasn't the first time, Evan thought.

"My place is with my sister." Inessa's voice was thick, horrible-sounding.

He grabbed a fistful of her hair, jerked her head back. "Soon enough you'll join her, but not yet. Hear me?"

She glared up at him, her lower lip extended in a pout. "I'll kill you," she husked, "after I kill *her.*"

Abd-El-Kader laughed. "What d'you make of this one?"

It took Evan several seconds to understand that he was no longer addressing Inessa. Another man had entered the room. Even staring at the face, even feeling the weight of his gaze on her, she could scarcely believe her eyes. "You," she whispered. "What are you doing here?"

"It would be unreasonable for me not to be here," Marsden Tribe said. "I just bought the Spider's business."

19

Major Juliet Korokova, wondering why Kata had sent such a lamb to her, watched the crackling fire consume Ivan Levrov's corpse along with any definitive evidence of what had actually caused his demise. That was her job; that was why she had been sent here on emergency orders.

That a member of Kata's directorate had shown up was hardly a surprise. Rodion, however, was. In the three days he'd been here she had made it her business to get to know him. He was no idiot, no unthinking drone Kata Hemakova had sicced on her. He was more, but how much more she had yet to determine. She had chosen him to help her wrap Levrov's opened corpse in a winding sheet in order to observe his nerve and stamina for foul odors. The portable heaters that had kept Morokovsky's fingers flexible during the autopsy had also had a deleterious effect on the body. The air around it was fetid with the noxious gases the corpse was still emitting in occasional furious mini-bursts.

Despite them donning rubber gloves and surgeon's masks, Rodion's motions were herky-jerky, as if he were trying to hide a trembling in his hands under wraps. His eyes above the mask were so big she could see the whites all around. It was clear that Rodion had no experience with either death or corpses. Why Kata had chosen him for Directorate O was a mystery she felt she needed to solve.

Korokova held no goodwill toward Colonel Kata Romanovna Hemakova. In their initial meeting a year ago, Kata had tried her best to dragoon Korokova into clandestinely working for Directorate O, never mind that she and her directorate were FSB and Korokova herself was GRU. By long-standing tradition, military intelligence and FSB were at each other's throats, continually fighting over territory. Every once in a while a mini-bloodbath would break out, quickly quelled, the ringleaders instantly vanished off the face of the earth.

They finished the winding and she sealed the sheet's outer end, then called for two of her men to haul Levrov's remains out to the pyre. She did not watch them go but rather kept her gaze steadfastly on Rodion. Rather than relaxing as the body disappeared through the tent flaps, his muscles stiffened even more and she knew he was anticipating what was to come. Stripping off gloves and mask, she left the tent; he had no choice but to follow.

From the moment of their first meeting, Korokova had wondered for whom precisely Kata was working. Of course she reported to Minister Darko Vladimirovich Kusnetsov, the head of FSB. Her meteoric rise through the ranks was nothing short of astonishing, fairly unprecedented, unless you counted the aborted career of Lyudmila Alexeyevna Shokova, who graduated out of FSB into the Politburo, only to flame out there within eighteen months. Her fall from grace was, so far as Korokova had been able to determine, shrouded in secrecy that even she could not penetrate. The Sovereign wasn't inclined to talk about it and she surely wasn't fool enough to ask.

There was about Kata a certain clandestine quality—well, that was, of course, to be expected, but it contained an edge of the subversive, which, to Korokova's mind, was unusual, not to say suspicious.

The flames crackled, rose higher, smoke curling over the blackened body like cupped hands. The smell of roasting flesh was too much for Rodion, who abruptly turned away and vomited up his last meal. The soldiers in a circle behind him and the major did not utter a sound. Their expressions were solemn, unbreakable. No one laughed at Rodion; no one would make fun of him, even behind his back. These men were far too disciplined, far too familiar with the major to step out of line in any manner. If they were curious as to the ritual ending for the victim, it didn't show on their faces. Theirs not to reason why. In their lives curiosity killed. Without exception.

When it was over, the pyre reduced to a caved-in jumble of charcoal and ash, Korokova headed back to her tent, Rodion at her heels. She stopped once, on the far side of the smoking remains, lifted her boot up and smashed it down on a partial row of teeth in Levrov's lower jaw. They shattered like glass, made distinct sounds like popcorn bursting in hot oil.

Inside the tent, she poured them both a drink—slivovitz, this time, one hundred proof, rather than vodka. They shot them down their throats in one go. Both their eyes watered. She cleared her throat roughly while

Rodion coughed and sputtered like an out-of-tune engine. He ran his tongue around the rim of his lips. The inside of his mouth seemed to have disappeared. He tried to speak but it was no use.

Korokova seemed to realize that. She smiled at him but not in a condescending way. Perhaps the shared exposure to death during the ritual of the winding sheet had drawn them closer, or maybe she was more inclined to gloss over his naïveté, which she had marked as a flaw.

"You know, Rodion," she said, "it occurs to me that I have been afforded a glimpse inside the Trojan horse your Kata sent here."

She made to refill his glass but he quickly placed his hand over the top, mouthed, *God, no.*

That smile again, made radiant by its benevolence. "Slivovitz is an acquired taste, I will admit." Her head tilted, making her seem younger, less formidable. "Didn't your father or grandfather ever give you a taste?"

"My—" He halted at the thin sound of his dry croak, tried again. "I never knew my grandfather. He died young, before I was born. As for my father, he drank only in bars and only vodka. My mother, all too aware of his predilections, wouldn't allow liquor in the house."

"A dry house." The major appeared amused. "In Russia, no less."

"And what about your parents?" Rodion asked.

"Mm, well, my father's father was half Swedish. My father used to call me his Little Valkyrie, a name my mother, being Russian through and through, hated. When she chided him about it he laughed." She looked away for a moment. When her eyes swung back, something had changed within them, they looked flat, almost dead. "They came from families with a long-standing hatred of one another. By marrying they defied their parents, uncles, aunts, sisters, and brothers. What did they care; they were in love."

She poured herself a bit more slivovitz, sucked it down as if it were a necessity for continuing. Possibly it was. "You'd think love would last— isn't that what books and films and TV shows tell us." She huffed. Her eyes turned glassy. "But their love turned to hate. They fell back on their respective families' old feud, split up. They live now in different parts of Moscow. They never see each other, never even talk to one another. And I—I scarcely talk to them. They have sunk back into the past where life is stoked by suspicion, hatred, and vengefulness. They've given up on each other."

Just then they heard the arrival of a helo, but to Rodion's ears the sound was different from the helo that had brought him here. This one was heavier, louder. He felt the vibration of its rotors sweeping through the air through the soles of his boots. Curious, he stepped outside the tent, saw a large military-style gunship. It was painted a glossy black with gold trim and a sigil on its side he'd never seen before.

Sensing the major beside him, he asked her what was going on. Without answering him, she moved forward until she was just beyond the rotors' radius, one hand shielding her eyes from the snow devils, the swirls of pine needles.

At length, the rotors swung to a stop. A door in the helo slid open and a smart-looking young man in a black uniform with gold trim stepped down. Immediately upon seeing the major, he stepped toward her. From the messenger bag slung over one shoulder he produced a large thick envelope, buff-colored with a thick black line along its borders. Even more curious now, Rodion came up behind her. He just had time to glimpse the Sovereign's seal at the top of the paper inside the envelope the major had quickly slit open before she noticed his interest and walked away.

Taking his cue, he turned away, stared at the black gunship crouched like a giant insect feeding on the fuel from the hose the major's men had inserted into its belly. Where had it come from? he asked himself. What division within the GRU could have such an aircraft? But then what did he know about the GRU, less than almost anyone. The truth was his eyes were always on the FSB; he had no interest in the GRU. Until this moment, that is. Now he was intensely interested.

Just then his sat phone buzzed. The call was from Kata. Briefly, he told her what he was currently observing.

"But the messenger and the helo are black with gold trim?" she asked him. "You're sure."

"I am. And the message that was delivered to her was from the Sovereign himself."

"What?" Kata's voice buzzed in his ear like an angry wasp. "How could you know that?"

"I saw his seal—the Sovereign's. There's no mistake."

The silence at the other end of the call stretched on for so long he felt obliged to voice her name. "Kata. You still there?"

"Shut up. I'm thinking."

He shut up. Looking over to where the major stood, her back still to him, he saw her rereading the message.

"Rodion."

"Yes." He snapped to attention.

"At all costs you must stay with the major."

Rodion saw Korokova torching the letter and its accompanying envelope, holding them by their corners until the very last instant before she allowed the remains to drop to her feet, where she ground the ash into tiny particles that turned the snow to black smut. He had a brief flash of the pyre; the stink of roasted meat still hung in the air. He was also aware of a certain tension in Kata's voice. Was it simply urgency or something else altogether?

"Is everything all right?" he blurted out.

"It will be if you do your job right," she snapped in return. "Listen to me, Rodion, you cannot let that woman out of your sight."

"But how—?"

"Romance her, take her to dinner, get her drunk—fuck her if you have to."

"What?"

"It can't be such a hardship for you, can it? I mean there's nothing in your file to indicate otherwise. Did we miss something?"

"Not at all," he said. "It's just that . . ."

"What? Morals, scruples? You left them at the door to FSB."

He heard her voice turn to granite and he shuddered. He did not want to piss her off. "It's just that what you're ordering me to do wasn't in my original remit."

"Everything changes, Rodion. Especially in the field. This is critical. Do you understand me?"

"I do."

"Good, then get to it. And Rodion . . ."

"Yes?"

"When you get back to Moscow get yourself a bagful of burner phones. When you've activated the first one text me to the following number." He memorized the numbers she recited. "Oh, yes, there's one other thing you should know."

He listened to what she had to tell him without interrupting her. He might have asked her a question or two afterward but she had already rung off.

■　■　■

Rodion's call reminded Korokova that Inessa was overdue for a sitrep. Stepping away from the mess she had made on the ground, she punched in a number on the sat phone. Inessa did not answer, and she did not leave a message, which would be insecure. Next, she called Taissa's cell, but again got no answer. Inessa was supposed to have checked in by now and, if not her, than Taissa. Concerned, she made a third call. Someone she didn't know answered the phone. "Abd-El-Kader is unavailable," he told her when she gave him her name. Obviously a newbie, she thought, annoyed. "Find him," she ordered. "He'll speak with me." But he wouldn't, the phone jockey told her. Clearly her name meant nothing to him. "I'll leave the message that you called," he said. "Don't," she told him, and disconnected. Something was very wrong. She called one of her permanent Russian contacts in Istanbul.

"She's gone," the contact said. "Lyudmila is no longer here."

"Then where is she?" Korokova snapped, her anger and anxiety rising as one.

There was a pause, so that she knew what was coming next. "We don't know."

The major growled deep in her throat. "And the female that was with her?"

"Of Evan Ryder there is no sign," her contact said. "She was last seen entering Alila International's warehouse."

This news shook Korokova. "She's with Abd-El-Kader?"

"It seems so. But . . ."

She snapped her fingers impatiently. "What?"

"That was yesterday."

"You said she was last seen at the warehouse. Don't tell me your people missed her exit."

"Well, that's just it," her contact said slowly and carefully. He knew his controller was one step away from exploding. "She hasn't reappeared."

"That's not possible." Silence in Istanbul. Korokova put her hand to her forehead, pressing against a migraine starting behind her eyes. She took a breath, then another. "Find out what's happened to her. If—When we find Ryder we'll have a lead on where Lyudmila has gone."

It was at this point that she became aware of Rodion coming toward her at a fast clip. His call had ended. "Get back to me—fast." Then she closed the connection.

He was staring at her with an expression entirely different from any she had seen on him before.

"What is it?" she said with a sense of foreboding.

"It's your pal Morokovsky."

"He's not my pal," Korokova said acidly.

"Don't I know it." He turned away from her, stepped toward the open field, where the black bristling helo crouched, all fueled up and ready to go.

"Wait a minute," she called after him. "Where d'you think you're going?"

"Back to Moscow." He turned around to watch her face. "Something detonated in Morokovsky's brain. Sound familiar?"

Korokova's face drained of color. "He's dead?"

Rodion grunted. "As a jackrabbit on a spit."

20

"All due respect," the Syrian said, "I'd prefer 'Abd-El-Kader.'"

Marsden Tribe's eyes bored into him. "In my experience 'all due respect' means 'fuck you very much.'" He lifted his head. "Is that what you mean? Örümcek." The Spider. "Because if it is you and I have a serious problem."

Abd-El-Kader's eyes lowered. "I didn't mean that at all, Dr. Kimble."

Tribe's gaze moved back to Evan. "That's my alias today, Ryder—Richard Kimble." His eyes danced. He wore a deep sea-green shantung silk jacket that must have been made for him, considering it would have been in style in the 1940s; jeans; and ankle boots. "Remember him?"

The hero of *The Fugitive.* "I do." She realized with an inner start that Tribe couldn't have done any better at lightening her heart. It was like coming back home from a long run overseas and watching an episode of *Friends.*

In an instant, Tribe switched gears. "You still with us, Ryder?"

"I'm still afloat."

He nodded. "I know the feeling."

She was willing to bet he knew precisely what treatment she needed better than she herself did. She had worked closely with him for over a year. Observing him keenly during that time she had come to recognize and absorb the quirks of his methods and behaviors. She had learned that what he didn't say or do was as telling as what he did say or do.

To that end, Tribe was already giving clipped orders into his cell phone. "Ayman, get my men in here ASAP. Have them bring a stretcher and the PA from the plane—what's her name? I forget. Honi Werner, is it? My friend requires immediate medical treatment. Right. Also there'll be a second female. Noncompliant, possibly violent, so a pair of steel handcuffs are in order, maybe an injection as well. The PA can take care of that if necessary."

Unable to keep her head up a second longer, Evan lay back onto the floor, unmindful of how many dead rat bodies she was using as a pillow.

"Hang in there, Ryder," she heard him say from far away. "We'll get you fixed up in no time."

She closed her eyes then, and she was done, returned to the sea of endless night and Rebecca's welcoming arms.

PART TWO

THEORY

Time crystals are a new phase of matter. Imagine a cube that becomes a hexagon, then reverts back to a cube. Now imagine a group of them—cubes, hexagons, cubes, hexagons. Though this cycling continues, the cubes or hexagons don't lose any energy. Try to imagine that. How can that be, you ask yourself. It's because—and here is the truly startling breakthrough—as time crystals they don't fall victim to entropy. But doesn't physics tell us that everything in the universe is subject to entropy? Yes, it does. Or did. No longer. Because time crystals defy the laws of classical physics. Fantastic, yes. But essentially useless until we find a way to manipulate them.

—from a TED Talk by Marsden Tribe

21

"What song did they sing you?" Isobel asked.

Ben sipped at his coffee. "'The Ballad of Betrayal and Patriotism.'" He took a bite of a freshly baked croissant.

Isobel was seated on an antique chaise longue, velvet-covered, with short hand-turned oak legs. They were in what back in the day was known as the morning room. Though it was close, dawn had not yet arrived. Isobel, who it seemed never slept or, if she did, for not more than forty minutes at a time—a habit born during her time in Israel's Shin Bet—had been waiting for his return. "An old chestnut," she said. "But often an effective one."

"They're convinced Tribe is behind Brady Thompson's death."

"Using what? Voodoo?"

"Close." Ben wiped his lips. "Qubits—quantum particles."

"Reade thinks Marsden has somehow found a way to weaponize qubits?"

"I think that's the premise they're working from." Ben sucked butter off his fingertips. "And it's not just General Reade and George Wilson and Wes Connerly we're talking about. There's also a woman involved, the brains, I think, behind the group. She claims her name is Zahra. A quantum physicist, heading up the government team working on quantum computers. According to what she told me, her mother was Iranian, father German. Oh, yeah, she claims Max Planck was her great-uncle, but with most records in Eastern Europe destroyed in World War Two it's impossible to verify her story." He expected Isobel's laugh and wasn't disappointed.

Isobel waved a hand. "Well, whatever this group is up to, Marsden's team is light-years ahead."

He nodded. "She admitted as much. Which is why they've sought me out, why they're making a concerted effort to recruit me. They want me to find the smoking gun that will prove Marsden was culpable for Brady Thompson's death."

Isobel hissed. "Did Zahra the Brainiac give you a motive? Why would Marsden want the secretary of defense dead?"

"I have no idea." Ben looked at her. "Do you?"

"Of course not."

"Okay, but all I know for sure is that he's the most secretive person I've ever come across and we both know that's saying a lot. As far as I'm concerned anything is possible. In any event, these people are going to believe what they want to believe. They know Tribe is way ahead of them. This is the way they've chosen to find out what he knows, or to slow him down so they can catch up."

Isobel's eyes narrowed. "There's your motive. Thompson's death set this all in motion. I'm betting they were the ones weaponizing—"

Ben cut across her. "I don't think their program is anywhere near being able to do that. Until yesterday I didn't even know it was possible. I'm still not sure they're right. We've been trying and failing to discover the cause of 'Havana syndrome' for a couple of years now."

Isobel shook her head. "Then it's impossible for qubits to be responsible. Three years ago full-scale exploration into the quantum universe hadn't even begun. It's still in its infancy; what we know about it is far less than what we don't know."

"Agreed," he said, "but the first attacks were debilitating, rarely if ever lethal. The attack on the secretary of defense was of another order entirely. The evidence they showed me—I don't know what else could have caused the mini-explosions in Thompson's brain." He took a breath and said, "What if they're right."

"About Tribe?" Isobel shook her head. "Impossible."

"I mean how well do you really know him?" He had deliberately elided over Zahra's insinuation that something was going on between Tribe and Evan. He didn't want to involve Isobel in that theory, at least not yet—not until he'd had time to verify it. His mind was also gnawing over the possibility that he was being played, that everything Zahra said to him was either a lie or a distortion of the truth. After all, he had admitted to Isobel that these people were living in their own form of reality.

Her eyes bored into his. "Has this Zahra gotten into your head?"

"General Reade and his people say one thing, privately she says another. In fact, she goes so far as to ridicule them. She thinks they're idiots."

"Well, in that she may very well be right." Isobel frowned. "But who is she that she's given such wide latitude?"

"I'm not sure it's her per se," Ben countered. "It may be the quantum initiative she's working on."

"Whatever the case, we need to know more about these people."

Ben nodded. "Agreed." And because he wanted to break Isobel out of her typical overseriousness, he added with a grin. "I could contact Ant-Man."

It took a moment for Isobel to return his grin. "If only we lived in the same metaverse."

She waited several beats, taking her time pouring more coffee, stirring in sugar granules. She took a sip and, over the rim of her cup, said, "I assume it was this woman, Zahra, you went back to see."

"What makes you say that?"

"Ben." She shook her head. "Don't be coy. It doesn't suit you."

"She wanted time with me without interference from the others."

"So she was the one who made the final pitch."

He nodded.

"And what did you tell her?"

"I accepted their offer."

Isobel spent long moments drinking her coffee, her eyes turned inward. Ben knew she was sifting through all the angles, knew better than to interrupt her.

When her gaze refocused on him, she put down her empty cup. "How do you feel about this woman?"

"I don't trust her."

"I'm certain the feeling's mutual."

"I'd be highly surprised if it wasn't. We scarcely know one another."

"Sure. But I'm sure General Reade's people have done a thorough background search on you. I'd do the same on her, but as we both know background checks can spew back the most fascinating disinformation."

He smiled. "Wherever she claims to come from, whoever she says she is—all of that's on shaky ground with me."

She nodded. "Okay, then. Go ahead. But be careful, Ben."

He rose, smiled down at her. "Aren't I always?"

"I mean with this woman, Zahra." She stood too. "All my instincts say she's poison."

He smiled. "You know as well as I do that for every poison there's an antidote."

She walked with him to the door. "Just don't take it too late."

22

Carat, one of the few all-night bar-clubs inside the Beltway, throbbed like a living heart in a nondescript building along Florida Avenue NW, just north of where it intersected with T Street. The club had no sign outside, just a mob of people trying to get in. The long entryway on the ground floor opened onto a disco for thirtysomethings and fortysomethings trying to be thirtysomethings. Above was a cabaret for the kinky set, below a basement of raves where the twentysomethings hung for the all-night thumpers that didn't get going until one in the morning. The bar, where Wilson was ensconced, lived on the third floor, accessed via stairs and, for the seriously drunk, an elevator.

It was where George Wilson, head of the Defense Threat Reaction Agency, had been coming at four in the morning five nights a week for the last three years, since his wife's death. From that time forward Wilson found sleep an enemy. Every time he drifted off he dreamed of his wife lying in a Walter Reed hospital bed in the biosecured wing, dying of a SARS-like virus no doctor knew how to treat. Wilson was not allowed in to see his wife—not on the last day of her life, not when her body was buried by six masked and gowned gravediggers. Not ever. No place for him to mourn, apart from the recurring dream that racked him to his marrow, something out of a postapocalyptic horror film. The dream from which he'd wake up screaming, drenched in sweat. The first time that happened he almost gave his security detail a collective heart attack. Now they were used to the sounds. They were the only ones who knew about his nightmares and cold sweats.

Inside Carat, Wilson found a measure of solace impossible for him to grasp elsewhere, even when he worked until after midnight. The echoes of soft footfalls in the maze of hallways, indistinguishable from one another, impelled him to keep the door to his office locked, disconcerting his staff, but especially his adjutant. Well, fuck them, he thought as he sat at the far end of the bar, which described two-thirds of a circle. At this ungodly hour only a handful of people were at the bar. Two businessmen going over paperwork—a contract or perhaps a divorce settlement. An old man with a crooked back, who looked like a hobo but Wilson knew was a billionaire, hunched over his bourbon. A bored-looking Asian woman at the opposite end nursed a cocktail, and, more or less in the middle, a brace of stunning high-end escorts, one Nordic blonde, one inky Black, heads together, laughing softly as they unwound with champagne after a long and, if Wilson was any judge, lucrative night.

In truth, Wilson was built for the clandestine services. With his specialized attributes he navigated through the infuriating government bureaucracy, rose to section head, which he ruled with an iron hand. He might look like a meek numbers cruncher; he was anything but. Once he was inside the services, his outsize intellect allowed him to rapidly rise through the ranks. He networked, knew the right people, memorized the upper-echelon codex. As a result he found it a snap to say the right things to the right people above him in rank, like General Reade. They liked his emphatically stated opinions, which he made sure jibed completely with theirs. So he continued to rise, all the while loathing his chosen profession and those around him. Not such an easy task. As Secretary Thompson knew well, Wilson possessed a wicked temper that was liable to flare up if he didn't keep it under tight control. No wonder he was plagued with ulcerative colitis.

And so, for the past three years, burdened by grief, misery, and dyspepsia, he had spent the last hours of the night and the early hours after daybreak at Carat's bar, drinking añejo tequila, numb to the effects of alcohol, even though his veins and arteries were flooded with it. He was well aware that the alcohol did his colitis no good, but he didn't care.

His security detail never accompanied him to Carat; only his driver/bodyguard Bruce stayed with him, sitting outside in Wilson's SUV, playing Wordle on his cell phone and checking the immediate vicinity at the same time.

Wilson was aware of her even before she sat down. He felt the stirring of the atmosphere, the scent of her—jasmine and black licorice—wafting over him when she was at his side. She dropped onto the low-backed stool next to him.

"You arrived early," she said, settling herself.

Of course, she was lying. She was late. But as was typical of her she would not apologize for it, let alone admit to it. She was not that kind of person, never had been, as far as Wilson knew.

"Zahra." He said it like a sigh, as if he'd been waiting for her for days instead of less than fifteen minutes.

"Long night of the soul."

"With Benjamin Butler, I assume."

She nodded, ordered her usual, an original Sazerac, made with cognac instead of rye and, of course, absinthe, said nothing more until it came and she took her first long sip. Wilson knew better than to rush her, which, he'd learned, could be a dangerous business.

When had women become like this, he asked himself idly—brash, liars, schemers. He supposed they'd always been like that, only now it was out in the open. These days you could not so much as lay a finger on a woman without an outcry being raised, your entire career in danger of going down in flames. Of course, men were better sheltered from accusations of any kind here in the military, but still he found the ascendance of women a bitter pill to swallow. Not that he had any intention of making a move on Zahra; the very idea was absurd. He had no intention of becoming the next General Petraeus. No, no, no—never, he told himself. Zahra had suggested their twice-weekly meetings take place here at the bar at Carat, where, she informed him, there were no CCTV cameras to record their conversations. Still, he wasn't immune to the intimacy of the space, which lent their meetings the veneer of a lovers' rendezvous.

"So," he said, hating that she was making him ask, "how did things go?"

She did not answer him right away. Instead, she stared between the precisely lined bottles at her own reflection in the mirrored back wall. "I think I was able to neutralize Reade."

"Butler doesn't like him."

"He's not too crazy about you or Connerly, either," she said. "Apparently, the only people he feels anything for are his partner, Evan Ryder, and their boss, Isobel Lowe." She sipped at her drink. "But back to Reade. Ben not only doesn't like him—worse, he has no respect for him; he thinks he's an idiot." She put her glass down, turned to him, a smile curving her lips. Wilson hated that smile—or more accurately he was afraid of it. It was like staring into the face of a serpent as its jaws slowly opened. "All to the good because I told him the same thing. And that led to him questioning whether his boss is responsible for Thompson's death."

"So I was right in culling you from the herd," Wilson said. "It's now you two against Reade and Connelly."

A vertical line appeared between her eyes, a sure sign of her annoyance. "You really can be a shit, George. You didn't cull me from anything. I'm not an animal." She leaned in close enough that he could smell the absinthe on her breath. Her hand on his sent a shiver through him. "Is that how you think of me, George? I mean deep down inside, do you see me as an animal?"

Did she require an answer, or did she already know? She was working her magic, making him feel small and ineffectual. He should have hated that, but he didn't. The truth was he reveled in it. Being here at this time with this woman, no one else knowing, sent a buzz through him like an electric shock. How extremely pleasant that was, almost ecstatic. For a moment, he glanced over at the two escorts, no longer appearing all that alluring compared to the woman so close to him he could feel the heat coming off her in waves. So close he could smell her sweat mingling with the jasmine and black licorice of her perfume, altering it subtly but absolutely. Another shiver ran through him, bone deep this time.

Reaching out, she lifted a drop of sweat from his hairline, put the tip of her finger into her mouth. That smile again. "Don't worry, George, if I bite anyone it'll be Ben."

Wilson took a ragged breath. "Will he come around?"

"He's agreed." Her nostrils flared as if she'd scented a far-off threat. "Whether he can be believed is another story."

He leered at her. "You know what will seal the deal."

The smile was gone now, her face settled into its battle expression. "You are such a pig."

"I state only the truth," Wilson said. "You're a master manipulator. You've used your father's family to gain outsized recognition. You use your, um, female assets, to the best ends possible. Are you now going to balk at using them on Ben Butler to get what we want?"

"I'm not balking at anything; I'm simply being careful. If I make a wrong step, if I spook Ben, we're out of options, get me?"

She drained her glass, called for a refill.

Her voice lowered even further. Wilson was mesmerized by her lips, wet and luscious.

"Look, George, we suspect that Marsden Tribe is behind the secretary's murder but only you and I know there's another player in the field—the

Russians. One of their top quantum physicists, Marius Ionescu, was spirited out of Moscow. Where is he? We don't know. Who got him out? We didn't. Tribe is the only one with the wherewithal to do it successfully. Evan Ryder is with Tribe, she's Ben's partner. We get to her, chances are good we'll find Ionescu. And we need him, George. Desperately. We're falling behind in the quantum race and you know why. Our government doesn't think physics is a science worth supporting in any major way."

■ ■ ■

An Binh had taught herself to lip-read when she was just a child, so her father could use her in his business dealings. She was better than having a microphone secreted on his adversaries. When they moved away from him to talk among themselves he turned his back, but his daughter did not, and she marked everything that was said between them. She liked lipreading; in her mind it was one step away from telepathy.

An Binh was the bored-looking Asian woman George Wilson had barely noted at the other end of the bar from him, and she was aware of every word said between Wilson and the young woman he called Zahra. She had come here through the intel derived from her own network of informants, which consisted of hotel night clerks, concierges, limo drivers and night-shift cabbies, salon workers, bartenders, doormen—in short, all the working people who were invisible, part of the wallpaper of life that no one paid attention to and who heard everything, shouting matches and whispered conversations alike.

She had never seen Zahra before but it was quite clear that Zahra knew Ben. In fact, she had been with him tonight. An Binh did not like this woman, did not like that she had been with Ben for so long. Zahra was beautiful in the way An Binh found certain reptiles beautiful—the way they held themselves perfectly still, the sudden surprising litheness when they sprang into action. She had eyes like those reptiles—gemstone bright, acquisitive, razor-sharp, even when half-lidded.

But most of all it was her parting remark, spoken against George Wilson's ear, that struck a needle of anxiety into An Binh.

"*It's pathetic how much you want to fuck me.*" Her lips touched his earlobe. "*Also, kinda adorable.*"

An Binh stayed at the bar long after Zahra and George Wilson left, long after the pair of escorts tottered down the stairs, giggling, heads tilted together, long after the old man fell asleep with his cheek in a puddle of bourbon the bartender was trying to mop up without waking him. Apparently this was a normal end to the old man's night. At some point thereafter the old man's chauffeur arrived and, in a fireman's lift, bundled him downstairs presumably on the first leg of his journey home.

She stayed because she needed to clear her mind of the magnetic pull of Zahra, and also because she needed to examine her anxiety. Eventually, she realized that her anxiety was not for herself but for Ben. Zahra had done something heinous: she had weaponized her femininity. An Binh had known Ben only a little over a year, but in working him through his physical disability and the psychological blocks it had caused, she had come to know him as well as either Evan or Isobel did—in some ways perhaps better. She did not think Ben could stand up long to Zahra. She saw how Zahra had handled George Wilson, running her psychological spear clear through him. Perhaps on some level he knew how he was being manipulated but didn't care. Either way, Wilson was hers body and soul. The thought of Ben being in thrall to Zahra was unendurable.

She paid her bill in cash, left a generous tip for the bartender. As she slipped off her stool and crossed to the staircase, she resolved to take care of Zahra herself. In her earlier life in Asia she had come across women like her, had dealt with some of them. She knew how they worked; she knew their thought processes as well as she knew the map of Vietnam. Their playbook hardly ever varied and even when it did it was not by much. And yet, as she descended the staircase, she was gnawingly aware of not underestimating Zahra. Only once had she made that mistake, and it had almost cost her an eye before she could gather herself for the final reversal.

That wasn't going to happen with Zahra, that much she knew for certain.

23

MOSCOW, RUSSIAN FEDERATION

When Rodion was eight years old his mother, on the phone with her sister, asked him to pour a bit of oil into a frying pan that had begun to smoke. As children will, Rodion, convinced he had a better idea, filled a glass with water from the tap and poured some into the pan. The inevitable result was scalded forearms and a scolding from his mother.

He had cause to recall this incident when he saw Kata step out of her armored SUV and cross to meet him and Korokova as they, crouching down to keep themselves safe from the rotors, scooted across the airport tarmac. Standing up beyond the slowing rotors' reach, Korokova stood stock-still. With Rodion at her side, she gave Kata the death stare that would have wilted almost anyone else. Not Kata, however, who was used to giving back as good as she got. In fact, she delighted in it. It was only one of the traits of hers that struck terror into the hearts of those who sought to dismiss or oppose her.

Like those sizzling drops of water, spattering him just before they turned to steam, the animus between Kata and Korokova pulled Rodion in and burned him. He tried to step away but found his boot soles mired to the tarmac, as if the ground itself had been reduced to tar by the ferocious heat scorching the air between them. He found himself blinking several times, as if otherwise all the moisture in his eyes would evaporate.

Korokova spoke first, each word forced out like raw meat through a grinder. "What are you doing here?"

She did not even do Kata the courtesy of addressing her either by her rank or by her name. *This won't end well*, Rodion thought. Was it his imagination or had Kata not blinked, even with the wind whipped up by the now almost still rotors? Was that even possible? he asked himself.

"I am here, Major Korokova, to update Rodion on his status."

Rodion looked stunned. "My status? Have I done something wrong?"

"Not at all." Kata studiously kept her eyes on Rodion, but her superb peripheral vision had marked out Major Korokova like a second-unit film camera. "I'm afraid Directorate O has been disbanded."

"W-what?" Rodion stammered. "How? Why?"

But it was Major Korokova who answered. "I see"—she addressed Kata—"that you've met Colonel Ferranov." She could not conceal the smirk, though it was quickly gone.

Rodion shook his head. "Who?" He was asking Major Korokova, not Kata.

"The colonel has been summoned to FSB by the Sovereign," Korokova said matter-of-factly. "He is the man I report to."

Well, there's something, Kata thought, though it was like pulling a tooth out of the fire—the only thing left after Ferranov immolated her career. Such an artifact was small but might turn out to be precious.

Rodion turned to Kata. "But what am I to do now? I feel like a man without a country."

"Don't worry, Rodion," Kata told him, "I'll find a place for you."

"Not in Ludovico Ferranov's new order." The major's sneer was back, this time lasting longer. "You can't help him, Ms. Hemakova. You can't even help yourself."

Rodion took a breath. "All right, then. I'll find my own way. I've done it before, I can—"

"You can't," Major Korokova said with the absolute authority of the new victor. "The service is no longer what it once was."

"When, what—?"

"You will become part of my staff, Rodion." The sneer turned into a smile. Kata had seen that kind of smile before, seen it used by seductresses and serial killers. And she ought to know. She was both.

"You can't do that." She put a goodly amount of aggression into her voice.

"Who's to stop me?" Korokova said. "You?" Her laugh sounded like someone pulverizing broken glass into concrete. "I don't think so."

"Regulations," Kata said, knowing this argument was weak at best. "Rodion is FSB. You're GRU. That isn't—"

"What? Allowed?" Major Korokova's eyes were bright as shooting stars. She was already drunk on her victory, Kata saw. "That was last week. In the here and now Colonel Ferranov can do anything he wants. So can I." She turned away from Kata, gripped Rodion's biceps. "You're mine now, Rodion. That my poaching you burns Ms. Hemakova's ass is the cherry on top of my sundae."

Kata watched them walk off with the gimlet eyes of the wary. She spat on the tarmac, hit the spot in which Korokova had been standing. Then she turned on her heel, climbed into her armored SUV, and slammed the door shut behind her.

"Home," she told the driver. But where exactly was home? she wondered.

24

Evan existed now solely in her memories. These were all good memories—of her childhood days with Bobbi before their split occurred, of her vacation in Southeast Asia with Lyudmila, of her saving Bobbi's two children, bringing them to their grandparents in Germany, the birth parents Evan herself had just met thanks to the intervention of Lyudmila, her time with them, the utter peace it provided. She lived in these memories; she felt safe in them. Nothing could touch her, and since she had already been grievously harmed no more of it could come to her. Nestled in her memories, she was rocked to sleep over and over again.

But inevitably she rose, as she must. No matter how much she wished to cocoon herself inside that peace, consciousness and with it the real world returned unheralded and unmissed. As she awoke to her pain she expected to see the face of the PA—she could not recall her name—Tribe had spoken of just before she lost consciousness in the Syrian Abd-El-Kader's Istanbul warehouse. Instead it was Marsden Tribe himself whose face hovered over her. She tried to speak but it was as if her tongue were plastered to the roof of her mouth. To her chagrin, she was able to produce only soft grunting noises. Never mind; Tribe seemed to know what she wanted. A moment later he was holding a rose-colored plastic glass of water with a bendy paper straw. Scooping one hand behind her head, he lifted it up, maneuvering the straw between her chapped lips. He did not have to tell her to sip slowly but he did anyway, a soft smile on his lips.

The water felt like velvet sliding down her throat. She choked and at once Tribe removed the straw from her mouth. She wanted to thank him, wanted to ask where she was, how long she had been unconscious, how the hell he'd known where she was, and why he had forced Abd-El-Kader to sell Alila International out, because surely he hadn't wanted to. Just to save her?

All of these questions swam in her head like fish around a reef, but be-fore she could utter one word pain sliced through her, making her wince.

"Now," Tribe said to someone out of her limited field of vision. "Again."

She felt a needle slip into the meat of her upper arm. A warmth suf-fused her, and she sank again into the deep.

■   ■   ■

Mouth raw and sticky, Evan arose once again into consciousness and, with a ragged breath, sat up. Tribe was still there. Or perhaps there again. She had no idea how long she'd once again been unconscious. Dizzy, she said nothing for several moments. To Tribe's credit he said nothing either, merely placed several pillows behind her back and head. So she wasn't in a hospital; he'd just have to push a button and that part of the bed would raise her from her recumbent position.

"Perhaps some tea?" he asked, clearly expecting her to be able to answer.

When she did, her voice sounded strange to her, as if it were being produced by someone else's larynx. "Do I look as bad as I feel?"

His laugh was soft and liquid. He offered her the cup of tea, which she took, swallowing the warm, sweet liquid with a sigh.

"You don't really want me to answer that, do you?" he said after a time.

"Lovely." She took another swallow of tea, looked at him, said, "Talk to me."

As usual he knew precisely what she wanted. "You're in Santa Cruz de La Palma. Canary Islands. I flew you here on my plane. Dr. Werner, my PA, maneuvered your right arm back into your shoulder socket, treated the rat bites and various other cuts and abrasions. Unfortunately, she couldn't do anything about the deep bruises—they'll have to heal on their own." He regarded her speculatively. "About that one, just below your sternum, it's big and deep."

"The result of my breaking the zip tie binding my wrists."

He stared at her, then whistled softly. "You're going to have to teach me that trick. Once you're feeling better," he added hastily.

"I've been out for how long?"

"Almost forty hours. You were in bad shape," he added unnecessar-ily. Although maybe it was for himself he'd voiced that, she thought. He needed things crystal clear in his mind and in the minds of the people he spoke with.

"You don't have to feel responsible," she said as he took the empty cup from her.

"Oh, I don't." That smile of his was both dazzling and puzzling. There were a number of emotions, she had found, that were not in his vocabulary—guilt, remorse, fear, they were as alien to him as a sunrise on Mars. "It's all part of doing business." He frowned. "Tell me, what were you doing at Alila?"

"I was attacked the day before by two females—the sisters," she said. "I was following up on a lead in order to find them."

"One of the sisters almost killed you before you killed her."

"They were Russian field agents."

"SVR."

Her eyes widened. How did he know that? "Actually, no. Their controller is GRU. A major by the name of Juliet Danilovna Korokova. I was trying to find them in order to get back to her."

Tribe considered a moment. He was extremely astute, and she wondered what he had sensed in her. It wasn't long before she found out. "This . . . mission you're on. It sounds personal."

"It's always personal when someone tries to kill me." When he stared at her, saying nothing, she shrugged. "Part of doing business."

He shook his head, as if negating her words. "No, I mean it's more *deeply* personal."

She panicked for a moment, sure he knew about Lyudmila, which meant disaster. No one could know about her relationship with the Russian ex-Politburo member. No one would understand; they probably wouldn't even give her a chance to explain, and even if they did they wouldn't believe her. Her career would be finished. She'd be in permanent exile. Limbo, the worst place for a field agent to be—neither living nor dead.

Putting the cup aside, she turned her head. "I'd dearly like a breath of fresh air."

He rose, crossed to the window, cranked the pane open. A soft breeze stirred the gauzy curtains, bringing with it the salty mineral smell of the ocean, the vague sounds of distant voices, a laugh. A dog barked. Through it all she heard the clatter of palm fronds. She closed her eyes. The sound reminded her of Southeast Asia, her time with Lyudmila, a time she had wished would never end.

"Were you alone when you were attacked?"

Her eyes popped open. Tribe was standing by her bedside. She looked up at him, hoping her frown appeared genuine. "What an odd question to ask."

He shrugged. "It's just a question."

She sighed. Her body's aches were gaining on her; she was a sprinter running out of energy. "Yes. I was alone." She frowned again. "I'm curious how you found me."

"Ah, well, that's simple. Your contact—the dentist, Dr. Enamiy—he's one of my informants. He told me you'd come in and what you'd talked about. I wasn't going to let that go."

She thought he was going to ask her again if she was alone, but once again he surprised her by saying, "Dr. Werner tells me you'll be able to have dinner downstairs in my dining room. She'll be in shortly to check on you and give you the details."

He stepped to the door. With his hand on the knob, he turned back to her. "Oh, by the way, the afternoon before I bought the Syrian's business a private seaplane took off from Istanbul."

Evan shrugged, which cost her, the pain in her shoulder lancing through her, squeezing her eyes shut for an instant.

"I know. It wouldn't mean much," he continued, "but the odd thing is that six hours later it landed in a cove here in Palma." His eyes bored into her. "Something of a coincidence, don't you think?"

Without waiting for an answer he turned on his heel, opened the door, and left her alone in the room. At least, she thought with bitter irony, she had something to chew over besides the constellation of pains from her injuries.

■ ■ ■

It wasn't long afterward that restlessness overcame Evan. She was unused to lying in bed for prolonged periods. Swinging her legs around, she dangled them off the bed, slid slowly to her feet. Her legs felt rubbery, and she held onto the wooden bedpost until the pain caught in her lungs subsided to a tolerable level. Looking around she saw a large square room stuccoed a pale yellow, with high ceilings, intricate crown moldings, and bas-relief cherubs dancing around a central chandelier, a fistful of crystal teardrops. An array of books on shelves filled one wall, a large painting of Palma another. A third wall was pierced by three large windows.

Slowly and carefully she moved toward the window Tribe had opened until she felt the breeze directly on her face. After glancing down at the street below the window, she closed her eyes momentarily, inhaling the soft air, the scents of an island in the Atlantic Ocean off a warm coast. She drank in the small sounds that drifted up to her, especially the cries, calls, and laughter of the children on the street, one running after another, trailing primary-colored kites behind them.

She opened her eyes and gazed out at the water, the top of the cliff face, the complex geometric pattern of the gray-blue rocks. Boats bobbed in the harbor, and farther out a regatta, sails billowing in the wind, passed by like the days and nights she had missed while unconscious.

At an insistent buzzing she turned. Her phone lay on the night table nearest her. She had not noticed it before. Tribe must have recovered it from the Syrian's warehouse. There it lay, vibrating for all it was worth. She went to it on stiffened legs. Her muscles were tight, cried out to be used.

She saw that someone—Tribe?—had plugged it in; the battery was fully charged. The instant she opened the line she heard Ben's voice, raised with urgency and anxiety.

"—the hell have you been? I've been trying to get through to you for hours."

In brief strokes, she told him what had transpired over the last two days, erasing Lyudmila from the recent past, so the attack in the Istanbul hammam was purely against her.

"Damn it, Evan. Every time—" Immediately the anxiety tightened his voice like the string of a drawn bow. He huffed. "Are you okay? And where the hell are you? Are you still in Istanbul?"

"I'm fine," she said, not wanting to get into the nuts and bolts of her torture, not now anyway, not with the way Ben was talking. Something was up, something big, and she didn't want to derail him with details that would only cause him greater anxiety.

"Can you just tell me where the hell you are? Are you still in danger?"

"You don't sound yourself. Are you all right?"

"Just tell me where you are." His voice was calmer, but strangely shaky, as if calming himself down was taking an effort.

"Ben—"

"Evan, just tell me. Please."

"The Canary Islands. More specifically La Palma. Tribe's villa, presumably. I'm still a little hazy on details. I've been out of commission for nearly two days." She heard him heave a deep sigh. "Don't worry," she said. "I'm with Tribe now. I'm safe."

"I'm not so sure about that."

"What?" Her legs gave out. She sat on the edge of the bed, her muscles trembling uncontrollably with pain, fatigue. "What is going on?" Apparently Ben's anxiety was communicable even over the phone.

He told her about Brady Thompson's sudden death.

Her first thought was that the FSB had discovered they had turned Thompson, that he was feeding them disinformation, but when she voiced this to Ben, he said, "That's what I thought. It's what I still think. Maybe."

"What do you mean?"

"Thompson was murdered in a very specific way, maybe Havana syndrome—"

"How? Havana syndrome doesn't kill."

"Correct. Something of a much higher order was used. A small group headed by General Philip Johnstone Reade is convinced someone has weaponized the—what d'you call them—qubits, the particles used in quantum computers."

She felt a chill go through her, shivered, teeth chattering. "I don't think that's even possible. How could it be?"

"What we don't know about qubits, about the quantum state itself, is legion. I think even your boy Tribe has just cracked the surface, but he's gone a helluva lot deeper than anyone else."

"Advances that anyone has admitted to, at any rate." She let the "your boy Tribe" crack go for the moment. "Everyone lies, Ben, especially in our shadow world."

"Well, one thing I can tell you for sure, this group—meaning us, the United States—doesn't have the capability."

"You're accusing Tribe without any evidence."

"Except his word that he's light-years ahead of everyone else."

"That's not evidence of anything," she retorted.

"You think not? Evan, try to be realistic."

She sat up straight, though it cost her in pain. "What does that mean?"

"I just . . . I don't want your relationship with him to cloud your professional—"

"So that's what you meant when you called him 'my boy.'" She was getting steamed despite herself. Or maybe it was just a reaction to her mounting anxiety, the thought that Marsden Tribe could be an accessory to murder. For what? An experiment on humans, the final trial in weaponization? She shuddered, eyes closed against the possibility.

"Over the last year you and Tribe have developed a . . . what shall we say . . . a certain rapport."

"What of it?" she said a bit too quickly. Defensive. Even she could hear it.

"I simply want to be absolutely certain that you will be able to leverage whatever you have with him to find out if he's behind this attack."

"Now it's your turn to be realistic, Ben. Why on earth would Tribe want to kill the secretary of defense?" But she had already thought of a reason. Maybe Thompson was chosen at random—that's how field tests were done, wasn't it? She wondered whether it could be the Russians who were behind this attack. Lyudmila had told her that they were working on advanced quantum theory. But then again she had no reason to think that they knew she and Ben had turned Thompson. As far as the Russians were aware, Thompson was their main mole within the American government. Besides, no one's research in quantum computers was as advanced as Tribe's. You couldn't believe any claim the Russians made. No, she was reasonably sure they weren't behind the attack.

"No idea, Evan. That's what you will find out. That's your new remit."

"Who else is in this group?"

"George Wilson, chief of the Defense Threat Reaction Agency, and Wes Connerly, head of the National Geospatial-Intelligence Agency. Of course, they knew I worked for Parachute security."

"Ben, you're telling me our new remit is to investigate the man who is paying our salary? At the behest of people you don't trust?"

"I'm saying Tribe needs to be investigated."

"Speaking of, Tribe told me a seaplane took off from Istanbul a day or two before he got me out of that warehouse." She needed to talk over him, even if it was just for the moment. Her head was buzzing with new intel, all of it conflicting. She felt overwhelmed. Dizziness forced her back until her head and neck were cradled by the pillow. Even then the ceiling seemed to be moving above her head. She forced her way through it, forced herself to focus. "According to him it landed here in Palma. I need to know who owns that plane."

"Okay, I just need to—"

"Do you not know me, Ben?" She also felt the need to assert herself firmly, strongly. But was it only for him, or was it for herself as well? "Do you no longer trust me?"

"Of course I . . . Hold on."

He was back three minutes later. "That seaplane is owned by Desiram Ltd."

"That doesn't help much."

"How about this? The chairman of Desiram is Bernhard-Otto von Kleist. Know him?"

"I know of him." Thank God this wasn't a Zoom call, otherwise Ben would have seen her flinch. "He's an international fixer or something, right?" She had of course never told anyone about her meeting with von Kleist last year. Von Kleist was attached to Lyudmila, or more accurately she to him. Either way she couldn't work out why his seaplane had landed in Palma two days before Tribe brought her here. Experience had taught her not to believe in coincidences.

And now that Ben had told her about Thompson, and their new remit to investigate Tribe, she suddenly didn't feel safe here with Tribe, even if she wasn't convinced of his guilt. How many of his people were in the villa and its surrounds? How many guards? How much security? She was gripping the phone so tightly it had grown hot against her ear, and for a moment she took it away. Staring at it, she felt another shiver run down her spine. She had noted when she first picked it up that the phone was at full charge. Did that mean Tribe or someone who worked for him had pawed through its guts, squeezing out whatever was in there? Had her sandbox been strong enough to resist whatever electronic pliers had been employed to crack it open and reveal its secrets—her highly confidential and inflammatory communications with Lyudmila Shokova, a former member of the Russian FSB, of the Politburo? Should anyone find out that Lyudmila was one of her main sources, even Ben would be quits with her, explanation or no explanation.

"*Evan?*"

She could hear his voice even without the phone against her ear. As she settled it back in place, she noticed with alarm that her hand was trembling, and this time it wasn't solely from fatigue.

"Still here," she said.

"Listen to me, Evan. Tribe hasn't done a SPAC or an IPO."

"He doesn't need to. He's got more money than—"

"The point is Parachute remains a private company, solely in Tribe's hands. That means he can do anything he wants, he's got no one to report to; no board oversight, no investors who become disgruntled."

"Ben—"

"No, hear me out. Tribe could be doing anything with his quantum computers. No one knows what's going on in his mind. Can even you tell me what his goals are for Parachute?"

"What do you mean 'even me'?"

"Come on, Evan. You know exactly what I mean."

She closed her eyes again. "This isn't like you—to keep harping on my relationship with Tribe."

"Look, let's say you're right and Tribe isn't the source of the quantum attack. That leaves the FSB, and if the Russians have somehow broken the barrier and managed to weaponize qubits then we need Tribe's help." He sighed. "The truth is I'm feeling a lot of pressure back here. With Thompson's murder—"

At last she saw it. Her eyes flew open. "The pressure coming from this group that's trying to recruit you."

"Evan—"

"Am I right or wrong?"

"Just carry out your new remit, that's all I'm asking."

"I get my remits from Tribe, not you." But seconds later she realized she was talking to dead air.

She put the phone down, knowing she hadn't told Ben the whole truth. What was of perhaps greater concern to her, however, was that her gut told her he hadn't been truthful with her either.

■ ■ ■

She must have fallen asleep despite her whirling mind, because when she opened her eyes her phone was blinking. She'd missed a call. Rolling over, she reached for the phone. A text from Ben: **you'll know what to do with these.**

Four files were waiting for her in the Parachute shared docs folder. They were enormous, high-res files. Curious, she opened one, which on her cell took some time. She stared at the image, mesmerized. Pulse quickening. Heart racing. When she had viewed all of them she could no longer remain in bed. It was time for a serious one-on-one with Marsden Tribe.

25

"What are you going to do with Morokovsky's body," Rodion said as he followed Korokova into the GRU morgue, "light a pyre under him too?"

Major Korokova strode down the gray cinder-block hallway as if she owned the building. "Not allowed," she answered, "within the confines of Moscow city limits."

"That was a joke."

"Amusing who exactly?"

Rodion struggled to catch her up, at least walk side by side with her. But instinctively he shied away from the walls; it was always winter down here. He was already behind the eight ball with her. Well, what else was new? And yet he knew he had to find some way of not falling into verbal traps he made for himself. Korokova was the most maddening creature he'd ever come across. She drew him like a lodestone. In her presence he felt at once subservient and exalted. Terrifying.

They came to the cold room, stepped in. Morokovsky's body was on the stainless-steel table, but the dictating microphone normally suspended overhead had been pushed aside. No familiar Y-shaped incision blemished the corpse, which meant the autopsy had not yet been started. The only other person in the room was a young blond woman whom Korokova addressed as Maria Mariskiovna. Beneath her leather apron, she wore the black uniform with gold edging he was seeing more and more of inside the GRU headquarters.

"Morokovsky's assistant," she said as an aside to Rodion. And to Maria, "Everything is prepared." Said as if Maria Mariskiovna's head would roll if it wasn't.

"The bone saw is right here," Maria said, tapping a wide-bladed steel implement with a pistol grip.

"And the container?"

"Just behind me," Maria said. Though she seemed to remain stone-faced, Rodion got the feeling that she was none too happy. "XLPE—cross-linked polyethylene plastic just as you ordered."

"Is it full?"

"Three-quarters," Maria said.

It was only then that Rodion realized that she was standing at attention, as if she were a soldier assembled for dress parade. Well, leather apron aside she was dressed for it. Was it normal to have a forensic pathologist in a soldier's uniform? He couldn't imagine so.

The major stepped up to the table, held out her hand. "Bone saw."

Maria passed it to her handle first. Korokova took it as if she were a forensic pathologist herself, making Rodion wonder at the breadth and depth of her skills. Seriously, sometimes she gave him the willies.

She stood level with Morokovsky's head. As Maria stepped to the head of the table, Korokova signaled her to move back to where she had been standing. "Rodion," she said, "take Maria Mariskiovna's place." When he gave her a questioning look, she said, "Go on." With a smile on her face.

He did as she bade.

"Closer," Korokova said, bone saw in hand.

He stepped forward.

"Closer." Bone saw raised.

Taking another step brought him up against the icy steel of the table.

Korokova nodded to him with the air of someone rewarding a good boy who knew how to take orders. "Now take hold of the corpse's head, one hand over each ear."

He looked at her, could not help the blood draining from his face. She was still smiling sweetly, as if they were having a coffee at a pleasant café. His arms seemed to move on their own. His palms closed over Morokovsky's ears. Rodion flinched. The skin was almost as cold as the table pressed against his hips.

"Hold on tight now, Rodion." Korokova was still smiling, or was it now a smirk? "You are about to get the answer to your facetious question. No pyre, as I told you. But *this*." Her eyes flashed as she brought the bone saw down on the base of Morokovsky's neck and began the pull-push motion, the large teeth sinking through flesh, tendon, cartilage, and bone as if they were a tenderized flank steak.

Rodion felt the vibrations, soft, smooth, rhythmic, and thought of silk scarves fluttering. That was until bile rose into his throat, the acid making him cough.

"Swallow, Rodion," Korokova said. "Calm yourself and swallow."

Shamed before her and Maria Mariskiovna, he struggled to speak. "I'm perfectly . . . fine." But, sadly for him, he released the head, crossed to one of the large stainless-steel sinks, and, bending over it, turned the spigot, the splash of water covering the awful sound of his retching. Not that Korokova and Maria didn't know what he was doing, but at least they couldn't hear him emptying his stomach of half-digested food.

After rinsing the foul taste out of his mouth, he wiped his lips with the back of his hand. Then, horrified, realized what he had just been using his hands to do. His palms seemed contaminated and felt numb. He wondered if he'd ever be able to warm them up.

As he was reaching for the soap dispenser on the wall over the sink, Korokova said, "Don't bother, Rodion. There's more to do." With a dropping sensation in his belly he returned to where the two women stood.

"Splendid." Finished, Korokova raised the bone saw and Maria took it out of her hand. The three of them looked down at the head severed from Morokovsky's body. "Interesting," she went on, "we could be looking at an art piece worth millions—who is that decadent Western artist—ah, yes, Damien Hirst. Yes, we ship the two parts of Morokovsky's body to Hirst, he'll preserve them in formaldehyde, but not before he studs the head with diamonds." She looked up. "What do you think Morokovsky would be worth then, Rodion? Twelve million dollars? Twenty? How high the moon?" She laughed, the sound oddly delicate, like the ringing of chimes.

She shrugged. "But of course we cannot do that. Shipping this body into the West. Impractical at best, no?"

"Not to mention illegal," Maria Mariskiovna said archly.

"Well, of course," Korokova said. "No matter. Profit is not our aim today, isn't that right, Rodion."

He nodded, not trusting himself to speak, his belly still roiling.

"Well, now, since I've taken on the part of Judith in Caravaggio's painting of Holofernes's beheading, I should complete the role of female assassin—sexually charged and deadly." Her smile broadened. "Sex and death, hand in hand, even you have heard of the little death, Rodion."

So saying, she took up Morokovsky's head by the hair and, holding it as if she were Aeneas lifting his lantern high to light his way into the underworld, she stepped toward the XLPE container.

"With me, Rodion."

He followed her like someone in a dream. Part of his mind denied that any of this had happened, that he had taken part in—

"Open the lid, Rodion."

Korokova had snapped the command. At once, as if obeying a force of nature, he gripped the handles on either side of the lid.

"Major." Maria Mariskiovna had come up behind Rodion. "Gloves are required—"

"Ah, no," Korokova replied, "where is the fun in that?"

"Please be careful," Maria said to Rodion. "Open it slowly. Very slowly. No, counterclockwise. It's a built-in precaution against opening it inadvertently."

"What's inside," he asked, as he began to turn the lid.

Maria supplied the answer. "Hydrochloric acid."

Rodion felt himself floating. He saw himself as if from above going through the ordered motions as if he were an automaton, as if this weren't him at all, rather someone masquerading as him.

Korokova held the head over the now-open container. "The opposite of formaldehyde, eh, Rodion."

He tried, but he could not turn away, as if his neck, his eyes were trapped in amber. Breathless, he watched as slowly, ever so slowly, Morokovsky's head vanished into the contents of the container, liquefying like lard in a smoking skillet.

26

Once upon a time, many hundreds of years ago, the Kremlin was a wooden fortress protecting the town that grew up around it. Over the centuries it had grown into a city unto itself, but the fact remained that it was still a fortress, created as its forebear was for war. And war had come. That it was of the Sovereign's own design made no difference. None at all. The Kremlin was on war footing.

The original fortress lacked many things the Kremlin now had. One of them, the most secret of secrets, was an elevator that descended from a hidden compartment in the Sovereign's quarters. It had a unique design—a layer of lead sandwiched between two layers of titanium. The elevator had only one stop as it descended from the Sovereign's quarters—a level below the basement and a trio of subbasements, the deepest of which contained the Sovereign's war room. Few people had ever been there. None but the Sovereign had been lower. The architects, engineers, miners, mechanics, and laborers who had designed and built the secret conveyance and what was attached to it were no longer alive, having been summarily dispatched with extreme prejudice the moment their services were no longer required. Therefore, it was accurate to say that no one but the Sovereign knew about it. Until today.

Today, Minister Darko Vladimirovich Kusnetsov, director of the FSB, stood in the elevator alongside the Sovereign. Were he a lesser person, someone with a less highly developed mind and, therefore, a less heightened sense of self-preservation, he would have been honored, not to say delighted, to be gifted with such preferential treatment. However, even before he had been summoned to the Kremlin this morning, when in the Sovereign's presence in recent days Kusnetsov's sensitive antennae had detected a change in the weather in the Moscow he lived and worked in. Storm clouds had arisen, piled higher than he could see; the wind had changed direction, picking up strength. There was a decided darkness at noon, and when the summons arrived at his doorstep in the crepuscular hour before dawn Kusnetsov was sure that he was about to be given a glimpse of what was behind those thick and threatening thunderheads. Either that or he would be disappeared in the same fashion as Comrade Director Stanislav Budimirovich Baev, his subordinate, head of the SVR. Former head, he'd corrected himself as he had showered, shaved, and dressed. He had already been up when the knock on the door sounded. He did not have to open the door to know what was about to transpire.

He had been driven through the city. Night was waning but daybreak was still a weak dribble in the east. Kusnetsov had initially felt a building sense of unease as he struggled to reconcile his mind to a new and unknown reality. His mind sensed a clear demarcation between the world that existed when he had fallen asleep last night and the world into which he had awakened.

Dawn light, pinkish gray, illuminated the walls of the Kremlin, setting them apart from everything around it, which, he thought, was entirely apropos of the occasion as well as of the hour.

He was expected, so admitted through three security checkpoints with a wave of a hand or a nod of the head. He was accompanied as far as the entrance to the Sovereign's private suite, then he was on his own. He passed through one room after another festooned with the Sovereign's mind-bogglingly precious collection that according to rumor he never looked at but nevertheless needed to possess: antique Persian rugs; gold samovars from the time of the tsars; paintings by Matisse, taken off the walls of the Hermitage Museum in St. Peterburg; a bishop's cloth-of-gold miter, the cross encrusted with diamonds, rubies, and sapphires, beaded with pearls. Kusnetsov, feeling suffocated, hurried on.

There were very few things in this life that caused him fear. He had gone through trial by fire when he was a teenager under the terrible pressure of his cruel uncle's apelike thumb. His uncle had reminded him every day what a coward Kusnetsov's father—his brother—had been for putting a pistol in his mouth and pulling the trigger, and that Kusnetsov was no better. Never would be. But when Kusnetsov became a young man, after the old man was felled by a fatal heart attack, whatever fears his uncle had instilled in him lost their grip. Kusnetsov knew he was no coward. But now, in this fearsome place he had never known existed, at this time of a sea change in the Kremlin—and therefore in the Russian

Federation—standing beside the absolute ruler of the Motherland, he felt a tiny worm of fear crawl through his insides like the devil made flesh.

Not that Kusnetsov had ever believed in the devil. His mother was reviled and finally thrown out of the house by his uncle for refusing to renounce her faith. She died in the arms of her family, the only ones to come to her funeral. His uncle never told him of her death. Only later, when Kusnetsov gained the wherewithal to search for her, did he discover the truth. At her grave. Yet now, in this moment, she was resurrected. The visage of Kusnetsov's mother rose before him. She was staring not at him but at the Sovereign. Her face was as pink-cheeked as it had been in the full bloom of her youth, but her eyes were black as fists of coal. She did not blink—of course she didn't blink! But Kusnetsov, who was still living, for the moment at least, did, and she was gone.

"We're here," the Sovereign said, so close to Kusnetsov's ear that he flinched and was immediately humiliated when the man beside him turned, gave him a penetrating look. The Sovereign was neither tall nor broad and yet his presence filled up the elevator to the point where Kusnetsov nearly choked. He wore a pitch-black suit, cream shirt, gold tie pierced by a tie pin that looked like a sigil. Perhaps, Kusnetsov thought, the color of the suit was meant to downplay how bloated the Sovereign had become. His face was both pallid and feverish, rounder than the last time Kusnetsov had seen him and yet somehow misshapen. The Sovereign had been secluded and alone for more than two years, during which time, rumors were, he sat brooding, planning the Russian takeover of Eastern Europe, his natural paranoia ballooning to outsized proportions. These days, it was said in whispers, he trusted no one—only the phalanx of doctors attending him for God alone knew what ailments real and imagined. At least some of them must be real, Kusnetsov thought. The Sovereign's neck looked as if he'd swallowed a baby python.

Thankfully the elevator door opened. They stepped out and Kusnetsov found himself standing on what could only be a subway platform. And yet it was nothing like any other he'd used in all of Moscow. It was narrow. Clearly not made for crowds but for a single man, who was now striding through the open door of the train that sat, clearly waiting upon his whim. The Sovereign took him on a tour just like any billionaire showing off his new multimillion-dollar toy. And yet this train was no toy, Kusnetsov sensed that right away. It consisted of three carriages: the first contained the parlor—divided into living quarters and office spaces.

Behind that was the dining room and kitchen. The third carriage was for the Sovereign's bedroom, though, from what knowledge Kusnetsov had of him, he rarely if ever rested; sleep was out of the question.

The living quarters in the parlor car were decorated and furnished as if for a tsar—polished teak and mahogany fittings, gold leaf filigree, silk upholstery. An ormolu clock sat atop a marble mantel, below it a trompe l'oeil fireplace, complete with cords of stacked wood and double eagle andirons, above a blowup of a photo of the Sovereign on horseback. He held a shotgun aloft, the stock on one thigh, while he gripped a dead wolf by the furred scruff of its neck. The highly polished teak floor, the walls sheathed in porphyry and marble, a crystal chandelier depending from the center of the car's coffered ceiling all lent the interior a disturbingly claustrophobic feel. Kusnetsov imagined he had descended into a crypt, or—even more disorienting—that he was inside the sarcophagus of a Venetian doge.

The moment they settled into opposing chairs the train began to roll. There were only three stations, the Sovereign told him. He looked around but saw no sign of the Sovereign's ubiquitous retinue of bodyguards, advisors, assorted apparatchiks—not even the assorted physicians. These forty or so members of the Sovereign's inner circle usually surrounded him like a swarm of bees surrounding its queen. Only this queen wasn't reproducing anything; he was Sovereign for life. After him, the deluge, Kusnetsov thought with a sour inner twitch.

The Sovereign's hectic gray eyes stayed on Kusnetsov, the dark half-moons under them standing out more starkly in the car's lights. Kusnetsov was a tall man, commanding in his own right, and certainly more pleasing to look at than the Sovereign. Like Napoleon, the Sovereign was sensitive about his height. He compensated for it by being demanding, inflexible, delighting in the ills and travails he impressed on others, especially the oligarchs who had grown rich as Croesus by his leave but failed to back him in times of unrest. Too busy on their megayachts plying the Mediterranean, the backyard of international billionaires everywhere. More than once Kusnetsov had heard the Sovereign opine bitingly that their wealth had overpowered their loyalty to Russia.

Had the Sovereign's guest been anyone other than Kusnetsov he would have considered asking why he had been summoned, what he was doing here. But the minister knew it would be a sign of weakness. The Sovereign was famous for deriding American presidents for their weakness, the foolish ways they confronted him, the arrogant way they assumed they knew him. Neither they nor their unjustifiably renowned clandestine services knew the Sovereign's mind in any conceivable manner. But Kusnetsov knew his mind—at least better than any of the oligarchs and apparatchiks fluttering around him. He knew the deep-seated rage the Sovereign husbanded like a deformed child at the slights and indignities he was convinced were thrust upon him and on Russia when the Soviet Union was disbanded, the Motherland's territory severely truncated.

The Sovereign rubbed his bloated face. "Darko Vladimirovich." He sighed, seemed to waver just slightly in his seat, sighed again more deeply. "Tell me, my friend, why did you divorce your wife? Was she cheating on you? Or did she find out you were cheating on her?"

Kusnetsov shrugged. "You're overthinking it. We lost sight of each other, that's all."

The Sovereign's eyes burned in his face like coals in raw dough. "But she was on your arm even while you attended your comrades' weddings?"

"Especially then."

"Appearances." The Sovereign nodded, indicating he understood completely. "It is far better to take a girl for a night—never more than one—and then forget her. To get tangled in feminine wiles is to court disaster, don't you agree?"

"Indeed I do."

"Mm." When the Sovereign closed his eyes he reminded Kusnetsov of an effigy, a mummified ruler, as if he were already dead. "Wars were started over a woman," he continued. "One need only look to the Trojan War for confirmation." He lifted a finger. "But the Romans—ah, the Romans—knew how to keep their women at arm's length. Well, most of them, anyway. Augustus and Julius Caesar being notable exceptions and look how they ended up—the one poisoned, the other stabbed to death by his own senators."

As the train traveled deep into the tunnel, the Sovereign opened a drawer in a table by his right side. From its depths he withdrew a crystal decanter and two slim vodka glasses. The decanter did not, however, hold vodka, but rather a deep ruby-red liquid, thick and slow-moving as it was being poured. It filled the carriage with the fumes of torture and death.

"Women are the root of all evil, my friend, never forget that. If you do you'll be doomed to make decisions not in your own interest. But you'll make them just the same, for your brain will have been turned off and then where will you be, hm?"

Without another word, the Sovereign handed Kusnetsov one of the glasses, took up the other, without ceremony tipped his head back, drained the liquid. Kusnetsov hesitated only a moment. Even before the contents of his glass touched his lips he knew what it was. The Siberian natives held that the blood from the antlers of the local red deer, ones young enough that their antlers were still growing, alive with blood and nerves, possessed miraculous healing powers. The antlers were cut off the living animals, the blood drained and sealed in airtight containers.

Kusnetsov had never tasted deer antler blood, had hoped never to do so, but now his time had come. He knew what an honor was being afforded him. Following the Sovereign's lead he tipped his head back, drank down the blood, nearly gagging in the process. The taste was sweet as well as salty, reminiscent of the minerals in icy water and Siberian granite, which were used in lieu of ice cubes in a number of Moscow's high-end restaurants. But unlike those it also filled his mouth with musk—animal musk that lingered on his palate, bringing with it like voices from a faraway place the clash of battle, the rigor of a steep climb through snow-covered forests, the stink of sweating hide, hooves through a crust of snow. Kusnetsov sat back against the violent draw of vertigo. At some point he became aware of the Sovereign studying him with the smallest smile he had ever seen.

The train was slowing, pulling into the next station. When it stopped, the doors to the carriage slid open and in stepped Colonel Bohdan Sergeyevich Petrov, head of First Division, overseeing intelligence and field agents in the Moscow region. He was a middle-aged individual, long, lean, hatched-faced. He wore his steel-colored hair short in typical miliary style. It made him look like a half-starved hedgehog.

"Colonel Petrov," the Sovereign said, "good of you to join us," just as if Petrov were responding to an invitation to a tea party. He did not rise from his chair; Kusnetsov followed suit, nodded briefly to the colonel, his face impassive, giving away none of his curiosity as to why the high-ranking GRU officer had, like Kusnetsov himself, been ordered to what was starting to feel like an internal summit. It seemed strange to him, not to say out of order, for the FSB and GRU to be asked to agree on anything. The organizations' mutual antipathy was the stuff of legends.

The door closed behind Petrov but the train remained in the station.

The Sovereign gestured. "Colonel Petrov, if you would be so kind as to unroll that carpet set against the wall behind you."

Say this for Petrov, he knew an order when he heard one. Turning, he reached behind him, pulled off the tape that had been keeping the carpet tightly wound.

"Good," the Sovereign said, as if addressing his child who had just returned from boarding school. That simile sprang to Kusnetsov's mind because the Sovereign had for many years exhibited the same symptoms as children educated at posh British boarding schools. He, like they, learned to be both defensive and protective of themselves. To do so they became stone-faced, emotionless automatons. They survived by dispensing orders, assuring dominance over the weak. They developed a deep-seated loyalty to their institutional tribe—in the Sovereign's case the FSB's forebear, the KGB, which had both nurtured him and indoctrinated in him an acute suspicion of outsiders. He, like they, was inculcated in the art of being a bully, completely fixated on winning every argument, every confrontation, every conflict.

What's next, Kusnetsov wondered now, was the Sovereign going to offer Petrov a cookie? But, no, of course not. "Now spread the carpet on the floor where you are standing." His most affable tone set Kusnetsov's antennae to quivering.

As the colonel complied, rolling out the carpet, Kusnetsov saw what at first sight looked like a fine Persian carpet, but upon closer inspection turned out to be a cheap imitation. Curiouser and curiouser, he thought, still maintaining his impassive façade.

The Sovereign gestured again, this time to a vacant chair. As soon as Petrov was seated the train pulled out of the station, gained speed, and went rocketing through the tunnel. To where? Kusnetsov wondered. There was a long-standing rumor that an underground system had been built below the dreaded Lubyanka prison as the chosen method of disappearing dissidents and oligarchs alike who displeased the Sovereign.

27

LA PALMA, CANARY ISLANDS

"It's the Syrians you're concerned about, the immigrants," Marsden Tribe said. "I appreciate that." He bit into a colossal shrimp after having dipped it in ketchup, not cocktail sauce—and not just any ketchup, but Red Duck, which illuminated his Portland upbringing. "Not to worry; the ones already in Istanbul are being taken care of. Those still in Syria will make the trip but under far better conditions and when they arrive they'll be given food, shelter, and a job—most of them at Alila International, the import-exporter I bought from Abd-El-Kader."

"That's a relief." Evan moved her shrimp around, wondering distractedly how the oxymoronic phrase "colossal shrimp" came into being. Why didn't it make people laugh when it was spoken aloud?

"Evan?"

She glanced up to see that Tribe's face had darkened. They were seated in the villa's dining room at a table far too large for the two of them. His brows were knit together. "I should have had your dinner served to you in bed. You're still recovering. I didn't think—"

"I'm fine, Marsden." *Except for my muscles aching and the headache behind my eyes,* she thought. She smiled. "Really."

"But something is wrong. You need to eat. You haven't eaten real food in days."

"I'll eat," she said. "But . . ." She sighed. "You need to see something."

"What?" He laughed, trying to lighten the mood, but the laugh was shallow and fell flat. He put down his fork. "Right now?"

She nodded. "We need a computer . . ."

He rose from the table and she followed him to a work room where there was a computer with a large monitor. She plugged in her phone, went online—every communication device at Parachute was quantum-encrypted, which by definition made it absolutely secure. She navigated to the site where Ben had left the enormous files.

Before she pressed the Enter key she turned to Tribe. "There are people high up in the administration—powerful people—who believe you're responsible for United States Secretary of Defense Thompson's sudden death."

"Curious." Hardly anything moved in Tribe's face. "Didn't he die of a heart attack?"

"Spin-doctor story for the press. In fact there was nothing wrong with him."

"Then . . . ?"

"Havana syndrome."

"Is this a joke?" But she wasn't laughing and neither was he.

"I wish. It was murder, Marsden. Brady Thompson was murdered."

"Not by Havana syndrome, surely."

"Well, no. And yes." She cleared her throat. "There's a theory floating around the small group in charge of investigating his murder that he was attacked by qubits that have been weaponized."

She expected him to exclaim or proffer both surprise and denial, but he said nothing, made no move. Had he been expecting this? she asked herself. Were his chickens coming home to roost, so to speak? Was she so wrong about him? It wouldn't be the first time she'd misjudged someone close to her, but, she had to admit, it would be the most bitter betrayal she had experienced. Aside from Bobbi's defection to the SVR, of course. But Bobbi was dead; she had put that betrayal behind her, making sure the passing years covered over the wound layer by layer until, in the increasingly infrequent moments when she still thought about it, it seemed as if it had happened to someone else.

"Okay, well, look at this." She pressed Enter, and the first of the images filled the screen.

Tribe peered in. "Brady Thompson's brain just after he died, I take it."

"Right." Evan said. "Note the three anomalies deep *inside* the brain. Now note the time stamp."

"16:31. Okay."

"So here's image number two." She continued. "Time stamp?"

"16:36, five minutes later." He shrugged. "Why would someone—?" He stopped abruptly. "Good Christ." His breath was hot on her cheek as he leaned in. "Is there another?"

"There is. Number three, taken at 16:41."

"Another five-minute interval."

"Yes."

"Now put them up side by side," he said.

When they were all up at once, he looked from one to another and said, "Thompson had been dead for how long when these were taken?"

"Two and a half hours, more or less," she responded. "Brain death was immediate according to the doctors at Walter Reed, where he was first transported."

"And yet . . ." He tapped his lower lip with a fingertip. "And yet the three anomalies, which almost assuredly caused his death, kept expanding after brain death." He gestured at the images. "Look, Evan, on each image, taken five minutes apart, the anomalies are larger."

"I see that. Which means?"

Tribe huffed. "Which means they're still alive independent of their target."

"What on earth could cause that," Evan said, "apart from quantum qubits?"

Tribe shook his head. "Not qubits."

She frowned. "If not qubits, then what . . . ?"

Though he spoke to her, his eyes never left the screen. "Everything in the universe is subject to entropy, that is, the decay of life to death." His hands gripped the edge of the desk so hard his knuckles shone white, as if the bones were about to burst through his skin. "However, I was speaking just now in received wisdom, taken as gospel by all forms of science. There is something that has been discovered inside a quantum computer that's fast enough to defy that wisdom. It's called a time crystal, so called because for whatever reason it's not subject to entropy. It moves from one state to another and back again—let's say a hexagon to a decahedron—without losing any energy. Because of their unique nature time crystals can be transmitted instantaneously over long distances."

She felt as if she had been punched in the stomach. "So you know about these time crystals."

"Of course I do. I've been experimenting with them."

She raised her eyebrows. "Anyone else?"

"Sure, but they haven't got nearly as far as—" He turned to look at her.

She was sick at heart. A silence as big as the villa enclosed them, thick with suspicion. "So then you are the only one." She pointed. "If as you say these anomalies that killed Thompson are the time crystals themselves, they have been weaponized." Her eyes searched his. "Talk to me, Marsden. For the love of God, tell me this wasn't you."

28

No one said a word. Petrov risked a glance at Kusnetsov, as if to say, *Do you have any idea what's going on?* Kusnetsov should have been amused by the other's clear discomfort, but for some reason he wasn't.

All at once the Sovereign started talking about his last hunting expedition, the gray wolf he had tracked on horseback for a day and a half until cornering it and shooting it through the heart. "That's a difficult shot. Not very many hunters can manage it." He looked from Petrov to Kusnetsov and back again. What was he looking for? Kusnetsov asked himself. Affirmation? Appreciation? Applause? "You can't shoot an animal through the head, it's disrespectful," he went on. "Never forget the animal is a worthy enemy. Also"—here he laughed, a raw, metallic noise more like a gunshot than anything that should be coming out of a human being's mouth—"a headshot will ruin the trophy. The head is meant for display, a testament to one's prowess." He spread his stubby-fingered hands. "And of course one's prowess is the entire raison d'être of the exercise."

He sat back, crossed one ankle over his opposite knee. "You know, when I was asked to come to Moscow from St. Petersburg, where I grew up and trained day and night, it was to join the government in the Kremlin under the auspices of a president who understood nothing about the Russian people. Curious, no?" He shook out a cigarette from a pack he kept hidden in his breast pocket, lit it, inhaled. He never smoked in public.

"Here in Moscow," he continued in a haze of bluish smoke, "I spent some months observing, keeping my mouth shut. I saw what others inside the Kremlin—especially this president—did not. We—the people of Russia—had had enough of democracy. We didn't know what to do with it and so it failed. Miserably." His cigarette, Turkish in origin, produced a sharp, acidic odor that permeated the carriage in less than a minute. As if he hadn't already marked his territory, Kusnetsov thought.

"Russia does not want or need democracy. The people have experienced for themselves the chaos, the decadence democracy breeds. They have universally rejected *dermokratia—shit-ocracy*. Our citizens have lived under an autocracy for longer than they can remember. Their fathers and mothers, their grandfathers and grandmothers all lived, worked, procreated, and died under regimes that tightened the screws on choice. They like that now, they're used to it, comfortable with it."

He inhaled, held the smoke as if searching for the way forward, didn't continue until his lungs soaked up all the nicotine the tobacco had to offer. "Like fools, we sat back, allowed NATO to expand its influence, we twiddled our thumbs when Belgrade was bombed, we turned a blind eye on the American incursions into Libya and Iraq. So here we are now with democracy squatting on our doorstep in Ukraine, in Poland, in territory that not so long ago belonged to the Soviet Union before we were downsized by the world to the Russian Federation."

"Indeed, Sovereign," Petrov intervened. "However, it's incumbent upon me to point out that we have taken control of the Crimea, infiltrated western Ukraine. We have successfully exported our illiberal ideologies to the West—the British National Party, Greece's Golden Dawn, France's National Rally, Hungary's Jobbik movement." Here Petrov was obliged to take a breath, as the beginning of his interruption had spilled out in a rush. Kusnetsov closed his eyes, anticipating the inevitable consequence. But Petrov was either unaware of the danger or desperate enough to ignore it. "But our greatest triumph was wooing the right wing of America's Republican Party," he continued. "Of course they followed their newfound savior. I mean to say their chief ideologist has been quoted as saying, 'Ukraine's not even a country.'" He spread his hands. "I mean to say we could not have put it better ourselves."

The rattling of the train carriages over the rails seemed to gain in power and significance in the ensuing silence. Kusnetsov opened his eyes. Ostensibly he looked at Petrov, but he carefully kept the Sovereign's expression in the corner of his vision.

"An ideologist," the Sovereign said in sepulchral tones, "is of course useful as a stooge, but this one is also a farceur. A buffoon. Not as useful as you seem to think, Bohdan Sergeyevich." He stubbed out the butt in an oversized ashtray beside his right elbow. "What you have seen fit to remind us of—" He swiveled his head to look at Kusnetsov. "Did you need reminding, Darko Vladimirovich?"

"Indeed not, Sovereign," Kusnetsov said forcefully without a hint of obeisance, which the Sovereign would interpret as weakness. "These facts are well-known to every person in the FSB."

In lieu of a smile the Sovereign showed his canines. "As well they should be, Darko Vladimirovich. As well they should." His gaze returned to Petrov with the heaviness of lead. *"Despite* these *well-known* inroads, Bohdan Sergeyevich, despite so many Americans finding an affinity with 'the strong hand' of governing, the Russian Federation and I in particular are in disgrace. A disgrace that must be remedied. I have inculcated the concept of Russian exceptionalism in our own people. I have turned our ideology outward. Now the time has arrived for the final step in the new Russian expansion. Today is the day that we begin to take back what was once ours. Today is the day we begin to make Russia great again."

As if the Sovereign had timed his discourse to the second, the train slowed and the platform of the third and last station appeared, a blurred string of columns, beyond the sliding doors' windows.

"Ah, so here we are," the Sovereign said as the train drifted to a halt. "At last."

The doors opened and Petrov leapt from his chair to greet his commander, General Mikail Maximovich Sidorov, first deputy director of the GRU.

"Now that we're all here," the Sovereign said, "we can begin."

Kusnetsov sat up straighter in his chair; he and the Sovereign were the only ones still seated. There was a knot in the pit of his stomach that no amount of deep breathing could unravel. In fact, it seemed to grow.

The doors behind Sidorov had not closed; the train remained at rest in the station, as if having fallen into a brief slumber. He glimpsed the trainman walking down the platform, heading for the rear car, which would, Kusnetsov presumed, become the first carriage when the train reversed its course. Then once again all was peaceful on the deserted platform.

The Sovereign switched from one buttock to another on his seat.

"Bohdan Sergeyevich, feel free to correct me if I'm wrong . . ."

Vot der'mo, Kusnetsov thought. *Oh, shit. Here we go.*

". . . but isn't it your job to oversee all GRU agents within the Moscow region."

Petrov nodded. "This is known, Sovereign."

"Of course it is, Bohdan Sergeyevich. And isn't it your job to ensure no defectors and enemy infiltrators are ever at large within your jurisdiction.

"Furthermore, isn't it your job to specifically see to it that these enemy infiltrators and defectors are caught, interrogated, and executed."

"Ah, without doubt, sir."

It was not a good sign when the Sovereign kept using your name virtually every time he spoke; it was akin to him delivering a sentence.

"Bohdan Sergeyevich, it has come to my attention that one Marius Ionescu has gone missing." The Sovereign cocked his head. It had the same effect as the cocking of a pistol. "Is this correct?"

Kusnetsov saw Petrov swallow before he said in a rather strangled voice, "Unfortunately—"

The Sovereign held up a hand, at which everyone else, not just Petrov, froze. "Explain your lapse of judgment, of reason, of the first protocol of vigilance. Have you any idea who exfiltrated this Marius Ionescu? No? Do you know how he was exfiltrated? No? Do you have any idea where this traitor is? No? Inside the Federation? Outside? Anything at all?"

Petrov's face looked drained of color. His shoulders slumped. He appeared not to have the strength to say "No" once more.

The Sovereign sighed. Looked past Petrov to his first deputy director of the GRU. "Mikail Maximovich, your opinion, yes?"

"Inexcusable." Sidorov's voice was as stiff as a knife blade.

The Sovereign grunted, waved a hand. "Take hold of him, Mikail Maximovich. Take him to the open door."

Sidorov's eyes opened wide. "Sir?"

The Sovereign came halfway out of his seat. "Are you deaf as well as derelict, Comrade General. This is your man. This happened on your watch."

Now Sidorov made the same mistake his subordinate had. "I will mete out his punishment by my own hands."

"Oh, yes you will." The Sovereign pointed. "Do as you are ordered."

Even as Petrov shrank back, Sidorov took hold of him by the scruff of his neck, frog-marched him to the edge of the carriage. Quick as a snake Petrov twisted away. He was about to leap onto the platform when Kusnetsov sprang from his chair, grabbed his jacket from behind, hauled him back into the car.

"Ah, yes, my dear Darko Vladimirovich." The Sovereign was standing now, took a step forward. "Bend him over. You know. Yes, like that. You understand."

An instant later the door slammed shut on Petrov's neck. He squawked like a chicken in the jaws of a fox. A lurch and the train began to move, the pillars whipping by faster and faster until, at the end of the station, the tunnel wall came up, smashing Petrov's head and neck, flayed off his shoulders.

"The carpet," the sovereign said, turning away, reseating himself. "Throw the body onto the carpet. Let him bleed out on it, not my teak floor."

29

"Yes, I've been studying time crystals for a while now," Marsden Tribe said. "And yes I have been experimenting with them. And yes it's occurred to me that their unique ability to defy entropy would make the possibility of weaponizing them irresistible—to some people."

Evan eyed him with more than a little uncertainty. "But not you."

"Not me."

They had returned to the dining room and he had picked up eating his shrimp as if nothing untoward had happened. There were three shrimp left on his plate—three out of six. He always ate six shrimp, no more, no less. She thought he chewed every mouthful a certain number of times but she couldn't be sure. She wasn't going to be caught staring at his mouth.

"I don't believe you." When he made no reply, she said, "I saw the look on your face the moment the first image came up on the monitor. You knew precisely what you were looking at—the attack and what caused Thompson's death."

"If I hadn't," he said, wiping his lips, "I wouldn't be worthy of owning a quantum computing company, let alone Parachute." He pushed his plate away. "Look, I can tell what you're thinking."

"Which is?" He knew how to nettle her.

"No matter what I say or even if I deny I was behind Thompson's murder you won't believe me."

"Did you murder him."

"No."

"I'm inclined to believe you."

He unwrapped a Snickers—his dessert of choice—and took a bite, chewing slowly. "Even so, there remains an ember of doubt in your mind that—"

"There isn't."

"Don't lie to me, Evan," he said sternly. "If this ember is not snuffed out, it will poison our relationship." His eyes were cool, unblinking. "And believe me when I tell you that before that happens I'll tear up our contract and boot you out the door."

"Charming." But her tone wavered. "Okay, there is something."

"Tell me." He looked abruptly alert and she knew she had his full attention.

"What I can't get my head around is if you're so far ahead of everyone else in quantum theory and experiments how this new weapon *couldn't* come from Parachute."

"I had the same thought."

Was he lying? Telling the truth?

"I'm already looking into it."

An anodyne answer that could mean something or nothing at all.

She thought long and hard, feeling they had come up against a brick wall without any way over or around it. There certainly was no way through it. After a time, feeling confused and defeated, she said, "So what do you propose?"

"Nothing tonight. It's too late. But tomorrow morning I'll take you to meet someone who may be able to convince you that I'm telling the truth."

"That seems unlikely."

He smiled. "Everything about me is unlikely, don't you agree?"

She didn't feel like giving an inch. On the other hand, she was damned if she was going to act like a petulant teenager. "I can't argue with that."

"Ah." His smile took on a sardonic edge. "At last a breakthrough." He slapped his thighs, stood up. "Time to get you back to bed. You need your rest."

"What I need more," she said, rising, "is to have a talk with Inessa."

Tribe frowned. "How do you know she's here. I might have turned her over to—"

"Playing coy doesn't suit you, Marsden." She broke out her own sardonic smile. "She's here. We both know it, so let's cut to the chase."

"You want to talk with her."

"Yes."

"Which means you want to interrogate her."

She snapped her fingers. "Damn, you're fast."

"No." The smile never left his face.

Her expression hardened. "Don't tell me 'No.'"

"I just did."

She shook her head. "You can't keep me from her."

"It's for your own—"

"Don't," she snapped. "Just don't." She watched him. They might have been circling each other at the showdown at the end of *Once Upon a Time in the West*. She could feel the tension between them, stretched to its limit. One way or the other something would have to give. "I'll find her wherever you've stashed her here in the villa. You know I will. Sometime in the early hours of the morning—"

"Okay, okay." He held up his hands, palms out. "In return you'll please take that look off your face."

"What look?"

"When I see that look of yours," he said, "all I can think of is death."

"Mission accomplished," she said dryly.

■　■　■

Inessa was strapped to a hospital bed by her wrists and ankles just as if she were in the psych ward of a hospital. She was dressed in a much-washed T-shirt and a pair of men's ragged shorts, clothes apparently given to her at the beginning of her incarceration.

"A one-size-fits-all villa, I see," Evan said.

Tribe had stepped into the room in front of her, signaling to a man—presumably a guard—to step away from his post at the side of the bed. "I insist on anticipating all possibilities."

"Good luck with that." She watched Inessa glaring at her, silent as a panther.

The room looked to be more or less the same size as hers; it was also on the second floor, but in the opposite wing. But unlike hers the walls were a glaring limewashed white, unadorned with any paintings or photos. The furniture consisted of a single wooden slat-backed chair. Evan crossed to the window, which overlooked the narrow streets of Santa Cruz de la Palma. Without streetlights the alleys had grown eerie blotches of light from lamps in second-floor apartments. At this late hour all the shops were shuttered, dark. The streets were deserted.

When Evan turned from the window and walked back toward the bed, the guard took over her spot, his back against the window. He did not take his eyes off Inessa.

Evan looked down at the restrained woman. "I can't talk to her like this."

"She's wild, nearly feral," Tribe told her. "When we first got her here she almost pulled the arm out of the socket of one of my men. She'll be restrained as long as she is in my villa."

Evan stepped to the bed, put her hand on one of the straps. "I need her free."

Tribe, following her, put a hand gently on her wrist. "Not a chance in hell."

Evan, gesturing with her head, led him to the other side of the room, spoke to him with her back to the bed so even if Inessa could lip-read she wouldn't know what Evan said. She did not want to take him outside; Inessa would rightly take it as a sign of weakness. "Marsden," she whispered, "I'm not going to argue with you."

He nodded. *Good,* he mouthed without making a sound.

"However, I will ask you one question: How many interrogations have you conducted?"

He glowered at her. "Is this a trick question?"

"Marsden, I know better than to try to trick you. So, no, it isn't. Now I would appreciate an answer."

He stared into her eyes for a long moment before he said, "I have never conducted an interrogation, no."

"Right. Second question: Have I ever interfered with your work on quantum computing?"

He huffed. "Of course not. You don't know anything about quantum computing." He took a breath; his expression changed. He sighed. "Evan, you killed this woman's twin. She'll rip your throat out the first moment she can."

"She's certain to try."

"I don't want anything to happen to you."

"That's an admirable sentiment, Marsden. Don't think I don't appreciate it. But now I want you to listen to what I'm about to say. Really listen. Can you do that?"

"Don't condescend to me, Evan."

She closed her eyes for a moment. "Just listen, okay? You're correct, Inessa will try to kill me." She took his gaze and held it steady. "That is the point."

Silence.

Then he signaled to the guard to follow him out of the room. As they crossed the room to the door, Tribe said. "He'll be right outside, hear me?"

"Loud and clear."

And then she was alone with Inessa.

30

"You can't shoot an animal through the head, it's disrespectful. Never forget the animal is a worthy enemy." Kusnetsov had cause to recall the Sovereign's words as he dragged Petrov's corpse onto the cheap rug, which Petrov himself had unrolled. It was, Kusnetsov considered, not unlike ordering prisoners to dig their own graves.

He had no doubt that the Sovereign had planned not only Petrov's death but the manner in which it was to be carried out before ever setting foot onto the train. And of course now his seeming aside about hunting made perfect sense. He had to not only kill Petrov for his stupidity in allowing the physicist from Directorate KV to escape but also do it in a way that disrespected him. Why this way, when there were so many others that would have humiliated Petrov just as well? Because the Sovereign was a hunter, and this is what hunters do, it is how they think. The manner of Levrov's death made it indelibly clear to everyone that the Sovereign had no respect for Levrov, and considered him less worthy than an animal.

"The trouble with you," the Sovereign said to General Sidorov, "is that you listen too much to the other generals." A vein stood out on the Sovereign's left temple. It throbbed with a life of its own, the only hint that he was working himself up into what Kusnetsov privately called a froth. Just like D'yavol, the Sovereign's beloved horse, after a long and full-out gallop in pursuit of his master's prey. "Everyone believes this is a war for oil, just as, it is said over and over, every war in this century and the last was fought over oil. But this war—*my* war—isn't about oil. Not at all. It's about expansion. So . . . as Ukraine goes, so go Poland, Slovakia, Hungary, Romania. You see it now, General Sidorov? Do you get the picture? *My* picture?"

"But, my Sovereign, fully a third of our forces have already perished. Our tanks—even our most advanced models—are being destroyed by missiles delivered by NATO countries. We are running out of attack drones and cannot quickly make more. We are being throttled, the Western European clients we thought addicted to our oil and gas have abandoned us. I humbly inquire where is the money to continue waging this war—*your* war—to come from?"

For a moment the Sovereign looked down at his perfectly manicured nails, a curiously feminine touch for such an overtly masculine man. "While you've been here with me, Mikail Maximovich, half the generals were placed under house arrest. Another quarter are in the Lubyanka." Looking up, he cocked his head. "Tell me, would you care to join either group?"

Sidorov rubbed a hand across his mouth, possibly to keep himself steady in the face of panic, Kusnetsov thought. A putsch was underway. The Sovereign was disappearing the high-ranking people he could no longer trust. Kusnetsov had seen the increasing number of officers in the unfamiliar black uniforms with gold piping, and now he understood. The new order had arrived.

"Neither option appeals," Sidorov finally said, taking too long to reply. He failed to hide the slight quaver in his voice.

"Ah, well, I didn't think so." The Sovereign eyed him with what appeared to be dispassion. Kusnetsov was not deceived. Though outwardly expressionless, the Sovereign did nothing with dispassion. "And yet . . . the generals decided even before the Ukraine reclamation. They commanded their men half-heartedly. Consequence: high casualty rate—death and desertions in unacceptable numbers. And did anyone anticipate the acres of fucking Ukrainian mud that stalled our ground forces, made of our vaunted tanks sitting ducks for NATO nations' anti-tank missiles? We were bogged down even worse than we were in Afghanistan. And on our own doorstep, mind you!" he thundered.

"Well, if we can't win the war," Kusnetsov said, "at least we can make Ukraine uninhabitable."

The Sovereign laughed with his whole body, deaf to the sarcasm of Kusnetsov's remark. Did the Sovereign know that each day that passed more and more young Russians were refusing to be enlisted in this war? Did he know that desperate aviation engineers were cannibalizing parts from civilian aircraft to repair damaged air force planes? Did he know that all leave in every area of Russian industry had been canceled indefinitely, even though in many cases industry was grinding to a halt for lack of raw material? Did he realize that bread was no longer readily available because of the war? What wheat was leaving Ukraine was destined for the West. Yes, more rice was being imported from China—rice that was a whole lot better than the disgusting large-grain homegrown variety. But then who the hell wanted to subsist on rice? And as for potatoes, the recent crops had been smaller, as if the potatoes themselves were protesting the war. *Every day,* he thought, *the stability of our life is slipping away from us.* Was the Sovereign aware of any of this? Of course not, and even if he was he'd refuse to believe it. But no, no one was going to tell him, least of all Kusnetsov.

"At last, someone who makes sense!" The next moment the Sovereign's face darkened. "But we cannot, we *will* not lose this war. Understand me?"

Rising to his feet, the Sovereign approached Sidorov. Only Kusnetsov's keen eye noticed the weakness in his left leg.

"Darko Vladimirovich, tell me." The Sovereign's voice reached imperial pitch. "What consequence should be meted out here?"

"You know my opinion on this matter," Kusnetsov said.

"Be so kind as to repeat it for the general, who I think has been inhaling the swamp gas expelled by his unfortunate comrades-in-arms."

"I am of the opinion that the GRU has become corrupt and incompetent."

At this, Sidorov launched himself at Kusnetsov.

Like an expert matador, Kusnetsov sidestepped the bull rush; the carriage doors slid open. Sidorov, off-balance, skidded toward rushing darkness. The howling passage of air took sound and breath away, as if Sidorov were falling into the vacuum of outer space instead of a subterranean tunnel. He went headfirst into the ground between rail and wall. Then all sight of him was swept away as if he had never existed.

31

Evan unbuckled the last of the four restraints holding Inessa to the bed and stepped back.

For several moments Inessa lay unmoving, staring up at the ceiling. Evan could see her chest rise and fall, the only evidence she was alive.

"*Ya ub'yu tebya,*" Inessa said, as if speaking to the room. *I'm gonna kill you.*

"Come and get it," Evan replied, using a voice stripped of all emotion.

In the space of a heartbeat Inessa sprang off the bed. But instead of leaping at Evan, she unwrapped one of the restraints, whipped it out. The far end wrapped around Evan's wrist. Immediately Evan drew her arm up and back. Inessa, drawn to her, stumbled for the space of an eyeblink, but she could not counter her forward momentum. Evan slammed the top of her forehead into the bridge of Inessa's nose.

Noting the gush of blood out of Inessa's nostrils, she said, "Your sister was the faster one."

Wrapping the restraint around her fist, she slammed it up against Inessa's jaw. She said, "Your sister was the stronger one."

She cuffed Inessa, palm against her ear. She said, "Your sister was the smarter one," as Inessa staggered back against the door with a loud thud. The door shivered as Inessa bounced back.

The guard must have had his ear to the door. It was yanked open and there he stood, snub-nosed pistol out of its shoulder holster.

"What the hell?" His eyes opened wide as he took in the scene. "Damn it, I knew you'd need help."

"What are you doing?" Evan took a step toward him. "Get out!"

But it was too late. Inessa had whirled. Slamming her knuckles into the guard's throat, she grabbed the gun out of his hand, turned it toward Evan. Evan knocked it free with the edge of her hand and scrambled to reach it. She calculated her distance to the gun, knew she wouldn't make it. Instead, she snatched the chair, hurled it at Inessa as she reached for the gun. Inessa's sprawling body spun the gun away through the doorway into the hallway.

Cursing mightily in both Turkish and Russian, Inessa turned on her bare heels, picked up the chair, raced across the room, threw it into the window. The glass shattered. With arms crossed over her face, she leapt through, disappearing from Evan's sight.

A commotion behind Evan—the sounds of pounding shoes—as more of Tribe's security, drawn by the sounds of the violent struggle, crowded the hallway. Shouts for her to get back, get back! The leading man lunged for her, but she wheeled away from him, sprinted across the room, bent over the sill, careful not to rip her palms to shreds on the glass shards.

Inessa was shinnying down a drainpipe that ran between the window and a large palm tree planted at the southwest corner of the villa. Without a backward glance at the security detail that had entered the room, Evan launched herself onto the drainpipe, began to slide her way down. The drainpipe was old, cracked in some places where the seams between sections were inexpertly joined. By the time she was a mere third of the way down, Inessa had reached the ground. Inessa gazed upward, and then, instead of fleeing, she grabbed a gardener's shovel from a nearby wheelbarrow, slammed it into the nearest floodlight, then swung it horizontally into the highest of the insecure joins she could reach. She made sure she was in the deep shadow of the palm; only Evan, continuing her descent, could make her out in the darkness between the upward splashes of the faraway security lights still working.

With each blow the drainpipe shuddered and rattled, forcing her to stop her descent and hold on for dear life. Inessa continued her attack until the pipe gave way altogether, leaving Evan stranded. Leaping from the dangling pipe through the fronds to the trunk of the palm, she gripped it with her knees and forearms. Sliding down was out of the question—she'd rip up her skin and clothes. But those same rough outcroppings, made when older fronds turned brown, now served as steps, making her descent faster.

By the time she leapt to the ground, Inessa was a mere shadow moving among larger shadows. She took after her, saw her rounding a corner, sped up. Reaching the corner, she turned in to the cross street only to receive an elbow to her chest. At once Inessa was on top of her, her knees pressing down on Evan's biceps, pinning her.

Inessa's face, distorted by rage, loathing, the thirst for revenge, the lunacy that comes with such extreme emotions, loomed above her. Her lips, feral in the inky shadows, were drawn back from teeth as savage, as tapered as a wolf's. She struck Evan's face over and over with white-knuckled fists soon enough stained with Evan's blood.

Evan struggled, but she lacked the leverage to throw Inessa off. Her limbs were useless. She arched her torso, rocking it back and forth in a desperate attempt to dislodge her attacker, but it was no use. Moments from now, she knew, her face would be reduced to a bloody pulp. It occurred to her that lying in a back alley of Santa Cruz de la Palma, night gentle as velvet closed down around her, was not how she imagined her death. That she had imagined it many times meant nothing now; she was facing it here, close enough to smell its rotten-meat breath. The chill of the grave swept through her, freezing bones clothed in gooseflesh gone blue.

"Who's the faster one?" Inessa hissed, throwing Evan's taunt back at her.

Another blow, hammer on anvil.

"Who's the stronger one?"

More pain, setting her nerves to screaming.

"Who's the smarter one?"

A sudden gust of warmth, the copper taste of her own blood filling her mouth.

"Who, who, who?"

Evan gagging, consciousness flickering like a candle flame beside an open window. Better to be there in the flickering light than here in the darkness.

In that instant the street was lit like a roman candle firing its energy. The brilliant light, dazzling, blinded Inessa as she instinctively looked up, threw a forearm across her eyes. Evan felt the loosening of her tormentor's grip. Heaving her hips to one side, she gained enough leverage to slide Inessa off her with her freed arm.

Even keeping her eyes turned away from the light, she felt it coming closer. And now she could hear the purring of an expensive car's oversized engine. Someone had turned in to the street at just the right moment. How? Why? No time for questions, let alone answers. She drove her knee deep between Inessa's legs, contacted bone.

Inessa groaned. The two of them, covered in blood, gained their knees. Their bodies threw grotesque shadows on the walls of the buildings on either side of the street. While Inessa was doubled over Evan toppled her onto her back, then grabbed her wrist and pulled her arm while at the same time stamping down hard into the hollow of Inessa's armpit. Inessa screamed as her arm separated from her shoulder socket.

Instead of rolling away as Evan had expected, Inessa managed to get to her feet. She kicked out, connecting with the point of Evan's chin. As Evan staggered back against a limewashed house façade, Inessa loped away down the street. The car's headlights illuminated her as she put her good shoulder against a door, but it would not give. Heading farther down the street, bent over, trying to recover from the kick to her crotch, she flickered into shadow.

Evan's jaw had begun to swell, was tender to the touch. The blow Inessa had delivered filled her head with the thunder of pain. As she came off the wall, she heard hurried footsteps, then the scent of Marsden Tribe. He had been driving the car that had saved her.

Thanks, she tried to say, but winced in agony. Instead of asking her how she was he asked her to open her mouth. When she did, he placed his thumbs at the hinges at either side of the inside of her jaw.

"Think happy thoughts," he said as he dug his thumbs in.

She felt a tiny pop, a burst of localized pain, and then a kind of quietude in her cheeks as he removed his thumbs.

"Where did you learn that?" she asked him, dizzy as a drunkard.

"All part of the first-class service," he said. "Can you walk on your own?"

"Of course."

He said, "Don't worry. I'm not taking you back to the villa. I know how vital Inessa is to you. Besides, I like nothing better than an adventure."

"Too dangerous."

"Don't I know it," he said, looking her over.

"Still."

He ignored her. "Only one way off this island." He winked. "I know where she's going."

He held the door for her. When she was settled in the Maserati and he was behind the wheel, they took off.

"By the way." He raised his voice over the risen wind, redolent of salt, sodium, and phosphorus of the sea. "Try not to bleed all over the full-grain napa leather."

She tried to laugh, but it hurt too much.

32

WASHINGTON, DC

Five P.M. on the dot found Zahra sitting at a marble-topped table at the Smoke & Mirrors rooftop lounge, situated between Capitol Hill and Navy Yard. She had arrived precisely seven minutes ago and had one hand snaked around an old-fashioned. She was wearing a blue wraparound dress and black pumps. She had dressed with care this morning, wanting to look alluring but not obvious when she met Ben.

Because she was looking for Ben she did not pay attention to the Asian woman who entered Smoke & Mirrors, looked her way, crossed the room, stopped silently at her table. Only then did she look up.

"I already have a drink." Her tone was dismissive, even a little annoyed. "As you can see."

A curious half-smile might have transformed any other face but on the Asian woman it kept her expression enigmatic.

"You have made a mistake."

She sat down beside Zahra, close enough for Zahra to breathe in her scent hinting of spice and smoked black tea. Too close for Zahra's liking, but she wasn't about to reveal her discomfort by edging away. Behind them a mirror flashed their reflections back at them as if mocking her.

"I don't make mistakes," Zahra said, slightly defensive. "Who are you and why are you sitting at my table? I'm expecting—"

"Ben has been unavoidably detained elsewhere," the Asian woman said. Zahra found her almost intimidatingly beautiful. She felt strongly the magnetism of the woman, as if the avatars of their respective beauty were going to war. "I am here in his stead."

Zahra's eyes narrowed. "Again, who are you? Why should I be talking to you? Do you work for Parachute?"

"I am an independent contractor."

"But you know Ben."

"Why state the obvious?"

"Nothing about you is obvious." Zahra was on the verge of raising her voice. She felt dislocated, as if a new reality had coalesced around her the moment this woman sat down beside her. "Not even your name."

An Binh told Zahra her name. "But I am not here to answer questions."

"Well, you damn well better answer mine."

"Mm, I don't think so."

Zahra, either disgusted or frightened, she didn't know which, rose. "That's enough for me."

"You haven't even touched your old-fashioned," An Binh pointed out.

"I've lost my taste for this conversation."

"I am not surprised." An Binh reached over, took up Zahra's old-fashioned, took a sip. "It's excellent, really. Why don't you sit back down?"

Zahra shook her head, gathered up her coat. "Not a chance."

"Suit yourself." An Binh shrugged. "In that event shall we agree to reconvene tonight at Carat?"

At the name of the nightclub Zahra froze. She cleared her throat if not her mind, which was threatening to spin out of control. "Carat?" She cringed. Had her voice cracked? "I don't know what that is."

An Binh cocked her head, took another sip of the old-fashioned. "Of course you do, Zahra. You were there just last night."

"Absolutely not." Zahra was regaining her equilibrium. This person was fishing in deep water, pretending to know more than she did in an attempt to get her to incriminate herself.

"I wonder if you recall seeing me there?"

"How could I, when I wasn't—"

"I was sitting at the other end of the bar." An Binh talked smoothly, compellingly over her. "But since you mistook me for a waitperson here, I suppose there's no reason to think you saw me at all. To you, I must have seemed like part of the wallpaper." The corners of her mouth turned up. "I suppose that's one reason I'm usually invisible."

Zahra felt compelled to lean forward. "Are you seriously playing the race card with me?"

"Heavens no," An Binh said so politely Zahra had the dizzying sensation of once again falling into an alternate reality. "We're both mixed race. However, we're hardly the same, you and I." She took a deeper savor of the old-fashioned. "I come from Vietnam and China. I have firsthand experience in being invisible, while you claim to come from an illustrious family and you've used that notoriety to be seen. Your goal has been to be recognized like a shiny celebrity. You've become an addict, while I understand that your addiction will kill you." Her eyes gleamed in the gentle luster of the small table lamp, making them look like holes into another universe. "Your world is entirely self-directed; that's a boon to people like me who are part of a shared vision."

An Binh shrugged powerful shoulders, revealed unexpected musculature; Zahra felt a moment's dislocation.

"I merely wish to point out," An Binh continued, "that even though you didn't notice me I was there when you met George Wilson for your clandestine rendezvous last night."

Zahra's blood pumped hard, the tolling of a bell presaging militant change. "Why would you use that particular phrase?"

"Why do you think?"

"You just said you were sitting at the other end of the bar."

"And you said you weren't at Carat last night, that you didn't even know that Carat was a nightclub with, it must be said, a first-class bar." She called for the waitperson passing nearby.

"I used the phrase 'clandestine rendezvous,' Zahra, because I am an expert lip reader."

Zahra, a dazed expression leaking into her face, slid back into her seat.

An Binh ordered another old-fashioned.

Zahra was abruptly overwhelmed by the scent of spice and smoked black tea.

33

They did not go far, or more accurately not far enough. Toward the quayside, the street squeezed down to a narrowing lane scarcely wide enough for a single person let alone the Maserati. Evan was out of the car before Tribe had a chance to stay her or even deliver a warning. She wouldn't have paid him the slightest attention anyway, so focused was she on catching up to Inessa. She could not allow her to escape the island, which seemed to be Inessa's plan B.

He vaulted out of the car without opening the driver's-side door. "You can't go without me."

"Watch me." Her mouth felt full of rocks. Her jaw had swollen even more, the flesh beneath soft as an overripe peach.

"You don't know the layout of this island." He came up beside her. "I do."

The blood was drying on her face but the throbbing from her neck up was hellacious, forcing her into prana—deep breathing coming from the base of her belly. She nodded, straining against her neck muscles, which had painfully locked up to protect the recoil her cervical vertebrae had suffered from Inessa's incessant blows.

She had no energy to waste arguing with him. Besides, the point he was making was irrefutable. Knowledge of the ins and outs of the island was something she lacked, knowledge that would surely give her an edge against Inessa. She had learned most emphatically not to underestimate the other woman.

"You should know," she said, the words forming but with difficulty and intense pain, "I injured Inessa's leg and shoulder badly, but that doesn't automatically give me an edge. An animal is most dangerous when it's wounded; when it no longer has anything to lose."

"I'll take that under advisement," he said, producing a Walther PPK from a shoulder holster under his whiskey-colored suede jacket.

"Who do you think you are," she said, "James Bond?"

"He should be so lucky. Isn't he dead or something?"

"Or something," she muttered.

They cautiously walked the narrow lane single file, Evan in the lead. No lights to either side of them, but far ahead they could make out the intermittent glimmer of the water, like the snow on a TV screen when a station has gone off the air.

And then just a few steps ahead she saw a different kind of glitter, as of light on oil. She stopped, Tribe just behind her.

"What is it?" he whispered.

She pointed as she knelt. "Look. Blood spatters."

He nodded. "A trail for us to follow."

"Maybe." She rose. "Or maybe it's deliberate."

"A false trail?"

"A trap," Evan said. "I know her now. I know how her mind works." She looked around. "She's luring us on into a narrow defile, a perfect place for an ambush."

"Seriously?" He brandished the Walther. "What would she use for a weapon?"

She placed her hand atop the barrel of the handgun. "Put that away before you kill someone." He made to move on but she stopped him. "Does this street lead directly to the harbor?" Her mouth was thick with words that for the moment seemed her enemy. She fought each word out through the pain they caused.

"It does."

"Okay. No point in both of us heading into a possible ambush. Go back to the car. Take another route to the far end of this street."

"By this time she may be already at the water?"

"I don't think so. I hit the nerve bundle in her groin when I gave her that bone bruise. She won't be going far."

She pressed on alone. He didn't protest, went back up the street. Perhaps this time it was he who saw the logic of her argument. She hoped so anyway.

Yet without him to keep her mind off her ravaged face the pain returned in wave after black wave, threatening to pull her under into unconsciousness. More than once she stumbled on a bottle or a discarded wax-paper wrapper, and once she found herself leaning against the front of a building not having any idea how she got there. Twice the pain in her head and neck amped up to an intolerable level, paralyzing her.

The lane continued to narrow, to a sliver of an alley whose sides pressed in on her, at times forcing her to turn sideways to fit through. The smell of the sea was much stronger, and now she could hear the slop and draw of individual waves hitting the low seawall. The rhythmic sound entered her brain, slowed it down. The pulse of the waves seemed to match the pulsing of her pain. She slid down the wall so slowly she wasn't even aware of it until her bottom contacted the uneven cobbles. Her eyes closed. She fell into her time in Sumatra with Lyudmila, surrounded by the clatter of palm fronds, the roar of endless waterfalls, the drone of nighttime insects, the clamor of tiny tree frogs, and beneath it all the hiss and suck of the sea against the wide scimitar beach.

She awoke with a hand against her throat. Her eyes flew open to see Inessa's face, to feel Inessa's breath on her own face. She lifted her arms, and Inessa's hand fell away; there was little strength in it, even less will. Inessa was on her knees in front of her, panting in agonizing pain. Her left arm fell loosely, hand, palm up, into her lap. They stared at each other, silent, intent simply on breathing.

"I'm sorry about your sister," Evan said after a time.

"No, you're not."

Evan could—or would—not answer.

"She tortured you." Inessa's voice, shrouded in inky shadow, seemed to come from far away. "*We* tortured you." She shook her head slowly, as if even that small movement exhausted her. "Taissa was crazy. The things she wanted to do to you. But you escaped. I was fucking amazed, how you managed it."

"Desperation is the mother of invention." Evan stared into Inessa's eyes, glittering like the sea just beyond them. "I didn't want to kill her."

"I know. She was like that, my sister. It was all or nothing, every time. She could never see the middle ground; maybe she didn't want to see it. I think it was easier for her to see everything in black-and-white."

"Isn't it possible we all want that?" Evan said softly.

Inessa closed her eyes. "You really fucked me up. My whole left side is on fire."

"Have you taken a good look at my face?"

Inessa tried to laugh, tears of pain and exhaustion leaking out of her eyes instead. "You sound like a bear trying to gargle rocks."

"Hey, fuck you."

They both tried to laugh as best they could.

Inessa stirred, moved so she was next to Evan, back against the wall. "I still hate your guts."

"Naturally."

They listened to the water, to the palm fronds' clatter, to the ping of rigging against masts.

"I never thought it would come to this," Inessa said at length.

"What is 'this'?"

"An impasse."

"Taissa would never put up with it."

Inessa huffed. "You're right about that." She leaned her head against the wall. "She was so fucked up."

"And you aren't?"

"I'm just a little fucked up," Inessa said, "though now you bring it up I no longer know what I am. I've been living close to death for so long I think I might already be half-dead."

"We'll have to do something about that."

A hitch in Inessa's breath. "So. Kill me then. I no longer have the strength to resist you."

"Don't be ridiculous," Evan said. "I never wanted to kill you."

"Then what do you want?"

"I want to know what you know," Evan said. "Everything you know."

Inessa bowed her head. "Take me back to the villa. Interrogate me. That's what you planned to do, isn't it?"

"Inessa, listen to me. Interrogation has now become the court of last resort."

"I don't believe you," Inessa snapped.

"I know." Evan shifted, her overtaxed muscles growing stiff. "But take a breath and think it through."

"Why should I? What's changed?"

"The circumstances. Look where we are—a long way from Istanbul. We've changed."

"No, no, no. You still want the same thing from me."

"Right now, I want your shoulder to be set and my face tended to. I'm not thinking past that."

"When at an early age someone you rely on turns evil you learn not to trust anyone."

Evan regarded her in a different light. "Your father or your mother?"

"My sister Taissa."

An icy sensation crawled down Evan's spine as she thought of Bobbi. Were their roles the same as Inessa's and Taissa's or the reverse? The night enclosed them, silent and obliging. She wondered if she should say something, but she didn't know what that might be. Possibly that was because she did not know how she felt. She lifted her head, relieved. "Here comes Tribe." She raised her voice as Tribe approached from the water end of the alley, shining his phone's flashlight app over them. "Marsden, show Inessa your Walther."

He took the weapon from its holster. Evan could feel Inessa tense through her pain, her eyes opened wide.

"Now holster it," Evan said with a grunt as she levered herself into a standing position, back still against the wall. She felt vertigo grip her. The edges of her vision field seemed tarred. "And get us the hell out of here before we both pass out."

34

"You need to put something in your stomach." Juliet Korokova put her hand on Rodion's arm. "Since you puked your guts out in the cold room."

She hurried him along; she wasn't much for comfort. Nevertheless, an inward shiver went through him at her touch.

They had stepped outside the door to the GRU's morgue. An ambulance sat idling, its driver and his partner smoking cigarettes and staring at Rodion's face, which, in the glaring overhead sodium lights, he was certain looked greener than an overripe round of Stilton cheese. He was certain they were laughing as he and the major passed by, and he was grateful to slide into the passenger's seat of her car.

"I think it's best if I go home," he said, aware that his voice was far from steady. The excruciating ordeal she had put him through had drained him; he could not scrape up the energy to be angry at her. All he wanted to do was crawl into bed, draw the covers over his head, and try to forget the sight of Morokovsky's head being slowly devoured in the vat of hydrochloric acid, skin and fascia curling up and bubbling off to give way to muscle and tendon, and finally bone, shining like bits of a baleful moon staring at him through coils of zinc-colored clouds.

"No, you don't." Korokova started the car and drove off in the opposite direction of his quarters. "We're going to put something hot in your stomach, along with half a bottle of excellent vodka. And we'll talk."

"About what?" he said miserably.

"Your initiation."

■　■　■

Like a princess in a modern fairy tale Major Korokova took him to a palace high above the city. With its magnificent views of the postmillennial commercial skyscrapers erupting into the air in the surrounding streets, it was easy enough for Rodion to believe he was in Shanghai or Dubai rather than Moscow.

"I'm still not hungry." He had entered a state of wonder the moment he had stepped off the high-speed elevator into this sprawling penthouse apartment. The question that had first sprung to mind was *Do you really live here?*, but it was instantly dismissed by the part of his brain still functioning normally.

Korokova watched him as he took in the sleek sofas and chairs, the glass-topped free-form cocktail table, the hand-hewn hinoki-wood sideboard topped by at least a dozen bottles of liquor, walls painted a blue as pale as a cool morning's sky. Four paintings were hung on the walls, depicting a fox, wolf, stag, and bear. There was something odd about them—their subjects' stance, perhaps, or the glazed look in their eyes? Rodion couldn't quite put his finger on it, until he looked at them from close up. He was startled to see that the artist had painstakingly reproduced taxidermized trophies. The dead animals were without context, floating on a background that wasn't quite white, wasn't quite blue, wasn't quite green. It depended on your viewing angle.

"What's the matter?" Korokova said. "Are you expecting a blood ritual?"

Rodion was so lost in parsing the paintings' meaning he all but started at the sound of her voice. With some difficulty he managed to ignore the magnetic draw of the paintings and turn to her. "After what you put me through this afternoon I don't know what to expect."

"Let me give you a piece of advice, Rodion. Don't expect anything."

They were fully ten feet apart, but her scrutiny seemed to obliterate the distance between them, quickening his breath.

"I guess you're right." He felt the need to sit down, hesitated, then said to himself, *The hell with it,* and plopped himself onto an oversized upholstered leather chair. The relief was palpable. "I thought we were going to a favorite restaurant of yours."

"A restaurant is no place to talk about matters that have real meaning." She slipped off her coat, and the individual hairs on its fox collar and cuffs lifted. Static electricity; even in death the animal seemed to be standing at attention. "Besides, there are times when I cannot stomach hordes of people."

It was at this point that, the fog of awe lifting, he realized there wasn't one thing of a personal nature in the apartment. Further, there wasn't a hint of the past anywhere in sight. She might have been a real estate agent showing him a model apartment for a new Western-style living complex. And, digging deeper, another thing he realized—there was nothing inherently Russian about the décor. Apart from the paintings, the entire living room was anodyne. The blandness must be deliberate, he surmised; it made the paintings even more disturbing than they otherwise would have been.

She crossed to the sideboard, hefted a bottle. "Do you like it here?"

She had mastered the knack of asking a question in a tone of voice that made it clear she had no interest either in it or the reply. Rodion wondered why; she certainly wasn't one for small talk.

He rose, crossed to the wall of windows, stared out at the chessboard of lights that pierced the glass-and-steel façades of the soaring towers. He could see into a couple; the lit offices seemed bare. "I need to sleep, not eat," he said.

She made no reply but came beside him, handed him a glass of vodka, sipped at hers.

He was astonished by the silence. Moscow was full of sounds, endless rivers of vehicles, diesel fumes, barked orders. But here, he found the city's lack of noise oppressive, even eerie. It wasn't the Moscow he knew. "Oligarch City," he said. "Who were these skyscrapers meant to house?"

"Foreigners," she said. "Foreign businesses. And now there are none."

"There are no more imports from the West," he mused. "Not even for the Bratva—the criminal gangs. Their black market has dried up." The vodka set fire to his throat and esophagus. "No one wants to come to Moscow."

"We no longer care for foreigners," she mused.

"Unless they're Chinese."

Her tongue clicked against the roof of her mouth. "And even then."

But she was either misinformed or lying. Rodion knew who was supposed to work in Oligarch City—the best and brightest Russian tech minds. But they had fled on the coattails of the oligarchs, poached by clever American venture-capital firms. He wondered how far gone the sanity of the Sovereign must be to eviscerate the country. The brain drain was as catastrophic as the embargo on Russian oil set in place by Britain and the EU, the only matter they could agree on since Brexit. The Sovereign, even as a young man in St. Petersburg, a patient man, had made three recent errors in his bellicose moves—militarily, politically, economically. The army was bogged down, losing men and matériel by the day; the invasion had awakened the sleeping giant NATO, now expanded and more solidified; Russia's oil and gas refineries had been designated for the scrap heap as longtime customers in the West scrambled to get their petro-fuel fixes elsewhere. The Sovereign had been clever in enticing Western Europe into dependence on Russia's cheap oil and gas. Yet the reverse had come to pass: the Federation's economy was built on providing oil and gas to the West. The ill-conceived war in Ukraine had shattered that mutual reliance. Now all the Federation had was its cyberwarfare directorates and the increasingly unhinged threats emanating from the Sovereign's designated mouthpieces on state-run TV and from the Sovereign himself.

"Settling in then, are we?"

Rodion turned to confront a man with, unless he missed his guess, Lenin's mustache and goatee, Trotsky's round small-lensed spectacles and electric hairstyle. There was a lupine cast to his face. Rodion thought of the fur on the major's coat standing at attention.

"I am seeing to it, Ludovico Aronovich," Korokova said. "Captain Molchalin and I just returned from the cold room."

"Took care of Morokovsky, did we?" Ludovico Aronovich wore a tailored black uniform with gold piping. A gold sigil was affixed to each epaulette.

"The captain and I shared that honor."

At Ludovico Aronovich's entrance the major had set aside her vodka. Rodion wanted nothing more than to finish his, sink into the carpet, and become invisible.

"We are pleased to hear it."

The royal "we," Rodion thought, just as Kata had. *Is this guy joking?*

But of course he wasn't. He stepped forward now, his long legs annihilating the distance to where Rodion stood. He held out his hand, which was thin and white and very strong, once Rodion gripped it. *Like a vampire.* He was so terrified he seemed to have lost control of his thoughts. He resisted the temptation to giggle.

"Colonel Ludovico Aronovich Ferranov," the Vampire, as Rodion was now fated to call him, intoned while Rodion's hand was still held captive. "The major has told me all about you, Captain Molchalin. You have been of great help to her."

"Thank you, Colonel." Rodion could think of nothing else to say; his mind seemed held in stasis by his terror of this man.

"No reason to thank me." Colonel Ferranov's eyes cut to Korokova and she excused herself.

With a sense of foreboding Rodion watched her as she stepped into the dining room, crossed it, and vanished down a hallway.

"So." Ferranov went to the sideboard, opened a door, splashed a fistful of ice into an oversized glass, poured a clear liquid into it.

Rodion could not read the label, so had no idea what the colonel was drinking. This disturbed him. What people chose to drink said a lot about them that they would never otherwise reveal. He consoled himself by drinking the vodka Korokova had poured for him, even though it was now more room temperature than ice-cold.

"You have been part of Kata Romanovna Hemakova's band of outsiders."

Rodion looked at Ferranov quizzically. "An odd way to put it."

"Hm." The colonel downed some of whatever was in his glass. "We can put it any way we want now that we have disbanded the Directorate O. Kata Hemakova works for us now." Was there a twinkle in his eyes? Surely not! "As do you, Captain."

"So you have culled me."

"We beg your pardon."

"Cut me out of the herd, so to speak."

Ferranov smirked. "Not so much of a herd, was it, Captain." He drew more of the liquid into his mouth. "No. In fact, it had become a dead end. Your remit regarding Directorate KV was null and void almost from the beginning."

By a herculean effort Rodion was vanquishing the paralysis of terror that had grabbed him by the throat. "The powers that be wouldn't tolerate it."

"Precisely."

Now there *was* a twinkle in Ferranov's eye; Rodion was sure of it. At that moment, Korokova reentered the living room. So transformed was she that he almost gave her a double take. She had changed into the same kind of tailored uniform in which the colonel was clad—black with gold trim and a sigil—though a different one—on her boards. She had slicked back her hair with pomade so that it glistened like a glass helmet. Her full lips were curled in a half-smile.

"Well," Ferranov said with a host's sweep of his arm, "now that we are all here, shall we go in to supper."

The glass-and-steel dining table was set for three. The walls were a forest green, and a chandelier hung from the center of the ceiling, its crystals twinkling like stars Ferranov had ordered up from a celestial broker. Two walls facing each other were adorned with what seemed to Rodion to be the preliminary pencil drawings of two of the paintings in the living room. For some reason—perhaps because they were starker—these were more off-putting than the finished output. Unlike the living room, strewn with rugs, this room had a floor of polished concrete, bare as a priest's pate. In this floor, Rodion realized the emptiness at the core of the apartment. There was nothing of value here, just a dark pit about to suck him in, and it was at this very moment that the loneliness that had been haunting him all his adult life, that he'd expended so much energy pushing away, rushed in; in its wake he found a nothingness too vast to be comprehensible.

He could not calm himself. He dragged his eyes from the floor between his feet, but that was of no help. He found himself in a standoff with the food served: a salad with fresh foraged mushrooms—Rodion could not abide mushrooms; thick slabs of meat, bloody as if from the butcher's cleaver, ribboned with translucent veins of fat, the melting runoff mingling with the blood, turning it viscous, opalescent. Rodion picked around the mushrooms in his salad as if they were the white fly agaric varietal, beautiful, tempting, deadly. Some years ago, one of his fellow recruits, mistaking them for champignons, had gorged on them while he and Rodion were foraging on a weeklong field exercise. Rodion could still see the young man, vomiting, bloating up like a dirigible on the floor of the forest, screaming while he knelt beside him, filled with a helpless paralysis. Already nauseated, he sawed into his meat, placed it in his mouth, swallowed without chewing. Chasing it down with the last gulp of his vodka, he contrived a circus barker's painted smile.

"Delicious," he said.

"There's more where that came from," the colonel said, not looking up from the meal he was busy demolishing.

"I couldn't." His voice was thin, attenuated. Korokova all but choked on the wedge of meat in her mouth. She glanced at him and winked—actually winked!

"I agree with the captain," she said, much to his amazement. "I think it's high time we got to the heart of the matter."

Ferranov looked up from the battlefield of his meal, wiped his glistening lips on a large linen napkin. "Always eager to get on with business, this one." Tilting his head toward the major. "Indispensable, she is." He nodded. "And she is quite correct. But for this part of the evening we shall require a cigar."

With this pronouncement, the person who had served their meal entered with a lacquered wood humidor, opened it for his master. He also wore the black-and-gold uniform. Ferranov looked over the contents as if each cigar were different, selected one, held it beneath his nose, inhaled. "Yes," he said to no one in particular.

They repaired to a smallish balcony on the other side of the apartment where, in the distance, the Moskva River gleamed dully in the haze of the city's light pollution. The familiar sounds of the city came to him then, but strangely muted, distorted as if they emanated from another dimension, and he felt even more cut off from his life before stepping inside the apartment. Rodion and Korokova stood, waiting, while Ferranov went through the protracted procedure of lighting his cigar. He stared fixedly at the burning end until the ash was of a length he found to his liking; then, quick as a fox, he looked up, directly into Rodion's eyes.

"Captain, we have for you a new remit. If you are as intelligent as Juliet Danilovna claims, you have already guessed that this remit is the reason why she brought you here, why we are present, why we have invited you to dine with us." He drew on the cigar, inhaled, let his lungs absorb the smoke's properties, exhaled in a blue cloud.

"We hear, also from the major, that you are somewhat attached to Kata Hemakova. This must cease. We are now in a new order."

"An order in which she has a diminished place," Korokova interjected.

Something akin to a smile crept along the lower half of the colonel's face without so much as touching his eyes, which were hard as marbles. "Or none at all."

Rodion was once more rocked to his core. This day, starting with the abominable trip to the GRU morgue, arriving at this place of deformed reality, the inedible meal, and now this, had shredded any sense of equilibrium he still harbored within him. Instead he felt cast adrift in this place, alien, implacable, disastrous for Kata and—he strongly suspected—for himself. But what was he to do? He was here now, in these people's service. As Ferranov said, it was a new order. Either he was in it or he would be swept aside, disappeared like so many others in the history of his country's political purges.

"Colonel," he said now, his face set and resigned. "My remit, if you please."

Ferranov nodded as if pleased by Rodion's direct response. "Major, you're on," he said, continuing his enjoyment of the cigar as he opened the glass door, stepped into the apartment, and disappeared from view.

Korokova turned to Rodion. "Kata Hemakova was explicitly ordered by the colonel to terminate her personal relationship with Alyosha Ivanovna. Alyosha Ivanovna is Kata's subordinate and therefore forbidden territory, as the regulations state."

Rodion knew of no such regulations and, even if there were, he knew full well this was not the real reason for Ferranov's order. He could not count how many such relationships were currently in progress, but they were all heterosexual. Kata's of course was not. Her relationship with Alyosha Ivanovna was considered deviant, hence the colonel's order.

"Not only has Kata not complied but she has flagrantly disobeyed the order by taking her inamorata out in public, to restaurants and nightclubs. This behavior cannot be tolerated."

Damn Kata, Rodion thought. *What is she thinking?* Well, Korokova was doing the right thing coming to him.

"I'll talk to Kata," he said. "She will listen to me."

"Unfortunately, Rodion, the time for talk has passed." She gave him her most penetrating look. "You will find Alyosha Ivanovna and you will terminate her."

"I don't—" Rodion's heart jumped in his chest. A terrible pounding took up residence in his temples. The shock split his mind in two. His instinct was to fight, but his rational half shut that down almost immediately. Korokova was ruthless; she had demonstrated a contempt for human life. And all at once the clouds parted. It now became clear to him why she had taken him to the morgue, shown him in what low regard she held a human. Part of him—the part that had been loosed by his forced participation in the horror of what happened in the cold room—was primed to kill Korokova, but then what? He'd still have to face off against Colonel Ferranov. Instinct gave him pause. Not only had he been trained not to contemplate such mutiny but he also now completely understood

Ferranov's unsettling paintings and drawings. They were trophies all right, but the postmodern kind. Taxidermists could preserve the bodies of the animals, but only an artist could capture their souls. He shivered, but there had been no gust of wind, and he thought, *God help me.* But there was no God, only him and the major, face-to-face, will-to-will. He looked across her shoulder. Beyond the building he could just make out the leading edge of the skyscrapers of Oligarch City. The oligarchs were all gone now, either fled to the West or caught up in the all-too-Russian sawmill of denunciation on a trumped-up charge, show trial, prison, world without end, amen. Despite the lights here and there—or perhaps because of them—the buildings of Oligarch City were empty as burned-out husks.

Korokova took a step toward him. "You don't what, Captain?" She used his rank deliberately; whatever friendship they might have had had been shelved.

"I . . . I think that's a terribly drastic step." He knew he'd already lost the battle of wills.

"Do you?" She put her hands on his shoulders, drew him closer so that he could smell the dead animal on her breath. "You know Kata better than I. Do you think she will obey orders? Do you think she will cast aside her lover?"

He felt every sharp angle of her; every shadow that cut across her face was a tear in his universe. He didn't answer her; the Rodion she was looking for did not exist and she knew it.

"Well, then, let me suggest another possibility: I shove you over the railing, as the coward you are, a traitor to the new order, and your cowardice will force me to turn Alyosha Ivanovna's brain to mush."

It might have felt as if he were coming face-to-face with a buzz saw, except she was empty, empty, empty.

Abruptly she grinned at him, took him by the hand. "Come." Opened the door for them to step back inside. "You must try on your new dress uniform. Black and gold are your colors. You'll look so handsome!"

As he allowed her to lead him back into the dread apartment where surely Colonel Ferranov lurked like a bear in its den, he knew he was well and truly lost. He had fallen in love with a monster.

35

At approximately 6 P.M. on an unsettlingly balmy winter evening, George Wilson, chief of the US Defense Threat Reaction Agency, sat in an anonymous conference room along an anonymous corridor in the Pentagon listening to the drone of reports from his heads of departments, as he had been doing for the last three hours. *Really, there is no end to it,* he thought. He wondered only half-jokingly whether he had been transported bodily from the Pentagon to the center of a beehive. Honestly, the oral reports meant as much to him as a bee's buzzing. At least he knew what the bee was after. Not for the first time, either today or in the past, he wondered what the point was. The truth was he hated conferences, hated listening to oral reports. He far preferred oral digests or, even better, written ones. But those had been deemed too insecure. These days, because of the hacker tsunami that was inundating them all, nothing of import was ever sent through the DOD servers—emails, texts, or anything in between. *We're back to the era of town criers,* he lamented to himself. *It's a fucking tragedy, is what it is.*

Truth to tell, even if he were more inclined to absorb what was being said the last place he wanted to be was here inside this windowless monolith that had always seemed to him more prison than think tank. Anyway, he thought morosely, wasn't "government think tank" an oxymoron? It certainly seemed so to him.

He wanted out in the worst way. And finally after years of searching he had found his path out of the government maze: Zahra Planck. Zahra was smarter than anyone else around this table—apart from him, of course. He'd been canny enough to intuit who she really was under all the façades she had fashioned for herself. No one else had, which was all to the good. His clandestine partnership with her around the quantum project would get them both out from under the government's thumb with untold billions in profits lining the horizon as far as they could see.

In fact, it was with Zahra he wished to be at this moment. He imagined them strolling westward hand in hand along the National Mall toward the Lincoln Memorial. They would stop midway, stare into the placid water of the Reflecting Pool before moving on at an even more sedate pace. Neither of them would want their time together to end.

Plunged deep into this daydream, it took moments for his mind to register the pain. Then the first explosion inside his brain detonated. In response he rocked back and forth in his chair, hands pressed against the sides of his head.

Around the table all talk ceased, all eyes rotated to him as if by an intense gravitational pull. No one moved, however; no one believed that any kind of physical human crisis could happen within the hallowed bunkered fortress of the Pentagon. They were all safe here, weren't they? It wasn't until the chief jumped like an electrocuted frog, the third detonation turning his brain to jelly, that someone finally broke stasis, called for the guards.

By then, of course, it was far too late.

George Wilson had slumped over, cheek against the tabletop, heart and mind stopped dead in their tracks. Goggle-eyed, hands over their mouths, terrified even to whisper among themselves, everyone else backed away as if from the plague. As one, they stampeded through the open door. No coherent thought, no backward glance. His colleagues, his team, didn't even give him the courtesy of a last goodbye. There was no loyalty in death.

Besides, in their minds he was no longer a human being; in that instant he'd become a statistic.

36

"Do you think she'll do it?" Tribe asked.

"Yesterday I would have said no." Evan stared at her bowl of soup, knowing she should eat. The trouble was she wasn't hungry. She glanced up at him. Every muscle in her body throbbed with pain. She took a sip anyway, swallowed. "Today, I think so. Yes."

"But you're not sure."

She shrugged. "With human beings you never can be, until the end, when it either happens or doesn't. It's especially true of Inessa."

They were seated at a round café-style table in the area off the kitchen where Tribe took his breakfast and, if he wasn't too busy, lunch. His first two meals of the day were unchanging: Grape-Nuts with fresh fruit and oat milk for breakfast, a salad of seaweed and Japanese mushrooms with sesame seeds and a ginger dressing for lunch. The space was cozy; above them puffy clouds rode in an azure sky across the barreled ceiling. No cherubs, though.

Tribe stirred, sighed. "That's what's so pleasing about physics. Everything in its assigned place all the time."

"Except in the quantum universe."

He smiled. "Well, but there too. You must know how to look and where."

"It's not easy."

He laughed now, a soft, subtle sound. "Far from it. You must learn to put all your lessons aside, everything you were sure was true and immutable, then search the world through Alice's looking glass."

"In a way it's like human nature, isn't it." She put her spoon aside. She nodded toward the bottle of vodka luxuriating in its icy bath. He raised an eyebrow but poured her some, watched her while she drank, put down the glass. "Neither abide by the hard-and-fast rules science has set down for centuries."

"Science is always evolving. You only have to look at the work of Gottfried Leibniz, Albert Einstein, Max Planck, so many others to know that. But I don't think human nature evolves at all." He pushed his plate away; it didn't seem as if he was hungry either. "Humans keep clinging to the roots of their baser instincts: sects, factions. Tribes. The more the world spins out of control, the more fear climbs, the more fiercely they hold onto those instincts."

He gestured. "Inessa is a perfect example. She's not going to do what you ask. She hates your guts."

"Doesn't matter." Evan finished off the vodka, the warmth sanding the spiky edges off her pain. "She respects me, and for someone like her respect means everything."

"She's got a whiplash tongue with you."

"And me with her. It's the only way we can communicate." She held up her glass for more vodka. "Anyway, whether or not she likes me or hates me is entirely irrelevant."

Tribe filled her glass. Months ago, he had intuited her penchant for good Russian vodka and her prodigious ability to hold it. And while she had gleaned a great deal about him as well over the past year, there was still so much that remained an enigma to her. Despite that, she found it difficult to believe he was behind Thompson's murder. For one thing, she didn't believe he was that good an actor. For another, she had had to deal with murderers of every stripe. She was familiar with their psyches. Tribe didn't exhibit any of the microexpressions—what the murderer knows and what they want to conceal—that she had mentally catalogued.

"I believe you," he said, "but I don't understand it."

"Ha, that's how I feel about your quantum world."

His eyes narrowed. "I can teach you."

"We don't have time."

"You underestimate my ability to turn you on to the quantum world. But I haven't underestimated your ability to absorb complex ideas." When she looked skeptical, he said, "Think about it. You're doing it all the time when you're in the field, calculating, vectoring on the fly. That's something I admire greatly." He shrugged. "I mean, I can't do it."

It was a rare admission that he wasn't indomitable. He certainly would never do that in public, which led her to believe that he had allowed her into his inner circle. At that moment, he took her glass out of her hand, drained the remaining vodka. Looking steadily at her over the rim while he did so.

■   ■   ■

A half hour later they stood in the room the doctor had assigned for Inessa, the one nearest the surgery, where she had popped Inessa's shoulder back in place and packed it in an ice wrap while she worked on the other odd and assorted wounds, scrapes, contusions, and the like.

"Well, aren't you a sight." Inessa was lying propped in a hospital bed. Her injured shoulder was encased in a hard cast that went down to the elbow. The rest of her looked like raw meat.

Do I look much better? Evan wondered. "How's your crotch?" she said.

A smile thin as a nail. "I can scarcely feel it, thank you."

Their private formalities out of the way, Evan took a step closer. "Tell me about Juliet Danilovna Korokova."

"She's a major in the GRU."

"And your boss."

"Yes."

"This I know. I want more."

Inessa blinked. "How much more?"

"All the up-to-the minute more."

Inessa blinked. "And if I don't?"

Evan shook her head. "Don't make me say it."

"No, no." Inessa had never lost that smile, like an evil Mona Lisa. "Go ahead. I won't be offended. Promise."

Evan leaned in. "I'll feed you to the sharks offshore."

Inessa's expression went dreamy. "What a lovely way to go. I like sharks." Her eyes focused on Evan. "So misunderstood, sharks. Don't you think?"

"Enough procrastination. Major Korokova. Now."

"You won't kill me," Inessa said. "I know you now."

She was right, of course. Evan had injured her enough. "We'll set you up on a beautiful island, maybe in the Seychelles. Someplace the Russians won't find you."

Inessa's expression hardened. "Don't play me for a fool. They'll find me, all right."

"Not Korokova," Evan told her. "That's a promise."

"Even if you can keep that promise. Someone else." A tinge of bitterness. "There's always someone else."

"Not if I have anything to say about it," Tribe said.

She looked at Tribe as if seeing him for the first time. A long silence ensued where their eyes locked. Then, she nodded. "All right." She returned her gaze to Evan. "Let's get this over with." She tried to turn in to a less painful position. "Okay, but, tell me you have my cell phone."

Tribe's eyes narrowed. "Why?"

"Because there are texts between me and Major Korokova in the sandboxed section you should read."

Evan looked at Tribe and he nodded. He'd kept Inessa's cell, but his forensic person on the island hadn't been able to break into the sandboxed section. Inessa letting them in was a big deal.

Inessa spoke for twenty minutes or more, her voice rising and falling with her pain and growing need for morphine. Evan was careful not to interrupt, not to ask questions; Inessa's confession was like a fine silken thread that could be broken at the least likely sound.

When she was done, Tribe handed over her phone. It had lost its power, so they plugged it into a nearby outlet, waited several minutes until there was enough battery power to turn it on.

"Here, look," Inessa said, showing them a short text conversation. "After Istanbul, you're Major Korokova's only hope." Inessa gripped the phone, her knuckles white, standing out like a skeleton's. She presented them with one text after another. "She knows you can lead her to Lyudmila Shokova."

"Wait." Tribe turned to Evan, his eyes wide with shock. "You know Lyudmila Shokova?"

Inessa looked from one to the other. Her silent laughter seemed to fill the space between Evan and Tribe, as if to drive them apart.

"You two remind me of an old Russian proverb," Inessa said. "*Lozh', kotoruyu ty khranish', ub'yet tebya.*"

She handed back the phone, and Evan immediately unplugged it, took out the SIM chip, ground it to grit under the heel of her boot. Even so, she was unable to keep the Russian proverb from pinballing through her mind like a circus tumbler: *The lies you keep will kill you.*

■ ■ ■

Sadly, the old Russian proverb was not wrong. Approximately four thousand miles away, Juliet Korokova's phone buzzed in the breast pocket of her black-and-gold uniform in a specific pattern to alert her to the fact that Inessa had activated her cell, specifically the sandboxed section. At once, she handed it to an adjutant.

"Find me the location of the phone at the other end of this signal."

Six minutes later she was handed the location along with her phone: La Palma, Canary Islands. Quickly, she chose her cadre of four soldiers under her command, trusted. Seventy-five minutes later, their gear securely stowed, they were helicoptered to the Kubinka military air base, where a jet was waiting for them on the tarmac. She was the last to board, checking that everything was as she had ordered. The moment she was seated, her bags stowed, the pilot took off the brakes, the plane raced down the runway, lifted off into clouds thick as whipped cream.

Somewhere nearby a rumble of thunder chased itself across the sky. Major Korokova closed her eyes. Smiling slightly, she drifted off into a dreamless sleep.

37

All government buildings were in lockdown following the sudden, shocking death of George Wilson within the walls of the Pentagon. The room where he'd died, and the adjacent corridors, had been cordoned off and were humming with FBI activity. The entire Defense Threat Reaction Agency was in shock, while still going about their assigned tasks, though in an unthinking, robotic manner.

The administration's spin doctors could no longer contain the story. An explanation for the deaths of two of a golf foursome made up of some of the highest-ranking members of the government could be delivered to the media in a logical, though completely false, format, and all ongoing questions stifled. But glossing over three out of the four dying suddenly was an impossible task, even for the veteran spin-meisters employed by the president. Questions were being asked by conspiracy theorists on both fringes of the political spectrum, which meant, inevitably, that a Senate subcommittee was being formed to look into the matter. That the subcommittee would spend months bickering as to its constituents and, after that, might, per usual, get nowhere, did not matter to Ben. At least, not at the moment. The slow grind of events on Capitol Hill was light-years away from the world he inhabited.

What did matter to him—mattered very much—was that following news of Wilson's demise, Zahra Planck had not returned his calls, texts, or emails. It was as if she had dropped off the face of the earth or, more accurately, dropped him off the face of the earth.

What the media didn't know, would never know, was that the victim was also part of the small group General Reade had put together to delve into the murder of Brady Thompson, also a member of the golf foursome. Did that mean whoever was responsible was targeting those four men? All were highly placed in the federal government, all had jobs that required them to handle top secret projects.

These were questions he wanted to ask Zahra, but she was nowhere to be found. The same for General Reade, who was and had been in meetings with the president at Camp David ever since news of Wilson's death made its way to the White House. Ben had, however, been able to contact Wes Connerly; they were to have dinner tonight, at which time Ben hoped for some answers, especially concerning Zahra's mysterious disappearance. Sitting in his car, down the block and across the street from the building in which she lived, he wondered whether she could be the one behind the murders. She was a manipulator and a liar but those traits didn't necessarily make her capable of killing someone. Another thing: so far as he had been able to determine she had no motive. She had of course been thoroughly vetted before she began work in the quantum directorate of the government's misunderstood and criminally underfunded physics program, but in these days hackers and criminals invading intranets had devalued the usefulness of old-school vetting. Zahra could be anyone, really, could be working for any one of a number of state-sponsored bad actors, and those were very bad indeed. Short of pulling her in and interrogating her there was no way to tell—white hat, black hat, something in between, though he could not imagine what that might be.

His phone buzzed with an incoming text. He glanced at the screen. Wes Connerly canceling dinner. Unsurprising but annoying nonetheless. He sent a middle-finger emoji as a reply—not the most diplomatic of choices but right now he didn't give a crap. He hadn't liked Connerly from the get-go, and his opinion of him had gone downhill ever since their first meeting.

Outside, night had fallen even if the temperature had not. He had rolled down the windows to gain the evening's hydrocarbonized breeze, not wanting to keep the engine and air-conditioning running. The streetlights were on here in Georgetown, quaint things that they were. It was unsettling to think that Zahra lived six blocks from his own home. Though he hadn't been there in almost a year, the knowledge of how close Zahra was to his home gave him the creeps.

The sidewalks were nearly deserted. What pedestrians appeared scurried like rats fleeing a burning ship, their eyes wide and staring blindly, as if they had been electrocuted by the air of existential menace.

Ben sat very still behind the wheel. He turned neither his head nor his body. He could not hear her, he could not see her, but her scent invaded the interior of the car several seconds before she pulled the off-side door open and slid into the shotgun seat.

Now he turned, saw her in a dark raincoat, matching her eyes and hair. Her face had been imprinted on his mind a year ago. "An Binh," he said softly, "what are you doing here?"

"This surveillance is useless," she said. "Zahra is not home." She turned her eyes on him, liquid charcoal. "She's not coming home."

He laughed, wondering if she was in some way joking. "Ever?"

She possessed the gravest of smiles. "Drive. I'll take you to her."

He did not doubt her for an instant. This was how she was; how their relationship worked. He trusted her; she had given him no reason not to. He started the car and she gave him directions. As he drove she spoke:

"Two nights ago, Zahra met George Wilson at a late-night bar. I was seated at the other end, having shadowed her. I listened to the entire conversation by lip-reading."

He knew he should ask her what the hell she thought she was doing, since he specifically told her to hang tight at the mansion, but good sense prevailed. What was the point? What was done was done. Besides, he had a sneaking suspicion he'd be happy she had disobeyed him.

She had pushed out her lower lip, a sure sign of her displeasure. "It's amazing what people will say in a bar. It's as if they have their head on a pillow dampened by sex."

She told him about the side hustle Zahra had going on with George Wilson, how Wilson was gaga over her, how she saw Zahra exquisitely twist him around her little finger. She gave him a look. "She's quite the operator."

Ben understood her meaning immediately. An Binh had ventured into the field because she was worried that Zahra was doing to him what she'd already done to Wilson—fractured his brain so he'd think with his dick. Sadly, he thought, she wasn't altogether off base. Though Ben had doubts about Zahra's motives, the erotic pull she had on him was strong and getting stronger, despite his misgivings. Zahra had indeed been twisting him around her little finger, even while he'd set his mind against it. The trouble was she hadn't been targeting his mind. Quite the operator, indeed.

"So you've stashed her somewhere," he said as she directed him down toward the Southwest Waterfront, an evolving area along the Potomac.

"Where no one but us will find her," An Binh said. "And in this lockdown no one's looking for her. They have bigger worries, don't they."

For several moments now her attention had been fixed on the water as they headed toward a ratty marina—the polar opposite of the ones to the northeast where the luxury boats were docked. Ben had never been down here, where lines of houseboats rocked gently at permanent slips.

She directed him to pull the car over several blocks away from the marina. "We'll walk from here," she said.

"A houseboat," Ben said as they approached the marina on foot. "That's where you lived?"

"I still do," she said. "It's been home ever since I moved here."

"Hold on."

She paused, turning to him. The soft slosh of the water carried clearly to them. Lights shone in the small windows of the houseboats. Folk music—Bob Dylan perhaps—spread itself like mist from someone's radio, adding to the retro feel of the marina. It was as if they had stepped into the final years of the sixties, when Flower Power was breathing its last before the coming storm of war, student protests, full-blown racial violence, the infamous Rolling Stones concert at Altamont.

"When we get inside, when we confront her," Ben told her, "I'll do the talking."

"Of course." An Binh's eyes seemed to grow large. "I am only the arrow."

"I should know this."

She stood immobile in front of him, not a hint of judgment in her expression or, he surmised, in her mind. "To be an arrow—and only an arrow—is to not care about the target or a need for revenge or a fulfillment of a mission. That is when the arrow is unerring, that is when it will always find its mark. That is freedom."

"I seem to remember your mission of revenge a year ago."

"That was your interpretation," she said. "Events, people arrive—that is life. But it is only ten percent of life. The other ninety percent is how your mind perceives and reacts to those events, those people. You have more control over your life than you think."

She gave him a wry look. "But, Ben, you already know all this."

A half-laugh from him. "In Buddhism I'm a rookie. I know it but I haven't yet incorporated it."

She nodded. "The *farang* Chaucer famously wrote 'Time and tide wait for no man.'"

Ben thought it interesting she chose the Thai word for "barbarian" rather than the Chinese "*Yěmán rén.*" But with everything she said or did it was a clue for him and him alone. She let him know that she spoke Thai as well as Mandarin, Cantonese, Vietnamese.

"You understand his mistake?"

Ben considered. "Chaucer had it the wrong way around. It's the mistake of all Western culture. Time and tide serve at the bidding of the Buddhist."

A genuine smile broke out across An Binh's face. "So well learned, Ben. Patience. All is patience."

They began to walk again, the lights of the marina reflected in their faces and then along the length of their bodies.

"With this woman you must exercise patience," she said in a lowered voice. "She does not know patience, she does not understand patience. This is your arrow."

An Binh's houseboat was moored at the southernmost end of the marina. It was painted a sea blue with faded yellow trim, making it as shabby-looking as all the others in the line. But as Ben was about to see, that timeworn appearance was strictly camouflage. They stepped aboard and went immediately down into the main cabin. Here, everything was neat, trim, and exquisitely rendered, from the silk-covered elm furniture to the paper lanterns that gave off jewel-toned light, to the niches in which were set what looked to him to be a collection of small Chinese imperial *yangcai* vases that, if real, dated back to the eighteenth century. If they were, indeed, real, Ben thought, there'd be many a museum willing to pay a fortune to acquire them. One thing was for certain, they weren't from Pier 1.

However, all the miraculously rendered Eastern atmosphere served only to further set off the prime exhibit: the woman tied to a chair in the middle of the room.

Her eyes opened wide when she saw him, and she broke out into a smile of such relief that Ben almost felt sorry for her. Almost.

"Benjamin, thank God. You've come to save me from this madwoman." As she spoke, her knees parted slowly and subtly, exposing the flesh of her inner thighs. And Ben, despite himself, felt a tightening, a certain heat roiling his lower belly. She knew her effect on him. There are ten thousand ways to smile, and, it seemed clear, Zahra knew them all. This one was unmistakable: it semaphored the silent phrase *Take me. I'm yours.* "And job number one would be calling off your attack dragon."

"A liar and a racist, to boot." Ben brought over a chair, positioned it facing the prisoner, seated himself. Behind him he could hear An Binh busying herself in the galley making—ah, yes—jasmine tea, by the scent wafting through the room.

In her extreme distress, Zahra let slip a frown. "Ben," she whispered, "what is this? What the hell is going on?"

He leaned his torso forward, matched her tone and low volume. "An Binh is making tea. A long, involved process if you do it right. And she will. She's a master."

Zahra shook her head. "I don't understand any of this."

"Well, that's the issue, isn't it?" he said. "Neither do I."

Her expression hardened, cracks showing in her makeup. "Listen, I'm a high-ranking federal employee, reporting to General Philip Johnstone Reade himself. I'm privy to things you can't even dream of." She jerked her torso back and forth without gaining any leeway from the rope with which An Binh had expertly bound her. "And certainly not your little Asian bitch."

Give An Binh credit, Ben thought, she did not even miss a beat in her brewing routine. How many times, he wondered, had that same slur been hurled at her. Was she so inured it no longer had an effect on her? Never mind, he was aggrieved enough for the both of them. He felt his muscles tense, his fingers curl into fists, but then he heard An Binh's voice in his mind, *"She does not know patience, she does not understand patience. This is your arrow."*

As if to affirm An Binh's read on her, Zahra twisted back and forth harder, for a longer time. Another person—a *farang*—would have told her curtly to stop, that her movements would only tighten the bonds because of the manner in which An Binh had affixed them.

"Get me out of here—now!" Her voice rising to the ceiling like soot from an explosion. "That's an order, Benjamin—a direct order from General Reade." When he made no comment, her cheeks and throat flamed pink. Her eyes grew wide and she bit back the words on her trembling lips, *Why aren't you answering me?* "Don't you fools understand that George Wilson has died, that I have to view the autopsy, direct the coroner to take the proper MRIs of George's brain?"

"Speaking of which," Ben broke his silence, "FBI forensics has been granted permission to exhume the body of Bill Fineman, the administration's late director of human resources and the fourth member of the golf party, three of whom are dead."

"Fineman died of a coronary," Zahra spat. "The results are official, a matter of record."

"Official but untrue. A new autopsy has been ordered with MRIs of Fineman's brain." He cocked his head. "What d'you suppose the new finding will be, hm?"

An Binh appeared holding a black lacquer tray. On it was a Chinese tea service for two. Setting the tray down, she poured a cup of jasmine tea for Ben before helping herself.

Zahra's upper lip twisted. "Oh, sure, I see how it is, *Ben*. She's not only your bitch, she's your *whore*."

Forcing his muscles to relax, Ben took up his tea, sipped it slowly and steadily while staring at Zahra over the rim.

Then she had a fit, throwing herself back and forth until the chair rocked on its left-side legs, then the right-side. Ben made no sound, no attempt to keep the chair from crashing onto its side. Meanwhile, Zahra threw her head back, howling like an animal. "Get me the fuck out of here! Someone will hear me, someone will come or call the cops. You'll see. And then I'll have you thrown in prison, sent to Guantánamo, where you'll rot in hell for the rest of your lives."

"No one will hear you." An Binh's voice was soft as a summer breeze. "No one is coming. No one will miss you." She smiled sweetly, with only the center of her lips, as only she could. "This is your Guantánamo, Zahra. This is your hell. You're never getting out of here. Never. Never. Never."

At last, Ben thought, she had allowed herself to respond to Zahra's hateful bigotry, but in her own time, her own way. Ben thought it terrifying, as did Zahra judging by the expression of dread on her face. Ben continued to sip his tea, inhaling the aromatic scent, delicate as a butterfly's wing. Patience, he thought as he slowed his breathing.

Hyperventilating, Zahra began to cry, tears overflowing her eyes, running down her cheeks. She grew very still, bit her lip. Her eyes implored Ben's. "Please," she whispered. "Please. I'll do whatever you want."

Another tool in her bag of tricks, he thought. Hyperventilating was a well-documented actor's trick. Usually, hyperventilation was caused by extreme anxiety or panic. But deliberate hyperventilating was another animal altogether, though the results were often the same. It constricted the throat, set up an unvirtuous circle of improper breathing, resulting in, among other symptomology, crying. Ben had seen this trick used before, a number of times; he knew how to differentiate it from its panicky form.

"Ben, please," she whispered, "I'm begging you. I can't take this—this confinement. I'm claustrophobic. I feel like I'm about to jump out of my skin."

Now the grotesque chameleon had turned herself into a helpless damsel in distress, warm, soft, in need of protection and ever so grateful for it.

More tears. "Untie me, at least," she implored. "Untie me. That's all I ask."

He stared at her stonily. The slippery slope of granting one blubbering-induced concession after another.

Her hair, damp with sweat, was plastered to her forehead. The stink of fear was coming off her in suffocating waves. "Where's your humanity, Ben? Have you no empathy? You must be crazy and numb. Dear God, have pity."

At his continued silence, she broke down for real, sagging as much as she was able, chin on chest. The real sobs coming from deep down in her belly. He was witness to all the false layers she had built up crumbling one after another. She had come to the bottom of her toolbox and found it empty. She now knew that all her false threats, her deceitful entreaties had fallen on deaf ears. The tricks that had always worked for her, always getting her what she wanted, had lost their effectiveness. Her power was gone.

Bent over as far as she could, she retched, vomited, kept retching even when there was nothing left to bring up save black bile.

Ben stood up. "Time to cut your bonds."

Her eyes rolled in her head; she drooled pink saliva.

"And then, like a dog that hasn't learned to obey, push your face into the mess you've made on your host's floor."

"Oh, God, no!" she shrieked. Looking up at him with bloodshot eyes. "You can't mean that! Ben, you can't!"

He stepped behind her.

"No, no, no!" she cried. "Oh, please, no!"

Silent as an owl, An Binh pushed Ben's chair out of the way, crouched in front of Zahra. Her nostrils didn't even dilate; she had smelled much worse in the backwaters of Vietnam and China.

So softly, Zahra was obliged to strain at her bonds to hear, "Tell him what he wants to know."

Zahra blinked. "Then . . . then will you let me go?"

An Binh stared at her, black eyes unblinking. "Tell him who you really work for."

"Will you? Free me?" Zahra's voice quavered despairingly; she already knew she was not going to get an answer. Her eyes filled with disgust, a visible admission of her understanding that there was no other path for her now but acquiescence. Was this how it was going to end, not with a bang but with a whimper out of her own mouth?

38

"You're taking an enormous risk coming with me," Evan said. Tribe, however, appeared unperturbed. Possibly, Evan thought, he was probing her own level of anxiety, which was growing with every moment he was with her. "If you were anything but my boss I'd forbid it."

When he laughed—really laughed, in private only, she had discovered—it took over his entire body. "But Evan, you know full well I thrive on taking enormous risks."

She liked him most when he laughed, primarily because he seemed almost unguarded, most human. He was an extremely closed-off person. Perhaps that was one of the reasons they got along so well. She had no idea what he really thought of her, how deep their friendship went. Possibly it was only skin-deep, but on the other hand he was spending an increasing amount of time with her, participating in her fieldwork. She hadn't asked for this, but she could think of no way of refusing him. She had tried that once—and only once. His reaction made it crystal clear that in all matters in which he took an interest he would do as he wished. Once he made up his mind, no one, nothing could dissuade him.

She had time to consider these matters, though not for the first time, as they crossed the tarmac of his private landing pad, where a white-and-black custom Airbus ACH160 helicopter hunkered down, a gigantic damselfly reflecting the early-morning sun. The acrid scent of aviation fuel and oil swirled briefly around her until swept away by the wind off the water.

"Where are we going?" Evan asked.

"Playa del Perdido."

Tribe climbed through the open door to the Airbus, and she followed. Inside the doorway, she stopped, stunned. The main cabin just behind the pilot's two-seat cockpit looked like first-class in a transpacific flight or a lounge in a high-end hotel: six wide leather-covered seats connected by sections wide enough to store laptops, pads, pens and pencils, along with pairs of cup holders. The middle and last rows were occupied by four men whom she did not recognize but who could only be bodyguards, judging by the semiautomatic weapons lying diagonally across their laps. Each one had a small chunky case on the floor between his boots. Some seemed indifferent, others averted their gaze from her battered face.

"Damn," she husked.

"It's on the other side of the island," Tribe continued, as if she hadn't uttered a sound, as if the guards were invisible to him, and very possibly they were; she imagined he'd been living with such people most of his adult life. "We'll be flying over the volcano. You'll like that—it's still seething from the eruption in 2021."

He was already seated next to the pilot, observing every detail of the preflight check.

"Okay, I give up," she said, standing behind him, "what's in Playa del Perdido?"

"Our friend."

Tribe made a subtle hand gesture toward the pilot only she could see. Her pulse began to race. She knew "our friend" meant Lyudmila. He didn't want her name mentioned in hearing distance of the pilot.

The engine started up and the rotors began to cleave the air above their heads. Apparently satisfied, Tribe rose, went past her to one of the seats in the first row of the main cabin. Evan followed, sat beside him. The noise rose and vibrations began, but in this luxury aircraft both were dampened considerably. Nevertheless, he pointed to a pair of headsets with boom mics. As soon as they had them fitted correctly, she heard Tribe's voice clear and strong in her ear. The headsets must be noise-canceling, she thought.

"We're on a closed circuit," he was saying. "No one can overhear us."

They rose into the air, the Airbus turning ninety degrees, and headed out across the island.

"I met Lyudmila eleven or twelve years ago. At that time I was making frequent trips to Moscow. Like other venture capitalists I wanted to take advantage of Russia's low prices and their not-quite-bright-enough oligarchs."

"They were smart enough to amass incredible fortunes," Evan interjected.

"But they weren't smart," Tribe said. "Clever, yes. Lucky, even more so.

But smart, no. That I found out firsthand. I was on the verge of making extremely advantageous deals with two of them when I was invited to a private party—oligarchs and high-ranking government officials only. Of course there were FSB officers present. They were always present, circling like vultures.

"Anyway, that night I met Lyudmila. From the start I was wary of her. First, she was an FSB major. Second, she sought me out, which worried me greatly. Reluctantly, I agreed to have coffee with her the next day. After that was settled, she disappeared and I didn't see her the rest of the night.

"The next day I met her at a café, the location of which surprised me. It was outside the ring road, meaning off the beaten path. She had told me in detail the route I should use to get there, using only public transportation. 'I'll take care of the rest' was the last thing she said to me before she vanished into the crowd."

"By which she meant surveillance."

"Yes. I don't have to tell you that I was surveilled almost all the time I was in Moscow. But she was a major in the FSB. If she wanted me alone, I had faith there would be no other agents around when we met."

"So you met her for coffee."

"Vodka-laced coffee was more like it."

Evan smiled as she nodded. "Yes. It was Lyudmila who taught me to love good vodka." She shifted in her seat. "So what did she want?"

"You must know what she wanted, Evan. She wanted an alliance."

Evan felt a little shock go through her. "Even then she was planning to defect."

"She told me how she had been treated ever since she joined the FSB, how the men around her resented her intelligence, her ability to get any job done, her fearlessness in the field and ruthlessness in HQ. The higher in rank she rose the more resentment she felt, the more harassment she received—anonymously, of course. But she knew who the perpetrators were—that, or she found out. Her punishment was swift and final."

"Her superiors didn't stop her—they didn't object?"

"They found her far too entertaining, she told me. Even then she was bitter about their callousness, their contempt for human life."

"So you agreed. You formed an alliance with her."

"I've never regretted it."

"And you had an affair," Evan said. "That would be Lyudmila's way of sealing an alliance with someone like you."

"Someone like me?"

"Smart, rich, handsome. Charismatic."

"Is that what you think of me?" He laughed. "My mother used to tell anyone who would listen that I was incapable of a long-term relationship. 'He's easy to like,' she said, 'impossible to be with.'"

"So nothing happened."

"Well, she tried," Tribe admitted. "But my mother was right—that was never going to work for me. We did kiss once and that was electric enough for me to be sure I was doing the right thing by keeping our alliance all business. Your brain shuts down during sex and that can be dangerous for someone like me."

Another reason, Evan thought, *why he's leery of anyone getting too close to him. But then here I am, closer to him than anyone else.* Was there meaning in that? She didn't know.

"Lyudmila's a complicated person—more than most," he went on. "But I expect you already know that."

"She's a good friend," Evan replied. "Though there were times she put me in danger I think it was—at least partially—to force me to become better under fire." She shrugged. "In any case, we've saved each other's lives."

"In the trenches of war," Tribe said, as if he were quoting a military leader, "the closest bonds are formed. Brothers in extremis."

"Sisters, too." It was a tacit admonishment and he knew it.

He nodded. "So your friendship with Lyudmila is extraordinary, isn't it; she's someone with whom you share the exhilaration of surviving what might have been your deaths."

"Exhilaration. I never think of it that way."

He looked at her. "Exhilaration counters fear. In the field aren't you ever frightened?"

"That's why I drink vodka." That came out from somewhere deep inside her. Had it even been a conscious thought? she wondered. "You learn never to talk about your fear."

"Wouldn't that be helpful—to get it out."

A thin smile on Evan's face, an element of ruefulness behind it. "You mean psychologically. Well, that may be true in civilian life, talking out your fears. But I inhabit the shadow world outside of society where fear is contagious, especially in the field. You learn to stopper that fear, stuff it into the bottom of the vodka bottle."

"Are you an alcoholic?" he asked, slightly alarmed. "That wasn't in your file."

Evan had tried not to think about that, she recoiled from it; the very idea made her angry. "I drink when I have to, never because I need to."

"I understand," Tribe said thoughtfully. "You need a way to distance yourself from the horror of injury and death."

Evan looked out the window. "Sometimes it works," she said softly. "Sometimes it doesn't."

They had passed from the touristed area that had built up La Palma's economy—the sleek hotels, oversized houses complete with Olympic-size azure pools, the billionaires' yachts on whose decks the bronzed bikinied bodies of models were stretched out like gorgeous flowers in the sunlight. Away inland were the clusters of small houses of the people who made life for the tourists effortless. In backyards, instead of pools, rows of well-worn shirts and shorts, pinned to lines, fluttered in the desultory breeze. No tennis courts here, only tiny postage-stamp gardens from which stalks of tomatoes, child-size trellises of cucumbers rose like trembling fingers.

Then these too were gone as the inhospitable true nature of the island showed itself in ridges and escarpments ever steeper, merging into the foothills of the mountain range that ran like the crooked spine of a disabled veteran—almost like the letter Q. And inside that Q, the volcano.

The helo rose higher into the steamy air as they flew past the Caldera de Taburiente, approached the volcano itself, a seething hellscape of red and orange, crawling across blackened fields of cooled lava.

Occasional vents of toxic steam shot into the air, blurring their view. Beneath those noxious clouds, the lava flows bubbled and crept from the burning magma deep in the layers of the island's subconscious.

No birds flew here; apart from the slither of superheated blood, no life at all. And yet, there was something compelling, almost hypnotic, about the aggressiveness of the landscape. A storm-roiled sea might be just as aggressive, but this outpouring changed forever what was beneath it.

■　■　■

The beachside village of Playa del Perdido basked in the late-morning sun as they set down on a flat area beachside. The eruption had turned the sand dark, rough, stubbly with chunks of lava, as if it had the pox. The flow from the volcano had destroyed many homes. Lives were lost, terrible damage had been inflicted, and where the red-hot streams had hit the water it created laze—lava haze—which was deadly, laced with hydrochloric acid. Explosions containing tiny bits of glass caused by the too-rapid cooling of the flow ensued, making immediate evacuation a necessity.

Now all was so quiet in Playa del Perdido after the helo's engines had shut down that Evan could hear the water's rush and suck against the tumbled rocks at the far end of the crescent beach. And yet, the aftermath of the destruction was all around her as she debarked, along with Tribe and their heavily armed escort.

No one met them, which she found curious. Together they trudged along the edge of the beach farthest from the water. Ahead, the end of the barrier road curved away to their right. Soon after rounding that curve, Evan saw the front porch of a wooden house—an oddity compared to the white stucco villas that clung like limpets to other parts of the shoreline. The house was set back into an outcropping of palms, their trunks curled by the onshore wind. Fronds waved at them, clattering, as if to announce their arrival.

As soon as they gained the porch, the front door opened and a figure appeared. Though it was in shadow, Evan immediately recognized the outline, accelerating her heart rate.

"Lyudmila," she said.

The palms clattered, the sea whispered against the shore. Overhead, gulls wheeled, calling, calling as if lost.

Instead of coming out to meet them, Lyudmila stepped back into deeper shadow. Tribe crossed the threshold, disappeared inside, but Evan stood rooted to the spot. Behind her, the armed crew spread out, quartering the immediate area around the house.

"Aren't you coming in?" Lyudmila's voice, wafted on the wind.

Evan still did not move. She could make out Lyudmila's tilted head.

"Am I such a surprise to you, being here?" She lifted her arm, held out her hand, and crossed the doorsill to where Evan stood. "I told you I managed to exfiltrate Marius Ionescu, the Directorate KV particle physicist. That's why I'm here. With him." She graced Evan with a familiar beguiling smile. "Come, darling. I would have had such little success without you."

Now both her arms were raised, and at last Evan stepped into the shadows. She inhaled the familiar scent, but this time it was a lit match to a fuse. She hauled off and slapped Lyudmila across the face so hard the other woman, unprepared, stumbled back.

"I was worried about you," Lyudmila said as Evan stalked into the house. She closed the door behind them, then hurried after Evan. "I know. Look at you. I went too far this time when I asked you to find Juliet Korokova. I should never have left you alone in Istanbul; that was a mistake."

"One of many." Evan finally found her voice. "But you wouldn't stay in such a dangerous place as Istanbul when you had me to investigate for you. Instead, you ran here to take care of Ionescu, another cog in the mysterious engine of your plan."

"Look, I helped you find Nemesis, didn't I?"

"And in the process I was forced to kill one of my sisters. Was that part of your plan, too?"

Instead of answering her, Lyudmila said, "I helped you with Omega."

"Where another of my sisters was killed." Evan had worked up an impressive head of steam. "Once I had three sisters, now I have none."

"And I led you to your birth parents." *But,* Lyudmila thought, *I never told you that your sister Bobbi is still alive, my agent inside the FSB. Some secrets need to be kept no matter the cost.*

Evan turned, stepped away from her, angry, bitter, dazed with conflicting emotions.

The curtains on the south-facing wall of the house were closed against the heat of the sun and also, Evan guessed, from prying eyes, though she had spotted no one on the curve of beach nor boats out beyond the shore. The flow from the eruption had rendered Playa del Perdido moot as a tourist destination. It was possible it would never regain the popularity it enjoyed once upon a time.

The house was small, but only by the standards of the whitewashed villas of Santa Cruz de La Palma. It contained a living room, dining area, large kitchen, along with, Lyudmila told her, three bedrooms with en suite baths.

"Evan—"

"Don't," Evan said. "Just don't."

Tribe was in earnest conversation, sitting opposite a small, thin man with a prominent nose above a brush mustache. This, Evan supposed, was Marius Ionescu. His hair, pushed back off his forehead, was pale as his eyes. The conversation broke off as with a herky-jerky motion Ionescu turned. When he saw Evan enter the living room, his eyes momentarily darkened in fear. As he rose, a question appeared on his face. Finding a reassuring answer in a gesture from Lyudmila, he regained his composure, and, in a courtly manner that reminded her of von Kleist, he came to her, shook her hand, and introduced himself.

"This is Evan Ryder, a close and trusted friend," Lyudmila said brightly, as if the altercation had never occurred, as if the rift that had opened up between them were a mirage. "And I see you've already met Marsden Tribe."

"I am very pleased to meet you," he said to Evan in his formal way. His brows crinkled. He appeared to be somewhere in his fifties. "Are you the one to get us to a safer place?"

"'Us'?" Evan repeated. "You mean you and Lyudmila?"

"No. Oh, no," Ionescu said. "Timur and myself."

Evan shook her head. "Who is Timur?"

Ionescu stepped out of the room for a moment, reappeared with his arm across the shoulders of a slender boy of seven or eight. He had white-blond hair and pale curious eyes. Marius brought him to the center of the room. The boy clung to him like a remora to a shark.

"Timur is Marius's son," Lyudmila said. "I'm sorry, Evan. I didn't tell you. Marius wouldn't allow himself to be exfiltrated without Timur."

"I'm a widower, you see," Ionescu said to Evan. "Timur is all the family I have. Impossible to leave him behind. I'd never forgive myself."

Evan stepped forward, knelt down in front of the boy. He stared at her, his eyes big and questioning. "My name is Evan, Timur. Yes. Funny name for a girl, right?"

"Woman," he said, dead serious.

"What?"

"I've been taught that only girls my age should be called girls. You're a woman."

She laughed. "You've been taught well." She gave Ionescu a quick smile and he nodded in return. "Anyway my name *is* funny, for a *woman*. Maybe my parents wanted a boy and got me instead." She smiled and Timur mimicked her, but his soft laugh was gone almost before it began. "I understand you've had a hard time lately." She took his hand. "But now that's all over with. You're safe now. We'll make sure of that, okay?"

Timur nodded. He seemed reluctant to let go of her hand, but at length he did, tracing the air around her face with his fingertip. "Are you all right?" he said in a whisper.

"Of course I'm all right, Timur."

"What happened to you?"

"I had an accident." *Think fast*, Evan told herself. "Surfing. Do you know what surfing is?"

He shook his head.

"It's when you take a board and paddle out into the ocean where the waves are and you stand up on the board and ride a wave into shore." She cocked her head. "It's tricky but sounds like fun, doesn't it?" He nodded. "Well, I was surfing and got careless at the end, fell off my board into some rocks. Silly of me. I won't do it again. Hey, maybe I can take you surfing sometime. Would you like that?"

He pursed his lips as if weighing the promised fun against her bruised face.

"I'd make sure nothing bad happens to you. I'd hold your hand the whole time."

"Yes, please," he whispered.

"Good. I'd like that."

She was about to rise when Timur threw his arms around her and hugged her tight. She felt his heartbeat close to hers. The sensation of his arms around her, the desperation with which he clung to her, pulled at her heartstrings, and she was reminded of her sister Bobbi's children, whom she had saved from their abductors. She was reminded most poignantly of Ben's daughter, with whom she had a long, guilt-marred history. She ached to see their smiling faces, to hear their laughter, listen to the stories of their adventures since the last time she had seen them. She yearned to hold them as she held Timur, to tell them how much she missed them, how much she loved them. But it was too dangerous for them, for her birth parents, the Reveshvilis, to visit them now.

She had carefully locked away these feelings in a corner of her mind, the better to do her job without the distraction of emotion, but Timur had smashed that lock. Flooded with so many feelings she felt ill-equipped to handle at the moment, she put her cheek against the top of Timur's head, inhaled the smell of his shampoo, the soap he'd used to wash himself— the scents of innocent childhood. Her eyes closed for a moment as he melted into her. She stayed with him for as long as he needed, for as long as she wanted. Slowly she calmed, then they broke apart. She turned to Lyudmila with a questioning look.

"No one else knew," Lyudmila whispered.

With a sweep of her hand, Evan dismissed her words. "Tribe knew."

"Actually, I didn't." Tribe had come over to them. "Not until I spoke with Mr. Ionescu."

Lyudmila reached out. "Evan, please don't be angry."

Evan held up a hand. "Timur, would you mind going with your father back to your room?"

Timur regarded her seriously. Then he nodded, took Ionescu's hand.

When the two of them were gone, Evan turned again to Lyudmila. "Listen to me, Lyudmila, you've been leading me around on a leash—a long one but one that nevertheless keeps me going where you want me to go, doing what you want me to do, irrespective of my own safety."

"Evan, you're being unfair. I've done everything in my power to ensure your successes in the field. You know that."

When Evan made no reply, Lyudmila looked stricken. And then quite suddenly her expression changed to one Evan had never seen on her before. To her utter astonishment, Lyudmila looked ashamed.

"There's something I want to show you." She turned on her heel and went down a narrow hallway, past the rearmost bedroom and out a screen door at the end of the hall.

Evan hesitated, her roiling emotions pulling her in two directions. Out of the corner of her eye she saw Tribe standing in the hallway outside the living room, inclining his head in the direction Lyudmila had gone. Still, she did not look at him directly, didn't want to. His alliance with Lyudmila, whatever form it took, was yet another factor kept from her not only by Lyudmila but by Tribe himself.

Finally, she broke her stasis, followed Lyudmila through the house. Rustling sounds in the trees let Evan know that Tribe's people were on guard all the way around the house even if she couldn't see them. In fact, she felt better not being able to see them; they were doing their job well.

When she emerged outside, Lyudmila turned to her, that strange look still on her face. "You're right," she said softly. "Everything you said is true. Mea culpa. Mea maxima culpa. I've been so self-absorbed with what I've been planning that I—"

"Just what *have* you been planning?" Evan took an unconscious step forward so they could speak in even softer tones.

Lyudmila sighed. "It's complicated." She waved a hand in front of her, as if to forestall any response Evan might make. "Okay, that was an all-encompassing anodyne cliché, but in this case . . ." Her voice trailed off for a moment. Then, as if coming to a decision, she shivered despite the heat. "You have to understand, extreme paranoia has informed every moment of my life for the last decade."

"How can I understand anything, Lyudmila, when everything you tell me has the substance of quicksand."

"I deserve that. And I deserved this." She put a hand up to her jaw, which was already darkening, puffing up in response to the blow Evan had dealt her. "Well, the truth now. No quicksand, okay?" She looked around as Evan had done moments before. "Five years ago I set an agent in place inside the FSB. I groomed them, made sure they knew what to do and how to do it. And they did. They were ruthless and clever. They kept climbing the FSB ladder. All well and good. I had it in mind that they should come to the attention of the Sovereign, that they would get close to him."

"And kill him."

Lyudmila nodded. "Precisely."

"A suicide mission, then."

"Something I made certain never to tell them."

"But it didn't work. Obviously. What happened?"

Lyudmila sighed again, and for once she looked tired. "The Sovereign's damn war happened, and with it, a changing of the FSB guard. My agent was sidelined."

It was at this moment that Evan noticed the dark rings under her eyes. She couldn't imagine the pressure her friend must be under. The first plan blowing up in her face and then the planning and extreme danger in exfiltrating Ionescu. But at this precise moment that was an observation, accompanied by no feeling at all. Her incarceration and torture in Istanbul had broken a line of trust that she wondered now whether she had been a fool to accept. Gone were the humid, sun-splashed days, the chittering moon-drenched nights in Sumatra—the easy laughter, the shared secrets, letting down their guard. Evan had to wonder now whether it was all lies, whether Lyudmila was even capable of letting down her guard. She stared at Lyudmila and wondered if there could be anything worse than a betrayal by a friend.

"So, on to plan B," Lyudmila continued in an even more subdued voice.

"As far back as eighteen months ago I had heard about the breakthroughs Directorate KV might be making in the world of quantum computing. I had heard a rumor they were trying to weaponize something called time crystals."

Evan felt the urge to tell her that Tribe had talked to her about time crystals but decided to keep her mouth shut. Better to hear about it from Lyudmila.

"Though sidelined, my agent was still operational. In fact being sidelined was helpful in them going outside FSB itself. They found the weak link."

"Ionescu."

"Indeed. He didn't like the direction in which the experiments were going. He was willing to leave but only if he could bring Timur with him."

"That must have made the exfiltration exponentially more difficult."

"I had planned for such an eventuality." A smile thinned by hesitation. "Now you know why I recruited von Kleist. He has the reach and wherewithal of all his clients."

"He helped with the exfiltration."

Lyudmila nodded. "And now that his usefulness is at an end he's gone back to his clients full-time and happy to do it."

"But what does Ionescu bring you?"

"Leverage," Lyudmila said. "The weaponization was discussed off his theories. Without him Directorate KV has been set back at least three or four years. By that time they'll be behind everyone else. More importantly, the Sovereign will be without the weapon he needs to keep himself in power."

Evan considered this, and her heart plummeted into her stomach. "So then it's impossible that the Russians are behind the quantum advancement of the Havana syndrome."

"So far as I know, that's right."

Evan's sense of foreboding was growing by the second. "Tribe told me that coming here would prove he isn't behind the weaponization of time crystals."

Lyudmila looked away into the trees, as if searching for something only she knew was there. Her expression was clouded by conflicting emotions. When her gaze returned to Evan, she said, "If he meant Ionescu that won't do it. Marius refused to be part of that."

Dread started to overcome her. This situation, this probability had pierced the internal wall she had built to separate her steely professional self from her vulnerable personal self. It wasn't even a wall, she realized; it was a membrane, always too thin, too delicate to protect her from her own feelings. What she felt for Tribe was now in the open, feelings she had long denied. Her words came back to her like a slap in the face: "*Smart, rich, handsome. Charismatic.*" That's what she'd said to Tribe in the helo on their way here. She winced. Had she been flirting with him all along?

She said, with a voice so shaky it terrified her, "That leaves Tribe."

She felt heartsick that it was Tribe, heartbroken that he had lied to her, over and over.

"I mean, who else has the expertise?" she said.

Why had he brought her here? She couldn't work that out; even looked at through this new prism it didn't make sense to her. But then she was lost in a forest. She could only see the trees nearest her, and these kept shifting from oak to aspen to pine.

"He's way ahead of everyone else," she added.

Lyudmila huffed. "Says who?"

"Says Tribe."

"You see what I'm getting at?"

That was the moment the trees nearest the rear of the house shattered, flew apart in a wall of deafening noise, a hail of semiautomatic fire.

39

It was well known that when Wes Connerly, head of the National Geospatial-Intelligence Agency, worked late he always ordered Chinese food delivered from Fun Wen, the restaurant five blocks away from the agency's building. This evening he ordered an egg roll, a quart of shrimp in lobster sauce, and kung pao chicken, extra hot. As he had done since he was a teen, he always asked for extra fortune cookies.

Security was so inured to his habits they scarcely looked at ID when the Chinese delivery person showed up. As long as they successfully passed through the metal detector, security was unconcerned. That this delivery person was female, that she was half Chinese, half Vietnamese, went entirely unnoticed.

Following Ben's instructions, An Binh had no difficulty finding the locked delivery entrance at the rear of the building. Nor did she have any problem disabling the lock. She let Ben in, and together they rode the elevator up to the third floor, where Connerly was ensconced in his office. The floor was manned by the night shift, who because of the emergency lockdown were so overworked they had no spare attention to notice personnel from a food delivery service.

Connerly sat at his desk, staring down at a stack of papers without really seeing them. His anxiety over Zahra's refusal to answer either his calls or his texts over the last eight hours had ratcheted up to an intolerable level. Beads of sweat decorated his forehead, his upper lip, the nape of his neck. His armpits felt swampy. He said, "Come," without looking up when the discreet knock sounded on his door, along with a soft voice saying, "Delivery." He had just picked up his phone to send yet another frantic text to Zahra, and was barely aware that the delivery person had set the plastic bag with Fun Wen's familiar red pagoda imprinted on it down on the corner of his desk.

However, at some point he became fully aware that there was still someone standing in front of his desk. "It's already paid for including a tip," he said distractedly. "But if you're angling for more—"

"I'm not here for money."

The female voice was more of a purr and had the self-assuredness no delivery person ever affected, two oddities that made him jerk his head up. But did he see her? She meant nothing to him—less than nothing, because to him she was invisible. Instead, his gaze was fixed on Ben, who stood with his back against the door he had just silently closed.

"Butler," Connerly said, "what the hell are you doing here? And what was the meaning of that—what d'you call it?"

"It's called an emoji, and I didn't appreciate you canceling dinner." Ben came away from the door. "You've been looking for Zahra, I imagine. But you haven't been able to find her, have you?"

Connerly's face darkened. "How dare you ask such a question."

"We know your backdoor deal with her," An Binh said.

For the first time since she entered his office he focused on her, bewildered that she was there. "What backdoor deal?"

"Your deal," An Binh said as deliberately as a judge rendering a guilty verdict, "to auction Zahra's creation—the weaponization of time crystals—to the highest bidder. Their breakthrough was an enormous opportunity for you two."

"That's preposterous! What utter slanderous nonsense," Connerly exploded.

"Time you mopped your face, Connerly." Ben stepped across the office until he was beside An Binh. "You're drowning in flop sweat."

Connerly stood up abruptly. "Get out. Get out of my office or I'll call security."

"Go on." Ben reached over, took the phone off the cradle, held it out to Connerly. "We'll be happy to direct those boys to Zahra, who can tell them everything she told us, along with the proof."

"She was secretly recording all her private conversations with you," An Binh said.

Ben shook the phone in Connerly's face. "That call will get us out of your office, I promise. It will also cost you your job, your pension, not to mention your freedom. But by all means call security."

Connerly grabbed the receiver. "I don't believe a word of this."

An Binh produced Zahra's cell phone, tapped the keys, and out came Connerly's voice, followed by Zahra's—the recorded litany of evidence, their deceit, their treachery, including duping Wilson, all laid out line by incriminating line.

Connerly opened his mouth to reply, then his jaw shut with a snap. He began to tremble so badly he was forced to sink back down into his chair.

Then the politician in him kicked into high gear. His head snapped up. "It was all her doing—Zahra's. She got her hooks into me and wouldn't let go. You can hear it in her voice, damn her. She sweet-talked me into it. She made it seem so easy, so simple. The future she laid out for the two of us—"

"The two of you," An Binh echoed. "There was no two of you, there never was. She was going to turn you in the moment she had the money from the auction."

"She had it all planned out, Connerly," Ben broke in. "Every minute detail. Using Wilson. Using you."

"A meticulous woman, your Zahra," An Binh said in her devastatingly quiet manner. "Give her that."

An odd glimmer now infused Connerly's face. "Well, not so meticulous as she'd like you to believe. The auction was called off." Connerly smirked. "Why? Because a buyer came to me and made a preemptive bid. It was an offer I didn't refuse; it was also an offer I never told Zahra about."

An Binh was wise enough to know that she and Ben were being baited and the best path forward was to say nothing, to let Connerly dangle in the vacuum they had made of his life. So when she sensed Ben's muscles tensing up, because she knew his body's signals so well, she immediately gripped his forearm to forestall him saying what had to be said, but not now, not yet.

"Well?" Connerly looked from one to the other and back again. The collar of his white shirt was now darkened by sweat. "I want a guarantee of complete immunity before I'll tell you the name of the buyer. That's what you want, isn't it? Of course. The buyer's identity is vital to you."

An Binh took her hand away and Ben leaned in. "Here's what I think, Connerly. I'm going to step out of the room for twenty minutes or so. I'll let An Binh do to you what she did to Zahra." A crocodile smile bloomed on his face. "How does that sound to you?"

Connerly's eyes were nearly bugging out of his head; he'd been sure they'd jump in a heartbeat.

"Zahra wasn't easy," An Binh said so softly it was almost a whisper. "She's a very determined young lady."

"It took you what, thirteen minutes?" Ben said.

"Twelve," An Binh replied. "Actually."

"Good God." Connerly cringed backward in his chair, but there was nowhere for him to go. "I'm ready to tell you, but I want immunity." His gaze continued to flicker between them. They could smell his fear. "I think that's fair, don't you?"

"Why would we want to be fair with you," Ben said. "You're a traitor. It's Gitmo for you. No one call, no lawyer, no trial. Just lockup. Sound good?"

Connerly stared at them as if he couldn't believe what was happening. As if this were a nightmare and he'd pinched himself hard but he didn't wake up—he was already awake. His lower lip trembled but no words came out of his mouth.

Quick as a snake, An Binh came around his desk and, hands on the armrests, shoved his chair back until it collided with the wall. Connerly's head snapped back and then forward, by which time An Binh had her fingers inside the collar of his shirt, jerking so hard the top two buttons flew off. Slowly and deliberately she unknotted his tie.

"Did you ever in your wildest imagination," she whispered in his ear, "consider that you would be strangled with your own tie." It wasn't a question and in any event it didn't require an answer. She whipped the tie around his bare neck, caressing the silk as she pulled it tight.

He stared up into her face, saw his imminent death imprinted there. His bowels turned to water. An Binh paid the stench no mind; after all, she'd smelled worse.

"All right, all right," Connerly rasped. His face was quickly draining of color. "The buyer's name is Ayman Safra." His eyes focused on An Binh, the death-bringer; silently pleading with her. "He's a lawyer with one client: Marsden Tribe."

40

There came a halt to the gunfire. By that time, Evan's hearing was in limbo. The entire world was a ringing silence, as if she'd been inside a clanging bell for the last hour. The initial attack lasted only ninety seconds, but it felt far longer, and in that short time an immense amount of damage had been done. Trees were lying on the ground, their trunks shredded, their fronds trampled into muddy paste. The rear of the house was riddled with so many bullet holes it looked as if the siding had been ripped apart by a horde of harpy eagles.

There must have been screaming going on somewhere around her— she could feel the vibrations, the high-low so different from the steady racket the submachine-gun fire made. The firing had stopped for the moment, but soon enough an answering fusillade vibrated in her ears as Tribe's men went to work, trying to cut down the intruders.

She stared at the shredded tops of the palms and at once found herself in *Apocalypse Now*, napalmed trees burning, smoke oily with chemicals and human liquids spreading slowly, thick as the silence that had descended on her.

Someone tugged on her arm. She started. Someone shouted in her ear and she turned, saw Lyudmila trying to pry her out of her temporary stasis. Together they dived to one side as the intruders' firing started up again, shattering the place where Evan had been standing just a moment ago. She had yet to see a single figure amid the fallen debris of the trees nearest the rear of the house.

Going back inside the house was a nonstarter, as it would only trap them rather than protect them. They needed to find Tribe, Ionescu, and Timur, get them away from the area, the quicker the better. Had Tribe's men already done that? Were they even now making their way to the helo? Would Tribe leave her behind to save his own skin? She didn't think there was any question about it; his concern for other human beings was radically limited.

Crawling on their stomachs, they made their way to the far corner of the house, slithered around to the side. Almost at once they came up against one of Tribe's men, his chest ripped open by at least a dozen bullets. Evan grabbed his submachine gun, Lyudmila ripped his handgun from its holster, both weapons slick with the dead man's blood. They kept going, keeping as low as they were able, hidden by flowering bushes of Canary laurel.

Evan's hearing was slowly returning and it brought the sound of continuing gunfire from the rear of the house. She could sense wooden boards disintegrating, wondered how long it would be before that part of the house was laid open.

There was no one in the house. They had reached the front, saw the door wide open, and, to their left, glimpsed furtive movement within the cover of the line of palms closest to the ocean. As Lyudmila moved off toward it, Evan asked herself why there were gunmen at the rear of the house and nowhere else. Of course a frontal assault would have been discovered before they came close enough to do any damage, but they could have crept along the palm line toward the side of the house. Maybe there weren't enough men to attempt an assault from two directions at once. There was another answer that filled her with fear, and, without taking another breath, she raced off in the general direction Lyudmila had taken. But instead of running just inside the first line of palms, she melted into the tree line, where thickets of salt wind-blasted junipers lent her heavier cover than the palms with their bare trunks. She was obliged to keep her back bent, as the junipers were only more or less five feet tall. A great deal of the island that hadn't been cultivated or planted for the millionaires was barren until the upper slopes were reached, where forests of three different pine species flourished. That was not the case here in the wide scar of solidified lava and ash that had gushed from the volcano. If she turned her head to the left Evan could glimpse that swath of barren land blazing in the slanting rays of the dying sun as if it were a gateway to another world—one of fire, choking fumes, and death, a battlefield heaped with the bleached bones of the dead.

Up ahead, she could see that the junipers were thinning out. Beyond, the final tongue of once-fiery lava, now a whitened wasteland, had destroyed all plant life in its path. Farther along the corniche began; nowhere to hide there. Where were Lyudmila and whoever it was she'd caught up with headed? Soon enough they'd be on open ground, sitting ducks for the assailants. And then, with a chill racing down her spine, she understood, her worst fears realized. She had to head them off before they reached the end of the palms that fringed the beach.

In the headlong rush she had lost sight of Lyudmila; she had no idea where she was and of course it was impossible to call out to her. In the next moment a shot rang out and nothing else mattered. She folded onto her stomach, aware again of the bruises and lacerations over her upper body. She took a deep breath, let it out slowly to manage the pain. Everything seemed to come to a standstill. Even the onshore wind had flattened and failed.

Had she heard a groan somewhere ahead of her? Eyeing everything in her immediate environment, she crawled forward, the weapon cradled on the inside of her elbows. Veering a bit to her left, she saw a figure lying in the brush: Lyudmila.

Quickly she made her way over to her, put a hand on her back. Lyudmila's head turned. She had bitten her lip. *My left thigh,* she mouthed. Crouching next to her, Evan ran her hand down Lyudmila's backside. The moment she touched the back of the thigh, Lyudmila winced. Evan saw the cloth of her pants leg, black, soaked with blood. A second rifle shot pierced the ground inches from Evan's hip. Instead of reacting, slithering away or returning fire, she went prone on the ground and froze in place. While she counted silently to one hundred she observed the hole the bullet had made in the ground. From this she was able to make a reasonable estimation of the sharpshooter's location up the slope. When all remained quiet, she flipped over onto her back, took a look at Lyudmila's thigh.

"Lucky. The bullet went straight through the muscle and out the other side." She ripped the sleeves off her shirt and used them to fashion a makeshift pressure dressing.

"Don't move an inch," she whispered. "Play dead. I'll be back for you."

Lyudmila nodded, going into prana breathing to oxygenate her body and minimize the pain. Her chest did not move; her lower belly did all the in-and-out work.

Evan backtracked, scurrying sideways like a crab, moving farther into the salt-dwarfed junipers, unmindful of them scratching her like thorns. Up and up she went, snaking her way around in a semicircle higher up than where she calculated the sharpshooter lay in wait for their next victim.

A flash of metal catching the last rays of sunlight caused her to pause, change course, moving slowly up and to her right until she was directly behind the sharpshooter. Gathering herself, she rose up into a crouch, descended in a straight line. She did not want to use her weapon unless it became absolutely necessary; no good could come from giving away her position.

She was almost upon the sharpshooter when he sensed her, turning in her direction up on one elbow. She kicked out, striking the elbow with such force the humerus bone ripped free of the ligaments and tendons attaching it to the shoulder. The sharpshooter grunted, whipped around his AK-308, swung the stock into Evan's already injured face. She bit back a shout as stars exploded behind her eyes. In the next instant the sharp-shooter was on her, his weapon jammed across her throat. He pressed down with his good arm in the center of the rifle, using the full weight of his body, severely restricting oxygen to her windpipe. He had pressed her arms to her sides with his knees.

She knew she had very little time before her body, depleted of oxygen, would lose strength. Jackknifing her legs, she trapped his head between her ankles, jerked him back, then let go and slammed the sides of her boots against his ears. He groaned, hands instinctively going to his ears in a vain attempt to limit the pain.

Evan, released, used his own weapon, thrusting the end of the barrel into the soft tissue of his jaw just above his neck. Blood spurted, his eyes rolled up in their sockets, and she shoved him off her.

She rose, gasping, rubbing the reddened area of her throat. She knew better than to touch the place on her cheek where he had struck her with the rifle's stock. It was already throbbing, hot and dry, the skin pulled taut by the swelling.

She made her way down the slope to where Lyudmila lay just as Evan had left her.

"Got him," Evan whispered in Lyudmila's ear. "How're you doing."

"I'll live," Lyudmila replied dryly.

"Okay, we gotta move. Think you can walk?"

Lyudmila shot her a venomous look, rose, and with Evan's strong arm around her, regained her feet. Together they staggered along, heads down, backs bowed. Evan prayed there wasn't more than one sniper in the attacking group. The odds were heavily in their favor; snipers were a curious bunch, always working alone, never in groups or even in tandem with another sharpshooter.

"Who the hell are these people?" she asked.

"Who knew we were here?" Lyudmila queried.

"It's got to be a small number."

Lyudmila gave her another sharp look. "But still unknown."

"I doubt very much one of Tribe's competitors would mount such an attack. That leaves your nemesis, Major Korokova."

"After Istanbul my security has been airtight. How would she know?"

"Well, wasn't it your partner von Kleist's seaplane that took you here?" Evan said sharply.

"*Former* partner. And yes, it was, but I've told you, he is not the leak. I know him. Drop it." Lyudmila's voice equally sharp.

Evan said nothing more, because her mind flashed back to the texts Inessa had shown them. Evan had timed it, made sure it was under thirty seconds so it couldn't be traced. But what if it had been? What if Korokova was somehow able to make the trace? That would explain the hit team's presence here. Except . . . It would have been easy enough to storm Tribe's villa on the other side of the island, but they didn't. They waited, tracked the helo to this hidden bastion. Which meant they were after not only Lyudmila but Ionescu, their rogue quantum physicist. They wanted Lyudmila dead and Ionescu back in Moscow.

All of this raced through her mind at lightning speed. For only a second or two she considered spilling it all to Lyudmila. But what good would it do? It was only a theory, after all. She might only muddy the waters.

"It doesn't matter," Evan said with finality. "We have to deal with the here and now. Later, when we're safely away, we'll have time to figure out why."

After a moment or two, Lyudmila nodded, but she looked deeply troubled. She didn't like loose ends. Neither did Evan, but this very well might be a loose end of her own doing. For the time being, at least, she needed to tuck away that possibility and get on with surviving this assault with their bodies and limbs intact.

"Promise me one thing," Lyudmila said abruptly.

Evan looked at her.

"Ionescu is my responsibility. I arranged his exfiltration, after all. But from here on out I can't keep my eye on both him and Timur."

"You want me to take care of the boy."

"This is my wish, yes."

"All right, but I'm not so good as a babysitter."

"You did just fine with your sister's children," Lyudmila pointed out. "You saved them when no one else could."

Evan saw no point in continuing to object. She bobbed her head in acquiescence.

At length, they reached the end of the junipers. Peering out, Evan saw three figures—Tribe, Ionescu, and Timur—huddled under the shelter of the last palm before the volcanic scree began. This was what she had intuited, why the assailants had sprayed only the rear of the house with semiautomatic fire: they were acting as beaters, people in the hunt to flush out the prey and herd them in the direction of those who would shoot them dead.

Evan knew they couldn't go forward and there was of course no turning back. But they weren't trapped. Lifting her head, she caught Tribe's attention, made a whirling motion with her forefinger. He nodded, mouthed *Thank God for you*, took out his cell, and punched in what Evan knew must be the number of the helo pilot. Moments later, the engine coughed to life and the rotors started spinning. In the next instant, the side door slid open and she signaled for the trio up ahead to sprint to safety. At the same time, she stood up out of the last of the junipers, began to judiciously pepper the upper slope of palms with fire from the weapon she'd taken off the dead security guard. Unlike in films where the hero or villain just kept firing, she did so in short bursts, moving the muzzle in an unidentifiable pattern. As a result answering fire was sporadic and desultory.

Once Tribe and his charges, forearms over eyes squinting against wind and debris, clambered into the helo, she held her free hand out to Lyudmila and they began their perilous trek. The helo's rotors were at top speed; it was ready to take off at an instant's notice.

The firing became steadier and Evan had to keep turning to cover her and Lyudmila, who was limping along faster than Evan had imagined possible. The strand became pockmarked by bullets, but the zigzag route the two of them took kept them from getting hit, though some of the bullets came scarily close.

At the helo, Evan pushed Lyudmila up as helping hands from inside lifted her off her feet. Two shots hit the side of the helo. It was not a war machine; it wasn't designed to take gunfire. Evan turned and, with slitted eyes, blindly emptied what was left in the magazine into the palms. As she turned to the helo a bullet almost got her. She could feel the hot wind of the bullet's passage. The helo's racket was deafening.

Then she was inside and the pilot lifted off, ascending as fast as the machine would allow, pushing it to the very edge of its ability. The helo trembled and shook, taking more gunfire from below. Then it was peeling off to the left, riding over the volcanic overflow, which now had darkened in the sunset's waning aura. Night was creeping in, which could only help them while they were still in range of the semiautomatic fire. Now far less accurate the higher they flew.

Lyudmila had crawled over the seats and was huddled between Ionescu and Timur. The boy's eyes were wide and staring, his breath hot in his mouth, but to his credit he wasn't crying, he wasn't panicking. It was impossible to have a conversation over the noise, but Tribe smiled at Evan, squeezing her shoulder. It was the first time since she had come to work for him that he had touched her. Odd and somehow sad that it came at this moment.

Evan's cell buzzed against her thigh, and, taking it from her pants' pocket, she read with mounting alarm the long text from Ben: outlining the conversation An Binh had overheard at the Carat bar between George Wilson and Zahra, Wilson's sudden shocking death, Zahra's sequestering, the revelation that it was Wes Connerly, not Wilson, whom Zahra was traitorously in league with, and Connerly's subsequent confession that it was Tribe who had outflanked the bidders for the breakthrough of weaponizing time crystals by making a preemptive bid. She glanced up to see Tribe smiling at her, nodding. But had his smile changed subtly or had her perspective on him caused her to think so. Either way, she didn't want him touching her again.

She was about to punch in a reply to Ben when she heard a whine like an armada of wasps.

"Watch—!" was all she had time to say before the ground-to-air missile struck the central stem holding the rotors in place. The craft bellowed like an elephant in mortal pain. It shivered and shook. Without the rotors it canted over, lurched heavily, hurtled downward in its death spiral.

Below them, the volcano seethed, steamed, glowing evilly. It ran red as blood.

PART THREE

ACTUALIZATION

Quantum teleportation is a demonstration of what Albert Einstein fa-mously called "spooky action at a distance"—also known as quantum entanglement. In entanglement, one of the basic concepts of quantum physics, the properties of one particle affect the properties of another, even when the particles are separated by a large distance.

—extract from the National Science Foundation,
July 6, 2020

41

Rotten to the core. That's what Minister Darko Kusnetsov thought as he put as much distance between himself and the Kremlin as he could, as fast as he was able. *The Kremlin,* he thought, *is like an old man who never bothered to take care of his teeth and now in ones and twos they're falling out.*

The first thing he did upon entering his sprawling apartment was to shuck off the horrific black-and-gold uniform the Sovereign had had made for him and which he had insisted Kusnetsov wear before he left his presence. *"I want to see you,"* he had said. *"I want to finally see the real you."* Even off his frame the uniform emitted the distinct odor of fascism, something he'd never have believed was possible in the Motherland.

If Kusnetsov had harbored any doubts about the rumors going around in FSB circles about the Sovereign's health his scarifying visit with him today erased all of them. It was eminently apparent that the Sovereign was insane. Perhaps the illness that had come upon him during the eighteen months he was incommunicado, holed up with only a dozen doctors, had started to affect his brain, or maybe he knew his time on earth was fast running out. Either way, Kusnetsov knew, he was a menace not only to the Western world but to the Federation itself.

There was no way he, Kusnetsov, could stand idly by and allow the Sovereign's increasingly irrational actions to completely destroy Russia. For a brief moment he thought about going to the Duma, the lower house of the Russian Federal Assembly. Almost immediately he recognized the foolishness of the idea. The Sovereign had neutered the Duma's power some time ago. Those who disagreed with him were arrested on trumped-up charges or simply disappeared. As he dressed in jeans and an open-collar shirt, he wondered how many bodies would be found if the Moskva River were ever dredged.

He looked at himself in the full-length mirror on the inside of his closet door. No natty Italian suit, no French shirt and tie for him today.

That kind of outfit would stand out like a rose among weeds where he was going.

■   ■   ■

The ghetto of Chelobit'evo, approximately thirteen miles north of Moscow center, was inhabited largely by Muslims, immigrants for the most part from Dagestan or Chechnya, most of whom spoke Tajik or Uzbek, rather than Russian.

As a young man, a raw FSB recruit, Kusnetsov had been assigned to take care of a drug-smuggling ring there. He went with two experienced officers a decade older than he was. Apparently, "taking care of" the ring meant shooting them all to death, confiscating their drugs, and selling them back to the poor inhabitants of Chelobit'evo at a price substantially higher than what they were used to paying. "The price of doing business," the older agents had told their buyers over and over again. Afterward, they offered Kusnetsov a tenth of their take. He returned alone later that night and distributed the funds to those most in need.

No trees, no medical clinics, no mass transit, and for love or money not a parking spot to be had. He did, however, drive past a Fix Price where everything cost ninety-nine rubles, several low-end groceries whose shelves were nowadays mostly empty, three "alcomarts" selling cheap liquor, the shops dotted amid monolithic apartment blocks erected with adulterated materials that cracked, split, and peeled six months to a year after they were built. The interiors, Kusnetsov recalled, reeked like a la-trine papered with rotting cabbage leaves.

In the distance he could hear kids yelling, calling to one another, taunting. Dogs took their heads out of overturned garbage cans to shoot him hostile looks as his car slowly rolled by. A pair of men of indetermi-nate age sat outside an alcomart, heads nodding, a line of empty bottles at their feet. Once in a while, a car would hiccough by, its engine wheezing like an asthmatic. Overhead what streetlights still worked sputtered on and off, unsure how close they were to death. Beyond, the sky seemed to phosphoresce, to have turned to liquid.

Hasan was waiting for him outside the halal butcher shop he owned. Hasan was a big man in every way—tall, wide, with a substantial belly that belied the speed and muscle he could bring into play at a moment's notice.

Kusnetsov drove up onto the sidewalk and parked. They greeted each other in the ritual way. Hasan's eyes, oily as black olives, sparkled in the light emanating from his shop. The harsh light made valleys of the creases and scars on Hasan's face.

"My friend," Hasan said in a low voice. He handed over a small packet. "Very difficult to get."

"Isn't everything these days."

"But this . . ." Hasan smacked his lips. "Very, very difficult." He gave Kusnetsov a price.

"What? You're robbing me blind, Hasan."

"On the contrary, my friend, I have given you the friends and family discount."

Kusnetsov laughed softly, handed over a roll of bills, which Hasan pocketed so fast it was barely visible.

"By the way," Hasan said, "you are being followed."

"Indeed."

"One of yours?"

"Not to my knowledge."

"Say the word and I will take care of him."

Kusnetsov had no doubt that Hasan would; he'd seen him in startling action. "Ah, no, Hasan, I have other plans for him." He set off with Hasan by his side. "Let's take a detour to Miryam's."

Hasan's face lit up like a will-o'-the-wisp. "Now there's a plan I can get behind. Remember the Katzenjammer Twins?"

"Is that what we called them?"

"Sure."

"Right. How could I forget?"

Hasan sighed. "Those were the days."

When Kusnetsov threw him a look he just laughed.

Here in the ghettos, nowadays off limits to the police, no crime was ever investigated, no offense reported. The ghettos of Moscow were worlds unto themselves. Muslims and non-Muslims alike frequented the alcomarts and places like Miryam's.

There were other brothels in Chelobit'evo, but none more renowned and certainly none as good. Despite her surroundings Miryam was a stickler for cleanliness and peace. Any patron who caused a fight or abused her girls was summarily kicked out, banned for life. Her place of business was fronted by a pawnshop trading in openly stolen goods. The proprietor was also open to providing personal loans at outrageously usurious rates. It was not unusual for one of his hired goons to go after deadbeats and fuck them up royally.

Miryam, with the selective blindness of pragmatism, ignored the goings-on at the front of her house. Her attention was wholly on her own domain—two floors of perfumed idylls for which her repeat clients scrimped and saved in order to forget their troubles, at least for one night.

Walking through the pawnshop, they passed cases of handguns, AR-15s, and other assorted assault weapons lit up by the hideous overhead fluorescent glare. In the rear of the shop a plain metal door opened onto a deliciously dim parlor straight out of the British 1880s, complete with velvet love seats, mahogany side tables, lamps with fringed shades. An ersatz fireplace was set into one wall, flanked by a pair of awful paintings of a horse race and a stag at bay.

Miryam herself greeted them, and not merely because they were different from her normal clientele in every respect. She greeted all her clients herself. Miryam had a Pre-Raphaelite figure and a face like Francesc Masriera's painting of Salome, which was to say like something between a seductress and a warrior princess. She deliberately heightened the effect by wearing a long skirt of orange velvet that only partially covered her diaphanous undergarment.

"To what do I owe the pleasure, gentlemen," she said, her voice as well as her eyes full of mischief.

"We'd like to book Chama's room," Kusnetsov said, "if it's available."

Miryam grinned, showing a gold tooth that winked at them as if in collusion. "For you two, it's always available."

They vanished up the stairs but did not go far, turning and waiting for whoever was tailing Kusnetsov to make his appearance. It took a while—perhaps he had thought to wait outside but got antsy, or maybe he took the time to make sure Kusnetsov hadn't slipped out the back. In any event a man finally did push through the metal door, took a look around the parlor at the paintings, the fake fireplace, the two young women indolently entertaining their johns on the love seat, sniffed at the air redolent with wafts of weed and opium. They could see his face darkening with righteous rage. As he stepped up to intimidate Miryam, Kusnetsov tapped Hasan on the shoulder, whispered, "You're on."

At once Hasan came barreling down the stairs, calling out, "Is this jerk bothering you, Miryam?"

"I can take care of myself," Miryam huffed.

"Not with me, you can't." The man brandished a Glock 17, pushed the muzzle into her face, making her back up so Kusnetsov, standing in the shadowed staircase, was positioned just behind the man.

Hasan gave it his best shout. "You can't fucking threaten her like that!"

As the man turned his head toward Hasan, Kusnetsov leapt down the stairs, chopped down with the edge of his hand into the side of the man's neck where the nerve bundle was hidden under skin and viscera. The man went down as if he'd been poleaxed.

As he and Hasan hefted the man, Kusnetsov thanked Miryam.

"Always a pleasure," she said with a crafty smile. "One of these days maybe you'll think of the perfect way to pay me back."

■　■　■

Chama's room was upstairs, through the last door on the left. It was always empty now. After Chama was murdered during a break-in, Miryam didn't have the heart to give it to another one of her girls, even the new one she'd hired in Chama's stead. Chama had been one of Miryam's favorites. Hasan had felt the same way, which is why he'd enlisted Kusnetsov's help in finding the perpetrators—the Katzenjammer Twins, as they came to be called. The two of them lasted three days, after which the room had to be hosed down with bleach and aired out for a week.

This was where they brought the man who had been tailing Kusnetsov. They sat him in a sturdy wooden chair. Hasan leaned over him, flipped open a gravity knife, stuck the point of the blade into the man's left nostril.

"I saw this in *Chinatown*." He turned briefly to Kusnetsov. "You ever see *Chinatown*? No time, huh? Too busy being a good little apparatchik."

Kusnetsov let out a snort. Far from being offended, he knew this was part of the personal bantering that went on between them. They were ostensibly on opposite sides of the law—whatever could be called law, which morphed to suit the regime's purposes that week, day, hour. Often, they both had a good laugh over that sad state of affairs.

"So," Hasan continued, returning his attention to their prisoner. "This ought to wake our sleeping beauty up." Pushing the blade in deeper, he twisted it with a deft flick of his wrist.

Sleeping Beauty not only woke up but screamed, jerking his body so hard he almost toppled the chair over, so that Kusnetsov was obliged to slap him hard across the face to calm him down. Still, blood spattered the front of his trench coat, and his eyes rolled wildly in their sockets.

Then they locked on Hasan and narrowed. "What the hell d'you think you're doing, cockroach?"

Hasan lunged with the gravity knife but Kusnetsov grabbed his arm. "Wait," he said.

"That's right, cockroach, wait," Sleeping Beauty said with a sneer.

Hasan pulled away from Kusnetsov. *"Nu vse, tebe pizda."* *That's it, you're fucking dead.*

Sleeping Beauty laughed. *"Potselui mou zhopy, zasranees."* *Kiss my ass, shithead.*

Hasan hit Sleeping Beauty on the side of the head so hard the man moaned involuntarily.

"Who are you?" Kusnetsov said. "Why were you following me?"

The man's eyes came back into focus. He inhaled a string of saliva drooling from one corner of his mouth. "My name is Fyodor Kovalyov and I'm here under express orders from Colonel Ludovico Ferranov."

"Why the order?"

Kovalyov shook his body back and forth. The flaps of the trench coat slipped off his thighs and Kusnetsov flipped them away, revealing the uniform underneath.

Hasan bent forward peering. "What the hell is that?"

Kusnetsov stared at the black-and-gold uniform. "New regime," he said. And to Kovalyov, "No wonder you were tailing me."

"Colonel Ferranov was right. You're a degenerate, another cockroach like your Muslim pal. Look at you, rubbing shoulders with this fucking Chechen in a fucking whorehouse in this hellhole where no self-respecting Russian citizen would be caught dead."

Still keeping Hasan physically in check, Kusnetsov said, "Who is Ferranov to give you orders to follow me?"

"Ha! Well. Colonel Ferranov is now head of SVR, soon to be head of FSB." He cocked his head. "FSB used to belong to you, Minister Kusnetsov, if I'm not mistaken."

"It still does."

Kovalyov spat onto the floor. *"Ja Pycckij pidaras,* Kusnetsov." *You're a loser.*

At which point, the ruble dropped and Kusnetsov understood everything. His summons to the Kremlin, his very VIP afternoon with the

Sovereign, was nothing more than a ruse to get him away from FSB HQ, facilitating Colonel Ferranov's Sovereign-sanctioned purge.

"In fact, you are mistaken," Kusnetsov growled. "Very much so."

He knew Ferranov, but only by reputation. He had been handling GRU's Directorate KV ever since its inception five years ago. Transfers between GRU and FSB were virtually nonexistent, but as Kusnetsov had discovered these were strange days inside the Federation. Anything, it seemed, was on the table and likely as not to be deployed. He was inside a madman's universe and he could think of only one way to climb out. He might very well lose his life as a consequence, but what was his life now? He seemed to have been off-loaded into a particular kind of limbo, one of the Sovereign's own design. Being in it made him feel as if an army of fire ants was crawling over his body. The present was intolerable, therefore it either changed or he swallowed the indigestible requisites of the new regime.

"It's done, a fait accompli," Kovalyov said. "Colonel Ferranov has already been installed. Tomorrow morning the purge will be complete. And where does that leave you, Minister? In the dark, in the cold, in your own private Siberia."

Hasan glanced at Kusnetsov. "Is this prick telling the truth?"

"I'm afraid he is."

"Then what's to be done, my friend."

Kusnetsov appeared to be staring at Kovalyov's face but in fact his mind was very far away. "What indeed." All at once he seemed to snap out of it. "Let him go."

Hasan's eyebrows raised in surprise. "What? Really?"

Kusnetsov shot him a look and Hasan nodded. He led Kovalyov out of the room to the top of the stairs. "Go on now," he said. "Get out of here." And promptly kicked him in the small of the back.

Down below, on the ground floor, Miryam watched the body's ugly progress down the stairs. A burst of blood flew through the air as the head smashed into a corner wall. She smiled grimly and spat.

42

LA PALMA, CANARY ISLANDS

Blackout.

A flickering as in an old movie—scenes of childhood, of her and Bobbi holding hands, her leading Bobbi down and down into the caverns where she would leave her sister overnight. Now she was gripped by an overpowering desire to return to that night, find Bobbi, and bring her back home, trembling and shaking, whispering "Sorry, sorry, sorry" in her ear. Taking a different path, one they could have shared instead of the divergent paths they had taken—paths of lies, deceit, hatred, husbanded deep inside both of them. Until Bobbi's death.

The earth began to weep beneath Evan. Her ears were filled with a mournful wailing, a recognition of everything lost forever rushing through her, tearing her apart from the inside out . . .

The stench of sulfur and hydrogen sulfide, the taste of ash in the back of her throat jerked her into consciousness. And yet she was still not fully awake; her mind was still filled with children, her and Bobbi. Her lungs were not working correctly. She longed to go back there, to change what had already been set in stone. Something deep inside her did not want to suck in this tainted air, but her autonomic nervous system insisted on continuing its work—which meant breathing in the deadly fumes.

Groaning softly, Evan rolled over onto her back. Just that simple maneuver cost her far more than it should have. She cracked open her eyes, almost immediately shut them again as the dry overheated air caused her even more pain.

That same something inside her—the will to keep on living—caused her to inch back down the slope on which she was lying, to get away from the blast-furnace heat and the caustic fumes. She knew if she didn't she would surely perish within minutes.

She tried to remember what happened, why she was lying here on the upper slopes of the volcano, but she couldn't quite get the images to line up or to even make sense. She groaned again as she worked her way down, sliding and slithering. Once the sole of her left boot grew so hot it caught fire and she was obliged to stamp down, to move sideways away from whatever had caused her boot to flame up.

Too soon, she had exhausted herself and lay panting in the broiling heat. Sweat evaporated as soon as it broke out on her forehead, the nape of her neck, under her arms, and between her breasts. The roof of her mouth felt seared, the back of her throat clogged so badly with ash she began to choke, could not even get out a cough to clear the passageway. She turned on her side as vomit mixed with bile erupted out of her.

But with that she felt better. She was dry as a bone, knew she needed to hydrate as soon as possible. Turning her head to the right she saw the twisted fuselage of a helo. Whose? Of course, Tribe's. Like a shock of electricity going through her, memory leapt through the fog clouding her mind. She was in the body of the helo with Tribe, Lyudmila, Ionescu and his son, Timur. Up front, the pilot. Lyudmila had asked her to keep Timur safe. Where was he? Where was anyone?

Slowly, agonizingly she crawled toward the wreckage. She must have been thrown clear on impact, but what about the others. As she neared the helo she smelled hot metal, melted plastic, burnt rubber.

Upon reaching the wreckage, she saw that the fuselage was intact. That, surely, was a positive sign. Had it blown apart in the air or upon impact the others would be dead. Gasping, she pulled herself up on the sill of the open doorway; the door itself had been ripped off and lay about twenty feet up the slope, barely recognizable as molten lava contorted it into what might be a flower.

Inside, the helo was a wreck. The seats had been uprooted as if by a giant hand, squashed, warped, pulled apart. In the cockpit, the pilot's body was half out of his chair, his head partially through the bulbous front. Dragging herself to a wall so she could stand up, she saw a slim figure, all its limbs broken, the back of its head a bloody pulp. Tribe? She closed her eyes as a wave of dizziness took her away from herself. When she opened them she made her way along the Perspex wall, closing in on the body. The dead man was Ionescu. A constriction in her heart gave way and she gasped. Her head ached with conflicting emotions. Despite what she had just learned about him she had found herself desperate for the dead man not to be Tribe.

Pulling herself together, she peered anxiously around the cabin. No sign of Lyudmila, Tribe, or Timur, only an unopened can of Coke on the floor amid the still-warm debris of metal shards, broken wires, shattered electronics. She bent down to fetch it and almost passed out. A ridgeline of pain rose behind her eyes and almost felled her. Swiping the can, she rose slowly, steadying herself with one hand against the Perspex. Popped open the tab and swallowed greedily. The sugar rush combined with the caffeine to shove her exhaustion into the background, though she knew she'd pay for the emotional lift later. She was past caring about things like that. Head clearing, she made her way up front across the canted floor, unsnapped the pilot's holster, slid out his handgun—a Smith & Wesson Military and Police pistol with a polymer frame that made it light and highly maneuverable. She checked the magazine, saw that all seventeen bullets were available to her.

As she picked her way back across the cabin, she saw that the Perspex on the opposite side had been smashed to smithereens. The fuselage was steeply tilted in that direction. She made her way over until she had a clear view through.

The only thing that caught her attention was Lyudmila.

■   ■   ■

At first Evan thought that like her Lyudmila had been thrown clear of the helo, but as she clambered out, strings and smears of fresh blood made it clear that Lyudmila had crawled out of the wreckage.

Scrambling down, she reached Lyudmila, who was lying on her stomach. Kneeling beside her, Evan put a hand on her back. Immediately Lyudmila began to stir, and, sliding the S&W into her waistband, Evan gently turned her over.

Lyudmila's eyes opened slowly; they took their time focusing. When she recognized Evan, she said, "Not to worry, darling, the pressured dressing you tied is still in place."

An eerie night had fallen, shot through with the sinister radiance from the slowly crawling lava, the stinking gas, the bloody light of hell.

Lifting up her upper body, Evan tilted the Coke can to Lyudmila's lips. Lyudmila drank it greedily. She wiped her lips. "What, no vodka?"

Evan was about to laugh in relief when Lyudmila's face distorted in pain.

"It's nothing," Lyudmila said. "Ribs. Only hurts when I laugh."

"This really is some shithole you've led me into," Evan said.

"What I've been doing for the last five years." Lyudmila took a breath, let it out. "Now comes the reckoning." She lifted her head. "Listen, d'you hear it? That's a helo."

"Lyudmila, how badly are you hurt. Really."

Lyudmila shook her head. "Quiet. They're coming."

Evan gripped the butt of her pistol. "Who? Who set this up?"

"Only three entities could mount an assault with this kind of military precision: the CIA, Mossad, and Major Korokova. The CIA don't know I exist, and even if they did they'd want to pump me for intel, not kill me; Mossad knows me and leaves me strictly alone."

"That leaves Korokova."

"The one and only." Lyudmila turned her head back and forth, eyes clouding with anxiety. "Where are the others?"

"Ionescu and the pilot are dead."

"And Timur?"

"Wait. You don't care about Ionescu? He's crucial to the next phase of your plan, isn't he?"

Lyudmila smiled wanly. "I really do have to stop lying, even if it's just to you." She started to cough as a gust of wind blew volcanic steam over their heads.

"What d'you mean?"

"I don't care about Ionescu," Lyudmila said. "He was nothing more than a means to an end. I made sure that everyone—especially von Kleist—believed I needed to get Ionescu out of Russia. In fact, it was Timur I needed to rescue."

Evan's brow furrowed. "I don't follow."

"My grand plan, Evan, wasn't to try to assassinate the Sovereign—that was a pipe dream, it was never going to happen. This quantum weapon holds no interest for me. These were all ruses—diversions—to keep my real purpose secret."

"Even from me?"

Lyudmila closed her eyes for a moment. "I'm sorry, darling. Sorry for everything I put you through." She sighed. "You were my most successful diversion of all."

Evan sat back on her haunches. "So Timur . . ."

"I've been trying for five years to wrest my son away from . . ." She turned her head away.

All the breath left Evan; it took her a moment to recover.

"Who is his father? Not Ionescu, surely."

"No." Lyudmila returned her gaze to Evan. Her ice-blue eyes were clouded with opalescent tears. "His father had no time for him, you see. But he refused to give him up. Ionescu became his tutor—I made sure of this. The first step, you might say, to Timur's freedom."

"If not Ionescu, then who?"

"The Sovereign."

Evan could not help an indrawn breath.

"I know. It's fucking embarrassing. But I was a different person then. I wanted a child. I wanted to make sure he'd be protected so I went to the source of all protection in the Federation. How stupid could I have been."

"No comment."

Lyudmila huffed. "I told you that I was pushed out of the Politburo due to rumors of lesbian liaisons."

"That was a lie."

"Well, yes—and no."

They heard the crunch of thick-soled boots. There was very little time now and Evan took out the S&W, made sure it was ready to fire.

"When I threatened to take Timur he vowed to ruin me," Lyudmila continued. "The Sovereign had his people spread the rumor to humiliate me. To get me ostracized. By then I was too well-known for him to have me killed or disappeared. I had developed a network of powerful people. But when I wouldn't stop trying to take my son from him, then he did call for my incarceration. That was when I used my contacts to get myself exfiltrated, when I began my exile from Russia and Timur."

"So all of your scheming was in aid of getting him back."

"An excruciatingly long and winding road, I know. But I was up against the Sovereign. I had to remain patient while I spun my web in as many directions as I was able. I had to keep his people off-balance, guessing—and I had to keep myself and Timur safe. Any hint that I—"

A rush of anger flamed Evan's cheeks. "So you used me as a stalking horse."

"I prefer to think you're part of the plan. A key part. You were the best—the only way . . . You were the perfect distraction." Lyudmila reared up, grabbing onto Evan's now sleeveless shirt. "Do you think I don't love you? Do you think my heart didn't turn over every time I sent you into peril?" Her eyes grew large as moons. "But this is about my son. It's about Timur. And now . . ." She gulped air, coughed against the volcano's caustic effluents. ". . . now I don't even know whether he's dead or alive."

Evan felt guilty that she didn't know where Timur was, whether he had survived the crash. In Lyudmila's eyes she recognized the demented terror of a mother whose child is lost, and despite all of the strife her friend had put her through, still her heart went out to her.

"He's alive, I know it," Evan said with no little force. "We'll find him."

Lyudmila shook Evan with unnatural strength. "I had so little time with him. He has no father—of course he doesn't. The Sovereign thinks of him as another of his possessions, something in his rage he has denied me." Her eyes slid away for just a moment. "And for all these years since he was a baby he's had no mother. Only caretakers. He's been brought up by mercenaries, you might say."

Evan's heart broke for her friend. She held her tightly for a long moment, feeling Lyudmila's inner trembling.

"Promise me you'll keep him safe," Lyudmila whispered hoarsely.

"You're his mother. You'll keep him safe yourself."

"*Promise me, Evan.*"

Evan had always thought of Lyudmila as beautiful—as in runway-model beautiful, which was true—but now that beauty looked hollow, blasted. Haunted. Evan felt a hitch in her breathing. "You have my word."

"And if Korokova shoots you dead?"

"Trust me." Evan squeezed her shoulder. "You have before."

A powerful searchlight flicked on, just behind three figures cresting a ridge lower down from where Evan and Lyudmila crouched. They were armed to the teeth, their heads covered in gas masks to protect them from the noxious gases. They looked like giant blister beetles, filled with venom.

They unslung their weapons. Three long black fingers blacked out the dazzling light, falling across Evan and Lyudmila like cudgels.

"It is often said that the shadows of guns cause as much fear as the guns themselves," Lyudmila whispered as if to herself. "Until now I found no reason to believe that."

It was at this moment that Evan realized that the fire inside Lyudmila she had found familiar and comforting had gone out. In its place was a different fire, more intense, finely attuned only to her son.

43

The creaking of timbers, the soft lapping of the water had lulled Zahra to sleep after Ben and the accursed An Binh had left her in the houseboat, but the nearby screeching of tires woke her with a start. She was tied to a much-worn wooden chair with cord as, apparently, the houseboat wasn't equipped with twist ties. Rocking the chair back and forth, she went over on her side hard. The old wood of the chair splintered. Grasping a saw-toothed piece in her hand, she levered it under the cord's knot, twisting it until the knot gave. Freed, she sawed through the knot at her ankles, scrambled to her feet.

Peering out one of the landward windows, she could see two suits piling out of a black sedan, heading out along the dock toward her, the pounding of their thick-soled shoes like the drumbeats of an enemy legion. She knew by the cut of their suits and the cut of their jib that they were FBI agents come to fetch her.

Without another thought she crossed to the water side, opened a window, and slithered out, down the hull of the houseboat, into the Washington Channel, a fairly narrow two-mile-long waterway that separated the Southwest Waterfront area from the man-made East Potomac Park, paralleling the Potomac River beyond the park. Normally, she would not have cared for the cold, but at this moment it served to wake her fully, sweep away the cobwebs, sharpen her mind.

Plunging under the surface, she struck out for the park on the far shore, holding her breath, husbanding her oxygen supply. She was strong, opting for two-hour workouts at five every morning; she had learned how to defend herself on rough streets, how to get by with two or three hours' sleep. Still, the channel's current was swift enough that despite her best efforts she was thrown off course. She came up holding a line securing a sailboat to its mooring. Head half out of the water, regulating her breathing, she watched as the government agents scoured the houseboat's interior for a clue as to whether she had actually been there and if so where she had gone. Watching them moving behind the houseboat's windows, bewildered and then growing angry at being stymied, was as entertaining as binge-watching *Stranger Things*.

"Your world is entirely self-directed," An Binh had said to her. *"That's a boon to people like me who are part of a shared vision."*

"Fuck you and the broom you rode in on," Zahra whispered just before she started to slip back into the water. She gasped, tried to haul herself up, but the rope was slippery and she could not maintain her grip with her cold-numbed fingers. Her legs flailed, and she began to panic, her breaths coming in short, sharp bursts. She closed her eyes in a vain attempt to stop the tears from welling up. *So close,* she thought. *I was so close to having it all.*

I don't want to die.

She must have said it out loud; a male voice above her replied, "You're not going to die."

Her eyes flew open, she looked up into the twilight to see a strong arm reaching down for her.

"Here. Take my hand." The fingers wriggled like eels. "Come on now. Up you go."

As if in a daze she reached up. As soon as she did so the hand grasped her forearm in a powerful grip, lifted her out of the water as if it was no effort at all.

He sat her on the gunwale of the sailboat. "Wait here," he said. She did. Shivering uncontrollably. In a moment he returned with a blanket, wrapped it tightly around her as if swaddling an infant.

"There," he said. "That's better."

He went to the cockpit, opened a locked door under the wheel and electronic navigation equipment. Brought back a bottle and two plastic glasses. "Nothing like bourbon to get your core temperature up, right?" He poured, they both drank. She winced but as the liquor flamed down her throat she felt the spark of life returned to her.

"I'm very grateful," she said, and meant it. "My name's Daisy."

"As in Daisy Mae?"

She laughed as if she'd never heard that joke before. "Not quite. But I'm flattered."

"Well, I'd have to see you in those cutoffs to be sure."

Now he was flirting with her; she liked that.

"I'm Rob, first-class sailor," he said. "But to be serious, what happened to you? Why were you floundering around in the water?"

She thought fast; she was a wiz at that. "A fight with my boyfriend, if you can believe that."

"Must have been some fight." He topped up their glasses. "Tell me about it."

She shrugged. This was something she didn't want to get into. The devil was in the details, and the more detailed your lie the greater the chances of getting tripped up. When it came to lying, she had learned early, the watchword was Keep It Simple, Stupid. "He was being an asshole one too many times," she said, taking another sip of bourbon, getting to like its burn. "I jumped ship, as it were."

"Abusive?"

"Uh-huh."

"Physical?"

"Hit me in the stomach with an old phone book he kept around."

"So ex-cop."

She shrugged again. "I'd rather not . . ."

Rob nodded. "Sure. Of course. Sorry."

"Nothing to be sorry about." She let the wrap of the blanket loosen around her front, revealing cleavage. Her wet shirt clung to her body. She never wore a bra.

His eyes traveled down to the V she had formed especially for him. "We ought to get you out of those wet clothes."

She gave him a look somewhere between cruel and seductive. Men loved that; like a dog to a whistle they knew who their masters were. She made herself shiver. "Let's see how else I can get warm." It was four hours to midnight, more or less. There were worse ways to idle away the time.

■   ■   ■

Three hours later, Rob dropped her off in front of the L'Enfant train station in Northern Virginia. He'd no doubt assumed she was taking a train to Manassas. She still had to wait an hour, but she'd grown bored with Rob and urged their departure earlier than she had expected.

"I'll dream of you in my clothes," he said through the open window of his car.

Either she didn't hear him or didn't want to hear him.

Fifty minutes later, the black SUV flicked its lights twice just before it pulled in to the curb beside her. She heard the door locks disengage and climbed into the plush backseat. The car was scheduled to be there every night at midnight beginning on the day that Bill Fineman died until Zahra was able to find a foolproof way to leave her job without causing questions. There was always the chance that she would be picked up and interrogated, which is why the rendezvous with the SUV continued night after night until she arrived, because nothing worked to plan in DC, especially not during a crisis.

As the SUV headed away from the station, she opened the manila envelope. Out poured two thousand dollars, a burner phone, a driver's license and passport under the name Daisy Mae Miller. No credit card, of course. Too easily traced. At least they didn't use Smith or Brown, she thought wryly. She could afford to be wry now; she was safe. She laughed, put the money, the phone, and the docs away. She was wearing Rob's clothes, which were too big for her but she had rolled up the cuffs of the chinos and the cuffs of the white shirt he'd been wearing, which gave off the scents of light sex-sweat and Tom Ford Ombré Leather. The problem had been shoes. Rob had solved that by stuffing newspaper in the toes of a battered pair of his Nikes. A jean jacket of his completed her disguise. All things considered, she thought, it wasn't half bad. Already her sweaty hours with him were part of someone else's life.

■ ■ ■

She was a clever child, such a precocious wunderkind she annoyed her father to no end. In fact, she enjoyed annoying him so much that finally, and against her mother's wishes, he hired her out to an elderly man, a professor emeritus in Göttingen, the German city in which they lived. Because he was a professor he agreed to pay her father more than he could get for her anywhere else. She was seven. It wasn't until three years later that the professor, in a fit of pique, told her that she had been sold to him. During the day he beat her, enjoyed it as if he were inflicting real pain. She accepted this time-honored male behavior as the cost of learning a series of disciplines with which she instantly fell in love. The old man was a professor in physics, an acolyte of Max Planck and the groundbreaking theories of energy quanta for which Planck won a Nobel Prize. At night, while the old man's snores resounded through the house, she would creep into his vast library and one by one absorbed his books on mathematics—algebra, geometry, trigonometry, all the applied maths, including calculus. These years of unique intimacy and intense study eventually, inevitably, led her to physics, both theoretical and experimental, and finally to quanta and quantum physics. She was surprised the morning she turned sixteen when he told her he was adopting her. He had many powerful friends, one of whom was a judge, who gave her the professor's family name, and because she asked for it, rechristened her Anna. By the time she was eighteen she had far outstripped Max Planck. By this time, the old professor had died, leaving her his entire estate, larger than she had imagined, with many real estate holdings. Within a month she had sold everything.

Moving to Poland, she sought out experts whose fathers had been in the East German Stasi. For the right amount of money they created another new identity for her. With this name and background she took entrance exams for several universities, stunning her elders, creating what amounted to a bidding war for her mind. Elated, she chose the most prestigious institution, achieving the highest grades. Upon her graduation, the quantum world was her oyster.

At length, she arrived in America as Zahra Planck, a grand plan already forming in her head.

■   ■   ■

Forty-five minutes after entering the SUV, she was seated in the plush leather seat of a slim private jet. She was the only passenger. Just before takeoff, she punched in a number on the phone. She could have made the call earlier, while she was in the SUV, but her MO was always to make them wait, especially if they were men. Men required an interval of anticipation to really get their juices flowing.

"I'm on the runway," she said when she heard his voice at the other end. "Time to take care of Connerly before the feds break him."

Without waiting for a reply, she closed the connection, put her seat back despite the requisite command not to do so during takeoff. Fuck that. She felt the thrumming beneath her as the jet picked up speed along the runway. The thrumming gathered between her thighs like a pool of warm slippery liquid. Eyes closed, she rubbed her thighs together, sighing. And then they were aloft.

Ten minutes later, while he was in the supposed safety of federal custody, Wes Connerly's head exploded from the inside out.

44

"Red and black," Evan said. "We need to stay in the red and the black." Meaning, stay out of the white glare of the searchlight. It was looking for them, that much was a certainty, a part of Major Korokova's military action.

Lyudmila had hardly nodded before Evan half-dragged her back and up into Tribe's ruined helo.

"We'll be safer here," Evan said.

"Not for long," Lyudmila replied. "You know that as well as I do."

"You're a pessimist? Now?" Evan said to lighten the dire straits they were in. But as she moved through the helo's interior looking for anything in addition to the pilot's pistol she and Lyudmila could use as a weapon it seemed to her as if time slowed down, got lodged behind her eyes. She had the distinct sense that while she and Lyudmila were moving, no one else outside the helo had taken a step, as if the three figures were stuck in hardened lava, motionless.

But then one of the gas-masked figures stuck the blunt snout of an AKS-74U assault rifle into the interior. Lyudmila lunged, tearing the weapon out of their hands, while Evan slammed the back of their head with the pistol butt. Together they hauled them into the helo.

Evan flipped the body over, tore off the gas mask.

"So sure, one of hers," Lyudmila said. "I have a record of all her people. He's 29155."

As Evan well knew, Spetsnaz Unit 29155 was a part of GRU special forces dedicated to foreign assassinations and the destabilization of enemy countries.

Lyudmila grunted. "Bugrov here was part of the team that poisoned Sergei Skripal, the double agent for MI6, and his daughter several years ago."

"Sounds about right from what Inessa's told me about Korokova."

Evan began to strip off Bugrov's clothes.

"What are you doing?"

"What does it look like? I'm going out there dressed in his outfit."

"There's only one," Lyudmila said.

"Please. Not in your condition." She hadn't expected Lyudmila to go but wasn't surprised that she wanted to. She looked up and saw her scrounging around in lockers whose doors had been sheared, twisted, or melted off.

"Look what I found." Lyudmila held up the object.

"Shades of *A Fistful of Dollars*."

Lyudmila shook her head.

"It's a Hollywood thing."

"If I have my cultural references right that's what we need now," Lyudmila said as she watched Evan layer up in the assailant's clothing. "A Hollywood ending."

Evan grinned as she pulled on Bugrov's thick socks, the heavy boots, doing her best to ignore the stink. She said, "I want you to know I forgive you." Lyudmila looked up at her. "For all the lies, the deceit. For everything."

"Look at you." Lyudmila gestured at Evan's wounds, bruises, contusions. "I never wanted you to be hurt."

"I know that."

"I don't regret using you."

"I know that too." Evan turned to her friend. "Without you I never would have met my birth parents."

"And without you I never would have been able to get Timur out of Russia. Time and again you provided the diversion that allowed me to work at prying Timur from the Sovereign."

Evan picked up the gas mask, about to put it on. "But we've been through this before."

"Not really. Not completely. Not here at the end."

"Please don't say that, Lyudmila."

Lyudmila's eyes narrowed; she put her hands on Evan's shoulders. "You know that I love you. You're the sister I wish I had."

Evan shook her head. "Now's not the time."

Lyudmila took a step toward her. "If not now, when?"

They stared into each other's eyes for what seemed a long time but might only have been a second or two.

Lyudmila unearthed something long held tightly deep inside her. "There's something else you should know—"

But Evan had already slipped on her gas mask and now stepped out the way Bugrov had come in.

45

Kata was standing in the shadowed doorway across the street from the kiosk within walking distance of FSB headquarters where she and Comrade Director Baev would have their clandestine meetings. Baev had been her boss when he was head of the SVR. He and Kusnetsov had been frenemies, accent on the latter, and he had tried to pull Kata into his schemes to bring Kusnetsov down. It was through Baev that Kata maneuvered her way up the FSB food chain. It wasn't difficult. Baev was in love with her and she had done enough to keep him on the hook without ever giving him what he most desired. In a frenzy of frustration he had gone from one mistress to another, wrecking their lives completely without compunction. As for his wife, he had lost interest in her years ago; even when he was in her presence, his thoughts were on Kata. He would have done anything to please her.

Now Baev was either dead or worse. In any case out of the picture.

Kata stood still as a statue, gazing fixedly at the kiosk that like many other businesses in Russia was shuttered, its starkness glaring in the streetlights. Behind it, on the far corner, had been a branch of an insanely popular American fast-food chain. After the Americans pulled out, a Russian entrepreneur had bought the empty store and installed his idea of a Russian knockoff. From the absence of customers it was clear no one was interested in the imitation; they wanted their Big Macs with good American meat.

"Missing Baev?"

She did not even turn to look at Kusnetsov.

"We used to come here, share a packet of warm chestnuts."

"And talk."

"From that kiosk across the street."

"Those days are gone forever." He jammed his hands into the pockets of his coat. "It's good you came."

"The decision wasn't an easy one. I no longer have a directorate." She gave him the side-eye. "When you called I had to hazard a guess as to which side you were on."

He was wearing a double-breasted charcoal-gray astrakhan coat with oversized black leather buttons. "I'm on the side of trying to survive the hash the Sovereign is making of the Federation."

"I was told you were with him earlier."

"That's true enough." Snow was starting and Kusnetsov shivered a little, but not evidently from the cold. "Now he's making noises about 'liberating' Poland." The snow, picking up the soot of the city, swirled gray as ashes from a crematorium. "He's well on his way to destroying us."

"With these black-uniformed storm troopers?"

"Among other increasingly insane notions."

"Those sigils they wear on their shoulders."

"The ancient Nordic rune *hagall*—havoc."

"Lovely," Kata said. For a moment she seemed lost in thought. "To answer your question, yes, Baev and I talked regularly off the grid."

"About me, I assume."

"Mainly," Kata replied.

"It must've been hell being friends with both of us."

She could not decipher his tone. "It wasn't easy; it wasn't particularly hard either."

"Not for you, anyway," he said dryly.

She decided to move on. "Running the SVR wasn't enough for him. He wanted your position."

"These days who the hell knows what my position is."

"I assume then you've met Colonel Ferranov."

Kusnetsov grimaced. "I haven't had the pleasure."

"A pleasure only a masochist would enjoy."

"That bad."

"Worse." Kata turned to him. "He's like a whipworm."

Kusnetsov's eyes narrowed. "What the hell is that?"

"It's like a tapeworm only more frightening. The female lays thousands of eggs in your intestines."

"Well, then," Kusnetsov said, "we've got to get that fucking whipworm out of the system."

"Really?" She put her fists on her hips. "And how d'you propose to do that?"

"Not me. Ferranov will make sure I won't be able to get within ten feet of him. Besides, I have to be elsewhere." He dug in the pocket of his astrakhan, brought out a ring with an enormous square-cut emerald. It was the one that Kata had taken off her namesake when she had killed her. The original Kata Romanovna Hemakova, a fearsome assassin of the first rank whose name Kata had taken several years ago, used that very ring to slit her targets' throats. He held it out to her. "But you—you've met him. He's already lording it over you."

"He dissolved my directorate—the one you created for me."

"Irrelevant. You're on a new path now."

"And what happens after? I get shot by three or four of his black-uniformed goons?"

"Leave that to me."

She gave him a level gaze. "So it's a matter of trust."

"It's always been a matter of trust." A thin smile played across his lips. "But I like you, Kata. Very much. We understand each other, don't we? So I'll tell you this much: I've made a deal with the devil. Two years gestating."

"In my experience," she said, "making a deal with the devil is never wise."

"Ah, but at least this is *my* devil."

At this, she acquiesced, and why not? She very much wanted her shot at Colonel Ferranov, fuck you very much. If this was what Kusnetsov was offering her, she was bound and determined to grab it with both fists. First step: she took the ring from him.

"Make it last, will you?" he said.

The ring—Kata's ring, the emerald of violence and death—felt heavier than she remembered, heavy as a Valkyrie's battle-axe.

46

The impact with the silica-laced basalt hit Evan hard, the force of it magnified by her wounds, juddering from her knees through her whole body, setting a new round of pain streaking through her. She released the pain through a steady hiss between her teeth, then moved off from the ruined helo.

She turned, hating the loss of peripheral vision the gas mask caused her, but she couldn't afford to take it off. For the moment, at least, she needed the edge that being hidden from Korokova and her people lent her.

Her first order of business was to shoot out the damn spotlight; she wanted to set the landscape back to its eerie black and red. This she did with precision, down on one knee, her right wrist steadied by her left forearm. But she paid for it. A shout echoed off the side of the helo and she heard the shots an instant after a plume of pumice spattered her thigh. She felt the heat of the bullet's passage even through Bugrov's uniform.

She spun rather than rising up, squeezed off two precious shots in the direction of the soldier who had fired at her. Then she moved, bent over, taking short, quick strides that would allow her to zig and zag as needed. Moving very fast, she leapt over one fissure after another, the heat instantly agonizing, but at least the gas mask allowed her to move freely through the eruptions of toxic smoke. She came at the sniper from the side, saw him sprawled on his stomach, the barrel of his rifle perched on an outcrop of basalt, a ridge that snaked downward from his aerie. Slowing her pace, she crept up on him. Gripping his gas mask as he began to thrash, she ripped off the canister in front, pushed his face down into the ridge of basalt. Again and again until his face was a bloody pulp. She pulled his rifle out from under him, moved off to her left until she sighted another of Korokova's Spetsnaz cadre who was following Bugrov's line straight toward the rent opening in the helo, probably wondering what happened to him. Evan sighted, put two bullets in his back. The dual impacts jerked him forward, smashing his head into the torn lip of the opening.

Now to find Major Korokova. A good thought, but as almost always happens in the field good thoughts evaporate in the space of a heartbeat. Up on one knee and in the process of rising to her feet, she heard a soft clatter behind her and, whirling, saw a figure holding a pistol on her.

"Hardly Bugrov, scarcely Dmitry," the figure said in a voice muffled by her mask. "You might be a good shot, but you're too fucking short."

The figure squeezed the trigger. One, two, three. Evan felt the impacts in her chest, deeper reverberations that sent a numbing kind of shock as she stumbled backward. Her fall seemed to go on forever.

47

Afterward, Kata had no taste for going back to HQ. Besides, the intel on Ferranov that Kusnetsov had sent to her phone gave her six hours. *"Timing is everything,"* Kusnetsov had told her. So instead of retracing her steps she turned left at the corner, headed for a small park some three blocks distant. What had been snow was for a time sleet and now rain, pattering on her shoulders, the sidewalk, the streets where vehicles hissed in their passing, when they weren't at a standstill. Another of Moscow's endless traffic jams.

She could have stopped at a café, but for some atavistic reason she felt the need to be out in the open. As an adult that ancient inner voice had served her well, and she followed it now. The park was small, almost always empty despite the red plastic children's slide at one end. There was something ineffably sad about that abandoned spiral—UV-resistant, rust- and decay-proof—a signifier for the sad state in which Russia and Moscow in particular found itself. She felt as if the country were drowning, going down for the last time. But was it much better in America, where she had spent her formative years? It came as something of a surprise to her that she had accepted the FSB offer to defect as the most effective way to hide— hide from the husband she had come to despise, from the children she had never wanted, from the DC inner circle that was suffocating her. She had thought of Russia as an adventure—a brave new world where she could start her life over. But it had turned out to be the same damn thing—a society whose rules were unbendable let alone unbreakable. Inside FSB she had thought she would be beyond the law—but FSB had its own set of laws, within which she found herself trapped. With the world burning there was nowhere to go where she would be free of her past, her memories of her sister. Every moment of her life she was haunted by Evan, by how both of them had screwed up their childhood. How they had never been there for each other, never sisters to one another. Shit! She turned her face skyward. The rain had morphed back into snow, large watery flakes landing on her cheeks like tears.

She entered the park and felt immediately calmer. The space was special to her. It was here in this out-of-the-way space that she often met Alyosha Ivanovna to be together without being observed, judged, ostracized, hated, with a judgmental stare, a swift turn of the head.

Tonight a lone figure sat on a bench near the slide—a man of indeterminate age, the collar of his greatcoat turned up around the lower half of his face. Though his head was down as if he was staring at the pavement between his feet, there was something familiar about him. Kata paused. It was the way he held his head.

Slowly, hands in the pockets of her coat, she crossed the park, sat down on the bench he occupied—not close, but not far away either.

"I suppose I should be surprised to see you here," she said as she stared straight ahead at the red plastic slide, "but in fact I'm not." When he made no response, she said, "I imagine you've spent enough time with Major Korokova."

"Too much time." Rodion's voice was rough, hoarse as if he had been shouting for a long time.

"Corrupted, are you?"

This dragged a laugh out of him, but it had a ragged edge. Buried in there somewhere was a sob. "Only in the worst way."

She waited for him to go on. The snow fell, thickening like paste.

"You've become her messenger now."

He turned his head, looked up into her face. "Alyosha Ivanovna needs to pay for your sins."

Kata felt a deep-seated chill like ice-slicked iron slide through her. "Is that how she put it?"

"She's enraged. She and Ferranov. She gave me an ultimatum. Kill Alyosha Ivanovna or be killed."

Kata ignored that. "Where is the major?" She made to rise, but Rodion put a hand on her forearm. She stared at it and he withdrew it immediately.

"She's not here, not in Moscow. She flew out yesterday."

Kata subsided, perched on the edge of the bench. "Where?"

"She didn't tell me, but I sneaked a look at the flight plan. La Palma. Canary Islands."

"What is she doing there?"

"Where is Alyosha Ivanovna?"

Kata sat back. "Safe from you, anyway."

Rodion sighed. "There's no way out of this—not for me, not for you, certainly not for Alyosha Ivanovna."

"I love her, Rodion. She's the first person I've loved since I lost my sister—and that was a long, long time ago."

"Still . . ."

"You cannot have her, Rodion."

He closed his eyes. "It seems I can't have anything."

A movement on his left side—the side away from her—alerted her. Jumping up, she moved in front of him. He was holding a pistol to his temple.

"Rodion. What the hell d'you think you're doing?"

"You know," he said. "You understand."

Like a snapped whip her hand reached out, gripped the barrel of the pistol. For a moment or two, they fought each other, the muzzle of the gun moving one way or the other, a life-or-death tug-of-war.

The snow continued to fall; the city sounds were muffled, then ceased to intrude upon the park altogether. At that moment across from them a child and his mother hand in hand entered the park. The mother could not see the silent struggle between Kata and Rodion. She smiled at them, said, "I know it's late, but it's his birthday. He's too excited to sleep and I don't have the heart to reprimand him." Her smile faded. "His father promised him a ride on this slide where he used to take him in summer."

They came closer, and Kata moved to block the weapon from their sight.

"His father is gone. Another woman. Forgotten all about his son, so now . . ." She shrugged, pointed at the slide.

Kata and Rodion watched as her son climbed the ladder, kicking aside the thin layer of snow that had accumulated on each tread. When he reached the top he looked back at his mother.

"Go on, brave boy," she said.

Her son, solemn as a judge, nodded almost imperceptibly, let go. Down he went along the spiral, pushing the snow before him. When he reached the ground he laughed and his mother laughed with him.

Kata felt the loosening of Rodion's muscles and she took the pistol from him, palmed it into her pocket.

The mother frowned. "Is something the matter? Are you two all right?" She colored. "Excuse me for prying but I could sense the tension from here. Please be all right." Her face seemed a manifestation of the loneliness inside her. "Whatever you two have you must fight for it. I didn't and now . . ." Her voice drifted off, her gaze returning to her son.

Kata could not help reflecting that this woman's very real sorrow seemed to put her concerns in perspective. Whatever her problems she would never experience the sadness crushing this woman, and that was a good thing, wasn't it? Once, she was perfectly sure, now not so much. She thought of her children, whom she hadn't seen in five years, and a strange and terrible pang went through her.

"You see, the thing is," the mother said, "I never really saw him until after he left. I didn't imagine he could betray me like that but he had it in him all along." She lifted her hand, let it drop. "Oh, I don't know why I'm telling you all this. Two strangers in a park in the snow. On my son's birthday." Her hand lifted again, fell. "But you know sometimes it's easier talking to strangers. Strangers never seem to judge you or if they do it doesn't matter because you'll never see them again." She gave them more of a smile, but it must have tasted bitter on her lips. "Apologies. Again."

"None needed," Kata said.

The mother turned, looking at her son climbing the slide again. He slid down with an exuberant yell. His cheeks were pink with life. "I remember being here as a little girl," she said, her tone wistful. "I loved the slide. It was metal then. It rusted and fell apart." She went to her boy, scooped him up, lifted him to her shoulder. "Come," she said to him. "Now it's time for bed." They began to move off, back the way they had come.

"Good luck," the mother said to them over her shoulder.

Kata nodded. "Better days," she said, and much to her astonishment meant it.

"Happy birthday!" she called cheerfully to the boy as he and his mother departed.

He turned his head, grinned at her, his face already a white oval, dissolving into the night.

Rodion stood up. He was quite close to her. For a time they said nothing. Then, "What will become of me now?" he asked.

There was only one answer she could think of. "Come home with me." Only one answer that mattered. "We'll find a way out together."

48

Right here, in the very spot where Evan lay on her back, the heat and smoke would have killed her had she not been wearing the Spetsnaz outfit and gas mask. As it was, she lay stunned into immobility. She found herself staring up into the face of Major Juliet Korokova. She seemed huge, built like an Amazon. Her naked face, however, was as stunned as Evan felt.

"Who the hell are you?" Korokova staggered backward. "How are you still alive? I pumped three nine-millimeter bullets into your chest."

Evan felt her heartbeat return to its regular rhythm; her breathing, temporarily interrupted by a second or two of blackout, resumed oxygenating her system. She knew she had to gather herself, to regain her feet as quickly as possible, to take advantage of Korokova's shock. She rose, keeping the trembling in her thighs under strict control, and as she did so a providential geyser of carbon and sulfur dioxides erupted just to the right of where Korokova stood. The major's arm went up reflexively while her other hand scrabbled to bring her gas mask down over her face.

In that moment of chaos, Evan launched herself, every muscle in her body screaming, the places where the three bullets had struck the tactical body armor that Lyudmila had found and that Evan had strapped on under Bugrov's outfit screaming like hell, as if a red-hot poker had been laid to them. But that was all in her body. Evan had shifted her awareness to her mind. Her body was simply taking orders, working strictly on muscle memory.

Evan's leading shoulder struck Korokova full in the chest, sending her hurtling backward onto a cross-ridge, which would have knocked the air out of every one of her cadre still alive. Not Korokova; she was made of sterner stuff. Though coughing, she was taller, heavier, and stronger than Evan.

From her position flat on her back she slammed the hard canister of the gas mask across Evan's already swollen cheek. Blood spurted as a cut opened up. Evan drove an elbow into the spot just below the major's sternum. Korokova's mouth opened spastically and Evan struck it so hard the back of the major's head slammed into the basalt.

They rolled over and over, each one trying to get into a dominant position. Closer and closer they came to a rivulet of lava, choking Korokova. With an animal cry she snatched off Evan's gas mask. Now they were both choking on the fumes, eyes watering, lungs laboring in the searing heat. Evan felt the moisture being sucked out of her face, the skin feeling tight, brittle, ready to crack apart like a thrown vase. Her throat tried to close up against the caustic sulfur dioxide, and she was assaulted by a nauseating vertigo. The ground seemed to tilt away from her; she felt herself falling, tumbling across the solidified lava field.

■   ■   ■

She must have blacked out then. The next thing she knew Korokova was on top of her, bearing down with her intolerable weight, her forearm across Evan's throat as she pushed her with her thick thighs along the basalt toward the twisting stream of superheated lava.

Evan could feel it on her hair, her scalp. A moment more and she would be fried to a crisp so quickly her flesh would start to melt before it caught fire, her blood literally boiling in her arteries and veins. A terrible, filthy way to die. She looked up into the major's eyes and saw in the red firelight the heady triumph of victory, the sure knowledge of causing an enemy's death, the pure pleasure of it.

She remembered her recent exchange with Lyudmila: *"But we've been through this before." "Not really. Not completely. Not here at the end."*

And here she was at the end, done in by this Amazonian bitch, the very person who terrified Lyudmila, who Lyudmila had sent her to kill. And now she really did forgive Lyudmila everything. She hadn't meant it before, not really, had said it because she thought it was what she was meant to say, because it was the right thing. But in this terrible moment everything between her and Lyudmila was reset, all the lies, the deceit, the scheming, crisped in this fiery, lethal landscape.

Part of her was burning; she could not tell which part but above her Korokova, with the strength of her outsize physique, had redoubled her effort to push Evan into the lava flow.

. . . here at the end . . .

And then Inessa's voice echoed in her mind: *"There's something else you should know about Korokova. She was shot just below her left shoulder; it never healed correctly. It's a weak spot."*

She had no leverage for a punch. Inches from the lava bubbling up from below she reached up, pressed her thumb into that soft spot just below the major's shoulder socket. Because of the outfit Korokova was wearing it shouldn't have meant much of anything, but in extremis Evan's strength was sevenfold, tenfold, for that moment when it counted most, almost superhuman.

Korokova cried out. As she tried to twist away from the deep-seated pain, Evan heaved her own torso from the hips, where her inner power resided. Dislodged, Juliet Korokova was briefly airborne before Evan, on her knees, hurled her forward, into the steaming lava.

The major's terrified scream was cut short as the skin of her face bubbled, peeled back, caught fire.

Evan sat back, pulled her gas mask back on, ignored the fumes, laced now with the revolting stench of broiling meat.

And so, you were wrong, Lyudmila, she thought. *It isn't over.*

49

Three in the morning was the best time to visit Directorate KV. This Colonel Ferranov knew, as did the physicists who toiled there. The directorate was housed in a gray Brutalist structure that to passersby looked like a bunker or a museum, had no signage on the outside or even a street number, just an anonymous door. The directorate ran pretty much 24/7; however, those inside were scientists, not soldiers. They needed their breaks, no matter what time of day or night it was, no matter what shift they pulled. Three A.M. was break time for the night crew, always had been.

Ferranov, striding through the string of labs, entered his office without anyone being the wiser. This was planned; this was necessary. Behind his desk, he brought out a satellite phone from within a double-locked bottom drawer.

He punched in one digit, listened to the hollowness of the line, the vague hisses and sputters as if the call was being routed through a ghostly dominion, which, in a way, was true. No one could hack these calls, though infrequently made. Ferranov saw to that.

The call went through and was answered at once.

"Where is the packet?" he said when the male voice on the other end answered.

"You haven't received it as yet?"

"No." Ferranov's elbows were planted firmly on his desktop, as if this aggressive posture could be transmitted across an ocean with his voice. "And I don't have the money I sent you either. I've paid for the packet. I want it sent now."

"The packet is in the mail."

Ferranov growled like an animal. "Don't be smart with me. Where is the packet with the formulae for the weaponized time crystals? I made a preemptive bid before your auction could start. I wired you the money, as instructed. Nothing has come back."

"That is a pity, Colonel. I do apologize."

"I don't give a shit about your apologies. They mean nothing to me."

"Again, a pity because that is all you're going to get."

"What?" Ferranov, apoplectic, jumped out of his chair. "Don't fuck with me. The end result for you won't be pretty."

"I am certain the result you have in mind is quite grisly, Colonel. But you won't find me. Not even your vaunted Spetsnaz will, this is my promise to you. My advice, forget all about the packet. You're not going to get it."

"I *will* kill you."

"Mm. I am certain you will try. But think of this, Colonel. Your money is lost. It is a great deal of money. How, I wonder, will you explain to your, er, superior its loss?"

"Fuck you." Ferranov paced around his office like a caged Bengal tiger. "I don't want your advice. I don't need—" But at that point he realized he was speaking to dead air.

He hit the button again. Nothing. And again, with the same result. "*Nu vse*—" He threw the phone against the wall. "—*tebe pizda!*" *That's it, you're fucking dead.*

It was at this moment that he caught a movement in the hallway just outside the door to his office. Was someone spying on him? Had they heard his side of the conversation? Intolerable. Whoever they were, he decided, they'd be dead too.

Taking a pistol from its polished black leather holster at his hip, he strode out into the hall. He turned this way and that. All he heard was the background hum of the electronics, the intermittent whirr of centrifuges, the imagined sound of neutrons being split apart. No voices, no footsteps. No one about.

What had he seen then? A specter? A floater in his eye?

A flicker at the periphery of his vision and he turned, his eyebrows raised.

"Captain Molchalin, what are you doing here?"

"I came to tell you that it's done," Rodion said. He'd never been good at prevaricating, but Kata was, and he was learning. "Alyosha Ivanovna is dead."

Ferranov's eyes narrowed. "Who?"

He doesn't even know her name, Rodion thought, all qualms wiped away. "Kata's inamorata."

"Ah, yes," Ferranov replied. "Well done, Captain. We may even decide to keep you around."

The last word was distorted, ended with a screech of shock and pain. A line of fiery agony extended from the back of his skull down his neck, between his shoulder blades, ending at his coccyx, causing him to arch his body. With a second cry of pain he whirled.

"You!"

Kata lifted the emerald ring, one corner of which dripped his blood. "You've made so many mistakes, Ferranov, they're beyond count. But the worst one was crossing me."

"You," he sneered. "You're nothing, part of the past. The new order is here. You're already dead, you just don't know it yet."

He lifted the pistol, finger already on the trigger. Kata's hand shot out like a snake. Instead of fangs, it was the corner of her emerald that opened the vein on the inside of his gun hand. He tried to squeeze the trigger but he'd lost control of his fingers. The pistol was useless. In frustration, he tried to throw it at her, but couldn't do that either. The weapon slipped from his frozen fingers, clattering to the floor.

"I have orders to make this last." Kata's eyes shone like marbles sent spinning through light. "What d'you think, Rodion? I defer to you."

Rodion's spine grew rigid. Even two days ago he would have hesitated, backed away, wanting to put as much distance as possible between himself and a thoroughly unpleasant part of the life he had chosen. The truth was that up until two days ago he had kept one foot outside this world, ready to panic-run at a moment's notice like a terrified rabbit. He had been afraid to commit to the crimes enacted here daily. But then, in the FSB morgue, Major Korokova had introduced him to another side of himself. It had been torture being made an accomplice to the horrific way she dispatched Morokovsky's corpse. Korokova was an animal; she had turned him into an animal, forced him to look inward at the worst parts of himself.

Afterward, Kata had introduced him to the ice, which he had mistakenly assumed would be to separate his mind from what at times his hands were required to do. But he was wrong. What was required of him was to unleash his mind, allow it to enjoy what at times his hands were required to do. Because of the torture Korokova had put him through, because of Colonel Ferranov's insidious intimidation, he found this transition surprisingly easy. Kata made him realize that he must be in or out, fully committed to her. As a result, ice now flowed through his veins.

His hands came up to the center of Ferranov's back, where Kata's lethal emerald had made its vertical slice. His fingernails dug into either side of the slice, and with a powerful jerk of both hands he ripped apart the colonel's hated black-and-gold uniform. Bits of skin and flesh adhered to the cloth, which was sticky with blood, making Ferranov shriek like a banshee. Rodion continued ripping and pulling until Ferranov was naked to the waist. He continued until there wasn't a shred of the uniform left above a ragged puddle around the colonel's ankles.

"Well," Kata said, staring into Ferranov's bulging eyes, "I guess we've got our answer, don't we, Colonel."

"Please," he whimpered, his entire body shivering as with the ague. "Please."

Kata lifted her chin toward Rodion. "What say, Captain? Thumbs-up or thumbs-down."

"Oppressors stripped of their power," Rodion said, "reveal themselves as cowards."

People were running down the hall in response to Ferranov's unholy yowls. The physicists, their break disturbed. Drowning in the mayhem, they stood immobile, rooted to the spot. Until Kata called out. Then they stepped back into each other, turned, and fled back down the hall. Doors slammed shut.

Rodion turned, saw a cadre of men, either huge as boulders or thin as scarecrows. All were muscular, however, and all appeared singularly focused.

"Who the hell . . . ?" he said, tensing.

"Relax," Kata said. "They're on our side."

Rodion's eyebrows shot up, but he made no further comment.

Kata laughed as the crew stalked past them; a private joke, then, Rodion thought. She was always full of surprises. The men spread out down the hall, kicking in closed doors to make sure none of the physicists and lab assistants communicated with the outside world.

"So, it's done, Ferranov." Kata's eyes grew dark. "Your brave new order has died in its infancy." She leaned in, smelling the stink of his fear. "I wanted you to see its death before."

"Before what?" He could scarcely get the words out.

Kata's smile was sharp as a scimitar. *"This."*

The emerald rose, sliced deeply from the right side of his throat to the other.

"Right." Stepping deftly away from the spurt of blood, the collapse of the body, she signaled to Rodion. "Let's go. Our work here is done."

Silence but for the machines continuing to do what they were programmed to do, unmindful of fear or pain or death.

50

Evan was engaged in what field agents euphemistically called "mop-up duty"—that is, killing the last of the people who had been hunting you down—when she heard the faint but unmistakable *thwop-thwop-thwop* of a helo's rotors though she could not yet see it. Hurrying now, she took down what her gyring sweeps had assured her was the last of Major Korokova's cadre and hastened even faster to the wreckage in which she had left Lyudmila.

She thought, *Lyudmila is wounded and I'm just about done. This second wave of Korokova's is perfectly timed because it will kill us both.*

So it was that she felt no relief, only an impending sense of doom, upon reaching the downed helo without further incident. There she found Lyudmila trying to get herself vertical by bracing herself against the side of the locker. She had found a long vinyl raincoat somewhere, probably in one of the lockers, and wrapped it tightly around herself to brace her cracked ribs. Bugrov, the first of Korokova's Spetsnaz casualties, was sprawled facedown at her feet, one arm extended as if searching for help. She didn't even want to look at Ionescu's shattered body.

"What's happening?" Lyudmila said without prelude; there was no time for niceties.

"First wave down," Evan replied.

"First wave? What d'you mean?"

Evan pointed skyward. "Hear it? Incoming."

Lyudmila closed her eyes for a moment. Her face was ashen, the blood in retreat.

Evan reached out to her. "You shouldn't be standing. You've lost blood from the gunshot wound."

Lyudmila shook her off. "And Korokova? What of her?"

"Facedown in a river of lava."

A sigh. "Well done, Evan."

The sound of the helos grew louder. They could hear the wind whipped up by its rotors; cascades of pumice and loose stones rattled against their temporary shelter, some of the detritus assailing the inside in blinding spurts. It was like trying to protect yourself against a sandstorm.

Evan handed Lyudmila one of the two AKS-74U assault rifles she had grabbed from the corpses outside. "We have to prepare ourselves."

Lyudmila looked at her, took the rifle. "For a helo full of Spetsnaz the most vulnerable time is just before they land."

"Also the most dangerous time for us," Evan said, shading her eyes against the inconstant hailstorm. "We'll hardly be able to see."

"Good thing a helo's a large target."

The ground began to tremble under them as if an earthquake were about to erupt. With a terrific roar a ragged crack formed in the floor of their helo, growing wider by the second. The noise was now deafening.

"It's now or never," Evan shouted.

Lyudmila nodded, but as Evan made to pass her, she staggered.

"Lyudmila!"

Evan dropped her weapon, grabbed hold of her friend as she started to go down. Evan tried to hold her up, but the rent in the floor cracked open and the entire helo juddered like a ship hit by a titanic wave. She lost her grip and they slid down together with a crash. The vinyl raincoat fell open to reveal a bloody torso that Lyudmila was still trying to keep together.

"Oh, my God." Evan moved Lyudmila's arm away, saw the jagged shard of metal stuck into her abdomen. "Oh, my God, what happened?"

Lyudmila grimaced. "It seems that Bugrov wasn't quite dead."

"He did this?"

"Just before I kicked his head in."

Evan couldn't get her head around this. Lyudmila couldn't be dying, she couldn't.

Tears filled her eyes. She could scarcely draw breath. "I won't let this happen," she gasped.

"Ah, well, darling, it's happened. No going back." Lyudmila tried to smile but gritted her teeth instead.

Even through her frantic ministrations Evan knew Lyudmila was right. A wound like this, in the abdomen, required immediate surgery and even then . . . Once the metal shard was removed, she would bleed out in a matter of minutes. Evan was now faced with a choice: take up both the rifles and step out of the helo guns blazing like Butch Cassidy or stay with her friend until the last breath.

Of course that was no choice at all. She moved closer to Lyudmila, held her tight. She bent her head; their foreheads touched. Outside, a great shudder. The helo had landed. Any minute now Spetsnaz boots would be thudding across the puckered landscape to take no prisoners. She was sure of that.

But part of her didn't mind—or more accurately didn't care. Here, at the end, she was with her friend, a woman closer to her than the sister she had lost. There was no word in any language for what they were to each other. In a world filled with bloody shadows, death, lies, and deceit they had found each other and formed a bond like no other.

Lyudmila coughed. Evan held her tighter, felt the rhythm of their hearts merging. From outside, the sound of boots on the ground grew louder and louder until their heavy tramp drowned out even the noise of the helo's rotors.

"You'll find Timur," Lyudmila whispered. "You'll take care of my son."

"I always keep my promise," Evan said.

"I know you do." Now a smile, however brief. "One of the many things that made me love you." More coughing, thick with strings of bloody phlegm. "Ah . . ."

"Lyudmila, don't go." Evan was sobbing openly. "Don't leave me."

"Don't be so maudlin, damn it." A flicker of the old defiant invincible Lyudmila shone bright as a sun through the pain and blood. "What a good friend you've been."

"Hush now," Evan whispered. "Save your strength."

There was a stirring behind them, a slurry of raised voices.

Lyudmila tried to take a breath but all that came out was a gurgle. Evan held her tighter, but Lyudmila was fading in and out. She rocked her like a child, whispered to her, cajoling her, begging her to hold on a minute, thirty seconds, ten, even one more second to still be together.

Then Evan felt hands on her, saying something she could not understand, trying to pull her away from her friend. Her shoulders flexed. "Get the hell off me." And then, softly, "Lyudmila. Lyudmila. I'm still here. Hold on. I've got you. No one's taking me away from you."

"Good. That's good." Lyudmila's voice was thin, dreamy, as if coming from another room. It was not Lyudmila's voice, not really. But against this inimical tide she still struggled.

"Timur." It was akin to the sigh of a very old, very tired woman.

"Yes. I will find Timur. I will tell him all about you."

A bloody smile formed on Lyudmila's lips. "But you don't know me." She shoved something into Evan's hand—a tiny rectangle coated with her own blood. She shuddered in Evan's arms. "I'm sorry." Her voice was like a weed in a storm, bent out of shape. "I'm so sorry."

Then the hands—more of them—did pry Evan loose from her dead friend. She screamed, struck out until strong arms wrapped around her, binding her tight. In one fist was hidden the sticky object Lyudmila had given her.

"Bastards! I won't tell you . . . anything," she cried in anguish.

"That's all right, there's no need," a male voice said in perfect English. "We're Mr. Tribe's men, Ms. Ryder. We're here to take you and Ms. Shokova to safety."

Evan's head came down. She was shaking so violently she thought she must fly apart. "No. You can't."

"I beg your pardon, Ms. Ryder. We will. We *must*. These are our orders."

"But look, look," she cried, weeping. "Can't you see she's dead."

51

"Poland."

"The magic word," the Sovereign said in Kusnetsov's ear.

"I've solved the problem. I know how to best open a second front."

Kusnetsov spoke into his phone while watching men in the weight room of Crocus Fitness go through their routines. He'd finished his forty minutes ago, had taken a steam, then a cold shower, and was now dressed in his black-and-gold uniform, which already smelled of sweat and very bad coffee.

"Excellent. Where are you? I'll have a car fetch you."

Kusnetsov told him and cut the connection.

Fifteen minutes later he was on his way to the Kremlin. The Sovereign had many residences. A few, such as Novo-Ogaryovo and Bocharov Ruchey, his summer homes, were publicly known. Others—many others—were kept a complete secret, denied by government spokesmen. But since his sequestering, the Sovereign had kept to his luxurious apartments in the Kremlin, a fortress in which he felt safest.

The Sovereign met him at the entrance to his apartments. His blood was high, tingeing his cheeks an unhealthy crimson; he was at once excited and agitated.

"Not here," he said to Kusnetsov in a rush, as if to forestall any further talk. "In these times there is only the one place for privacy."

Kusnetsov nodded. "Of course." It was what he was counting on.

The Sovereign was wearing his black-and-gold uniform, but it was rumpled, creased here and there as if he'd been living in it since the last time Kusnetsov was here. He looked a bit more bloated, his eyes yellow, feverish.

"No one followed you," he said as they descended in the private elevator.

"Not at all," Kusnetsov said, barely disguising his surprise.

"Good, good." The Sovereign pursed his lips. His hands were busy brushing imaginary lint from his uniform. "One hears rumors now, dark tidings, ominous omens."

"I don't understand, sir."

The Sovereign shot him an evil glance. "I didn't expect you to," he said shortly.

The mood swings are worse, Kusnetsov observed. But full disintegration was still a ways off, and in the meantime, the Federation was balanced unsteadily on crumbling foundations. Defaults on sovereign debts were piling up, and no matter how hard the Kremlin flunkies tried to spin it the disastrous ramifications would be felt for years to come. No one but the Chinese and North Korea to buy Russian oil and gas—and North Korea had no money to speak of. The army decimated, far worse losses than anyone had the nerve to tell the Sovereign, least of all his generals, reduced to a mutinous lot. Chaos in Ukraine, the mighty Federation reduced to shooting off rockets like Hamas. Abject humiliation. The madness of the Sovereign had to stop.

The moment they took their seats, the train pulled out of the station beneath the Kremlin. No doctors, no security—no one but Kusnetsov and the Sovereign. This was how the Sovereign's mind worked now—irrationality and paranoia were the norms.

They sat in the parlor carriage. While the train gently rocked on its rails Kusnetsov opened a topo map of Poland, which he had marked with various lines and symbols. He laid out his plans for attacking Poland in such excruciating detail he could tell the Sovereign's eyes were about to cross.

"Yes, yes, Darko Vladimirovich, this is all quite excellent, well thought out." The Sovereign smacked his lips. "And yet I must admit all this talk of invasions has made my throat dry." He turned, opened the drawer on the table at his side. He withdrew the crystal decanter filled with Siberian deer antler blood, along with a pair of sparkling champagne glasses because, he said, they needed to drink more this time. The viscous ruby-red liquid filled the glasses. As before, it also filled the carriage with the fumes of the poor young animal's torture and death.

Kusnetsov palmed the small packet he had bought from Hasan in the Chelobit'evo ghetto. Hasan had a myriad of connections, a poisonous spider sitting in the center of a worldwide web. Luckily he and Kusnetsov were fast friends of many years, having helped each other out numerous times. In this instance, Kusnetsov had taken advantage of Hasan being an importer of all manner of illegal substances. He could evade the West's embargo mainly because most of these substances were smuggled out of China and Tibet. This particular packet was filled with a dun-colored powder so fine it dissolved in liquid almost instantaneously.

The Sovereign held his glass high. "To bringing Poland into the Federation's fold."

"To success," Kusnetsov said, the only one aware of the words' double meaning.

As the Sovereign was about to put glass to his liver-colored lips, Kusnetsov leaned forward, put his glass on the corner of the map, reached out with a forefinger, tracing it along one of the main lines he had drawn. "Now right here, I forgot to tell you . . ." And he embarked on another pointless and convoluted tactic the Russian advance forces needed to take.

As he spoke, the Sovereign leaned in as well, put his glass down next to Kusnetsov's. In due course, over no longer than several seconds, the dun-colored powder blended with the deer antler blood.

Kusnetsov's oration complete, the two men sat back and drank deeply from the glasses. This was a solemn ritual into which Kusnetsov readily immersed himself since this was the last nauseating salute to the Sovereign's life.

The powder worked quickly, as Hasan promised it would. It was a concentrate of the leaves and unripe fruit of *Physalis alkekengi,* also known as the Chinese lantern, a relative of bittersweet nightshade. Within moments, the Sovereign clapped his hands to his head as the intense headache started.

With eyes made rheumy by the pain, he pointed. "You, you." Sucked in a breath. "Of all people, you."

Kusnetsov, stoic, blank-faced, said, "You brought this on yourself."

The Sovereign frowned, fissures scored across his wide glistening forehead. "I don't understand."

"That's right," Kusnetsov said softly. "And you never did."

The Sovereign reached for him then, fingers like an animal's claws. "I'll . . . I'll . . ." He groaned, his tongue protruded, lolling. This was Kusnetsov's cue to back away. The vomiting came next, copious quantities of food, deer antler blood, bile, and lastly the Sovereign's own blood. Kusnetsov thought of the slain deer that gave its blood only to have it end up on the expensive carpet of the Sovereign's private train roaring through its tunnel under Moscow. What a long terrible journey—and for what?

Kusnetsov, disgusted, turned away even before the Sovereign's dead body slid off the chair into the reeking muck. Stepping to the Sovereign's own communications center, he first put in a call to General Zakhalin.

"It's done," he said. "Stand down the missile launchers and all air-to-ground weapons. Tell your company commanders to pull back—but slowly, we don't want to give the wrong impression of a defeat. Bring them back home over the next ten days."

His next call was to Pavel Lagunov, spokesperson for the Duma, the lower house of the Federal Assembly. Again, he began with the words "It's done. Call a session for tomorrow morning. I'll address the entire body, then you can say what you will." His next call was to Portonov, head of the Federal Council, the assembly's upper house.

"Can this be done, Minister?" Portonov squeaked. "Actually done?"

They're sheep, Kusnetsov thought. *They've all been trained by the Sovereign to be meek and to take orders from him. It will take time to recondition them. Generations of Russians have been brought up under autocrats—first the tsars, then the communists.* The short-lived Glasnost was an abject failure. No Russian knew what to do with freedom. With no one to tell them what to think, what to do, they were terrified.

His final calls were to some close friends of the Sovereign and then to Maxim, at the Politburo. Fortunately, with foresight Kusnetsov had accumulated files on almost all of them, stuffed with documentation detailing their various crimes, misdemeanors, embezzlements, affairs with undesirables from Moscow's lower depths.

"I have ordered the president, the foreign minister, all the high-ranking officials to attend what I've led them to believe is a Sovereign Ball," he informed Maxim, just as he'd told the others. "They will come—even, especially, the Sovereign's mouthpieces. They will be all together in one room. They will be dealt with."

The Security Council was another matter entirely. They—ultra-hard-liners and Sovereign tail-waggers all—had dispersed at the first sign of trouble. He had sent FSB detachments out to run them down, but so far they'd had no luck. He'd have to watch his back extremely carefully, be on the lookout for any sign of a violent pushback.

Those important tasks completed, he went forward, stepping through the work area of the parlor carriage into the operator's cabin.

The man's head jerked around, his eyes opening wide. "Who are you?"

"A favored guest of the Sovereign. He's ordering you to stop at the last station, wait there with the doors open, then take us back to where we began. Clear?"

"Yes, sir," said the operator, clearly trained to take orders without asking the whys and wherefores.

But just to make sure, Kusnetsov stayed beside him as they rocketed past the second station. At length, the operator slowed the train, slid it into the third and last station. If he was surprised to see the horde of men standing on the platform, he made no remark or sign. As the train came to a halt, Kusnetsov ordered the operator to open the doors, and to remain in his cabin.

The men poured into all three carriages. They were built either like boulders or scarecrows. There were a hundred of them, two hundred, three hundred, all piling into the carriages—Kusnetsov counted. Unlike their compatriots now in control of Directorate KV, their sleeves were rolled up, showing the constellations of crude tattoos made from graphite or coal dust and urine criminals gave themselves while inside prison. Not all of them had been inside; others were either unmarked or had necks, shoulders, or biceps inked by professionals, some of them beautiful as any artwork. All of them were heavily armed.

The last to step aboard was Hasan. He was flanked by Agulov and Gulov, the heads of the two largest and most powerful Bratva, Russian crime syndicates. Gulov carried a bottle of Siberian vodka whose label Kusnetsov had never seen before.

He gripped Kusnetsov's hand. "You're as good as your word, my friend." His eyes narrowed. "Is he dead?"

"As a side of beef."

A great smile burst across Hasan's face. "This I have to see."

Kusnetsov extended an arm toward the living area of the parlor carriage. "Be my guest."

Hasan moved into the carriage, and Kusnetsov gestured to the Bratva chiefs to join him on the now-empty platform. Without taking his eyes off Kusnetsov, Gulov swung the bottle against the edge of the open carriage door. The glass shattered, the vodka exploding like lava from a volcano, leaving him holding the neck and jagged bulge. He held this aloft, shaking it.

"Our friend Hasan may be joyful," he said to Kusnetsov. "However I am anything but. If, as you claim, the Sovereign is dead, this is, of course, good."

"Very good," Agulov interjected.

"You, Minister, have accomplished what I never could have believed possible."

"You managed to induce Gulov to the negotiating table," Agulov interjected again, earning him an annoyed look from his new compatriot. "That is hardly a little thing, isn't that right, Gulov."

Gulov made a disgusted noise. "It was either come together or lose our businesses to the trade blockade. Iran's stuff was top-notch but there was too little of it and we began to fight over it. Of course we did, the Chinese imports were dogshit, adulterated with sawdust and melamine, impossible to sell a second time to even the almost-gone drug-heads."

"Well, but we were boxed into a corner with no way out," Agulov countered. "The minister provided us with an exit."

Gulov grunted. "But now comes the true test. Even with the Sovereign dead, even with your partners in the generals and the Duma, we have a terrible fight on our hands. The Sovereign was deeply entrenched. In death as well as in life he had many powerful friends."

"But more powerful enemies," Kusnetsov pointed out. "The oligarchs will return. We will prevail."

"But the Sovereign's Iron Curtain has come down," Gulov said. "I doubt the oligarchs will return from their self-imposed exile anytime soon. We're fucked, cut off economically from everyone but our untrustworthy and conniving so-called allies. For myself, I despise them all. I'd kill them if given half a chance. Counting on them for anything would be a grave mistake."

"To say nothing of our reputations," Agulov said, his bitterness coming to the fore, Gulov's pessimism starting to work on him.

"We have control of the media," Kusnetsov told them. "I've seen to that."

Agulov nodded. "Understood."

"What about social media?" Gulov asked.

"It's all good," Kusnetsov said. "The usual suspects are out with conflicting stories, muddying the waters. As usual."

"Even so we are facing a civil war like no other."

"Would you back down now after having come so far?"

"We back down from no fight," Gulov said.

"Still, at the end of the day, we are criminals, Minister," Agulov protested. "No one will see us as anything but."

To this Kusnetsov replied, "Everything in Russia is mutable. Villains become heroes and vice versa; this is part of our culture, part of who we are. It's happened over and over in our history. Why? Because we keep rewriting our history. This moment won't be any different. Why? Because we have already begun to rewrite our history once more."

Neither of the chiefs said a word.

Kusnetsov went back into the car, into the operator's cabin, grabbed the trembling, ashen-faced man and began to walk him through the carriages to the other end of the train, where an identical control cubicle was awaiting him. On the way they passed the Sovereign. The operator gagged and vomited. Kusnetsov was obliged to hold him by the scruff of his collar in order to keep him upright. When they reached the last carriage, which was to become the first one, he clapped the man on his shoulder. "Get in there. Take us home."

"H-home?" The operator stared at him, stupefied. "Where?"

"The Kremlin," Kusnetsov said. "Where else?"

52

THE FOG OF WAR

Evan had the vague sensation of flying, then not flying, then nothing but a black hole, then flying once more. During this time she was never fully conscious. When she did finally open her eyes she found herself in her room in Tribe's Santa Cruz de La Palma villa. For what seemed a long time she did nothing, while a troupe of doctors prodded, poked, gently manipulated her. Once she was sat up, a portable X-ray machine pushed against her chest. Later, alone, she drank copious amounts of water. The first time it came right up and she found herself on her knees in front of the toilet, head lolling. During this time her thoughts were completely with Lyudmila. In the first forty-eight hours of consciousness, she was certain that she would break, that Lyudmila's death was the last straw, causing her to lie in bed and never get up again, no matter what cocktail of drugs Tribe's doctors injected her with.

It was too much to think of anyone else, even—especially!—Tribe and his betrayal. She could not think of Timur, even though she had promised Lyudmila. She had not even absorbed the story of how Tribe and Timur escaped the wreck, the side of the hellish volcano.

Lyudmila's death shattered her. She knew this and she didn't. Her world was too small, too filled with Lyudmila and herself to admit any light into the darkness into which she had been plunged. They circled each other like blasted planets locked in a death spiral.

Outside her tiny universe, others had made attempts to talk to her, of course—first Tribe, then a neurologist, a therapist specializing in grief counseling and PTSD. She resisted all of them; she was in no mood to talk, let alone open up about what had happened. She did not even want to look at Tribe. There was no room. For one thing, she had taken Lyudmila into herself and thus filled to the brim could not countenance any intrusion. And for another she could not at the moment deal. His betrayal of his country and of her made her sick to her stomach. She did ask about

Timur. She needed to be assured that he was alive and well taken care of. She told the grief counselor to talk with him. "He needs your empathy," she recalled saying. "I'm fine." But of course she wasn't fine. Whatever the opposite of fine was, that was where she now lived. And there came a time when a small hesitant knock on her door announced Timur. The door swung inward and there he stood, bruised here and there but thank God physically none the worse for wear.

She left her bed, padded over to him in the striped silk pajamas Tribe had provided, and knelt before him.

"Timur," she whispered. "I'm so happy you're okay."

"But Aunt Evan," he said, eyes brimming, "you're not."

"Oh, honey. I'm fine. Truly fine now that you're here." She opened her arms, he stepped into them, and she enfolded him, she felt his heart beating against hers and she whispered in his ears, "Whatever happens, Timur, know that you are protected and that you are loved, by me and by everyone around you."

He put his forehead against the hollow of her shoulder. "I know about my mother."

Evan's eyes welled up, blurring her vision. "You must miss her."

"I don't know." His voice was thin, reedy, trembly. His thin shoulders shook. "I should, shouldn't I?"

Evan had no clear answer for that except, "Honey, whatever you're feeling—or not feeling—is okay. Nobody can or should tell you how to feel. That comes from inside you."

"But I never knew her," he wailed, and she held him until even his crackling energy waned and he slumped against her.

Evan sighed, kissed away his tears. "Oh, honey, none of us who loved her knew her."

■　　■　　■

Even Ben's repeated calls went unanswered. Ben was used to her protracted silences when in the field but that didn't mean he had to like them. Accordingly, he got permission from his boss, Isobel Lowe, to fly out to where Evan now was, where in due course he presented himself at the front door of Marsden Tribe's villa. He was welcomed with Tribe's usual aplomb. Others might call his demeanor remote or distracted. For Ben it was a signifier for being spaced-out. He had never liked Tribe and he sure as hell liked him even less now that he knew it was Tribe's own personal lawyer who had made the preemptive bid for the weaponized time crystals, taking it out of auction. However, his easy smile did not betray that secret knowledge.

Evan was of course unaware of any of this, nor in her present state would she have been all that interested if she were aware. She had deliberately kept him in the dark about her friendship with Lyudmila. But then Ben was under the misapprehension that he was her mentor, when actually it was Lyudmila from whom she had learned every trick in fieldwork. Now here she was sunk in the pit of the moment when she left Lyudmila in the wreckage. Why hadn't she checked to make sure Bugrov was indeed dead? She had been too busy trying to defend the immediate vicinity around the helo. She knew that was why—of course she knew, but still her guilt got the better of her. It was difficult, drowning as she was, to consider this rationally and to forgive herself. The loss of her friend had punched a hole through her in precisely the same way Bobbi's loss had. Bobbi had been recruited during the trip on which Evan had taken her for her seventeenth birthday. Unaccountably, Bobbi had been restless in the laid-back tropics of Sumatra, which Evan loved so deeply and dearly. She had been desperate to get to Copenhagen, their next stop, and for good reason. Unbeknownst to Evan, Bobbi would meet with an SVR recruiter code-named Leda; a formal deal would be struck. From that moment until her violent death five years ago at the hands, both Evan and Ben believed, of the FSB itself, Bobbi was an SVR agent embedded in the center of American political life. What had Bobbi done to deserve her death? Had she turned against Russia? Had she inadvertently leaked some of their secrets to her late husband? Had her use run its course? Had she been found wanting? No answers, not even an educated guess.

Lying back on the bed, one of the stack of ice packs by her bedside against her swollen cheeks, she closed her eyes. No sleep approached her on little cat feet, dwelling stubbornly on a distant shore to which Evan had no access. The strange energy of insomnia worked inside her, engendering in stark detail a recurring dream . . .

. . . of being in the stream near their house. Bobbi is with her. They are children, prepubescent. Bobbi is laughing at her, repeating over and over, *I have the power, not you. Never you,* but in the manner of dreams, she doesn't understand what that means. Anxiety builds in her to unbearable heights.

That's when Bobbi reaches out, places both hands on the crown of

Evan's head—*You want power? Here's power*—and pushes her down under the water. When Evan struggles, Bobbi wraps her legs over her sister's shoulders, and keeps her down . . .

Evan's eyes snapped open. Her chest was rising and falling as if her mouth and throat were full of water. Instinctively, she turned on her side, gasping air into her lungs. She knew she was hyperventilating but she couldn't seem to stop. Her limbs moved spastically, scarcely under her control. The back of her left hand smacked the side table, unsettling the water jug and the plastic glasses nesting one inside the other. Her cell phone slipped off the corner of the table and dropped to the rug. As she struggled to lean down far enough to fetch it, her hand struck the corner of the drawer, which had partially slid out. She scooped up her phone. Up on one elbow, she started to close the drawer and paused, her hand in midair. There, resting inside, was the SD card Lyudmila had pressed into her hand at the last moment. The sides were caked, black with her friend's dried blood. She was about to push the drawer closed but something stopped her. Afterward, she will think of this moment and wonder what caused her to pluck out the SD card instead of shoving the drawer home. After a time she will realize that there is no answer, and anyway the question is irrelevant. It's the SD card—or rather what is on it—that matters.

Slowly and carefully she rotated the SD card, then using a bit of water cleaned it off, mindful of keeping the flat copper pins free of moisture. Reopening the drawer, she found a paper clip in a far corner, opened it, used the end to pop open the tiny tray on the right side of her phone. She swapped out the SD card she used for extra space with the one Lyudmila had given her, slid the tray home. Then she turned on her phone, navigated to the SD card. Though it could hold 1 GB of data, there were only two files. One was a JPG image, the other was a PDF text file.

She brought up the JPG first. It was a color photo, a portrait of sorts with the subject in three-quarter view: blond hair, blunt-cut down to her earlobes, a lupine aspect to her heart-shaped face. No makeup, no earrings. At first glance Evan found herself wondering who this might be and why Lyudmila wanted her to see the photo.

"I'm sorry. I'm so sorry."

Then she caught something in the face she thought might be familiar. She turned the photo this way and that in order to see it in different light. Then, as if magnetized, her head lifted up and she saw her own reflection in the mirror on the wall opposite her bed, saw past her skin mottled by bruises, small bandages, her flesh distended here and there:

A lupine aspect to her heart-shaped face.

Her heart skipped a beat and she looked again at the photo.

No, she thought. *It can't be. It's not even remotely possible.*

But there she was, staring at her sister. Bobbi. Older. *Not dead.* A blonde. *Not dead.*

"I'm sorry. I'm so sorry."

Lyudmila's voice and the photo of Bobbi seemed to collide in some strange space inside her head—some fantasyland where wishes were flying horses. She blinked, rubbed her eyes, stared again at the photo, which was indeed her sister, Bobbi Ryder. And yet something about her face, the expression, the new lines, even the set of her head, was subtly different.

To stop her heart colliding with her rib cage she turned to the PDF file. At once, a rapid pulse started up behind her eyes and she gasped for breath. What had come up was unmistakably an SVR eyes-only file. How in the world Lyudmila had hacked it she had no idea. There was a name on the file but it wasn't Bobbi Ryder.

Kata Romanovna Hemakova.

Who the hell is she? Evan asked herself.

Then she began to read, and everything else in the world ceased to exist. Bobbi Ryder exfiltrated out of DC, out of the country, her "death" staged by her SVR handlers. Bobbi Ryder, who was given the operational name of Kobalt, and when Kobalt was officially retired, she became Kata Romanovna Hemakova by—and here Evan had to stop to keep her vertigo at bay. When it became unbearable not to go on, she did and discovered that Bobbi became Kata Romanovna Hemakova by murdering the real Kata Romanovna Hemakova, an FSB assassin. Breathlessly, Evan read the list of the original Kata's assignments, kills, honors kept secret among a small cadre of high-level FSB officials including Minister Darko Vladimirovich Kusnetsov, director of the FSB.

Evan read on as if in a stupor. The more she read about her sister the more unreal the whole thing became, the more she questioned Lyudmila's sanity—and her own.

At length, after she had run through the file three times—three times!—to make sure she'd read everything correctly, that she wasn't hallucinating—although she knew she wasn't; the SVR watermarks on every page were real—she switched back to Bobbi's photo, stared more deeply at it. This was Bobbi's face, all right. Not only older but harder, more determined. Also, she had developed the muscled shoulders of a swimmer.

Abruptly, she slammed the phone facedown on the bed. She lay back, slowly willing her tightly bunched muscles to relax. She closed her eyes, let the tidal water of memory close over her.

"Bobbi," she whispered. "What have you become?"

But with an icy shiver down her spine that terrified her, that tensed her muscles all over again, she knew the reality was even worse. Kata Hemakova wasn't what Bobbi Ryder had become. It was what she had been all along.

■   ■   ■

Night arrived. She could tell even through the drawn curtains, but once again sleep was out of the question. Was it only now after years in the field that she was aware that exhaustion and sleep were not synonymous, did not even live in the same house?

Rising, she padded to the bathroom, took a shower to wash the sweat off her, not caring if the needles of water peeled away a couple of the bandages that had been so diligently applied as well.

Wrapped in a thick white bath sheet, she stepped to the window, pulled aside the curtain, then stood stunned, rooted to the spot. She stared, dumbfounded. No boats, no harbor leading to the Atlantic Ocean. She overlooked a courtyard with a fig tree on one side and a lime tree on the other. In its center a beautiful, tiled fountain. Her gaze was drawn to the sky above the courtyard's far wall, into which, some distance away, rose the slender minarets of the Sultan Ahmed Cami, the Blue Mosque. As if in a dream she watched her hand float out to unlatch the window, allowing the sounds of the people setting up dinner in the courtyard to wash over her. Turkish. She heard Turkish voices, querulous, singing, speaking of politics—always politics.

She wasn't in La Palma. She wasn't in the Canary Islands at all. She was in Istanbul.

53

ISTANBUL, TURKEY

It was time to see Ben. Notes had been slipped under her door several times following his arrival. She'd ignored them as she had ignored all the other notes Tribe had sent her. To his credit she had to admit that he hadn't invaded her privacy when he so easily could have. After all, she assumed like the one in La Palma he owned this villa—the color scheme was similar, as were the décor and the room dimensions. Only the rugs were different, a detail she'd been too preoccupied to notice until now.

But before she arranged to see Ben she removed the SD card, put the original back into her phone, and sealed the tray. She slipped out of bed, dropped the SD card on the bare floor outside the circumference of the carpet, crushed it with the leg of a chair. Then she took the residue and flushed it down the toilet, along with any tiny bits left on the floor. She carefully placed the chair back in its original position. She got dressed, crossed to the door, opened it, called for one of Tribe's security people to fetch Ben Butler.

■　■　■

Ben's frown was so deep it gouged new furrows into his face. Evan sat in the chair she had moved, watching him like a hawk. She expected a dressing-down for keeping him and Isobel out of the loop. But then she'd been with Tribe all the time and he was their boss, even Isobel's.

"Hey," he said.

"Hey yourself."

There might have been more in this vein had Tribe not followed Ben through the door. Quietly, he closed the door behind them. The black stitches set diagonally across his forehead attested to the damage he had suffered in the helo crash. The skin around the stitches was swollen, pulled unnaturally taut.

"I imagine you've worked out where you are," Tribe said. She wondered if he was angry with her, but his voice and his expression were neutral, calm if not entirely relaxed. Something was up. Something they knew and she didn't. She hated being in this position.

"Do you own this whole city yet?" she said.

Tribe laughed. "Just the important parts." He had an easy laugh, inviting you to join him, so she did. Ben didn't even crack a smile, but then Ben was all business, all the time.

"I suppose you're wondering how Mr. Tribe and the boy managed to escape the fiasco on the volcano," Ben ventured.

"That's okay, Mr. Butler." Tribe made a sweeping motion with his hand. "I'm perfectly capable of speaking for myself."

"I never doubted it," Ben said trying to recover. "I just thought we might cut to the chase."

"Admirable," Tribe said without trying to keep the sarcasm out of his voice. "But wrongheaded."

Ben swung toward Tribe. "Are you saying you know Evan better than I do?"

"I'm saying I've spent more time with her recently than you have." Tribe's voice was mild but there was no mistaking the underlayer of steel. "Surely that counts for something. Especially now. In this situation."

Evan looked from one to another, wondering how to short-circuit a pissing match Ben could never win. "What situation?" she said sharply. "Will one of you and for the record I don't care which tell me what the hell has been going on while I've been out of it? I mean I don't even remember being flown here."

"You wouldn't," Tribe told her. "You were unconscious. We saw to that."

"You what? Drugged me?"

"It was the only way. You needed to heal. You still do, from what the doctor tells me."

"What do doctors know?" she spat.

That stopped everyone in their tracks. As the silence beat on, Evan glowered at both of them. "Okay, will one of you read me in?"

"That's—" Ben began, but before he could say another word, Tribe said, "I know what 'read me in' means." Tribe opened his hands in a gesture of truce if not yet rapprochement. "Briefly, what happened was this: I contacted my people just after the helo was hit." Evan nodded, remembering seeing him on his cell phone. "They came in a speedboat—a cigarette—which is faster than any other power boat. Anyway, the boy was out cold. I picked him up and made my way down the slope with him in my arms. I made it to the beach, where we were picked up. I turned to go back for you and Lyudmila but my security people wouldn't allow it. They had to physically restrain me."

"Bully for you." Evan looked at Ben. "Haven't you told him?"

"I've told him everything, Evan," he replied.

"Of course he denied everything."

"Hey," Tribe protested, "I'm standing right here."

"You," she said, "I don't trust."

"You don't trust anyone," he replied curtly.

"That's what keeps me alive."

"It also," he said, "keeps you from knowing anyone."

Another tension-filled silence, into which Ben interjected his voice. "Evan, Mr. Tribe did not authorize Ayman Safra, his lawyer, to make that preemptive bid for the weaponized time crystals."

When Evan's gaze switched back to Tribe, he said, "I've been working with time crystals for over two years. I happened across the theoretical process to weaponize them a while ago, but I kept it in-house, strictly a secret. I recognized the extreme danger immediately, turned my research to other more productive aspects of the crystals."

"If that's so," Evan said, "if you're telling the truth, how did the algorithmic formula escape Parachute?"

"There never was a formula," Tribe said. "Not as such. As I said, it was just a theoretical construct."

"Could someone else have stumbled on it?" Evan asked.

"Anything's possible, especially when it comes to qubits and time crystals," Tribe replied. "But I doubt it."

"Well, then the most likely explanation is that someone inside Parachute stole it."

"But how did Zahra Planck get—" Ben snapped his fingers. "Wait a minute. Mr. Tribe, someone inside Parachute must have had a relationship with her. Can you—?"

"Done," Tribe said and made a call on his cell.

Evan took a breath, let it out. "Ben, why don't you back that up to the beginning?"

So he told her everything he and An Binh had discovered through Wes Connerly and Zahra Planck, the lead physicist on the US government's quantum project. "Connerly and Zahra had a falling-out. Now Connerly's dead—which means the entire golf foursome has been killed, by the weaponized time crystals, it turns out. A second autopsy was performed on Bill Fineman and the cause of death changed."

"So, what, you expect me to believe Tribe's attorney bought the process? On his own?"

"Again," Tribe said, spreading his hands. "Still here."

"No," Ben said. "We believe he had help." He paused a moment, before sighing. "Also Zahra Planck has vanished. She's much cleverer and more resourceful than we imagined."

"She didn't vanish. She's on Ayman Safra's boat," Tribe said. "And I have the answer to your question. There is someone—or there was. He quit last month." He gave Ben all the details.

Ben called Isobel, relayed the information. "We'll find him," he said as he disconnected.

Evan nodded. "So Ayman Safra and Zahra Planck," she said. "Who else?"

Ben shrugged, and Evan made a disgusted sound.

"The boat is currently here in Istanbul, taking on supplies," Tribe said. "It's due to depart at midnight."

"Which gives us—" Ben glanced at his wristwatch. "—a bit less than four hours.

"Once it leaves Istanbul, once it reaches international waters," Ben continued, "we'll have to involve INTERPOL and a fistful of other inter-country services. We'll be drowning in red tape while they're off to God only knows where."

"There are so many ways to track them," Evan pointed out.

"True," Ben said, "but while you were recovering two more deaths have been reported—our secretary of the treasury and the Russian foreign minister."

"They want to go beyond a proxy war," Evan said. "They want to start an actual war between us and the Russians."

"Exactly." Ben nodded. "As of now the deaths are unexplained, but it's only a matter of time before the truth comes out, causing a worldwide panic."

"War and panic," Tribe said.

"And it may already have started," Ben said. "Russia has gone media silent. Ditto the Kremlin."

"As for social media, it's a shit show," Tribe said. "And I ought to know since I'm a big part of that particular shit show. I like seeding chaos into disorder."

Ben cut his boss a disgusted look. "Bottom line, no one knows anything, and if they claim they do you can be damn sure they're making it up."

Ben took a step toward her. "Look, Evan, I hate to ask this of you after what you've just been through, but I can't take point in the field. Zahra knows me."

"And after what happened up on the volcano," Tribe said, "I'm more or less a prisoner of my own security forces."

"And rightly so," Ben pointed out. "You had no business being up there. You could've been killed—or worse."

"What would be worse?" Tribe asked.

Ben ignored him, turned to Evan. "So that leaves—"

"I know." Evan rose from her chair. "Brief me."

Ben eyed her. "So you have a plan."

"Always," Evan said.

54

THREE-MASTER

The moon waning, clouds building over the water. Halfway across, a light rain began to fall. Lights blazed in the cabins of the custom three-masted schooner owned by Ayman Safra. A hundred feet if it was an inch, Evan estimated. Crew of four, plus a chef, this she was sure of. He must be one hell of a lawyer, she thought, to afford an eight-figure yacht of this size and workmanship.

Wrapped in shadow, she was on a tender, part of the crew bringing fresh meat, spices, and produce to the schooner. Evan was in charge of the lamb, Tribe having bribed ipar Et, Istanbul's finest butcher shop, to substitute her as porter.

She was part of a trio of delivery people—the only woman, which she didn't like. Standing out in any way was to be avoided in the field, but in this she had no choice. The driver sped on, the schooner rose above them, eventually blocking out much of the sky. What small slice of moon there had been was overrun by clouds by the time they made fast to the schooner's leeward side.

A Turk with the build and glower of a professional wrestler guided them down to the galley, where the chef showed them where to store the provisions. The air was redolent of onions and turmeric. The chef—a small, mustachioed Lebanese—insisted on personally checking the provisions. When it came to the lamb, his hands, small, reddened, with neat nails, turned over the saddles, shoulders, and legs, all the while glancing up into Evan's face.

"You're new," he said in an indifferent voice. And then more sharply, "I was not aware that ipar Et employed females."

"We're shorthanded," Evan told him. The less interaction she had with him the better.

The chef grunted, turned over the last saddle of lamb, then waved at her dismissively. "Out."

Obediently, she exited the kitchen. She was the only one from the tender left on board. She made her way up the gangway into the salons, all fitted out in gleaming wood—floors, walls, sconces, bookcases, nooks within which sat small sculptures of marble and stone. Everything built in, including tables, sideboards, tufted red velvet sofas. She passed through the dining room with its mahogany table affixed to the floor and its crystal chandelier depending like an upside-down mushroom from the cream-painted ceiling.

"What are you doing here?"

She turned, saw the wrestler type glowering at her.

"You should be back in the tender by now."

Instead of turning tail, which he expected, she placed herself squarely in front of him. "I was taking a minute to admire the interior."

He stalked up to her. "This is forbidden."

"Okay, okay. I'm almost finished," she said.

"You *are* finished."

He straight-armed her, his palm impacting her chest. She did not move, even an inch. His eyes grew wide. She chopped down on his forearm with the edge of her hand. At the same time she slammed the heel of her other hand against his chest. He lurched and fell backward. At once, she was on her knees over him. A sharp jab to the side of his neck into the nerve bundle just beneath his ear rendered him unconscious. Dragging him to a locker was no easy task, but she managed to stuff him inside, close the door.

Rough hands on her shoulders tried to pull her away from the locker. Cocking her left leg, she smashed the heel of her boot into her assailant's crotch. She heard the air go out of him, twisted her torso to the left, grabbed him around the neck, jammed his forehead into the locker. The crew member went down and stayed down.

The less time she spent on the schooner the better, so she left him lying there, stepped over him, and entered what looked to be Ayman Safra's study. In fact, the lawyer was in residence. He sat bolt upright in a wooden swivel chair in front of his built-in desk, his back to the entry. On it were three cell phones, lined up like rank-and-file soldiers; a laptop; a pad; five pens, also perfectly aligned; a cut-crystal diamond decahedron paperweight, art glass with swirls of gray at the bottom. Open in front of him was what appeared to be a ledger, bound in buckram leather, its visible pages filled with lines of neat, precise handwriting. He was alone and undisturbed.

Stealing silently in, she crept up behind him, was about to slither an arm around his throat when she realized the man sitting in the chair was dead. Pulling his head back, she ascertained that he was indeed Ayman Safra. She also ascertained that he'd been strangled with what appeared from the mark to be a wire. A silent coup? she wondered. In that instant, she caught a glimmer of movement in two adjacent facets of the decahedron on the desk. Instead of whirling around, she waited until the last instant, until she caught the scent—a woman's scent. She allowed the scent to come to her, then dropped to her knees. A metal belaying pin struck Safra's shoulder, then the desktop, splintering it. He crashed out of the chair sideways, and now Evan whipped around. Balanced on one leg, she struck the woman on the ankle with the toe of her boot, then, rising, smashed down on her instep. The woman's head came up and Evan recognized Zahra Planck from the photos Ben had shown her.

Showing no sign of pain, Zahra attacked her with the belaying pin, lunging, bringing the weapon down in an overhead smash. Extending her left leg and bending it at the knee, Evan swiveled to her left, bringing her fists together, burying them in Zahra's stomach. Zahra had no reaction—none at all. Evan struck her, opening her top hand, slashed through fabric and skin with the tips of her fingers and her nails. Again nothing, not an iota of pain flashing across Zahra's face, no flinching of her body, no contraction of her muscles. That's when Evan realized that Zahra had CIPA, a rare congenital disease. Her pain-sensing nerves were disconnected from the part of the brain that would normally react to pain. No matter how hard Evan hit her, no matter the cuts she might inflict, Zahra would press her attack, oblivious. She would continue until her last breath was expelled.

She came at Evan then, the belaying pin slashing back and forth in a blur. Evan felt a heavy blow on her left forearm, then right biceps. She could feel her strength being replaced by numbness, then weakness. What kind of training had this physicist had? Evan wondered. The way she attacked with purpose but without discipline, with pure fury, surely must have come from back alleys and moldy basements.

Zahra came on, relentless, her eyes narrowed, the belaying pin switching from hand to hand so that Evan could not tell the direction of the next blow, let alone time it. There was a strange dislocation in fighting someone who couldn't feel pain. It was as if they were superhuman, as if their body defied all the laws of hand-to-hand combat. It gave them an advantage she had never before faced. It was disquieting and illusory, as if she were fighting multiple foes or a shadow that could inflict a mortal wound. Evan feared that she was not up for this, not after everything she had been through—the tension, pressure, pain, guilt, and grief. *With doubt creeping in,* she thought, *I've already lost.*

But muscle memory was so ingrained in her that she allowed Zahra to get close—very close. She held the belaying pin in front of her like a knife, intending at the last instant to whip it around in a blow to Evan's abdomen. Evan's arms were still all but useless, but that was okay, she could deal with that, in fact the numbness made her more like Zahra.

Just as Zahra brought the head of the belaying pin back to gain momentum for her horizontal strike, Evan twisted her torso from the waist and, engaging the power in her lower belly, used her legs to drive forward. Now behind Zahra, she drove her elbow into the small of Zahra's back. But there was minimal force behind the strike. Zahra whirled and, grabbing the cloth of Evan's shirt, slammed her back against the desk so hard the entire desk shivered, pens flying every which way. A sharp pain ran down Evan's back into her legs, and she sagged against the desktop. All the breath went out of her; her face was ashen, and Zahra grinned, seeing her victory rising up before her.

She jabbed the head of the belaying pin into the soft tissue just below Evan's sternum. Evan grunted. For an instant her eyes rolled up. Zahra closed for the kill, her eyes burning like lamps in her skull. Evan could scarcely catch her breath. Her lungs seemed to have forgotten how to do their job. She gasped, on the verge of blacking out. Then her left hand, searching for a handhold to keep her from collapsing, closed around a jagged shard from the splintered corner of the desktop.

The belaying pin swept down, targeting the top of Evan's head. Evan swung the wooden shard up and across the bridge of Zahra's nose. The nose collapsed, blood gushed out, but that hardly mattered. Zahra only paused to wipe the blood off her face. The belaying pin bounced off Evan's ear, onto her shoulder. Evan groaned. Her entire body was on fire. Only one chance now to stop this unfeeling killing machine, and she took it. She drove the sharp end of the shard into Zahra's right eye, pulled it free, then buried it in Zahra's left eye.

There was only so much a human body, even one afflicted as Zahra's was, could take. She collapsed on top of the lawyer's body. Evan drove the wooden shard home. Zahra arched up, bloody lips drawn back from bloody teeth in the rictus of death.

Thighs trembling, Evan sat down on the swivel chair, turning it away from the two bodies, one atop the other. That's when she looked up to see the cook standing in the doorway, aiming a small .22 Browning pistol at her. They stared at each other for a moment.

"Goodbye," he said.

Three shots pitched him forward flat on his face. She saw three bright flowers blooming in his back; heart, left lung, right lung.

"Perfect," she said as Ben stepped over the dead chef. "But what the hell took you so long?" Her head hurt, her shoulder ached, and her body was still shuddering with excess adrenaline and the aftermath of terror at having gone hand-to-hand with what had seemed to her as something inhuman—a demon.

Ben, who had driven the tender, came over to her, cupped her head in his hands. "You look—"

"Don't you say it." They locked eyes. "You ever go up against anyone with CIPA?"

His eyes cut to Zahra. "Her?"

"Could feel no pain—none at all."

"Like a machine."

"Yes."

"Anyway." He sighed. "Thank God."

"So, you . . ."

"Hey, listen. It was no piece of cake what I had to do. Tie up the delivery personnel, then take care of the two crew you didn't take out."

Evan gestured with her chin, winced at the pain. "Except him."

"Yeah, I forgot about the chef. Who thought he'd be so loyal?"

"Lebanese like his boss. Wouldn't be surprising if he was a family member." Her head lolled on her neck.

"Evan . . ."

"Job's not finished, Ben."

He looked over her shoulder. "What have we here?"

She turned. "Ayman Safra's ledger, I think."

Ben picked it up, turned it in to the light. "Right you are." His finger stabbed out. "And now we know who ordered Safra to make that bid on the weaponized time crystals." He turned the ledger so Evan could see.

"Ludovico Aronovich Ferranov."

Ben nodded. "Colonel in the GRU. According to our sources he was in charge of the Russian team experimenting with qubits and time crystals." His finger poked the page again. "And here's a scribble on the margin. This fucker never sent Ferranov the goods."

Evan's head fell again, her chin hitting her chest. Ben put the ledger down, knelt in front of her, took her hands.

"Listen, you're nearly out on your feet. We've got to get you to a doctor—maybe even a hospital."

At the last word her head snapped up. "The algorithmic formula is still here, Ben. We've got to find it."

He looked at her. "You're not going anywhere until we do, is that it."

"In a nutshell."

He sighed again. "You are the most stubborn human being I've ever met."

"Give me the medal later. Let's get to work."

"Right." He moved the laptop over so he could access it. He turned it on, waited, frowning. "Well, that's out. The hard drive is fried." He pressed keys, tried to get into the BIOS, the core of the computer. "No dice. I can't get anything out of this. It looks like the hard drive was reformatted before it was fried."

"So Zahra sabotaged it."

Ben nodded. "Looks that way."

"Then there must be a thumb drive." Evan pointed. Slowly but surely feeling returned to her arms. "Check her person."

Ben turned and knelt beside Zahra's body, went through it like the true professional he was. He turned back to her. "No joy."

"Well, it must be here somewhere."

Ben looked around. "Not in plain sight it isn't." He stood, hands on hips, quartering the study with his gaze. "It could be anywhere on this schooner."

"I don't think so. She had just killed Safra and was waiting for me. She wouldn't have had time—"

"Hold on." She swiveled the chair back around until she was facing the desk.

Ben stepped closer. "What is it?"

Evan's eyes narrowed, her gaze falling on the crystal paperweight. "What if it *is* hiding in plain sight."

The paperweight was engraved: TIFFANY & CO. Tiffany did not make art-glass paperweights, not in that shape anyway. So what were those gray swirls? She picked up the diamond decahedron and there, lying underneath, was a thumb drive.

55

Overnight in the hospital was all Evan could tolerate. Over the advice of the surgeon who reset her shoulder she returned to Tribe's house, accompanied by Ben, who filled her in. The thumb drive did indeed contain the algorithmic formula for weaponizing time crystals. The mechanism for deploying them was found on the schooner. Naturally, the US government claimed ownership of the mechanism, as Zahra had been their employee, but since it was based on stolen Parachute intellectual property it came into Tribe's hands.

"He trashed it," Ben told her. "I was witness to it."

"Astonishing that it could send time crystals across thousands of miles within a matter of milliseconds."

"According to Tribe time crystals are unimpeded by either distance or time."

They were sitting in the courtyard under the shade of the fig tree. Beyond, the fountain splashed, and beyond that the lime tree rose. From their position they could see the very tips of the Blue Mosque's delicate minarets. The sky was clear. The long afternoon lay ahead.

"He insisted on it," Ben continued. "But still I don't like him."

Evan smiled. "You don't like anyone you work for. Except for Isobel."

"Yes." Ben squinted into the sunshine. "She is different."

The sound of the muezzin came to them, melodious and alien, floating like a sail above the sea.

"We caught Parachute's ex-employee. He was on his way here supposedly to meet Zahra."

"She entrapped them all, didn't she?"

"You put an end to that."

There was a small silence between them. They'd known each other a long time, had been through difficult, life-threatening times in the field.

Once lovers, once friends, now perhaps only compatriots. But possibly, Evan reflected, that was enough.

"And Russia?" she asked.

"There's a strong rumor going around that the Sovereign and his inner circle of advisors have been purged," Ben said. "There's even a photo of him dead circulating on social media but no one can come to a consensus as to whether it's real or a deepfake. The White House still hasn't been able to contact the Sovereign, so maybe there's something to the rumors. As you know, with all the disinformation being floated it's often difficult to get to the truth inside Russia. But Russian troops do appear to be pulling back from the Ukraine border, though there's still fierce fighting in Odessa. As for a war all signs point to it being off the table. Thank God."

The muezzin's voice flowed and ebbed like the tide. The spice of cumin and chilis mixed with the rich scent of spit-roasting lamb. The fountain splashed, rippling the water in the hexagonal bowl.

"He likes you, you know," Ben said seemingly out of nowhere.

"What?" Evan turned to him. "Who?"

"You know. Tribe."

"You're nuts."

"On the contrary. Remember when he said that you don't trust anyone?"

Her eyes narrowed. "I took that as a compliment."

"He also said that lack of trust keeps you from knowing anyone."

"So?"

"So that's as close as Tribe is ever going to come to admitting he likes you."

Ben might very well be right, but in truth Evan's mind was elsewhere. Though she sat here with Ben, she was imagining a different scene, where she sat in this same spot beneath the fig tree with Lyudmila, Timur, and, strangest of all, Bobbi. They talked and laughed, about what she had no idea. It was only important to her that the four of them were together, that neither hatred nor death kept them apart.

Moments later, Ben stopped talking. She did not notice, not then, not when he rose and left her to her dreaming.

AND THEN . . .

On a night not very far in the future, Rodion Molchalin went out for a walk along the Moskva. In point of fact he did this every night sleep eluded him, which was almost always. He found a bench and sat for a while, the soft glow of the city washing the river clean. The air was frosty, the city unnaturally silent, as if covered in a blanket of snow. Far above, luminous clouds slid over the city like deep-sea creatures. To his right rose a semicircular pillared arcade in the center of which lived a bronze statue of a World War II general who died defending Stalingrad. The arcade was deserted; no one visiting the fallen hero. To his left, across the river, rose the twisted towers of Oligarch City. It might have been his imagination but it seemed to him there were more lights on there, as if slowly but surely new life was being breathed into the city within the city. And Rodion stuck between these two symbols, belonging to neither.

After a time he rose, stepped closer to the steep riverbank. The river, wide, calm to the point of somnolence, appeared sheathed in iron or ice. In these moments of utter solitude, alone amid the sleeping metropolis, he could not help but think of Juliet Korokova. He did not know where she was, but something inside him knew she wasn't coming back. He did not miss her—not exactly. He knew he loved her as much as he hated her and wondered how these two opposing emotions could abide side by side inside him. If he felt he was pining for her he would be very cross with himself, though occasionally he felt himself slipping into this dangerous and self-defeating fissure.

At length, having drowned his sorrows in the Moskva, fed up with his self-abnegation, he turned, expecting to go home. However, on this night his feet turned in another direction, leading him to Tverskaya Street, not far from Red Square, where he saw ahead of him the entrance to PP&J, a bar, a nightclub, a strip joint, and, on the top floor, a private club for FSB officers of a certain standing.

Inside it was appropriately noisy, sweaty, and very, very loud. It was, he realized, a place to get lost in, and perhaps because he was lost himself he felt comfortable here—more comfortable than in his narrow military bed surrounded by an empty apartment, anyway. He spent no more than three minutes up in the VIP room, disgusted with people he knew and didn't want to know all acting, talking, hitting on women with the same tired lines.

Down in the bar it was quieter and he began to relax. He ordered an iced Jewel of Russia vodka. Only Russian vodkas were available, of course, but Jewel of Russia was one of his favorites.

The bartender set the glass in front of him, poured the drink, and Rodion lifted the glass in a salute, downed the vodka, asked for another.

"Leave the bottle?" the bartender asked with a grin.

Rodion was about to say, *Hell, no,* when a voice to his right said, "Maybe you should."

He looked over at the woman who had slid onto the stool next to his.

"Maria Mariskiovna," she said as the bartender poured from the bottle. "Remember me?"

It took Rodion but a moment. Blond hair, beautiful eyes, pouty lips. "Morokovsky's assistant, right? We met at the GRU morgue."

She flinched. "Don't remind me. That was a gruesome afternoon, even for me."

They clinked glasses and drank.

"I've taken over his position," she said.

"Do you like it, working there?"

"Do you like working for the FSB?"

Touché, he thought, and smiled. "It's all I know, to be honest."

"Me, too."

By mutual consent they moved to the lounge. A corner table had just opened up, in a nook away from the madding crowd.

"So," she said. "What are you doing here?"

"You mean alone?"

She threw her head back and laughed. She had a beautiful laugh, he thought.

She put her hand over his. "Who says you're alone?"

■   ■   ■

"It's so beautiful," Timur Shokov said as he and Evan started down from their jungle villa heading toward the wide curving expanse of beach. "Sumatran emerald and turquoise all over." They were carrying surf-boards. Timur's was emblazed with the Guns N' Roses logo—two revolvers twined in thorned rose stems, a bleeding red bloom on either side. Guns N' Roses was his favorite band. Evan wondered what Lyudmila's favorite band had been, or even if she had one. *"But you don't know me,"* Lyudmila had said.

Amid the cries of the macaques they hit the beach for Timur's surfing lessons. He wasn't good yet, but he was very keen on trying, which, Evan felt, was more important. Anyway, he was an exceptionally fast learner, just like his mother. Before they hit the beach proper she dug out suntan lotion, made sure he was slathered up—her as well. What a maternal thing to do, she thought. She realized then that he was staring at her.

"Aunt Evan . . ." His voice, thin and reedy, came to her in a drift. He licked his lips.

"Go on, Timur," she said. "You can ask me anything, you know that."

He nodded, his hand reaching out. "Your scars."

Evan smiled. "Battle scars. Your mother had them too."

His eyes opened wide. "She did?"

"She was the best fighter I've ever met—strong and smart."

"That's what I want to be," he said with a jut of his chin. "Strong and smart."

"Timur." She placed a hand on his shoulder. "Whatever you want to be you *will* be. But don't be in such a rush to grow up. This is your time for fun; embrace it. You will never pass this way again."

After an hour or so in the curls, rising, falling, balancing, riding, fall-ing again, laughing, they retreated, dripping, salt-crusted, to the shade of a palm grove and sat without toweling off. Evan opened a wicker basket that had been left for them on the large blanket provided by the resort's staff, who treated them like royalty mainly because the resort was now owned by Marsden Tribe. He had wanted to come with them but Evan shut that down at once—this was her time with Timur—and after what she had done for him and his company he knew better than to argue with her. He was a quick learner too.

"I used to come here with your mother," Evan said, as she handed

Timur a sandwich. "We loved it. The only place on earth where we could find peace."

"Did you and my mother love each other?"

Evan smiled. "As best friends love each other, yes."

A frown appeared on his face. Evan had the urge to smooth those lines out with the pad of her thumb.

"She never told you about me, though."

Leave it to children to cut through all the bewildering adult clutter. For a moment she envied him. "Not until the end." His frown urged her on. "Your mother knew she had only one chance to get you out of Russia. She planned and planned—so cleverly."

"She didn't want you to help her?"

"Oh, but she did want that. And I did."

"But she didn't tell you."

"She felt it was better that I didn't know," Evan said. "And she was right." She was acutely aware of a softness inside her for this boy who had been dropped in her lap, and for Lyudmila, her friend. A special warmth with which she was not well acquainted. "Your mother was almost always right."

His gaze dropped to the sand between his legs. "You must miss her."

"Oh, Timor." Her heart broke once again and she gathered him to her, kissed the crown of his head. "I know you miss her, too."

Abruptly, he pulled away, looked her straight in the eyes. "Will we love each other?"

"That, Timor, is up to you." She ruffled his hair. "I already love you."

"Is that why you . . ." He nodded toward a corner of the basket, in which resided a bronze urn.

"Timur," she said. "You're very young. This is not something you have to be part of." She lifted the urn. "You can just watch or go back to the villa. I can do it at night while you're asleep."

He touched the side of the urn with the tips of his fingers. "This is what she wanted, right?"

"She will be as happy here in death as she was in life. She will become part of this place." Evan swept her hand out. "Part of everything."

Timur regarded her with his serious eyes—an adult's eyes—grown up far too fast. Evan realized that she had to find a way to return his childhood to him before it was too late.

"I don't want you to do it without me," he said. "I want to be part of it."

"Right." Evan nodded, unscrewed the top, lifted out the plastic bag, gray, opaque, with Lyudmila's remains. "Let's do it then."

Astride their boards, they paddled out past the breakers, floating, rocking in tandem. She opened the bag. They held it together.

"Ready?"

He nodded and they overturned the bag, the contents spilling out, darkening the water between them. But only for a moment as the tide took Lyudmila away from them, out into the deep.

"Now this will be our place," Timur said when they returned to shore. He wiped his eyes, unembarrassed to be crying in front of her. It wasn't the first time nor, she thought, would it be the last, which was fine. Which was as it should be.

Our place, she thought. Her mind of its own accord had turned to her sister. Bobbi alive. Seeing her photo, reading her jacket had been like grinding salt into a wound she hadn't realized was still open.

Timur took a bite of his sandwich, chewed thoughtfully, then swallowed. "Tell me about my mom."

This wasn't the first time he'd asked her about Lyudmila; he never asked about his father.

"She was a complicated person." Evan always started this way. "She was the keeper of many, many secrets."

"Like Circe," Timur said. "Or Dumbledore."

Evan smiled. "Yes, just like them." The thought of Lyudmila passing into legend made her unaccountably happy. "But her biggest secret—her secret of secrets—was you. Everything she did from the moment I met her was bent toward the two of you being reunited." Evan popped the top on a cold bottle of Fiji water while she took time to consider a moment. "Timur, your mother was very smart, very influential, very beautiful. She could have had anything in the world if she put her mind to it. But all she ever wanted was you."

Timur had stopped eating but he accepted the water from her. His eyes were large and wet. "She was a good mom, then, wasn't she?"

Evan's heart broke and she reached out to take the child's hand. "Yes," she said. "Yes, she was."

■　■　■

Wrapped in her lover's warm arms, Kata Romanovna Hemakova, once known by the code name Kobalt, born Bobbi Ryder, lay in that nighttime place between dreaming and waking. Every time Alyosha Ivanovna moved in her sleep Kata moved with her, as if they were one person.

Kata was dreaming or perhaps imagining a beautiful woman and a young boy—a mother and son?—in a land of emerald and turquoise. This land kept shifting as if it were the sea itself. She heard birds calling, insects whirring—and laughter, lots of laughter, echoing into the sky. It was only at the last moment of the dream or the imagining that she realized the woman was her sister, Evan.

But when she woke to gray Moscow rain, Evan and the boy were gone from her memory.

ACKNOWLEDGMENTS

First and foremost:
Mitch Hoffman, agent extraordinaire
Victoria Lustbader, my first and always editor, the love of my life
Second and foremost:
Linda Quinton, my second editor, always advocate, and partner in
publishing
Also:
My entire tireless team at Forge Books. You make my life infinitely
easier and happier.

ABOUT THE AUTHOR

ERIC VAN LUSTBADER is the author of twenty-five international bestsellers, as well as twelve Jason Bourne novels, including *The Bourne Enigma* and *The Bourne Initiative*. His books have been translated into over twenty languages. He lives with his wife in New York City and Long Island.

ericvanlustbader.com